SUGAR AND SPICE

Anna MacRae is only five years old when her mother dies in childbirth one bleak wintry day in 1940. She is left with twin baby sisters and a father fighting somewhere in Europe. They are taken in by Elsie and Bert Dixon and are moved to the countryside. Anna is a gifted child, with a warm personality, but not so her twin sisters: something is not quite right with them. Years later, after giving birth to twins of her own, must Anna make peace with the sisters who tried to ruin her life, if she is to find her own true happiness...?

SUGAR AND SPICE

SUGAR AND SPICE

by

Ruth Hamilton

Magna Large Print Books
Long Preston, North Yorkshire,
BD23 4ND, England.

British Library Cataloguing in Publication Data.

Hamilton, Ruth
    Sugar and spice.

    A catalogue record of this book is
    available from the British Library

    ISBN   978-0-7505-3466-6

First published in Great Britain 2010 by
Severn House Publishers Ltd.

Copyright © 2010 by Ruth Hamilton

Cover illustration © Kerry Norgard by arrangement with
Arcangel Images Ltd.

The moral right of the author has been asserted .

Published in Large Print 2012 by arrangement with
Severn House Pubishers Ltd.

Magna Large Print is an imprint of Library Magna Books Ltd.

Printed and bound in Great Britain by
T.J. (International) Ltd., Cornwall, PL28 8RW

This piece is in memory of Michael Neophytou,
who died tragically aged seven
while playing in his garden.
God bless you, Michael. God bless your lovely
family.
Ο Θεός να σας, ευλογεί, Michael
From Linda next door, aka Ruthie xxx

One

Wagons roll at about the same time every Monday. By ten in the morning, mothers in the village are on their way to the baby clinic, some in search of reassurance, several as part of a fashion parade and to demonstrate how well they are losing their baby-weight, others to fill a gap created by a hiatus in career. The making of friends who are in the same bracket is a comfort when life becomes so monotonous and lonely.

I go because I feel guilty. The secret I hold fast to my chest is a burden I must carry alone, because few would believe me and fewer still would attempt to understand my ridiculous predicament. I am not a normal mother. I make few friends, invite no confidences and, were it not for Mrs Battersby, no one at all would have any concept of my position. Mrs Bee lives next door with her daughter and son-in-law. She wears a wrap-around flowered apron, makes wine from improbable kitchen debris, believes in red flannel, and cleans shoes with the inner side of banana skins. She is a relic and I am glad to know her.

The side door opens suddenly and loudly as it crashes into the wall. 'Anna?'

'In here.'

She waddles into my living room and places a

11

bottle of her deadly parsnip wine on the coffee table. 'Eeh,' she wheezes. 'Aren't they bonny?' She refers, of course, to the twins. They are propped in the pram, one at each end, clean, clothed and angelic. 'Yes,' I reply. My girls are pretty. They are healthy, rosy-cheeked, excellent feeders, and strong-limbed. One is stronger than the other, but it's only a matter of differing birth weights. I have to believe that. I'd like everyone else to believe it, too.

Sharing a bed with a man whose sperm count is low allowed me to cease to expect motherhood, but my status altered radically long after I decided that childlessness was fine. I worked with children, and eventually harboured no wish to produce any of my own. Children complicate life; motherhood has destroyed mine.

'And they've made you look younger, an all,' announces the ageing Manchester immigrant. Years earlier, she followed her daughter down the East Lancashire Road and settled here, in Hesford, a satellite of St Helens. 'Nobody would ever think you were forty,' she says.

Forty? I feel eighty, and then some. The days grind along relentlessly while I feed, clean and watch my twin jailers, while I launder their clothes and prepare food for their father, a man I can no longer pretend to love. That is probably my own fault, because everything is my own fault. I am arrogant, self-indulgent, exhausted, worried and clinically depressed. This wonderful old lady has me down as 'mithered', and she is only too correct.

Mrs Bee has placed herself in an armchair.

'He's reading again,' she announces with the air of a speaker at a summit conference.

'What's he reading?' I ask. The 'he' in question is her son-in-law and my erstwhile boss. He owns the patience of a saint, which is probably just as well.

'A book.' She spits the four-letter word from her throat as if clearing it of phlegm. The presumably wise head shakes despairingly. In her opinion, no good ever came of books. She has lived her whole life without indulging in them, as she has been too busy doing. Doers have no time for reading, radio, television or theatre. Which is a pity, because she might have made a hilarious comedienne. 'Book about psychology,' she snaps.

I am trying not to smile. Wanting to smile is a new sensation, yet I dare not indulge the need. 'He's a head teacher, Mrs Bee. He has to read in order to keep up with the system.'

'System?' she cries. 'System? A damned good hiding and bed without supper's what they need, not bloody books. Mind, it is a thick one. He could use it as a weapon, I reckon, when some of the little buggers kick off at playtime.'

There is no cure for Mrs Battersby, and I am glad about that. She is a ray of light in an otherwise dark sky, but I am lucky, as she radiates sporadically in my house. Paul and Jenny next door live a life that is constantly illuminated by this woman, and they often look drawn and tired. When in full flood, the old woman might even register on a Geiger counter, and radiation sickness could become a distinct danger.

'Pity you didn't move here earlier before having

13

them.' She inclines her head in the direction of the pram. 'You could've made friends. Mind, you'll happen meet a few gradely folk at yon clinic.'

I doubt that. The conversation is embedded in projectile vomiting, pyloric stenosis, brands of baby formula, rashes, colds and teething. On a good day, some quiet revolutionary might mention *Coronation Street* or the price of salmon, but such subjects usually receive a premature burial under layers of nappies, some disposable, others of the terry towelling variety.

'You miss your job,' announces Mrs Bee. 'You thought you'd get away without kiddies, didn't you?'

I nod.

'Have you thought about one of them opers?'

Rooting about in the depths of my handbag in search of keys, I ask her to repeat the question. 'An oper. Mind, they sometimes turn out to be no opers, them girls from abroad. They can be all spaghetti and no English. That builder up Tithebarn Road got a pole.'

Anyone else might have got lost somewhere along the way through Mrs Bee's meandering, but I am used to infant schoolchildren, so I manage to navigate the misty path. 'A pole? Do you mean a Polish au pair?'

She nods rapidly. 'That's what I said, isn't it? An oper. I think she were a Pole, any road. She were all funny sausages and red hot tea with no milk in it. She fair scalded one of the kids before she left. I said to our Jenny, "She'll never last, because all she knows is yes, no and disco." I

14

were right. Three or four months later, she forgot the word "no", finished up pregnant and on her way back to somewhere with about twenty letters in its name, mostly zeds, exes and the odd Y. You don't want one of them, do you?'

I don't care, but I daren't say that. A nanny might be a good idea. A nanny would come in with no pre-knowledge and no opinions about my situation. Like me, she would learn the hard way and become my witness. Help in the home is affordable, as I intend to divorce him only when I am back to normal. Normal? I wish he'd go. I wish he'd go now, and to hell with normal.

'You'll be all right, you know.'

I look at her. The grey, frizzled hair is thinner than it used to be. She once showed me a wedding photograph, and she has been beautiful, with long, dark hair and very surprised eyes. 'I suppose I shall.'

'Lass, it's trowmatic, is giving birth. And you've had no mam to show you how to fettle. Some women don't take straight away. But tell me, Anna, what would you do if somebody harmed them two twins?'

My answer is automatic. From deep within my animal core, the words arrive. 'I'd kill.'

Again, the steely head nods. 'At your age, most women's kids are coming into their teens or twenties. Babies is very tiring. Two coming at once is more than twice as bad as one, if you get my meaning, like. None of it's your fault, love. You got caught that little bit later in life than most folk, and it's hard. But you'll get by.'

'Yes.' I move my pram towards its launch pad

15

near the front door.

'Will I get my coat and come with you?'

This time, my smile arrives properly. I am imagining her rattling round the clinic, chest wheezing, fingers prodding babies' limbs, advice on gripe water and goose-grease delivered in broad, flat Lancashire tones. 'No. I'll see you later for coffee.' After locking the door and making sure that Mrs Bee gets home safely, I begin the walk up Beech Grove.

The troops are on the move. I marvel at the number of new mothers who place their precious darlings in frail-looking buggies. Cars have suspension and springs to absorb bumps and dips in the road, yet newborns are placed in what seem to be flattened pushchairs, no support at all. These younger women note my age and my twin Silver Cross, probably have me down as an old-fashioned freak with an unnecessarily ornate chariot, but at least I cared enough to buy solid transport, especially when informed that I was expecting a double event.

No one speaks to me beyond the odd 'hello' accompanied by a brief bow of the head. I don't care. Do I? Again, I allow a grin to visit my face. I wonder how many of these got arrested for diving semi-naked into a fountain on Trafalgar Square? They haven't lived. I have. Is it over? I don't want it to be over. The me that is buried under the label 'mother' must come through. That's selfish, isn't it? Charlotte and Emily should be more important than the vessel that launched them into the world. Yet I cannot plead completely guilty to loving me, because depression is hatred of self.

The waiting area is small and packed with people, each with a child. I have two – one on each arm. Weights, Measures and Vaccinations Ltd are represented today by two nurses in white uniforms and navy blue cardigans. They exclaim over the beauty of each customer, place younger clients on scales and mark the card accordingly. But on this occasion, my attention is fastened to a small, dark-haired girl who sits directly opposite me across the square space against whose walls our chairs are placed. Her skin is unnaturally white, and she stares at the floor, her gaze skimming the top of her baby's head. She isn't with us. I know that feeling.

'How old are they?' asks the person next to me.

'What? Sorry, I was preoccupied.' I rewind the tape in my head until I find an echo of her words. 'Eight weeks.'

'They're lovely,' declares my next-chair neighbour.

'Yes,' I reply. I offer no comment about her offspring, so she turns her attention to next-chair-but-one. I feel sorry about this, as I am talkative by nature, but I must not let anyone in. The girl across the room is blinking back some wetness in her eyes. No wedding ring. Perhaps she removed it during the pregnancy if she became slightly water-bound; perhaps she mislaid it. There is no white mark on her tanned I-am-spoken-for finger. Then she looks at me.

A cold fire burns in brown eyes that should be warm. She is half my age – might even be a teenager. An automatic movement of her knees is

17

employed to keep her baby happy. She is having one of those robot days. I incline my head slightly, and her lips part as if to take in a short, sharp breath. This tenuous contact is severed when the names Fairbanks and Hughes are called. I am the former. She is the latter.

Sometimes, we do things that we might never explain. Touching the arm of Somebody Hughes is a similar happening. I don't know why I do it, and I worry about consequences.

She leaves before I do, since I have two to be weighed. When I gain my release, I look across the road to where a tangle of prams sits outside the chemist's shop. Most pram-owners are inside, but Somebody Hughes is standing there as if waiting for... For what? For a bus? No. Her pram, probably second-hand, is not a folder; like mine, it is coach-built and not quite the thing these days. But she might be waiting for a bus. Or a lorry. Stop this, Anna. You don't know her, and she is very unlikely to be suicidal. Not everyone is like you. Very few go to bed praying for a nice died-peacefully-in-her-sleep outcome. A vehicle would hurt, and one or the other might survive.

When the twins are strapped down, I cross the road. 'Hello, Somebody Hughes,' I say stupidly.

She stares right into me and, for a moment, I wonder whether she might suffer from something worse than post-natal whatever. 'Hello,' she answers eventually. 'You were in the clinic.'

'Yes.'

She is searching me. I can almost hear her machinery as she registers every aspect of my exterior self. Good clothes – click. Good pram –

18

click. Very tall – click. Blonde – click. Rather old to have those babies – click. But, in the end, she allows me a measure of trust. 'I'm not myself,' she manages.

'I know.'

'How do you know?'

I shrug. 'Our eyes met across a crowded room and you reminded me of me.'

'Oh.'

'Sounds a bit Barbara Cartland,' I tell her. 'But if you need a friend, someone who understands a bit – well – I'm Anna Fairbanks and ... and here I am. Come on. Let's leave these three outside The Mustard Pot and grab a coffee. If we sit near the window, we can keep an eye on our sprogs.' Is this a good sign? Or have I just adopted another daughter? She is Susan, she is young, and she is fragile in both mind and body. Can one oddity heal another? Can the process of trying to help her mend me? Is this yet another symptom of my terrible self-interest? All my life, I have found people who needed me. Almost invariably, they have supported me in return. She needs someone. It might as well be me.

Susan Hughes is starving. She demolishes three halves of toasted teacake while I eat just one half. Her mouth must be lined with asbestos, because she drinks hot coffee in a few desperate gulps. After a deep breath, she speaks. She is unmarried. She dares not identify the father of her baby, because he will kill her if she does. The house is crowded. The baby, a boy named Stephen, occupies a box room with her. 'It's like a cupboard with a window,' she tells me. 'My mam's a bit ashamed of me. Well, I think she's more angry than ashamed, because she wanted me to have a proper job and a future. My dad's always drunk.' Oh, God – I know how that feels. 'He beat me up when my belly started to grow, then he hit me again when I wouldn't tell him the father's name.' She sighs heavily. 'By the time I've bought the baby's food, I've hardly any money left.'

My mind rushes along like a Grand National horse that has deliberately unseated its unwelcome passenger in order to clear Becher's Brook. For the first time in weeks, I feel almost alive. 'Come home with me,' I command. Sometimes, I can't quite manage not to sound like a teacher. 'Two heads are better than one, even if they're messed up.' She needs to divorce her family. I need help in the house. And I am definitely and absolutely crazy.

Mrs Battersby agrees. 'Have you gone twice round the bend and met yourself on the road back? You don't know her from Eve. She could be a thief or summat. And what about Den?'

I shake my head. What about him? I need him like a fish needs a lifeboat. He doesn't 'do' babies, seldom plays with them, never bathes or changes them, refuses to take them for a Sunday morning walk while I cook lunch. 'He won't notice.' I reply. My husband should have been Victorian. Or, perhaps, from some Middle-Eastern culture where wives know their place and walk several paces behind the men.

'Where's she gone now, this Susan?' is Mrs Bee's next question.

'Home. Somewhere on the council estate.'

20

She bridles. The arms fold themselves beneath an ample bosom, her chin juts forward and thin lips clamp in the closed position while she prepares for battle. The wait is a short one. 'In the caravan? You're shoving her and a kiddy in yon caravan?'

I nod. 'It's a luxury van, Mrs Bee.'

'Will your fellow mind having a kid with a kid in his mam and dad's caravan?'

'She'll be in the house when he's abroad.' Surely one of his gaggle of females will entice him away forever in the not-too-distant future? I often dream of the husbandless state and, if I could choose, I would probably opt for widowhood, as it carries a degree of respect. Divorce is nasty. Den is nasty. As for me – well – I can be fluent in nasty if provoked. Since the death of Den's father, the caravan has been left on the extra acre we managed to extract from the Earl of Derby when purchasing our house. The caravan's a decent size, and is certainly better than a box room.

'You don't know her,' repeats Mrs Bee.

I cast my mind back to that small crumb of time when I noticed Susan in the clinic. There's a clear photograph of her – dead eyes, drooping shoulders, absenteeism. I cannot explain this to Mrs Battersby, as she doesn't begin to understand how life is for people like Susan and me. In fact, Susan's excuse for being 'not the full quid' is far more acceptable than my own. I have everything. I have a husband who works, a four-bedroomed house, a bit of land and two perfect daughters. Perfect? Like normal, it's a debatable concept.

21

'We'll support each other,' I say. 'She'll help in the house – she might even become one of your opers in time.'

Mrs Bee snorts. 'Is she Scouse?'

'There's a Liverpool accent, yes.'

The diatribe that follows is amusing. Do I want my twins to talk with an accent thicker than treacle? Is she trustworthy? What if her family come round, what if, what if, what if...?

Blood and stomach pills – can my neighbour not hear herself? Her vowels have been treated with a flat iron, she uses 'nowt' for nothing, 'owt' for anything, 'summat' for something. Having gone straight from school desk to factory, Dora Battersby has graduated to 'posh' by hanging onto her daughter. Jenny married well, speaks well, and has given Dora a good standard of living. So the old lady forgets her roots and, like so many others, retains the accent and vernacular of her yesterdays. But she is now a cut above the ordinary, because she lives in a detached house on the edge of countryside. I cannot dislike her, since she is a product of environment, as are we all. But sometimes, she can be slightly annoying.

'Let's agree to differ,' I suggest.

'And if it doesn't work out?' she asks as she walks to the door.

'I deal with it.'

After feeding, changing and settling the twins, I have my Anna time. For twenty-odd hours a day, I am a mother; for one hour each afternoon, I am me. I am lighter today, because I have found a punctuation mark who will, I hope, help interrupt the tedious paragraphs of the daily grind. 'She's a human being, not a semicolon,' I tell myself aloud.

We walked down Beech Grove just a couple of hours ago, Susan in shabby jeans, I in a fairly decent dress and coat. She declared herself 'made up' with the caravan and wept a few tears of gratitude while I stuck to business, instructing her on the use of gas, the daily emptying of the loo, where to store her pram. She was so excited. 'But it's got a proper bedroom and a sink and a cooker,' she exclaimed.

'My husband's father owned it,' I told her. 'After his wife died, he used it as a sort of granny flat. It meant that he lived almost with us, but the van gave him a degree of independence.'

She looked at me then with wide, hopeful eyes. 'Tell me he didn't die in here.'

'He died in hospital. And he was probably the best man I ever knew, so worry not. If any trace of John remains, he will be here to do good, not harm.' I could have gone on to say what a pity it was that John's son had not turned out more like him, but this new and improbable relationship between Susan and me is still in its infancy. 'If you don't like it here, we can find somewhere, surely? You don't have to stay with your parents, especially if your dad is abusive.'

She blinked again. 'Why are you doing this for me?' she asked.

'Because you need somewhere and I need help. We both need help, don't we?'

She gazed down at her son. 'Sometimes it's hard to love him.'

'Yes.' I placed an arm across her shoulders.

23

'You're too young for all this, and I'm too old. Adjustment isn't easy.'

A sudden moment of recognition arrived in her face. 'Hey – didn't you used to teach up at Hesford Junction Primary?' she asked.

I replied in the affirmative. 'Teachers are mostly normal when allowed off the lead at three-thirty,' I told her. 'But there are rules, Susan.'

'Oh. Bugger.' At last, she smiled. 'Go 'head, then,' she said in her best Liverpool 8 accent. 'Let's have it over with.'

'OK. One, while there is food in my chest freezer – it's in the garage – thou shalt not starve. Two, while there's baby powder in my house, Stephen shall not starve. Washing machine's in my kitchen, use when it's available. Let me deal with my husband. He's a twit.'

The laugh she delivered at that point was almost melodic. It deteriorated into hysteria, and I pushed her along the garden and through the side door. The weeping stopped abruptly. 'Oh, God,' she exclaimed repeatedly as she walked through the house. 'Look at that. Is it antique? Is it real? Does the clock work? It's older than Adam. There's a lot of books.'

I placed her on a sofa. 'Stop being impressed. I feel guilty enough without all that, Susan.' Sitting on a footstool, I gave her some idea of my life. Not too much. Not yet. 'I come from poverty. I worked hard, got out, got a boyfriend who almost amused me until he became my husband. All you see around me has been acquired throughout almost twenty years of teaching. Den doesn't buy furniture – he's into stocks, shares and trying to

24

get his mitts on krugerrand. I did all this myself. Never expected to have children, so I occupied myself by home-making.' I sighed heavily. 'This is all just salad dressing, Susan. But there's no substance in my marriage. I'm here just for a while. I'm waiting for the next ... thing.'

Her brow furrowed. 'Next thing?'

I shrugged. 'Don't ask.' I didn't tell her I'd been tired of Den for years, that the twins and their accompanying problems were wearying. Nor did I bother to inform her that I was always waiting for the next 'thing' even though I usually had absolutely no idea of what I was expecting. Except for the twins, of course... There was a list some-where. Items like 'write a book' and 'do something political' were part of an agenda I would probably never follow. 'Have a love affair' had been done and dusted, but that had to stop. Would the presence of Susan have an effect on those illicit and delightful meetings?

When she calmed down, there was a quiet thoughtfulness about her that pleased me. She is not a typical tearaway, I believe. Yes, she's made mistakes, but she is sensible, intelligent and very afraid of her family. There is more to this than meets the eye.

'I'll come tomorrow while they've all gone out, but I have to leave a note for Mam,' she said before she left.

So, she is coming tomorrow. What have I done? Is Mrs Battersby going to become difficult, will my husband throw a fit, will her family descend on us and burn the house to ashes? Emily is coming to the boil. She is in the dining room,

25

while her smaller and slightly younger sister is upstairs. It has to be like this. For some reason known only to God and, possibly, to the devil, my twins need to be kept apart. Don't ask. Not yet. I'll get round to all that shortly.

By the time I have dealt with my children, Den is home and I am just about to pour soured cream into the stroganoff. Sometimes, he smiles at me and I catch a glimpse of that long-dead boy, the lad who pushed me through the West End of London in a wheelbarrow, he who debated with and thrashed verbally most of his contemporaries at Imperial College. Today, I catch no glimpse of the shivering creature I held during the first and second breakdowns; today, he is happy. There is something wrong with Den, and I don't know enough about illness to make a judgement, but he appears to be two separate people. He gets as high as a kite on life, then enters a trough so deep that it might have been sculpted by Dante.

'Good day?' he asks.

'Mixed.' I allow his kiss to touch my cheek. I can't go through it again. Another breakdown, and I shall join him in one of the Inferno's lower circles. 'There's a young girl who needs Pa's caravan. She has a baby and no support. Just on a temporary basis, you understand. Is that OK with you, Den?'

He stands silently in the middle of the kitchen. My kitchen. He doesn't do kitchens. 'Another of your lame ducks?' he asks. I hear the contempt in his voice, but its undercoat is resignation. He is giving in to his wife because he has that power

26

and is demonstrating his magnanimity. It is not his fault, and I am guilty yet again of the sin of arrogance. I stay one step ahead of him as a matter of necessity, but I should not call him a twit. The man is ill, and I ought to respect him.

My shoulders slacken in relief. He has, in fact, given in to me for years while I've brought slower children home for secret lessons in the dining room. 'Yes,' I reply. 'And it won't be for ever – just until we find her a flat or a house to rent. She needs to get back on her feet.'

He goes to change his clothes while I thank God that this is a good Den day. I would have got my own way eventually, but the process of achieving it would have been tiring. Grating nutmeg into the pan, I wonder anew about my husband's life. There seems to be no core to him. He depends for support on status, the job, the car, the house. And, of course, the women. His skeleton is near the surface, rather like that of a cuttlefish. He appears to measure himself through the eyes of others, and he is frail.

I should have moved on years ago, because I cannot delete him completely from my life, since he is the father of Emily and Lottie, and I have little time for women who try to separate children from their father. The twins are not bargaining tools, and I shall aim for a civilized divorce. When I'm ready. Will I ever be ready? I'm ready.

'Smells good.'

He is behind me and is moving his hands to my breasts. Stay solid, Anna. This is not your biggest problem. Just eat, then lie down and think of

Wales. It will make a change from England.

Emily still requires at least one night feed. Lottie, who sleeps in the bedroom next to ours, manages to last until morning. The baby monitor on my bedside table brings Emily's strident demands into my left ear at ten minutes past two. She requires her servant and she requires attention *now*. I collect the necessary items and walk to the other end of the house. I change her, feed her, and try hard not to fall asleep while she is in my arms. How tightly she holds onto my housecoat; when I open my eyes, she is staring hard at me. I can hear the words she doesn't yet know – 'You're mine, just mine.'

The lavatory flushes, a tap runs, then Den's tousled head inserts itself into Emily's room. 'Still keeping them apart, then, these two little enemies?' The mockery is noticeable.

'Yes. Emily wakes Lottie.' I don't bother to opine that Lottie has no temper, no ill-will, no nastiness.

'Hmm.' He strokes the stubbly chin. 'But it will stop soon, won't it?'

I nod. The man whose moods swing from elated to flat-as-a-pancake judges me insane, because the arrangements regarding the twins seem to be eccentric. He goes away and I breathe a sigh of relief. I find the situation impossible to explain to myself, but it is real. Emily hates Lottie. It is my belief that the antipathy began in the womb, but no one would ever agree, I am sure.

Rodney Street. Mr Evans-Wright laughing at me over the tops of his half-moon spectacles.

'They're just moving, Mrs Fairbanks. Be grateful.'

'They're fighting,' I informed him.

He shook his head. 'These are not identical twins. They're fraternal, so each has its own sac. It's impossible.'

How hard I worked at believing that until I found myself in the dentist's waiting room some weeks later. Stuck there for an hour, I began to digest an article in one of the many scattered magazines. One in eight of us is probably a twin. We commit our first 'murder' long before we are born, usually at the embryonic stage. The stronger digs in deep and deprives the weaker of nourishment, so only the fittest survives. My tooth was filled eventually with amalgam, and my mind was filled to bursting by dread.

I place Emily in her cot and go to sit with Lottie. Both started life in incubators. A nurse told me that most twins fare better in a shared unit, but mine became distressed when placed together, so they had to be separated when they reached the grand age of two days. Emily's birth weight was almost five pounds, and she overcame her breathing difficulty very quickly. Lottie, who weighed just over three and a half pounds, needed longer. She was born bruised. The damage was declared to be birthmarks that would probably disappear very quickly, and only I knew the truth. The sacs were separate, but they were not made of concrete. Emily had managed to hurt Lottie in spite of their natural separation.

And I now live with the reality. In the twin pram, I use a sausage-shaped pillow fashioned

29

from a draught-excluder. Without that, Emily would kick the living daylights out of her sister, and I might be blamed for mistreating my child if Nurse Hawkeye or Dr Breast-Is-Best saw the bruises. I close my eyes and pray. Loving Lottie is so easy, but I have to beg God for the strength to love Emily.

The medics have awarded me a title, at least, a mooring marked 'post-natal depression' alongside which I am supposed to drop anchor and wait for the pills to work. The months and years stretch before me, all invisible, all inevitable, all there to be feared. My daughters will grow. I shall need a buggy, and the handle I push will have to be positioned so that the girls face me, as I shall need to protect Lottie closely. There is always the chance that she will fight back, and that could make things even worse.

They will walk and play and fall, and I shall not always be there to supervise closely enough. They will go to school and, unless I warn the teachers, Emily will batter her sister at playtime. 'Please, God, make me wrong,' I beg. They will grow out of this, surely? Emily will settle and become quieter, while Lottie will learn to guard herself. I have heard that teachers and nurses make the poorest mothers. Help me, God.

Our Maureen arrives at noon. She is plump, jolly and rather squashed in an ancient Mini containing 'our Susan's clobber'. 'Maureen,' she breathes before dropping half a dozen supermarket bags at my feet. 'Our Susan's on her way. Only she's had to wait for our Marie to go out. I couldn't have fitted her in my car, anyway, and her pram's not a folder.'

I open my mouth to reply, but Maureen has rushed back to her rusting vehicle. This time, she returns with three cardboard boxes and a broken nail. 'Bugger,' she says as she chews at the latter item. 'Gone right in me quick, that has.'

Her third visit is accompanied by a sack of children's toys. 'I have to go,' she mutters. 'No tax, no insurance and no bloody tread on me tyres.'

As the Mini screams away in a cloud of smoke, Susan dashes round the corner with her pram. 'That was our Maureen,' she explains breathlessly. 'Sorry about the mess – she's in a hurry.'

'So I gather. No tax, no insurance, no tread and no fingernail.'

'Oh, heck,' moans Susan. 'And she's a bridesmaid on Saturday.'

'Who is she?' I ask.

'Our Maureen. I think she's me cousin, but you can never be sure with my family.'

'And our Marie?'

'Oh, yeah. That's me mam.'

I shake my head and guide her into the living room. This young woman's possessions are in a couple of boxes and a few small plastic bags. Stephen remains outside in his pram. 'How big is your family?' I ask.

Susan shrugs and advises me that she lost count some years ago. Her mother comes from a family of about ten, but there could be more here and there depending on her grandad's behaviour at any given time. Her dad has three brothers, one a

31

drug addict, one in jail and the third competing with her dad for Drinker of the Decade. Her own generation is not easy to track, as some are un-married parents, others twice married, and a few have stepchildren. 'There's all half-brothers and half-sisters,' she complains. 'I can't keep up with it at all. Can I leave the big pram in your garage? I'll be using the folding one more, I suppose.'

'Of course. My husband uses the carport.'

She grins. 'Oh, I do feel better,' she tells me. 'I'm moving house. My own little cottage with a dining room and a kitchen and a bedroom. There's even a telly. I can watch Corrie without our Ian keep switching over to the football and our Gary wanting the motor racing.'

It is becoming clear that I have taken in a member of a dynasty. Still, our Maureen, who, I have gleaned, lives 'somewhere near Sefton Park, but she keeps moving', seemed keen to get our Susan out of the family home. With any luck, Susan won't be missed unless they call a register every morning – even then, they might think she'd got buried under the sheer weight of com-peting personalities.

We drink coffee, and I find myself hoping that Mrs Bee won't pop in. I don't want poor Susan to spend her first morning being tortured by the Spanish Inquisition.

Hope fades when the side door clatters against the wall. Should I pad that area? Better not. The crashes let me know when my wonderful, opin-ionated neighbour is granting me an audience. She's in. After helping herself to coffee thinned from the contents of a hot water jug, she sits

32

opposite my non-paying guest. 'You're here, then,' she says. 'Do I know you?' Oh, God. Here we go.

'I don't think so.' Susan is dunking a ginger biscuit. In twenty-four hours, she has gained the ability to look someone in the eyes. The someone Susan watches is a noisy drinker. Mrs Bee hoovers the coffee into her mouth. I sometimes wonder whether she might own the ability to drink when placed three feet away from her cup.

I perform the necessary niceties, taking care to address Mrs Bee first. 'Mrs Battersby, this is Susan Hughes. Susan, meet one of my next-door neighbours.'

Susan swallows her biscuit and studies the intruder. Again, her mechanism is almost audible. Wrong side of seventy – click. Apron from World War Two – click. Face like a prune – click. Thinks she knows everything – click. 'Hello,' she says. 'I'm having the caravan.'

'Hmmph.' The old woman folds her arms.

But Susan has the measure of her. In flat, almost disinterested tones, she brings Mrs Bee up to date. When the facts are laid out, my neighbour shakes her head. She wants to know what the world is coming to, but Susan did right in choosing not to abort, and she'd be all right in the caravan, better than a bloody box room.

My shoulders relax slightly.

'How could he beat his own daughter?' asked Mrs Bee. 'And on top of that, how could any man hit a daughter with his grandchild on board? Bloody criminals, some of these folk. Just don't let him near me,' she adds. 'Because I've still got

33

one of my hubby's shotguns.'

Susan's jaw drops. 'A gun?'

'Oh, yes. Best poacher for miles, Ernie. In fact, he were that good, he got a job as a gamekeeper. Set a thief to catch another, you see.' She nods wisely. 'Other than that, he weren't very bright. I don't know where my daughter got her brains, because her dad thought manual labour were a left wing president of some South American country.'

Susan and I laugh. It is only too clear where Jenny got her brains. Had Mrs Bee been educated, she would have been dangerous – even now, she is a force to be reckoned with. I try to imagine her as a university lecturer, but the flowered apron would never fit in.

When the Speaker of the House has left us, I show Susan her bedroom. 'Den is away a lot, so, sleep here if you want to when he isn't here. Three babies waking him would be worse, so it's the caravan when he's in residence.'

'You don't like him.' There is no question mark at the end of the sentence.

She is right, but I say nothing. I have discovered rather late in life that liking a partner is more important than loving him. Husbands and wives need to be friends, not just lovers. The space between us is now our own Grand Canyon, and nothing will ever span it. Growing apart has little to do with love, though the erosion of friendship has, in my case, affected my ability to feel affection for him, and I no longer want him to touch me. There is no real communication; the only ground we supposedly share is our children, and

Den has little interest in them. He wanted a son, but got two daughters.

'Anna?'

'What?'

'You've wandered off.'

'Yes, I do that sometimes.'

'So do I. You don't love him.'

'The friendship between us died, Susan. As for the rest of it – I think the course of true love is closed for major road works.'

'It's a bugger isn't it?' she says.

I agree with her. 'It's a bugger in a bucket.'

'What's one of them, Anna?'

'Oh, it's a Mrs Battersby-ism. I think she believes a bugger in a bucket would make a lot of noise.'

Susan's laughter is too shrill. Today, she has left behind the only family she has known. Today, she has made a decision that will affect her future and that of her little son. On the one hand, I am a life-raft that has saved her from stormy waters; on the other, she has deleted a form of semi-security that she has come to understand, at least. The abusive father is still her dad, while the ashamed mother is the only one Susan has. But Stephen will not always be two months old; soon, he might begin to notice the disquiet around him, and he could well become afraid. 'You'll be fine,' I tell her.

She swallows noisily. 'I hope so. I want the chance to get to know my baby.'

'And to learn to love him?'

'Yes.'

This child and I understand each other thoroughly. I don't know why, and I wish someone could explain to me how a glance across the baby clinic could lead to so sudden and complete an understanding. 'This is my second lot of twins,' I tell her.

Susan's eyes are wide. 'You what? Did they die?'

I shake my head. 'Still very much alive, I'm afraid. My mother died when they were born. I was five years old, the war was on, so the country had a lot to worry about. New babies with a five-year-old sister were not high on the agenda.' I stared at the floor so that Susan might be spared the self-pity in my expression. My childhood was stolen, and I have no power to eliminate that fact. I am a firm believer in coping skills. We can all reach back through the years and blame a happening or an injustice that changed our lives. But we have to get past it, or our history becomes a winner. Yet I wish I could have played more often like the rest of the kids, regret not joining in with rounders, tag and hopscotch.

'So were your foster parents nasty?'

I laugh. 'Not at all. They were the same as everybody else, trying to scrape a living, trying to manage my sisters.'

'Naughty?' she asks.

I am not ready for this, not just yet. The fact that history may be repeating itself is obvious, but only to me. I come from a family that regularly produced twins – three of my mother's sisters gave birth to fraternals – but my sisters and my daughters are the only ones who have been ... difficult. 'Let's get you sorted,' I say to my companion. 'There will be plenty of time to talk.'

The afternoon is hilarious. We make up the double bed and bring in a carry cot for Stephen. Susan gets involved in rearranging the kitchen, and there is much clattering of pots and pans. The babies are out in the garden, mine in two separate prams. She doesn't ask why, and I offer no information. Like children playing house, we produce tea and toast, then Susan makes the miracle happen.

Determined to show her home to Stephen, Lottie and Emily, she brings them one by one into the caravan, propping them up with cushions on a long sofa. Emily punches Lottie, and Susan deals with the situation in a way that has never been available to me; she places her son between the two girls. The one-sided war stops. Emily grasps one of the little boy's arms while Lottie holds the other. Peace. Perfect and absolute peace. I refuse to react, though tears sting my eyes. It seems that God is good after all, because a woman I didn't know until yesterday has applied a dressing to my soul. Emily is smiling. Lottie, who has not had a great deal to smile about, is gurgling. A milky froth appears on her lips, and she blows her first perfect raspberry. The sound startles Susan's son, but Emily chortles.

This is a day to remember. I got one phoob (Susan's word for raspberry) and a laugh out of my other child. Emily is beautiful when she laughs. I have not noticed before how lovely she is.

'You all right?' Susan asks.

I nod, as I do not trust my voice to carry words in one piece.

'Depression's a bugger, isn't it, Anna?'

'In a bucket,' I manage finally. 'But we'll be OK, love. I just know we are going to be OK.' We have to be. One middle-aged woman, one teenager and three children between us. We will get there one day. Because we must.

Two

The winter of 1940 would be talked about for several decades. Most people had stopped looking up in expectation of German planes overhead, but the sky remained the source of a problem so huge that the north-west of England almost ground to a halt.

The town of Bolton, Lancashire, placed as it is in a dip between moors, was in serious trouble, because the lowest of its streets became snowbound to the point where people could not leave their houses. Thus far, the war had been a quiet one; now, at the end of January, it was as silent as the municipal graveyard.

But, in 13 Broom Street, there was noise enough to waken the dead. At each side of the blackleaded range, plaster that had already been crumbly was pitted with holes inflicted by a heavy poker. The news had eventually been passed to the top of the street, and digging had gone on all day. Frankie MacRae was in labour. Men and women had conveyed this information by leaning out of bedroom windows and yelling the message until it reached number 1. A brave soul went to fetch a doctor, a midwife or anyone else with the ability to deal with a birthing – even a vet would have done.

Anna, Frankie MacRae's five-year-old daughter, had been carried next door by Mr Dixon. Snow banked at each side of the cleared area was unsteady, and Mr Dixon looked rather like a snowman by the time he deposited the child at his own fireside. 'This one's terrified, Elsie,' he advised his wife. 'You'd better go now, love, and sit with Frankie. She's in a hell of a state.'

So Anna was left with a childless and middle-aged man who had no idea of how to entertain an infant. He was a nice fellow. Anna had always loved Elsie and Bert Dixon, so she decided to look after him. Looking after Mr Dixon took her mind off all the worry next door, and the young Anna was a born entertainer, so she wrote him a story and drew some illustrations. At the back of her mind, she could still see her mother battering the wall with the poker, but everything would be all right now, because Mrs Dixon was with Mam.

After what seemed a lifetime, Mrs Dixon came back. She stood in the kitchen doorway and shook her head. 'Twin girls,' she announced. 'Doctor's still there.'

'And Frankie?' asked Bert Dixon.

No reply came from Elsie Dixon's lips. She simply stared at her husband and blinked back some tears.

'Mam says I can pick their names, so they have to be Katherine and Rebecca, and she doesn't mind if they get called Kate and Beckie,' said Anna. 'When can I see them? When can I see my mam?'

Elsie Dixon pressed a balled fist against her mouth before fleeing the scene.

Bert picked up Anna and sat her on his knee. Her mother was dead. Newborn twins required

40

care and attention, but who would bother while there were guns and tanks preparing for battle across the English Channel? Kiddies had been scattered to the four winds, some to Wales, some to Scotland, others to parts of England in which the Nazis might take little interest. The children of London were in the most serious danger of becoming orphaned, but no one in any town was safe. Bolton, just a few miles from Manchester, was scattered generously with munitions factories, engineering works, mills, foundries. What would happen to Frankie's girls? Would they be removed and stuck on some remote Welsh farm? Would they be separated from each other? 'No,' he muttered. 'Not as long as I draw breath.'

'I can't draw breath,' said Anna, whose hearing was acute. 'I can draw a house and a tree and my mam, but... Don't cry, Mr Dixon. It'll be all right, the Germans won't get us.'

'My wonderful girl,' he sobbed. 'You're a credit, that's what you are.'

Anna, who had no idea what a credit was, knew something terrible had happened. Death had already paid a visit to number 13, because Smoky, Anna's half-Persian, had been poisoned by a pigeon fancier in the next street, so she had witnessed one departure. 'Is Mam dead like Smoky?' she asked tearfully.

Bert sniffed. The trouble with kids these days was that they knew too much too early. It was likely that the war had made them old– Sweet Jesus! What about Billy? Billy MacRae was possibly still in England, but he might be shipped off at any time. Where the bloody hell was he barracked these days? He needed to be told that his wife was dead and that he was now father to three daughters.

The door opened and Dr Moss appeared. 'A word, Mr Dixon? Please?' He backed away as if intending to retreat to the narrow lobby.

'Is she dead?' Anna asked before the two men could escape.

The medic stopped in his tracks. There was something about Anna MacRae that demanded and deserved the complete truth. She was five, but she seemed to be nearing forty. 'Yes. It's very sad, Anna, but we couldn't get your mother to the hospital. She needed ... erm.' Transfusion was rather a difficult concept. 'She needed an operation, and we were unable to take her to town.'

Anna turned her back on the two men and stared into the fire. 'Pictures in the flames,' Mam always said. But she wouldn't be saying it any more, would she? Smoky had been so still and stiff after his fit. Mam was like that now, Anna supposed. Without the fur, of course, but still and stiff. They would take her away and put her in a box in the ground – that had happened to Grandad. Lots of flowers, people crying, black clothes, beer afterwards, everyone singing and pretending to be all right.

'What will happen now?' she asked without turning to face the others.

'I'm not sure,' the doctor replied.

'We'll mind them for the time being,' promised Bert Dixon. 'Welfare department's got enough on its hands.'

Peter Moss swallowed hard. 'I'll ... er ... make it

my business to ensure that you get financial help, Mr Dixon. There are committees, charities, organizations. I'm sure you will be awarded assistance.'

When Dr Moss had left, Elsie made her appearance with the two babies. She placed them on the rug, and Anna stood over them. They were funny-looking creatures, faces all crinkly like balloons with some of the air let out. Anger hung in the air above the red-faced newborns, and their cheeks burned bright, shining wet with tears. Anna bent down and dried their faces. 'This one can be Katherine,' she announced. 'She's got the most hair, so we'll be able to tell which is which.' They wore little white nightdresses, mittens and bootees. These two people had come out of Mam, and she had died afterwards. They had no mother. She had no mother.

The tears came then, and Anna realized that she was easily as angry as her little sisters. She screamed and howled while Mrs Dixon prepared baby milk, while Mr Dixon tried to offer comfort. Anna wanted to beat the walls with a poker, just like Mam had done. She wanted to burn the whole world, kill Germans, because they had taken her dad away. Had it not been for that piled-up, suffocating snow, she would have run all the way to town, just to get away from ... from everything and everyone. 'I want my mam,' she screamed.

The babies tried to compete, but their sorry wails were nothing compared to sounds produced by a pair of healthy, five-year-old lungs.

'It's not fair!'

Bert Dixon grabbed the child, picked her up

and cried with her. 'We'll mind thee, lass,' he said repeatedly.

She was sad, lonely, frightened and furious. With tight fists, she beat her kind neighbour on his shoulders, neck and face, but he continued to hold her close. 'It's all right, Anna,' he told her. 'Hurt me all you like, because I know your pain's bigger than mine.'

She ran out of steam eventually, and was placed on the horsehair sofa under the stairs. Elsie Dixon handed her a baby and a bottle, then showed her how to feed Rebecca. 'I'll do the other one in a minute,' she said.

'You're crying as well,' hiccuped Anna.

'We all are,' came the reply.

'Not Mam. Mam won't laugh or cry ever again.' The baby took a few sucks, then fell asleep.

'Tickle her feet,' ordered Elsie, her voice quiet and cracking slightly. 'Keep her awake, petal. You're not the only one missing her mam.'

Bedtime arrived. Elsie stayed downstairs with the babies, who were housed in two padded drawers carried down from an upstairs tallboy. Anna found herself alone in the back bedroom, and she was scared all over again, as she had always slept with Mam since Dad left for the war. When everything was quiet, she made her way downstairs. Silently, she pulled on her teddy-bear slippers and went outside. Snow towered above her, and she prayed that it would not collapse, yet she was determined enough to make her way back to number 13.

Mam was still here. Stretched out in front of a cold range, Frankie MacRae waited for the undertaker to make his way through the product of a severe blizzard. She was white, very pretty, and like a lying-down statue.

Anna collected tablecloths, the green baize table cover, some coats and two cardigans. After wrapping herself in the clothing, she wound the rest of her finds around herself before lying down with Mam. Very gently, she took hold of an ice-cold hand, then, as quietly as possible, she sang Brahms' Lullaby, but she could not quite manage the 'red roses I'll spread, all over thy bed', because Mam had loved roses. There had been roses on her wedding day – Mam had shown Anna the photo.

When morning entered the kitchen via a pin-prick in blackout fabric, the little girl found a brush and a comb for Mam's hair. The water was cold, but it didn't matter now, did it? With a clean flannel, Anna washed her mother's face and hands. The fingers were slacker now, not as fastened to each other as they had seemed in the night. She found her mother's Missal and rosary, winding beads and chain round those poor, chilled fingers before placing the Missal on Mam's chest. It had been given to Frankie when she had made her First Holy Communion, so it should go with her to the grave.

Anna sat at the kitchen table waiting for someone to come. It was wrong to leave Mam alone in this lifeless house. Frankie MacRae had been the centre of everything, the caregiver, nurse, washer-woman, cook and mother. Like Smoky, she was very dead, but the body that had housed Anna's female parent was deserving of respect, and Anna

45

would award that to the woman she had loved with all her young heart. Smoky had been different – just a beloved pet. The lady on the floor was special, and Anna wanted to make sure that everyone knew that.

There was a big noise outside. She ran into the parlour and saw that the snow was moving again. Some big shovels appeared and, attached to them, the nose of a snow-spattered green tractor put in a partial appearance behind the twin blades. They were clearing the way for Mam. It should have been done last night, then the operation could have happened and Mam might have lived. But Anna was too cold and exhausted for anger, so she simply returned to the kitchen and waited with Mam.

After some shouting and the clatter of hand-held spades, the door opened and the world walked in. Anna lifted her head high and looked a black-clad man full in the face. 'I did my best to get her ready,' she said. 'But there's blood on her clothes and I couldn't get them off her. She's too big.' This experienced undertaker bit hard on his lower lip before speaking. When he did manage to produce words, they arrived at a pitch higher than usual. 'Have you been here all night?' he asked.

Anna nodded. 'I washed her and combed her hair and gave her the rosary and Missal. Then I waited for you, because she's special, you see. And I slept with her. I always sleep with Mam when Dad's away.'

He squatted down in front of her. 'You know we have to take your mother away now, don't you?'

46

Of course she did! Did this man think she was stupid? 'She doesn't like pink. Don't put anything pink in the box. She likes red roses and nearly white ones, creamy-coloured, and her church is Peter and Paul's. She'll want Ave Maria, and the hymn with dark sataninic mills – something like that, anyway. Her favourite priest is Father Brogan, but keep him away from the whisky.' An important thought struck. 'You'll not get roses in January, but no pink flowers.'

The man had never seen such composure, certainly not in a bereaved child. He picked her up and passed her over to Bert Dixon. 'Take her home and get her warmed up,' he said. 'She's frozen halfway to death herself.'

Those were the last words Anna was to hear for many weeks. In the arms of her would-be foster father, she lost consciousness. Spring had arrived before she heard that presses local and national had nominated her a war heroine, that owners of businesses had pledged money enough to feed and clothe her for some time, that her real dad had sat with her for over two weeks before leaving for foreign shores. Not for a while would she learn that the Co-op hearse had provided the means of getting her to the infirmary before returning to pick up her wonderful mother's body.

It was pneumonia. Double pneumonia seemed so impressive and important, as was the framed item above her bed, a message from Buckingham Palace signed by King George and Queen Elizabeth. It was all very lovely, but Mam was still dead and Anna had not attended her funeral. She hadn't the strength for tears, so she remained quietly sad for several days. They were trying to build her up. Building her up involved a great deal of food and learning to walk all over again. The once robust child had lost much of her upholstery, and her legs were so weak that they didn't make any sense.

Recovery was slow. But, once Anna managed to teach her lower limbs the difference between straight ahead and going round a corner, she had the best time ever. Bolton Corporation sent people from the Town Hall to talk to her, and newspaper reporters interviewed her and took photos.

Slowly but surely, the scales approached figures commensurate with her age and frame. Eating ceased to be a chore and became a pleasure, because she was better fed than she had been at home. Unlike others on the ward, Anna had a savoury tooth, and often chose a second helping of dinner rather than a pudding. She was finishing a bowl of hotpot when the Man From Welfare arrived.

He sat down and told her his name was Mr Sugden. 'You all right now, love?' he asked.

She nodded, because her mouth was full.

'Only we wondered whether you might like to get fostered somewhere in Wales – on a nice farm, perhaps?'

Anna swallowed. 'With Mr and Mrs Dixon?'

He shook his head. 'No. They'll be staying here.'

'Mam didn't want me vacuumated,' she told him. 'She said the Yanks would come, then Hitler would be...' She searched for her mother's words. 'He'd be a spot of grease on the road and a dirty

48

page in the history books.'

Mr Sugden nodded. This child was a celebrity, so he had better mind his manners. In most cases like this one, the kiddies would have been moved at the stroke of a pen, but Anna was one of Bolton's heroes, and Bolton might well want to keep her. 'If we found somewhere up in one of the villages where Mr and Mrs Dixon could be with you, would that be better?'

Anna shrugged. 'You'd have to ask them. Grown-ups decide, don't they?'

Like many who had met Anna MacRae, Bernard Sugden wanted to take her home and give her the best life possible in these difficult times, but she was part of a package and, if possible, siblings should be kept together.

Father Brogan, who had administered Extreme Unction on Anna's second day in hospital, came to visit the afternoon following the Man From Welfare. 'God bless you, child, you're a sight for sore eyes, and isn't that the honest truth on a rainy day?'

She smiled as she remembered her mother's words. 'He's a lovely man, but he will put himself outside half a bottle of scotch every day.'

'Did you do Mam's funeral?' she asked, although she already knew the answer.

'I did. The church was packed like a sardine tin, and she got the full Requiem. There's a headstone now with her name on it – people have been very kind. There was nothing pink. The Co-op said I was to be sure to tell you that.'

'Thank you, Father.'

He took a flask from a pocket and poured some

of its contents into his mouth. 'Medicinal purposes,' he said with a wink.

Anna chuckled. 'My mam liked you,' she said.

'And I liked her. She's missed by the whole of the parish, but there's many a good soul in this town who'll want to help after the tragedy.' He held her hand. 'Mr Dixon's to work in the countryside with the Land Army, and Mrs Dixon will look after you and the babies in a cottage outside Bolton. I baptized them – Katherine Joan and Rebecca Frances. They're doing fine, so they are. Mortallious troublesome when hungry, but isn't that ever the way of it? You'll be home soon. God bless.' He left.

Anna wasn't sure how to feel about any of it. Nothing could be done to retrieve the life she had known, because nothing could be done to bring back her mother. Jesus had resurrected Lazarus, and his sisters had been as happy as Larry, but Jesus wasn't here. So, unlike Martha and Mary, Anna couldn't sit and wait for her Saviour to come along and fetch Mam back. She didn't want to leave hospital. Although either Elsie or Bert had visited every day, they had never brought her sisters, and she was ashamed to admit it, but life in the celebrity lane had been preferable to the thought of living with those two angry, red-faced little people.

Anna decided to make herself indispensable. After finding her way to the geriatric wards, she visited daily and read aloud from books, newspapers and magazines. The patients were delighted, as some had few visitors, and many were not long for this world, so the new presence on

50

the wards was a source of great pleasure to them.

However, the powers in the paediatric department noticed that Anna MacRae was becoming institutionalized, so she was released into the community at the beginning of April. Staff and patients wept when she was driven away by one of the doctors, and many expressed the opinion that the infirmary would not be the same without her. 'Bright as a button.' Sister Morton dried her eyes, then dragged her reluctant nurses back inside. 'Come along,' she snapped. 'There's a war on, you know.'

Anna was driven around the edge of her very large town, and she recognized little of what she saw. The world was very green and there were no mills, few shops, no tall chimneys staining the sky. 'You'll be safer and healthier up here,' said Dr Openshaw. 'Your foster parents have jobs. Mr Dixon will work on a farm, and his wife will help some evenings at a home for mothers and babies. Hitler won't waste his bombs out here.'

Anna gulped. She would miss Peter and Paul's, would even miss the nuns, many of which number were humourless, sour-faced and swift to punish all offenders, however minor their crimes. Two or three of the sisters were pleasant and very stimulating when it came to education, and the lay teachers were mostly all right. But she had lost everything. She had no mam, a dad who was away killing Germans, no friends, no home, no school, no expectations. What did people do out here in the countryside? There were cows, horses and sheep, but so what? She couldn't play hopscotch with a sheep. 'Where's my school?' she asked.

51

'Just a bicycle ride away,' came the answer.

'I can't ride a bike.'

'You'll learn,' the doctor promised. 'And riding will make your legs stronger. You can have your own hens, so your own eggs will be collected daily. You'll be able to run in the fields and help with your sisters.'

Ah. She hadn't forgotten Kate and Beckie, but she'd chosen not to dwell on them. At the back of her mind lingered the small suspicion that the twins had killed her mother, that Frankie MacRae would still be alive were it not for the babies and the snow. It was better to blame the snow, because accusing her sisters was not nice.

The car stopped outside a stone-built cottage. It was in a row of four, so there would be neighbours, at least. 'Can I go in?' she asked.

The doctor nodded, but stayed where he was while Anna went through the gate and into the house.

It smelled empty. There was no furniture, and her footfalls echoed along stone floors. She found a front room, a big kitchen, and a huge rear garden that needed immediate surgery. Upstairs, there were three bedrooms, plus a small bathroom with a metal bath that was stained below the taps. She almost laughed. There was a real bath! Grandad used to have one of those, and water had been heated in a boiler behind the fire downstairs.

She returned to the car. 'There's no gas,' she said.

Her chauffeur nodded. 'Oil lamps and candles, I'm afraid. But at least you have mains water and

52

a back boiler. No one can have everything, child.'

It was Anna's opinion that some people had nice cars, good suits and jobs that didn't make their hands dirty, but she said nothing. Her mother and the nuns had trained this child well, as she remained anxious not to upset anybody. 'Thank you,' she said dutifully. 'I'm sure I'll learn how to ride.'

'Good girl.'

A thought struck. 'Is it a Catholic school? The one I need a bike to get to? Is it Catholic?'

The doctor cleared his throat. As far as he knew it was an ordinary state primary school, but he wasn't a hundred percent certain. 'Not sure,' he replied.

Anna, knowing that she had struck gold, thanked him politely and stepped out of the car, automatically steering herself in the direction of number 13. It looked different. The step hadn't been stoned, and Mam always... She turned her head and saw the enormous pram outside number 11. They were propped up and making noises. Ignoring the twins, she stalked past and opened the door to a future that had to contain the Dixons and two strangers in a pram. But there was hope; that hope rested in Father Brogan's boss, the Bishop of Salford.

Within days of her return, Anna found herself caring for the babies. She was not expected back at school, which was just as well, as her days were packed with changing and feeding two very young infants. It wasn't Elsie Dixon's fault. She was getting on in years, and she wasn't used to children, as she and Bert hadn't had any of their own.

'Anna,' Elsie said as they were finishing supper one evening. 'Don't you think you and the little ones might be better off with somebody a bit younger than me and Bert? I mean, if we move up to the country, he'll have to do farm work, and I'll be expected to do my bit a couple of evenings a week because of the war. It's not easy, love.'

Bert cleared his throat. He wanted to keep the three girls, but he understood his wife's misgivings. 'Think on, Anna,' he said. 'We love you to bits, but it won't be easy for any of us.'

The child thought for a moment before replying. 'It would be better if we stayed here,' she said. 'That house smells funny and it's got no gas mantles. It's all grass and trees, sheep on the hills and cows in the fields. No picture house, no shops, no nothing.'

'There's a bus into town,' said Elsie.

Anna was ready for this. 'And do you take the twins on the bus? Who looks after them while you go to town and I go to the Proddy school and Mr Dixon works on the farm?'

Elsie, too, was ready. 'They can stay where I'll work,' she replied. 'Mrs Mellor has a big house full of young women and babies – she looks after them – so two more won't be a problem. Me and Bert are looking forward to getting away – we'll all be safer.'

Anna sighed dramatically. 'All right,' she pronounced. 'But my mother wouldn't be happy with me sitting next to Protestants. When my dad gets

54

back from the war, he won't be pleased, either.' The bishop would save her. He wouldn't sign to say she could get taught by non-Catholics.

'When do Kate and Beckie start sitting up?' Anna asked.

'A couple of months yet,' answered Bert.

A couple of months? What was she supposed to do in the mean time? Sit in a field making daisy chains among a few dozen cow pats? Feed chickens, do sums next to a Proddy and learn to ride a bike? 'When do we have to go, Uncle Bert?' She had been instructed to name them Auntie and Uncle, and had decided that it seemed to be a good idea.

'Next week,' he said. 'The bishop's given his decision. You can go to the school, and a priest will come to the house and teach you on a Saturday.'

Great. The list was growing again. She'd lost her mam, her dad, her house, her school, her town, her friends and her Saturdays. She'd almost lost her life, and she'd almost become famous, but she still had to do as she was told. Upstairs, she made her first *THINGS* list. Something would happen. There was always a next thing. So she wrote what she wanted to happen, then said a decade of the rosary. She could do no more. Like a buttercup in a field, she bent every time the wind blew. But it wouldn't always be like this. Would it?

Tom Brogan had to walk away. As a priest, he was used to raw emotion, because he counselled the bereaved, forgave the sinner, attended the dying, baptized the newborn. But the tragedy embodied by Anna MacRae, whose faith shone from every pore, was more than he could cope with. She was talking to her mother. In Anna's mind, Frances was seated at the right hand of God, so the child was speaking to a saint. He wished with all his heart that his own beliefs could be so pure, so simple.

'They can't even sit up,' she said. 'They just dribble, drink milk and wet their nappies.'

Even two graves away, he could hear her. Several sips from his hip flask helped a little, and he steadied himself on a headstone belonging to Somebody Riley. He wasn't drunk. His vision was clouded by tears, not by alcohol.

'We're going tomorrow, and our new address is number three, Weavers Row, Eagle Vale. It's all right. It has a bath with taps and the water comes from behind the fire. If you want to visit us, that's where we'll be, but God will give you directions if you forget the address. Come and see us. I'm not frightened of your spirit.'

This was the last straw for Father Brogan. He sobbed into a handkerchief until Anna touched his hand. 'It's all right, Father,' she advised him. 'When the lining came away, she started to lose lifeblood and it couldn't be helped. It wasn't the twins' fault. It could have happened when I was born.'

He stared at her, his sobs slowing. 'Anna? Who told you that?'

'Mam did. When I was asleep.'

'Oh. I see.' She had probably overheard a conversation between Mrs Dixon and another woman. This had transferred into her sleep, and she believed that her mother had told her. 'That's

56

good, then, isn't it, Anna?'

She nodded. 'Oh, and Mam said if you don't stop drinking, you'll be dead in five years.'

'Did she say that when you were asleep?'

'She's always said it. She could even smell it at confession, because it came through the holes in the whatsername.'

'Grille,' he said helpfully.

'So I want you to pour what's left in your pocket onto Mam's grave. She'll get rid of it for you.'

Angels came in all shapes and guises, the priest decided. Tramps, thieves, vagabonds, the elderly and the young had been his teachers for many a year. He stood over the grave of a beautiful woman and poured away his scaffolding. 'I'll go back to Ireland,' he told mother and daughter. 'There's a place in Dublin for priests like me who take a drop or a gallon too much. For you, Frankie, and for you, Anna, I'll get dry.'

Anna laughed. 'You'll not be dry long, Father. Here comes the rain...'

The cart arrived to take them and their belongings to their new home. The horse ambled along and began the long trek through town and up Tonge Moor Road. The rain held off, at least, so that was one happy circumstance. Anna sat with her mother's table, dresser, parlour furniture and rugs. She was taking all that was left of Frankie MacRae and putting it in a house made of stone and uneven plaster work. Folded near her feet was the green baize cover she had wrapped herself in when her mother had been dead just a few hours. It was difficult to know how to feel, because although she was happy to have her mother's things, she was sad about moving them.

'You all right, love?' asked Bert.

She nodded. She had to be all right, since she needed to learn to ride a bike and go to school with a load of Proddies. There were very few houses. Field after field spread all the way to the horizon, and Anna swallowed hard. Why did people choose to live up here in all the silence? Where did they buy bread, see a doctor, go to the pictures? But she had to admit, however begrudgingly, that the countryside smelled and tasted good. It smelled and tasted of raw peas straight from the pod. The taste was green. Could a taste own a colour?

They reached their own tiny hamlet and found a young woman in the front garden. 'Welcome,' she said cheerily. 'I'm Land Army, but I've been posted to you for the day. Still, at least I don't have to do any mucking out, which is the best news ever.'

She talked funny and she had pink hair. Later, Anna would be told by Elsie that the colour was strawberry blonde. Lifted down by Bert, Anna studied the Land Army. It had no uniform – just overalls and a pair of heavy boots. 'I'm Anna.'

'Pleased to meet you, I'm sure,' answered the Land Army. 'I'm from Essex, but I'm here for the duration because I asked to come here. My grandparents live just over the hill, and I help on their farm. Anyway, aren't you the famous one? Everybody knows your name. I'm Linda, by the way.'

'Hello, Linda-by-the-way. We have to live here because of my pneumonia.'

'You'll get used to it,' Linda promised. 'There are other houses over the hill, so don't think you have just these immediate neighbours. Decent people. Nice little school, and there's a bike inside for you. Second-hand, but good condition. When we've got you settled, I'll put the saddle right for you and teach you how to use it.'

Linda Harris was filed immediately under the *good people* label in Anna's mind. She talked funny, dressed like a man, smelled a bit of horse poo, but she was a good-people lister, as were Uncle Bert, Auntie Elsie, Father Brogan and Dr Moss. There were a lot more good people than bad. In fact, if it wasn't for Mam being dead and 'bloody' Hitler remaining alive, the world would be a wonderful place. So Anna decided to be as happy as possible and walked with Linda into her new home.

Three

The Battle of the Bulge took place a couple of days after Susan moved into the caravan. I named the riot rather appropriately, as I had never seen so many beer bellies flopping about above too-tight waistbands of jeans. This display of sartorial elegance was further improved by T-shirts that had either shrunk in the wash, or simply failed to keep up with the growth of their owners. The possessors of bellies and ill-fitting clothing wanted our Susan, but our Susan didn't want them.

Fortunately, Den was away. He would never have coped, since his main concerns in life are his position at work, his membership of Round Table, his beautiful car, and the opinions of his neighbours. Because I have absolutely no patience with bullies, I sent for the police. They came screaming round the corner in a car christened a jam butty by Susan, who is clearly used to the sight of a vehicle with a red stripe across its middle.

Two jaded constables leaned nonchalantly against the parked vehicle and enjoyed the beauty of the scene. They were so 'excited' that they might have been seeing a Renoir for the first time. My front lawn was scattered with beer bottles and broken plant pots. Dog dirt was smeared on the door, and the biggest of the men – our Gary – was screaming at the lesbo inside. According to him, I

60

am a predatory lesbian who has stolen his sister, but the police were not impressed. 'Right,' said one before calling for backup. 'Shut it, Hughes.' He clicked a switch. 'Send a wagon,' he told his radio. 'It's the Hughes boys. Yes, it's them again, and I'm sorry – get the disinfectant. Over and out and a happy Christmas.' It was nearly August, but he didn't care.

'The paddy wagon'll be here in a minute,' Susan advised. 'Then we have to get an injunction off a solicitor. If they come anywhere near, they'll go straight to jail, do not pass go, do not collect a red cent. Daft buggers.' Thus she dismissed her family before promising to clean up the front once the paddy bus had removed her offending relatives from the vicinity.

Mrs Bee had to get involved, of course, but she had the sense to leave her gun inside. I came out of the house and whispered, 'Mention no guns,' before talking to the constable who had moved Christmas on his calendar. 'Susan's in my house,' I advised him. 'She's sleeping in a spare room at present, but she has a caravan in the back garden. They had no room at home, and I am not a lesbian.'

He chuckled. 'Listen, love. I wouldn't let my mother-in-law's cat live at the Hughes place. It's like Bedlam, but with a colour telly, and God knows how they came by that. That girl's the only decent one. She deserves a break.'

Mrs Bee was having a word or three with the men in handcuffs. 'Dog shit?' she yelled. She went on to inform them that if the cops didn't shift them fast, she would scrape off the offending mess and shove it and her spade sideways right up–

'All right,' said the other policeman. 'Don't get too graphic, or you'll be giving the boys ideas above their station.'

But her dander was up. Watching and hearing her magnificence in full flood was a privilege, and I sat on a low wall while she spat venom. 'Come round here again and I'll separate you from your future,' she promised. 'Hitler wasn't all wrong, you know. Folk like you should get casterated, then you couldn't breed and fill the world with fat bastards.'

'Hang on, love,' urged the nearest policeman.

'Two bloody world wars, I've lived through,' she went on seamlessly. 'Good men gone and buried, some of them not even buried because we couldn't find them. Did they get blown to bits so's you lot can sit in the house all day drinking beer? Did my brother lose half a leg for you?'

The offending articles were finally locked in the back of the van.

She carried on shouting about 'casteration' and National Service and idle bastard Scouse gits. It was like watching a film or an early episode of Coronation Street when Ena Sharples had ruled the snug in the Rovers. Tony Warren knew what he was about when he invented the Street, because those powerful women had come through a couple of wars, and therein lay their strength. Though I had to admit that Mrs Bee's language was a great deal more colourful than anything emerging from a soap opera. 'Get in here,' I told her when she stopped for breath. 'I mean it. You'll be ill if you

62

don't calm down.'

Mrs Bee looked straight through me. 'I'll get me bucket,' she said.

Between them, the two women cleared up the front of the house while I phoned our lawyer. The injunction was to be sought, but the solicitor, a close friend, became almost hysterical when I told her about Mrs Bee. 'It's not funny,' I said with great solemnity. 'She could have a stroke or a heart attack, because she can't help herself.'

When I returned to the living room, the unmistakable smell of Dettol rose from both occupants. They were having a glass of the famous parsnip wine, but I refused to partake, as I had no intention of being charged with some felony like being drunk in charge of a pram.

'Can me mam still come round?' asked an anxious Susan.

'Yes. I knocked her off the list.' And it was quite a lengthy list. How so many could fit into a three-bedroomed house I would never understand. 'Don't drink any more of that,' I told her. 'You'll be seeing double and walking like a ruptured duck.'

She giggled. It was already too late, because her system hadn't become inured to Mrs Bee's wines. It is my belief that a person needs to work hard and slowly before setting foot inside a three-yard radius of Mrs Bee's alcoholic beverages. Even a small dose can be nearly lethal, as I had discovered after imbibing a couple of sips of her rhubarb 1969.

Mrs Bee went home. She travelled in a line that was less than straight, and would probably sleep off her problem in her favourite chair. But Susan had a baby to care for and– She was snoring softly, and I needed to amend my opinion. 'Anna,' I said. 'Today, you have three babies.'

It was, in fact, easier with three. Stephen lay between my girls and all was well. All was nearly well. I shivered. He was too quiet, too good, too perfect. The little lad was just ... there. An occasional smile, a gurgle, a small movement of the arms... Beyond that, there seemed to be little in him. The day of the dog-shitty door was the day on which I began to worry about a small creature whose name was neither Lottie nor Emily. They could lift their heads, sometimes trying to raise themselves up on their arms when face down on the floor. He stayed where he was put. An icy finger travelled the length of my spine. There was possibly something wrong with little Stephen Hughes.

We both like the graveyard behind St Luke's in Hesford. We walk under the lych gate and along shale paths until we reach the back of the church. Older stones bear names of some very young occupants. It is easy now to believe that early in the century, one in five children died before they achieved a second birthday.

She hasn't said anything about Stephen. I have dropped a hint or two, but Susan insists that boys are always slower than girls until they reach their teens. Our prams are parked under a tree, and we rest on a bench nearby. 'Susan?'

'What?'

'He doesn't play, does he?'

She looks towards the prams. 'I know, but he doesn't kick the daylights out of Lottie, either, so let's count our blessings.'

She is right, of course. But while my older twin is troublesome, she is developing, as is Lottie. They always reach for me, 'talk' to me, laugh at me. 'He doesn't often cry, does he?'

'I'm lucky,' Susan says.

Running out of options, I decide to go for the full works. There is a baby involved and, much as I like that baby's mother, he is the one who is truly important. This is not going to be easy. Shall I wait until we get home? Oh, God. 'Susan, have none of the nurses at the clinic said anything about him?'

She blushes slightly. 'Not much, no.'

'What have they said?'

Susan turns and looks hard at me. 'One said he wasn't ... wasn't coming on as he should, but he might catch up suddenly. They do, you know.'

'Yes, they all have their own speed. Emily focused properly weeks before Lottie did.'

'There you are, then.'

'He's a bit floppy,' I say.

'Leave it, Anna. Please leave it.'

Looking at her now, I see the girl I first caught sight of in the village hall on baby clinic day. She is lost, lonely and terrified. 'I can't talk about it,' she tells me. Fear blazes behind unshed tears. She begins to rock back and forth like some long-neglected inmate in an ancient mental institution. 'Please, Anna,' she repeats.

I move closer and pull her into my arms. Her hair smells of my shampoo. She is young, tiny, beautiful and immeasurably afraid. 'You can say anything at all to me, Susan. If he needs hospital tests, I'll go with you. I will never, ever betray you. I won't take the caravan away from you, and I'll deal with any trouble like I dealt with your brothers. From the age of five, I've lived with fear and emptiness. But I stamped on it. I still have to manage it. My dreams and nightmares are not controllable, but I cope. Give me your burden.'

'At home,' she answers. 'Let me think while we walk home.'

To my extreme disappointment, Den's car is on the driveway. I send Susan to the caravan and go into the house. It's deadly silent. Perhaps Amsterdam has worn him out, because the house feels empty. Without knowing why, I creep upstairs and along the landing. He is in the bathroom and hasn't closed the door. My husband is sitting on the loo picking at his pubic area. Whatever he harvests goes into the washbasin.

I stand there for several seconds. This person, managing director of the largest company in the area, is collecting crab lice. I remember Auntie Elsie's weekly safari for nits when I was young, then I clear my throat. 'Would you like me to see if the chemist has a little fine-toothed comb for your pubes?' I ask, my tone light and pleasant.

Red-faced, he jumps up. 'They mustn't have changed the sheets,' he cries.

'Bollocks,' is my immediate response. It's appropriate, at least. 'You come back from Amsterdam with crabs? They don't live in sheets. You've picked them up from a whore, you stupid man.'

'She wasn't a–' His face reddens even further.

'Whatever she was, there was wildlife on her body. Now. Listen to me, Denis Fairbanks. Come near me again, and I shall not be answerable for my actions. Remember, I'm post-natal, so it wouldn't be murder. Get out of this house now, and take your crabby little friends with you. I want you gone by six, otherwise I phone the doctor and tell him about your little visitors.'

'But Anna–'

'Bugger off. I mean it, Den. You are a despicable, spineless little shit.' I descend the stairs and he tries to follow me, trousers and underpants round his ankles, sweat pouring from his brow. He reminds me of one of those Brian Rix oops-the-vicar's-lost-his-dignity farces, and I find myself laughing. Bad mistake. He has a sense of humour until he becomes the subject of ridicule. Is he really English?

'Don't talk to me like that, you bitch,' he shouts.

For some reason or other, I cannot take this man seriously. He wants patting on the head and praising several times a day. Like a dog, he needs to be told how precious he is. 'Hear me, bird-brain,' I say. 'Get out, or I'll go and ask Mrs Bee if she knows a remedy for crabs. She'll start off with a recipe, I daresay, but I'll soon put her right. Get to a clinic and, when you've got rid of your sexually transmitted lodgers, find yourself somewhere to live, because you, too, are a louse.'

When I get outside, I am shaking so much that I can scarcely steer the pram. My bolster is still in place, but Emily is getting so strong that she will soon be able to kick it out of the pram. Lottie is asleep, and Emily glares at me. She always has to be placed at the end facing me. If I put her at the other end, she screams like a banshee. I am fed up with everything, but Susan needs help. My divorce will be sooner rather than later; I must sit it on a low light for a while, as young Stephen deserves my attention more.

But I don't get the chance, as Susan is learning fast. She's becoming very astute when it comes to the assessment of people. 'What happened?' she asks. 'Something's happened – I can tell.'

So I tell her. If I am expecting her to open up her heart, I have to be prepared to do the same.

'Bugger in a bucket,' she says. I can tell she is truly shocked. When she has placed all three babies on a soft rug – Stephen in the centre, of course – she asks me what I am going to do.

'Divorce,' I say. 'Then, perhaps I'll go back to work. You cope with the kids and you get free bed and board, plus all child allowance and a small wage on top. OK?'

'Fine,' she replies. 'What if it had been something worse than crabs, Anna?'

I shrug. 'Life's a bitch, then you get syphilis.'

'Don't say that,' she chides.

'I'm joking. Do you think I'm going to let him near me again? He's got till six to sod off, then, if he's still here, I phone the doctor and tell him about Den's new pets.'

'You wouldn't!'

'Just watch this space if and when,' I tell her. 'And put the kettle on.'

Susan makes three bottles for the babies while

I change their nappies. It's half past five. He has half an hour to bugger off out of here. If necessary, we can all sleep in the caravan, because I am not going inside the house while he remains. I already feel itchy all over every time I think about those blinking lice. I don't give a damn about all his women, but he should keep the filth away from me and my kids.

'So I'll live in the house when he's gone?' Susan asks.

'Yes. But he won't go without a fight, love. This house and the extra acre are evidence of his success. He has a position to maintain, and I am his wife – he owns me. And it's all the fault of womankind – his mother reared him as if he were another Messiah.'

'What are you going to do?' she asks.

I allow her a tight smile. 'Just watch a professional at work, babe. Then, when the road's cleared, we'll talk about Stephen.'

Six o'clock comes, and he is still in the house. I can open none of the doors, as he has put the bolts on. OK. I leave the children with Susan and walk to a telephone box on the main road. After informing our doctor that I have had to move into the caravan with three babies and another mother, I explain that I cannot share a home with a man who has a venereal problem. Next, I phone our solicitor and give her the same news. 'Before he jumps in and asks you,' I tell her, 'I want you for my side of the divorce.'

Smiling grimly, I go into the pub for a quick brandy. It's early, so the place is empty apart from a couple of old men playing dominoes. The landlord asks me if I am all right and, after swallowing the alcohol, I tell him I am fine and dandy, thanks. Feeling slightly more optimistic, I walk home and remember my childhood beliefs, the strength of my faith in the Catholic Church. No divorce. Divorce is a sin, but no one ever mentioned prostitutes and crab lice, did they? No longer bound by archaic law, I march down Beech Grove and knock at my own door.

'Come in,' he says after opening it.

'I'll come in when you're out. I've started divorce proceedings, and the doctor knows why the twins and I are living in the van. Get out now, or I go to Mrs Bee. And I am sure the firm would like to hear about your jaunts on the continent. A word with Mrs Bee, and the whole village will know within the hour. Get packing, Buster.'

He looks at me with those big, doggy eyes. He's scared to death of another breakdown, of being alone, of not owning a wife, a house, an acre and a couple of kids. I can almost read his simple thoughts – because he is simple. He will have to start applying for jobs elsewhere, will need to convince everyone that he has ended the marriage, will want to find some female clown who will take him on and do kitchens and bedrooms. Really, he requires a cook who works as a concubine on the side. He should advertise. 'You need to be married,' I tell him. 'I need not to be married. So find somebody PDQ and pray she doesn't have the brains to see through the sham that you are.'

He blinks rapidly. 'Are you serious?'

'No,' I say. 'I'm joking. Let's go upstairs, make

70

mad, passionate love and give your tenants a future. We could set up our own little farm and sell them to people who want to plant evidence. Grow up, for God's sake.' I take a step back. 'Hello, Mrs Bee,' I say, turning my head as if in response to her presence. She isn't there, and neither is Den – he's stepping away.

He closes the door and I hear him running up the stairs. He'll go. He'll have to go in case I start alerting the neighbourhood about his carelessness. Mrs Bee continues to be absent, but he thinks she's with me. She's probably inside like all sensible people, will be helping her daughter to prepare the evening meal.

Back in the van, all babies are asleep in a row along the sofa. Susan and I are a bit cheesed off, so she dashes off to the chip shop while I stay with the offspring. It's all been a bit musical chairs, and I sink gratefully into the sofa next to our children. Asleep, Emily is nothing short of gorgeous. Lottie is pretty, but Emily the Terrible is a thing of beauty rather than a joy for ever. It's so hard. This post-natal disquiet from which I am supposedly suffering should make it impossible to love either of my babies. The awesome truth is that I adore Lottie and am scared to death of Emily.

We eat our fish and chips from the packaging in which they arrive. When we have finished, Susan delivers another shock. Still. Perhaps it's best to have everything pushed into one day? After informing me that my husband's car is now gone, she sits opposite me and we're back at the clinic on that first day. I watch as she empties her face of all emotion. 'They were all out,' she tells me

71

eventually. 'Mam had gone the bingo, and I didn't know where the rest of them were. Then he came back and ... he raped me.'

'Your dad?' I ask.

She shakes her head and informs me that her dad has probably suffered for years from brewer's droop. 'My brother.'

And here I sit, putting crab lice into perspective. 'So Stephen is your nephew as well as your son?'

'Something like that.'

There are some split seconds in life when the world shakes without the help of a fault in its structure. I can't see properly, can scarcely hear. Adrenalin surges through me like an express train with failed brakes, and I need to kill someone. This young woman has raised herself, has made the best of the circumstances into which she was born. Say something, Anna, I tell myself as the earth crashes back into its proper place. 'Does your mother know?' My heart is threatening to jump out of my chest. I will kill him, I will.

'No.'

'Does anyone know?'

'Just you, me and him.'

I can't help myself. 'Which one of your brothers?' I ask.

'The honest truth? I don't know.'

This information I find difficult to process.

It pours from her. She has to spit it out quickly to get rid of the taste. In a dark room, she woke to find herself struggling to breathe, because someone had placed a pillow slip over her head and was tying it with a cord. In spite of this restriction, she managed to identify the attacker as one of her siblings. 'They all smell of the same sweat,' she tells me calmly. 'And they're all about the same size. When he'd ... finished, he told me in a whisper that if I grassed, he'd kill me. It was my first and only time. Even their voices are alike, so the whisper meant sod all.'

There's a cold hand in my chest, and it seems to be trying to choke the life out of me. 'What were you going to be, Susan? If Stephen hadn't happened?'

'A vet would have been out of my reach, so I was going to be a vet nurse. I was saving up – had a little job cleaning and another in a clothes shop. I've got ten subjects, and four of them are top marks. Then this awful thing happened. Mam and Dad turned on me – it was a nightmare. I put bolts on my bedroom door and lived in there. In the end, I was a skeleton with a big belly.' She smiles at me. 'Then you found me.'

It's a long time since I prayed. I thank God for sending Susan and Stephen to me. 'I won't say a word to anyone,' I tell her.

'Thanks.'

'Who was in the house after it was all over?' I ask.

'Nobody. It took me a while to move, because I had to untie the knots in my dressing gown cord.' She hesitates. 'I think it was our Gary. He had scratches on his face, said he'd been in a fight at a club in town.' For the Hughes family, 'town' means Liverpool. 'He brought them all round here to trash the place because he's frightened that I'll tell you. But I'm not a hundred percent certain it was him. Anyway, I think my son's the real victim here. It's like the Spanish Royal family from way back. They were affected because of inbreeding.'

She's a clever, well-read girl.

And she hasn't finished. 'When he grows up...' The four words hang in the air for a while, and I know she is omitting *IF he grows up.* 'Well, he'll have to be told, won't he?'

'Possibly,' is all the answer I can muster.

'He can't go round having kids,' adds Susan. 'Because he could pass whatever it is along down the line. His genes are wrong, Anna. And it's not his fault, yet I'll have to tell him he's not normal. The stuff goes round and round in my head all the while.'

This is another factor that puts me in my place. I have worried myself to the edge of sanity because Emily seems to hate Lottie. But my kids are what Mrs Bee would term 'all there'. They are developing physically and mentally, are vocal and capable of watching life and taking it in. Stephen just stays where he is put, and that's a terrible problem. 'You haven't told the doctor that the child is your brother's?'

'No. Can you imagine what he'd think, Anna, if I said I don't know which one? He'd probably decide I've slept with all of them – he might not believe the truth. Which one? I'm not sure, Doctor. Think about that.'

Emily delivers her usual performance, and I go to feed her. Susan comes in, face wet with tears. She tells me he never wakes to be fed, that she has to rouse him and force him to take milk. I tell her it's none of her fault, that she's doing her best, and I'll work on him. Somewhere in the deepest recesses of the roof space, I have books on child development. The library might be better, more up to date. I am not going to tell Susan not to cry. She probably never cried at home, but she can let herself out here. Her problems outweigh mine, so I cannot return to work until things settle. Clearly, I shall require gigantic maintenance from the dear departed.

'How can I thank you?' she asks.

'By being here and by being yourself. That caravan is still your own space. Use it when you want to get away by yourself.'

'You're my miracle,' she says before speeding out of the room.

Susan and Stephen, who are not my family, are precious dependants, and I shall carry them as far as possible and for as long as I am needed. I know how it feels to have not just a rug, but a whole fitted carpet dragged from beneath my feet, and that is why I understand her. My partially stolen childhood is reflected in the loss of her virginity, an act so cruel that I cannot allow myself to consider it for any length of time. I still want to kill Gary. He was the ringleader when it came to the destruction of my garden; he was the one who called me 'lesbo'. There is no shadow of doubt in my mind. Gary is the rapist and the father of a child who probably has special needs.

It's a criminal family. The mother – our Marie – is bogged down beneath the weight of so many dysfunctional sons, and her husband's a waste of space. Out of that compost heap has emerged an intelligent and lively flower whose nerves have been shattered by an animal. Animals. She likes them, doesn't she? Dogs I have read about, and they are used for the blind, for the deaf, for the disabled. Stephen might respond... At last, I sleep.

The most wonderful thing about Juliet Anderson is that she can make almost anything happen. She knows just about everyone in most professions, and can be depended upon for discretion. Her motivation when it comes to helping people originates in her genuine affection for the human animal, and I am happy to count myself as one of her favourites in that large category.

She is my solicitor. At first, she probed gently with a view to finding out as much as she could about my needs, but, once furnished with the information that everything had to be top secret, she went to work in the dark and came up trumps within a week.

The phone rings. 'Can you talk?' she asks.

'Sort of. What is it?'

'Where do you want him?'

'My house.'

'Thursday afternoon at two?' she suggests.

'Fine.' I say goodbye and join my lodger in the sitting room. Now, I must begin. Susan has to trust me. If she doesn't, the whole thing will have to be called off. 'Susan?'

'What?' She is knitting a blanket for her son's pushchair.

'If you need to see a specialist, you normally go to your doctor for a letter. Right?'

She nods.

'I've ... er ... I've got round it, pulled a few strings, called in some favours. If you will allow it, a man called George will come on Thursday to assess Stephen.'

She drops the knitting. 'Bloody hell, Anna. You said you'd never betray me, never let me down – now this? A bloody doctor coming to stare at my son because he's a freak?'

The child in question chooses this moment to lift his head from the pillow. He has never done that before.

'George knows nothing,' I tell her. 'And, when he comes, you can go out or stay in. If you're out, I'll just say I'm concerned about the baby's development. If you're in, you tell him as much or as little as you like. I'm doing this for Stephen, not for you or me. Susan, I'm just a teacher. I don't know a great deal of medical stuff. But I've read some journals in the library about children of incest – yes – it's a nasty word and, unless the behaviour goes back through generations, most of them are OK.'

She blinks rapidly. 'You sure?'

'Yes.' I can't say any more, because something is happening. He's staring at me. He's glaring, actually. It's as if he's telling to take my nose out of his affairs, to bugger off out of it and mind my own business. A miracle? Perhaps not, though it's a definite happening. 'A-bah,' he pronounces before allowing his head to become too heavy to carry. I burst into tears. It's another of those moments, isn't it? Life throws up boulders, and they are either obstacles or stepping stones. I dry my eyes and walk over this one.

'Anna?'

'Give me a minute, Susan.' She heard it, too. She's grinning from ear to ear. I compose myself. 'Remember the day we met?'

'Of course I do.'

I swallow a lump of emotion. 'Did you go out at all after he was born? Before we met, did you go out? Apart from the clinic?'

'No. We stayed in the cupboard. I didn't want to see anyone in that house, so I made myself scarce.'

She had made Stephen scarce, too. For the last few days, he has been out of prison and is now listening, seeing, copying Emily's 'a-bah'. We need to teach him how to play. The little lad has become used to the idea that no one expects anything from him, that he can remain a newborn with no need to do the growing up bit. I suppose I understand him. Life grabs at us the minute we emerge from the womb, and it can get hard. He's had a rest, but I intend to make damned sure that he catches up. In this moment, I am incredibly happy.

'There's nothing wrong with him, is there?' Susan asks.

'We won't need George,' I tell her. 'Not just yet, and hopefully never. But you'll have to get him moving, love.'

It is clear that Stephen has a good sense of timing, because he chooses this moment to break wind and kick at his blanket. I am going now to cancel George.

We have four babies. The last of the quartet arrives at ten minutes to six exactly one week after the Battle of the Bulge. He is rather large for a pram, but he has clearly thrown all his toys out of the playpen and wants them back. Now.

As soon as he appears, Susan takes herself and the other three babies through the French window, across the huge lawn and into the caravan. She's a clever girl – she can carry three at once. I'd send her the fourth, but she doesn't deserve him. 'Well?' I ask.

'You've changed all the bloody locks.' It's strange how I've never noticed before that his thick, lower lip is rather slack and wet.

'Yes, I've changed the locks. What do you want?'

'I want my house back.'

'The house is for the children, Den. When they're eighteen and have finished school, we'll talk about the house.'

'What?' The Paul McCartney eyes are round and shocked. 'Where the bloody hell am I supposed to live? This is my house, and I've worked hard for it.'

I fold my arms. 'For the bricks and mortar, maybe. But I made this a home – I worked, too. Anyway, none of that matters, because I am going for full custody, and no judge on earth will throw out the twins. It's their turn, Den. It's their house, their home.'

He staggers back. 'Can't I just live here? I'll sleep in another room.'

'So that people will see how OK your life is? So that no one will talk?'

The man nods. 'That's it. That would suit me.'

'Oh, bugger off, will you? I can't be bothered – talk to your lawyer.'

'Yes,' he screams. 'And you got Juliet, didn't you?'

'I did.'

And it just happens. One minute, I am standing at the front door; the next finds me on the floor in the hall with him on top of me and his hands closing around my throat. It's true. Your life does flash before your eyes, and I am back in a cold kitchen with a dead woman, then up in the countryside, teaching a class, giving birth. A sudden, desperate surge of adrenalin allows me to move my own hands and tear at his face. Blood drips. It tastes metallic.

He jumps up, blinks stupidly and runs away. 'You're not worth it,' he calls over his shoulder. He means I'm not worth a life sentence, I suppose.

His car roars off the drive, and I remain on the floor. Those small pinpricks of light that arrived with strangulation are beginning to disappear. Susan dashes in. I can't speak. She screams, weeps, then dials 999. I listen while she demands an ambulance and the police. 'Get a bloody move on,' she shouts, 'because she's been half killed.' When she passes by to get back to the children, she gives me a wide berth. 'You're a crime scene,' she says. She's been watching too much television of late.

Susan has clearly been working hard and going through my phone book, because once I'm at the hospital Juliet turns up and bursts through the curtains. She hasn't done her hair. Never before

80

have I seen Juliet Anderson dishevelled. Am I dying?

'Anna–'

'You didn't even knock,' I say huskily.

After a few 'Oh, my Gods', she asks me how I am and what happened.

I can't be bothered. I love Juliet like a sister – well – not like my real sisters, because they don't deserve much, but that injection they gave me is sending me to sleep. The last thing I hear is Juliet saying, 'We've got him now, Anna. The divorce will be a cinch. He may not be prosecuted, but there was a crime, and that crime is registered with the police.'

No dreams. Perhaps injections stop a person having dreams. I wake in the morning with a headache, a sore throat and a thirst that needs Niagara. Then I go home.

Being looked after is a terrible thing. People come with flowers. Mrs Bee is all poultices, beef tea and eggs chopped up with butter and soft breadcrumbs. Her visits are short, because she has a duty to perform; her real job pro tem is to use her telephone to blacken my husband's name left, right and centre.

'There's a man on the phone,' says Susan. 'Says he's a colleague and he's heard about your trouble,' she adds with the air of a mother about to berate her teenage offspring. Mrs Bee's smoke signals are clearly working well if the news has travelled all the way to Hesford Junction.

'Tell him thanks, and we'll talk when my vocal chords get back to normal.'

'Is it him?'

'Who?'

She jerks her head in the direction of the phone. 'Your fellow.'

'He's a fellow teacher, I suppose.'

Susan lowers her tone. 'Have you had it off with him?'

Two can play this game. 'What off?'

'It. Thingy. Sex.'

'Go and ask his name.'

'Geoff Schofield, I think he said.'

'Yes.'

'Yes what?'

'Yes I've had it off with him.'

She sniffs before going away to inform him about my vocal equipment, only to return immediately. 'He says can he come round.'

'No.'

'Er ... do I give a reason?'

'No.'

She stares at me open-mouthed for a moment before going to do my bidding. When she has settled back in her chair, she starts to giggle. Between fits, she tells me that she has seen more of life in the last three weeks than in her previous nineteen years. We've had a riot, an attempted murder, hospital, parsnip wine, poultices and signs of improvement in her son.

'And chips from the chippy,' I remind her. 'We don't often have chips. And listen, you. Don't tell me you haven't seen crazy stuff at your house. They all live on the cusp of criminality.'

'Oh, I kept out of trouble,' she answers airily. 'Women can rise above all that sort of thing.'

Perhaps she did rise above it, but one of her brothers rose above her, didn't he? That same cold anger settles in the pit of my stomach. It isn't the sort of rage that visited Den when he tried to strangle me; his was a hot fury and was totally out of character. Mine is icy cool and ready to plan. I don't know where or how to start planning, but revenge is a satisfying dish with no calories. So I have to work at it, because I don't know the recipe. Yet.

'Where are the kids?' I ask.

'I put them in the oven – the gas helps knock them out.'

I love this girl's answers.

'They're in three prams. Emily's on one.'

'On one' is, I believe, Scouse for in a bad mood.

'I do hope she grows out of it.'

Susan looks at me hard and long. 'She's like you. She's stubborn and she knows what she wants. Lottie has your sweetness, but Emily hasn't shown it yet. I do think Lottie will fight back, though, because she's got you in her as well. When they start walking, we'll need eyes in the backs of our heads.'

She's right. Arrangements will have to be made, and nothing will be ideal. I suppose ideal would be two separate continents for them, but I can hardly engineer that. And they have to be together. Here I go again – echoes of childhood when I insisted that Kate, Beckie and I should be together. A great deal of trouble might have been avoided had we been separated, but...

'Glass of parsnip 1974?' she asks.

I throw a cushion at her. 'You,' I say, 'are getting on my bloody nerves. Put the kettle on and

83

behave yourself.'

'Yes, Miss.'

Lists. I carry on with my scribblings. *Hang onto house. Get a good monthly income from him. Get Gary. Evening classes for Susan. Write a book. Try those disposable nappies. Hurry divorce. Burn his old clothes. Borrow a different car, follow him.* Yes. If I follow him, I'll find him with one of his local 'business associates'. Then I'll get a name. A name is better than a couple of dozen dead crab lice in a matchbox, photos of a bruised throat, plus adultery with person or persons unknown. Shall I cite Round Table? Because for Den, charity never did begin at home...

The shocks come thick and fast these days. Just as I get my voice back, and when the bruises begin to fade, I am called by the hospice in Bolton. Elsie and Bert, who stayed together in the countryside long after we had all left, are now dying together. They always did everything as a pair, and it seems that they are travelling hand-in-hand towards eternity. Both now well past the age of eighty-five, they have served their time and are far too frail to continue earthbound. There is a pain in my heart, and I will not cry, not yet.

'I can manage,' Susan insists. 'Just leave me enough money, and I'll get help if I need it – next door or my mam – whatever. You've got to go, Anna. They were there for you when your mam died – eh? So go.'

'I'll come back every night,' I tell her. 'It's only forty-odd miles. Even if I have to go for days, I can come back and help at night.'

84

'Just phone me.'

'I will.' Again, I thank God for sending me this girl.

The hospice is a serene place with gentle, caring staff. These brave souls deal with death on a daily basis, and they sit me down in an office with a cup of tea, biscuits, and a very nice woman. 'The Dixons are in the same room,' she tells me. 'We broke all the rules, because those two have been together since they were children. It won't be long now.'

I scarcely recognize the two good souls who raised me from the age of five, and my twin sisters from birth. They are unconscious, and both are plugged into morphine pumps. Tiny, bird-like and twisted, they are curled into positions that face each other. I wipe their dry lips with 'lollipops' made from pieces of sponge on sticks. Elsie and Bert are desiccated and beyond revival, and the care is now merely palliative.

A nurse joins me, takes their pulses, wets their lips, checks the medication. She tells me that there is a sandwich for me in the office, and a coffee making machine in the entrance hall. But I am too exhausted for any of that. In an arm-chair at the foot of those twin beds, I fall asleep and dream of long-ago days when Elsie stopped fearing cows and learned to chase them out of her garden, when she learned to love the sight of her washing hanging in good, clean air. I hear Bert's heavy boots clipping the garden path as he walked home from the farm, listen to his stories of newborn lambs and calves. We walked, just he and I, to a stable where I watched the birth of a foal, saw the dam licking it clean, stood open-mouthed in shock when the new baby struggled to its feet on legs like thick knitting needles.

'There's a copy in the drawer,' says Elsie, but I am too busy looking at the foal.

'See, lass, that's life going on, is that,' Bert says now. 'The bloody Germans can't stop it – nobody can. Birthings still happen and nowt can be done to spoil any of it.' The Americans were coming. There were millions of them, and they would cut Hitler to bits. We would all be safe because of the Americans.

'In the drawer,' says Elsie again.

Precious moments away from Kate and Beckie, just Bert and his Anna with new life and the scent of hay. Blackberries picked on the way home, fallen apples carried in my held-out skirt, Auntie Elsie at home with pastry so short it melts in the mouth. These two are my people, special, precious people.

A hand touches my shoulder and I wake with a start. Elsie is going on about something in a drawer as I open my eyes and see the nurse. 'Sorry,' I say. 'I was tired.'

'It's all right, love. They've gone. It was peaceful and I think they waited for you.'

I am so weak, I can't even cry. Although days have passed, the trauma of Den's assault is still etched in my head and I am simply not over it. 'I heard her speak,' I say. 'Something about a drawer?'

The nurse nods. 'That happens sometimes. They come in spirit to relatives just before they go to their rest. It was her last message, and there is something for you in a drawer. I'll get it for you later.'

I am alone with the shells that used to contain my guardians. They are still warm, and I stroke their faces. They did their best. Eventually, they realized that responsibility for the twins was too much for me, but many children born in the war were cared for by older siblings. I was never ill-treated, except by my sisters. I was never punished, never slapped. Elsie and Bert Dixon, now gone from this earth, saved us from being sent to strangers.

'Thank you,' I whisper. Then I go to speak to the nurse in charge.

'No post-mortems required,' she informs me. 'And they asked me to give you this envelope. I know you live in St Helens, so we'll help all we can with arrangements.'

After I leave the hospice, I sit in my car and read. In simple language, Elsie tells me that they won the pools in 1961, that they spent some, used some during retirement, but that the rest has been invested for me. For me. The tide overtakes me, sweeps me along on a wave of grief so powerful that I can barely keep breathing.

'They loved me,' I sob, aloud to myself. 'And I should have saved them from...' I can't even say it to myself. I should have saved them from my sisters.

When I finally get home, I sleep for two days. Susan, who knows me better than anyone – even though our acquaintance is young – leaves me to it. I have killed my marriage, and my foster parents are dead. Sometimes, only sleep will do.

Four

'Uncle Bert?'

'Yes, love?' He put down his evening paper for the third time. Anna was in a questioning frame of mind, and it was best to get it over with.

'You know that woman with the white hair? She's in all the photos with the king and the queen and princesses. Never smiles, loads of jewellery, very tall.'

'Queen Mary, you mean. She used to be the queen till the other George died.'

'Mary of Teck. She comes from Teck.'

'Right. She married George the Fifth, our king's dad. What about her?'

Anna scratched her head. 'Whose side is she on in this war we're having?'

'Our side.'

'Are we sure? I mean, if England went to war with France, and if I married a Frenchman, would I have to be on the French side? Because I'd still be English, wouldn't I? Just because you end up living in another country, you don't have to change who you are. I'd be on England's side.'

'Yes, but you see, the way it works—'

'So she could be sending secret messages to Hitler, couldn't she? She's a German.'

'She might be part German, but she's not a Nazi. Any road, her dad was German, but she was brought up here all her life. And she married

88

a king, so she's English Royal Family. It's different for them.'

'But what if I married a French king?'

'They haven't got any kings.'

'Why not?'

Bert copied Anna's action, removing a flat cap before scratching his scalp. 'They cut all their heads off.'

'Who did?'

Bert was getting a bit bogged down. The trouble with Anna was that she was permanently hungry, but not for food. He prayed that he wouldn't have to go through Dunkirk again, because she complicated history with the simplest questions, and the simple questions were always the most complicated when Anna was involved. 'The French people did. They lined them all up and cut their heads off with a thing called a guillotine.'

'Why?'

'Er ... because they had nowt to eat.'

'So did they eat their heads?'

'Eh? No, no. They just wanted rid of the aristocrats – the posh people – for summat called liberty, equality and brotherhood. I think.'

'So they cut their heads off? That's not very nice, is it?'

Bert sighed. It was like talking to someone who was fifty rather than six years of age. 'Where are the twins?'

Anna shrugged. 'With Auntie Elsie, I think.'

'Take them out for a long walk, Anna. Give Auntie Elsie a chance to do her ironing.'

'I'd rather learn my catechism.'

'You know your catechism. Please, Anna.'

So she got on with it. Finding them was the first job. She dragged Kate from under a chair, washed and dressed her, strapped her in the pram. Beckie was in the kitchen eating a bit of rather grey, raw pastry. She was treated similarly by her older sister and, when both were clean, clad and fastened down, Anna set off. She would take them for a long walk, all right.

It was miles to Bolton, but mostly downhill. She didn't think about coming back uphill; she simply set off to take these two troublesome creatures away from a household that would have been peaceful without them. They were communicating now in some language known only to them and, once tired of 'talking', they fell asleep, lulled by the movement of their baby carriage.

Exhausted, she leaned against a wall near a window belonging to Preston's of Bolton, a large jewellery shop. Eight miles was a long way, and she needed a rest. Then the girl came along. She said how pretty the twins were, how much she would love to take them for a walk, and that she would bring them back in an hour.

Freedom. But what use was liberty when legs didn't work and feet felt as if they were on fire? After a few minutes, Anna bestirred herself in an effort to make use of this precious span. Would the girl come back? Or would she take them home and persuade her parents to keep them?

Fear struck. The enormity of what she had done hit her in the ribs like an invisible sledgehammer. Anger had sustained her over all that distance, but now, ready to collapse from exhaustion, weakened in body and mind, she wondered at her own terrible stupidity. They were her sisters. Good, bad or indifferent, those were her mother's children.

Police would get involved. She would be questioned for hours, and she would have to confess that she had tried to lose two defenceless babies. It was a sin. It was all a terrible, mortal sin and she would not get into heaven. Just like all the Proddies at the new school, she would be excluded. Oh, God.

Anna ran blindly through the town, Deansgate, council offices, shops, Bradshawgate, Churchgate. In the end, she was forced to stand again outside Preston's, because the hour was almost up. From here, she could see in four separate directions, so that was a bonus.

The girl brought them back. 'They did nowt but cry,' she complained. 'And they stink to high heaven. I think they've both filled their nappies.' She glared at Anna as if blaming her for the hellish hour the twins had given her. Anna grabbed the pram. All she knew was that she couldn't walk all the way back to the house. It was too far, and she was too tired. The bus wouldn't be any use, because she would need to abandon the pram and inflict terrible smells on all the other passengers. 'Think, think,' she told herself.

There was only one thing for it. Like most of her generation, Anna had been taught to be honest and to ask for help whenever needed. The people to ask were the police and, as long as you told them the truth, they would help you. Thus it came about that Bert and Elsie had their charges returned, complete with pram, in a large, blue police van.

'Don't shout at me,' was Anna's first plea. 'Uncle Bert, you told me to take them for a long walk while Auntie Elsie ironed, and I did. I walked and walked and walked until I couldn't walk any more. So these policemen brought us home.' She stalked off in the direction of the front door, stopped on the step, turned and delivered her afterthought. This was a good time for the whole truth – not that it would make a great deal of difference. 'I wish I could have left them in town, because they get on my nerves. They both stink, they're hungry and probably thirsty, because they don't like Vimto.' On this note of high drama, she entered the cottage.

Elsie was hard on her foster daughter's heels. 'Why, love?'

Anna thought for a moment. 'Because there was just me, Mam and Dad. Then there was just me and Mam. Then there was no Mam and THEY were here. I don't like them. They're just not nice, they're pests and they get me down.'

'But ... but they're your sisters.'

'I know they are. If they hadn't come, I'd still have Mam.'

Elsie dropped into a chair. 'That's terrible, Anna. You can't blame–'

'You want me to tell the truth, don't you? I can stand here, if you want, and say they're lovely and wonderful and I'm glad. It would be lies. It would be marks on my soul.' She ran upstairs and shut herself in the bedroom. At the top of her voice, she screamed at the closed door. 'I know she could have died having me, only she didn't. She was alive. She died having them, because there were two of them and that's too many.'

Elsie attended to the filthy and starving twins while Bert made a pot of tea for the constables. They drank up, said not to worry, and went off to do their duty elsewhere. Elsie passed one of the twins to her husband. 'Here. Get that bit of soup down her – and I mean down her throat, not her clothes.' She wiped her face with a handkerchief. 'I'll see to the other one.'

Later, they sat together, one at each side of the fire. The twins were asleep, and the quiet was wonderful. 'We bit off a lot,' said Bert. 'We bit off a mouthful we can't chew.'

'I know. But what else could we have done?' Elsie dragged a hand across her aching head. 'Frankie's family couldn't cope – they've all got loads of kiddies. And it's not too bad. I'm getting used to being up here, and Anna's looking a lot better. I suppose I depend on her a lot, especially when you're at work – but who else is there?'

'Only that Mellor woman up at the hall, and she's got her hands full, hasn't she? You're there two evenings a week, so you know about them poor young girls with their unwanted babies. Any road, haven't we always said we wanted these to have a normal family life? Frankie would spin in her grave if she knew we'd put them in some sort of institution.'

'And the clean air in Anna's lungs has done her the world of good,' said Elsie. 'She's not breathing in all the muck from the mills, and that makes a difference.'

Bert closed his eyes and stretched out his legs.

'You know what, love?'

'Eh?'

'I think we should stop here for good now. I'd never have thought about coming to live up on the tops like this, but it's gradely, isn't it?'

Elsie nodded. 'But what about her?' She pointed to the ceiling.

Bert took a sip of beer. 'She'll come round, because she'll have to – just you wait and see.'

School wasn't bad. At school, there was no Kate, no Beckie, and Anna got to play once during the morning, after lunch, then again in the afternoon. She brought a packed lunch in the little basket on her handlebars, and each school day was a blessing, because the twins were not a priority during those precious hours.

Her teacher was Miss Burke, and she took a keen interest in Anna, who was top of the class in most subjects. She noticed how slowly Anna left the building every day, saw the bicycle wobbling along the lanes at a speed that scarcely kept it in an upright position. Unlike the child who went reluctantly to school, this one would have lived there had she been given the choice. After looking into the little girl's background, Cora Burke found some answers. This was the one who had been in all the newspapers after staying with her dead mother and finishing up in hospital with pneumonia. Anna was a character, and the woman she would become was already on show, since she had matured at an unnaturally fast pace.

In the playground, Anna MacRae was an

organizer. She made up the games, invented the rules and generally kept order in her corner of the yard. She was lively, imaginative and funny. Yet she was not happy. So Miss Burke decided to question her. Was anyone hurting her? Did her foster parents treat her well? Did she like living in Weavers Row? Why didn't she want to go home at the end of the day?

Anna studied the plainly dressed woman. A different hairstyle might have been a good idea. And some better shoes. 'I don't want to go home because of the twins,' she replied. After all, wasn't honesty best?

'Your little sisters?'

Anna nodded. 'But it'll get better when they're about two or three, because there'll be no nappies and I can teach them to read.'

'Perhaps I'll come home with you this afternoon and meet your sisters.'

Anna rode home like the wind that afternoon. After clattering her bike to the ground below the front window, she ran inside screaming breathlessly, 'The teacher's coming. Miss Burke. She'll be here in a few minutes.'

There followed a blur of activity involving Anna and Elsie. Bert was on an ordinary shift, because the weather wasn't too raging hot for working the fields. Anna piled clean nappies on the dresser while Elsie swept and dusted. 'Where are they?' Anna asked, her words still starved of oxygen.

'Playpen. Back yard,' replied Elsie. 'Straighten that cushion on Uncle Bert's chair, love. I'll go upstairs and try to make myself look halfway to–'

'Hello?'

Anna sighed, shook her head, then went to welcome her teacher into the house. Elsie, after throwing up her arms in despair, put the kettle to boil and found some home-made biscuits that hadn't had their edges chewed by the twin girls' incisors. 'Pleased to see you, I'm sure,' Elsie said when the woman came in. 'Sit you down, Miss Burke. Have you come to talk about our Anna?'

'Just a visit,' replied Cora Burke. 'She's a very clever girl, so I thought I'd take a look at her sisters, because if they are anything like Anna, they will be stars.'

Anna smiled. Stars? Unless coal-eating and nappy-soiling became sports, the only marks they would leave were the messes they made of just about everything within their reach.

The little girl sat and listened while her teacher coo-ed and chuckled over the playpen at the back of the house. They were beautiful, they were clever, they reminded Miss Burke of their sister. Anna tutted quietly. She was a person who tried to be good; they made no effort whatsoever. Two years old in January? They acted like newborns.

A scream from Elsie had Anna jumping out of her chair. What on earth had they done now?

The question was answered almost immediately. Kate and Rebecca stumbled into the living room. They could walk. Oh, God, they were on the move. A whole new chapter stretched in front of Anna now – they would be able to get her toys, her books, her drawings. She would ask Uncle Bert for shelves they couldn't reach.

Elsie came in behind them. 'On the same day, too,' she exclaimed.

'They learn from each other,' was Miss Burke's contribution to the occasion. 'Splendid.'

Splendid? They would be through the hedges, under the feet of cows, up and down the lane, round corners – it was going to be a nightmare.

'Isn't that wonderful?' Elsie dried her eyes.

Anna had seen enough. She smiled politely at Miss Burke. 'I have to go,' she said. 'I'm due up at Holcroft Farm to watch the harvest coming home. My friend invited me, and Uncle Bert will bring me back.' After glaring at the twins, she left the scene at a speed that precluded any dissuasion.

She ran all the way, stopping only when a stitch in her side made running painful. Linda would understand. Linda was usually busy, but she was definitely on Anna's side.

When she got to the yard, there was quite a party going on. The harvest was almost gathered, and the rain was holding off. Men in clogs sparked ironclad soles on cobbles while a concertina played. Linda was hopping about with a handsome lad, while even Mrs Mellor from Berkeley Hall was tapping a foot as she sat on a stool. Anna was swept up by Uncle Bert, who twirled her round until she felt quite dizzy.

'Is that Linda's boyfriend?' Anna whispered.

Bert grinned. 'Not if Iris Mellor has owt to do with it. She'll have him down for marrying somebody with land and money.'

'Linda has land and money, Uncle Bert.'

'Has she? Oh, well that's all right, then. Mind, they'd have to make a long road between here and Essex to join them together.'

'Don't be daft,' Anna chided playfully. 'This is her grandad's farm, isn't it?' All the same, she felt a bit sad. Linda usually played with her, but she was currently fastened to a young man who gazed at her adoringly. Linda was letting her down.

'Uncle Bert?'

'What, love?'

'They've started walking. The twins. Can I have some high-up shelves and cupboards? I don't want them getting hold of my writing pads and drawing books. And I'd like a lock on my bedroom door.'

He set her down on a bale of hay. 'You can't have a lock in case of fire. There's no way of getting away from them, lass. They're your sisters, and that's the end of it, nothing more to be said or done. I mean, I understand. Our Arthur used to drive me twice round the bend, but I got used to it. You have to try, Anna. You're the big girl – they're the babies.'

'I know. I'm horrible, aren't I?'

He shook his head. 'Nay, lass. You're honest – that's your main trouble. You see it, you say it, and you suffer for it. Like we keep telling you, you've had a tough time what with your mam, then your dad off fighting, us moving you up here, two new babies – not easy for any of us.'

'No. But it would be easier without them, wouldn't it?'

He sighed. 'Anna, they exist. They're a fact of life, and they're ours till your dad gets home.'

She knew she was being selfish, that she wanted all the love, not just some of it. What she failed to comprehend was that her reaction was normal under the circumstances, that she had lost both her primary carers and had been landed with a pair of sisters for whom she had to take partial responsibility.

'Too young, but too old,' said Bert, not for the first time.

They walked homeward, Anna disappointed because Linda hadn't spoken to her, Bert wondering what the two little beggars would get up to now that they could walk. They were naughty – Anna was right about that. But they were babies and they had to be given a chance.

'I think I'll join the navy,' Anna muttered as Bert opened the gate.

He grinned. With such a sense of humour, she wouldn't go far wrong ...

It was murder in full, living colour. There was nothing black-and-white silent movie about life in the Dixon house once Kate and Beckie were on the move. There was sometimes an element of Keystone Kops in the lunacy that occurred, but the speed at which the pair operated defied science. They climbed, they fell, they screamed, they escaped and, with the efficiency of those long-ago Egyptian plagues, they destroyed all in their path.

Poor Bert made a gate for the bottom of the stairs, gates for doors front and back so that the house might be less than stifling, put a padlock on the coal bucket lid, and built new fencing for the back garden. The chickens were no longer safe, so the poor creatures had to be cooped up when the twins were outside, and were allowed out in their wire run only when the menaces had been removed from the scene.

Anna went to live upstairs. She emerged for baths, school, lavatory, food and drink, but the rest of her time was spent in happy solitary confinement. She felt sorry for Auntie Elsie and Uncle Bert, but there was little she could do to help. The German army, air force and navy paled into insignificance, because the real enemy was now within, without and all around like a London fog.

She heard them, though. 'Aga borra Anna?' one would ask.

'Anna borra,' the reply usually came.

It was plain that they were daft or foreign, because they weren't speaking English. Perhaps they were Germans sent to spy? Even so, Anna kept reminding herself of the promise made to her dead mother. She was supposed to be educating her sisters. They had been hard enough to catch when crawling, but now, containment was virtually impossible.

She sat on her bed reading a fairy tale book. But she couldn't follow the story, because she felt guilty. Uncle Bert was at work, while Auntie Elsie, who did all the cooking, cleaning, washing and ironing, was stuck with Those Two. She put down her book, then gazed through the window. Something had to be done and, as no one else seemed prepared to do it, it was up to herself to make something happen before poor Auntie Elsie ended up in the graveyard. Think, think, think.

She tidied her hair, walked downstairs, opened the little gate and stepped into the living room. They weren't here. They were probably in the kitchen or in the back garden with Auntie Elsie. Right. 'Here goes,' she muttered before letting herself out of the house.

With every step she took away from Weavers Row, she concentrated on what she had to do. It had to be done properly and carefully, or she might do more damage than good. She needed to be brief, polite and successful.

A young woman answered the door.

'I need to speak to Mrs Mellor,' said Anna as bravely as she could manage. 'It's urgent.'

She was taken to a sort of library where Mrs Mellor sat, telephone receiver in one hand, cigarette in the other. She motioned for Anna to sit at a small table near the window. Then she yelled at the phone. 'Don't tell me there's a war on, because I have noticed. I am overcrowded by five and I need more help.' She threw the phone into its cradle. 'Red bloody tape,' she muttered before turning to Anna. 'Hello, young lady.'

'Hello, Mrs Mellor. They aren't all babies here, are they?'

'Sorry?'

'You have some that can walk and all that?'

'Oh, yes. We have little ones of all ages here. So. How can I help you?'

Anna took a deep breath, then launched into the speech she had prepared. She told Mrs Mellor about her mother dying, her father in the army, the twins, Auntie Elsie and Uncle Bert. 'I hope I'm not being cheeky, but they're making

101

Auntie ill because she's a bit old for them.' They were making everybody ill, but that factor was best left out of the equation. 'So I wondered whether they could come for a few hours every day like to a nursery, because I don't want Auntie Elsie to wear out and die.'

'Neither do I,' replied Mrs Mellor. 'She's here Tuesday and Thursday evenings, and she's a damned good worker. Forget the damned – you're not supposed to use that word.'

Anna giggled. 'I can work for you if you want,' she offered. 'Like with the older children – I can read to them and show them games.' She decided to allow this woman to set one foot inside the truth. Through a small chink in her armour, Anna disclosed the fact that the twins spoke a strange language. 'Playing with other young walkers, Mrs Mellor, they might start to talk in English.' She paused. 'Please. I'll do anything.'

'I know you will, child. You're a good girl. The answer is yes. They may come every weekday morning at first, then for a full day. We have a trained nursery teacher...' She paused and glared at the phone. 'And we'll soon have more help once I strangle the authorities with their own red tape.'

Anna walked home on this glorious September day. Trees were just beginning to turn, some yellows, some reds, some pale browns. Auntie Elsie was safe, though she might take some convincing. The twins would not be sleeping in an institution; they would merely be attending a nursery. It made sense, but would the Dixons see it that way? 'And it won't do me much good,' she muttered to herself. 'They'll be there when I get home from school.'

Anna walked in to chaos. They had broken up a newly-baked loaf of bread and scattered it hither and thither. Elsie was in a rocking chair. She was also in despair. The newly-arrived Anna caught up with the twins and smacked their hands hard.

'NO!' screamed Elsie.

The twins didn't cry. Beckie spoke to Kate, 'Anna bogga borra.'

Kate replied. 'Anna borra,' and they laid themselves on the hearth rug and fell asleep.

Anna sat down. 'I've sorted it out,' she said airily. 'Someone had to do something, and they're my sisters. So I've done it.'

'What have you been and gone and done now?' Elsie wailed. 'Can't you see I've enough on without–'

'They start nursery next week. Up at the hall. They'll still live here, but you'll get a few hours without them. It's best, Auntie Elsie.'

Elsie sighed. This child had just walked in on landed gentry and negotiated with a woman who was seen as a pillar of the community. The kiddy was brave, and she never ceased to surprise those closest to her. 'Thank you, Anna,' she managed while fighting to hold back tears. 'They are getting a bit much.'

'They always were a bit much,' came Anna's dry reply. 'You need time to do all your jobs. They might get better when they have to mix with other babies.'

They would have to get better, Anna concluded

103

inwardly. School and mingling with her peers had taught her that co-operation and blending in were important. If a person wanted to stand out, it was better to do it through good work, not by being different and badly behaved.

'Do you think they'll be all right?' asked Elsie anxiously.

All right or not, they were going, because Auntie Elsie needed rest. If the twins behaved badly, they would be dealt with. There was something about Mrs Iris Mellor that spoke volumes about her attitude – she would suffer no fools. 'Don't worry,' Anna advised. 'It'll be the best thing that ever happened to them.' Satisfied with herself, she returned to her room and to Hansel and Gretel. The children in the story were twins. They tried to demolish a whole gingerbread house! Clearly, this behaviour came with the territory...

The two young MacRaes fitted in perfectly. After just one morning of tantrums, they calmed down like everyone else and, apart from eating a bit of plasticine and throwing some sand, they settled, listened and learned. When the nursery teacher got out the words and things baskets, she discovered that they could read. She held up an apple, and Kate gave her the appropriate word; she held up the word 'duck', and Beckie brought a yellow plastic bird to her. It seemed that the occasional lessons forced upon them by their older sister had left a few deposits.

They were also fully capable of understanding English and were able to speak some of it. Yet they

104

continued to communicate with each other in a language that defied interpretation by the rest of the world, and were judged by their teacher to be extraordinarily intelligent. She was heard to opine that infants who created languages were going to be adept at most subjects, particularly languages ancient and modern. Anna, who helped at the nursery when she could, kept her mouth shut, because she thought her sisters were daft, and judged the staff to be sorely misguided.

But one evening after school, the twins invaded Anna's bedroom. Kate smiled. 'Anna borra,' she said sweetly. 'Please, Anna borra.'

'Anna borra borra,' echoed Beckie.

'What's borra?' Anna asked. She was annoyed with herself for leaving the door open.

'Pretty,' they chimed in unison.

'And what's bogga?' asked the older child.

'Swearing,' grinned Kate. 'You read now.'

They climbed onto the bed, one at each side of her. This time, they tore no pages, and even pointed out some of the words. She began to read aloud, moving an index finger under lines of print, leaving out the odd word and trying not to smile when they struggled to fill in the missing letters. But they managed. 'You are clever,' she told them. 'So why act daft?'

The reply was simple. Both answered, 'Bogga.'

To that, Anna found no answer.

Five

We are both making lists now, so I have managed to make Susan almost as daft as I am. Her lists are more sensible than mine, though. She is collecting information on child development and is working hard at stimulating Stephen to give him the chance to catch up. I am putting together three or four pages of Den's incomings and savings, all his misdemeanours, all his faults, all stocks and shares. Crab lice in a matchbox have become a bit crumbly, but Juliet took them away and had them identified. I am guessing that there would not have been a line-up in some police station, since one crab louse looks much like another as long as no one wears a hat or a false moustache.

She lays down her pen and stares through the French windows. 'I think he'll be all right, Anna. Probably not top of the class, but nowhere near the bottom, either.' She looks at me. 'Have you told Juliet that you inherited a small fortune and two houses?'

I shrug. 'Might have mentioned it.'

Bert and Elsie bought the house next door with some of their winnings. If adapted, the two cottages together would make a very nice place. I suppose I'll have to cough up and admit to having an income from rents, plus a decent inheritance. Honesty is the best policy, isn't it, Auntie Elsie?

A double funeral, double the flowers, double the tears. Going into the house afterwards was awful. Empty teapot for the first time ever, no cooking smells, no balls of wool and half-knitted garments. At the funeral, no Katherine, no Rebecca. I avoid contact for the most part, but I had to let them know that their foster parents had died. Nothing.

As predicted, both are linguists. Katherine teaches Latin, Greek, French, Spanish and German. Her professorship at Oxford is attached to Greek. Rebecca translates for several big businesses and for governments, lives abroad for months on end, has a flat in Paris, occasionally stays in London with her twin. On the surface, they are successful, happy and wealthy women, but no one knows them. I know some of their story, but not everything. I shiver.

'You cold?'

'Not really. I think my sisters just walked over my grave yet again.'

'They don't do graves,' replies Susan. 'They certainly didn't do the poor Dixons' grave, did they?'

'No.'

'What happened with you and your sisters?' she asks.

I smile. 'If we had a week, I'd tell you half of it. Better wait till the book comes out and they prosecute me.' They wouldn't dare, and I know it, but I carry on with the pretence. 'In fact, Susan, you won't need to read – just hang on until they get me in Crown Court for libel or whatever.'

She swallows audibly. 'Is that the book on your list?'

'Yes. It probably won't get written. I'm guilty, too. I ran away and left Elsie and Bert to deal with...' With monsters. 'With my sisters.'

'Where did you go?'

I am so tired. 'To my dad.'

'But what—'

'Not today, Susan.' I don't want to think about my dad, because that's another painful place in my soul. The way he was when he came home from the war, the issue of what he had become gradually dawning on the child I used to be. My father was alive, yet I had lost him.

'Was it ever easy, Anna?'

'Some days were absolutely wonderful,' I tell her. 'And that's the truth for almost all of us. But yes, it was difficult on the whole.' Homework missing, teachers disappointed in me, my clothes ruined, the thefts from shops, the terrible rows that came to blows...

She crosses the room and hugs me. She is the mother I lost, the Elsie I loved, the daughter I should have had twenty years ago. Like me, she is bruised, but not quite broken; like me, she is almost indestructible. I need her, and she needs me. God has usually sent someone to help me through the bad times; Susan and Stephen can assist with the second lot of twins in whose upbringing I have been forced to play a part. This time, I know it has to come out right. Surely it will? Please tell me it will.

This is crazy. Marie, Susan's mother, is the only one of us displaying sense, because she has stayed in my house with the three babies. Cramped into the tiny interior of our Maureen's Mini, Susan, our Maureen and I are kangarooing down the Hesford bypass towards St Helens, metropolis of the area. The car is unwell. When started, it coughs like an asthmatic with secondary emphysema. It doesn't like bumps in the road, takes corners with great reluctance and a lot of fuss, has poor brakes and bad tyres. We are, I conclude, in a dangerous situation.

We are aiming for the Highwayman and, if Maureen's driving gets any worse, any highwayman will be a victim of hit-and-run, and even his horse will be a goner. But it's the pub we need. The Highwayman's a happy hunting ground to which bored housewives repair at the end of another boring day with a boring family. They search for a bite of someone else's apple, and my apple is probably in there now with his latest huntress. Descriptions of the would-be Diana are scary. She has hair dyed jet black, wears at least three pairs of false eyelashes, and has a bosom big enough to preclude the need for a table at meal times.

'Worrif she's not there?' asks Maureen, who has become excitable due to the misbehaviour of her car. Her pronunciation tends to deteriorate when she's stressed.

'Diana? She'll be there,' I answer.

'Is that her name?'

I shrug. 'Goddess of the hunt. No idea of her name, but she's been seen pointing her arrows at Den, so we need to get the real name for the divorce petition.'

Susan and I wait in the Mini, because Den

might recognize her – he'd certainly remember me. Maureen squeezes her bulk through the driver's open door, and I find myself waiting for Maureen to get stuck.

'It'll be all right,' Susan tells me. 'She knows what she's doing. She'll know him from the photo you gave her, and she'll see you right, I promise.'

'She'd better. She'll get no car out of me if she fails.'

'There you go, then,' Susan says. 'She's got a good incentive, so–'

'Why has she left the engine running?' I ask.

The answer arrives in the shape of our Maureen plus two handbags, one of which is clearly not her own. She tosses these items at the two of us in the rear seat, squeezes herself into place, then roars off the forecourt and round the corner.

'Jesus.' Susan was speaking for both of us. 'It's terrifying, Maureen. Have you done a bank robbery or something?'

'As good as,' she says as she waits for the bypass lights to change. 'I pinched her bag. She never noticed and neither did he – they were practically glued together.'

I pull myself into some sort of order. 'That's because he has a gob like a suction cup – they may need to be separated surgically. Maureen, keep your eyes on the road, love. I want to get home in one piece and preferably without being charged with theft.'

Maureen laughs. 'This is nothing, mate. Good job you don't live by me – your nerves'd be shredded. They come home with three-piece suites, pianos – one feller turned up with a coffin last week for his mam, and she's not even dead yet. She's nearly dead, like, but not quite.'

Oh my God. All I wanted was a name. Person or persons unknown could be OK, but a name is better when it comes to adultery. I wish we'd never bothered. I'll be having a heart attack at this rate – coffins, pianos? I am in with the criminal element! When we turn right at the roundabout, I get the distinct feeling that we are on two wheels, because our Maureen is bigger than the rest of us, and we are listing to starboard. Or is it port? Whatever, we're in a mess. Please, God, just get us home. It's starboard, I think.

We enter the house and throw ourselves onto chairs. Marie is watching TV and hardly notices us.

'That,' I tell our Maureen sternly, 'was a waste of time. You were supposed to get her talking, find out her name in the general run of conversation.'

'Run of conver-bloody-sation? She was halfway down your husband's throat, girl.'

I sigh. 'Look. She'll notice that her handbag is missing. If she puts two and two together, she might just realize that I've got her name, address and so forth out of that missing handbag. The evidence is useless if it's stolen.'

'You weren't there.'

'I was. I was outside in a car. Of sorts.'

Maureen stands up, leaves the room and returns almost immediately with a cloth and a pair of Marigolds. She dons the rubber gloves, cleans the outside of the bag, then tips its contents onto the

111

floor. Susan copies down all she needs before watching while our Maureen puts everything back.

'Where are you going now?' I ask as Maureen turns to leave the scene.

'To put the handbag back,' is her answer. 'I'll borrow your driving gloves off that stand in the hall.'

Susan and I jump up.

'Stop where you are.' Maureen has clearly had enough. 'I am going by myself, because you two are as much use as concrete cushions.'

At last, Marie looks up. 'Has something happened?' she asks.

I can't help it. I double over with laughter and tears stream down my face. The perfect stupidity of the situation has me in pleats. Concentrating on a soap opera has allowed Marie to miss everything. I suppose she's used to this sort of carry-on; I am not.

'What's up with her?' Marie asks her daughter. 'And where's our Maureen gone again?'

Oh, the pain of it. I sink to the floor and curl like a baby in the womb.

'Is she always like this?' Marie further enquires. 'Is she on tablets?'

It seems that Susan isn't coping too well, either. She leaves the room and I hear the door of the downstairs loo slamming home.

'Anna?'

I look at poor Marie. 'Yes?'

'What are you laughing at?'

I can't tell her about the dyed-haired, huge-breasted goddess of the hunt. I certainly can't tell tales about poor Maureen, because poor Maureen is up to her neck in it already. I stand up. 'I'll ... er ... I'll put the kettle on.'

Susan joins me in the kitchen. 'What if she gets caught?' she asks. 'How will we know?'

'Oh, stop it. She'll be back soon, won't she?'

Susan shrugs. 'Or she'll be in a cop car. Whatever happens, our Maureen'll take it in her stride.'

'But she can't go to prison, Susan.'

'Why not? They keep her bed aired between visits. Just calm down, because my mam thinks you're ready for a straitjacket.'

We carry tea through to the living room, but Marie is engrossed again in a television programme. She's forgotten me, and I'm glad about that. I keep glancing at my watch and looking at the clock. If Maureen gets picked up and charged with theft, I'll never forgive myself.

A sound like gunshot makes me rush to the door. Thank God. That antiquated little Mini has served its time and is backfiring because it's worn out, poor thing. Maureen gets out of the wreck. 'Never again,' she says, her eyes fixed on me. 'I've had enough now, Anna. Let me in.'

She steps inside. 'She'd come up for air after kissing your husband, yon Diana–'

'Dolores,' Susan says.

Maureen ignores her and motors on. 'She was on her hands and knees looking for her bag. Your feller was on his hands and knees looking for her, because the place was pretty full. So I dropped me bundle, and I says to the woman next to me, "Hey, what's that under the chair?" and it's the

113

handbag. So the woman next to me's an 'ero, and I cleared off sharpish.'

'Shush,' orders Marie. 'I'm just getting into this.'

My life thus far has been eventful and interesting, but the colours added by this family are primary shades. No pastels or delicate greys for the Hughes clan – they remind me of Laurie Lee, who wrote in great splashes of colour, but you never knew where his next spillage would settle. 'You are amazing,' I tell Maureen from the bottom of my heart.

'And you owe me a car.'

I can't help myself. I throw my arms as far as they will reach around our Maureen, and burst into tears.

The adverts are on. Marie stands up and touches my shoulder. 'Listen, love. You want to see a doctor about all this – laughing your head off one minute, whinging the next. I had an auntie like that. Finished up in the funny farm for a month. They plugged her into the mains a few times, then she was great. Well, she was quiet, which was a big improvement. Have you tried evening primrose?' Her play has started again, so she can't wait for an answer.

It's a white Hillman Imp so-called estate, very square, and with a rear door so that Maureen can easily stash her shopping. Or shoplifting. My friend from Skelmersdale has brought the car round, and is about to load the defunct Mini onto a breakdown vehicle.

Maureen walks round the Imp. 'Looks like an

ice-cream van,' she says. 'All I need is a jingle-jangler and a bit of a fridge – I could coin it in down Crosby beach. Few lollies, ninety-nines, wafers.'

'Someone has the franchise,' I tell her. 'Please stay out of trouble, Maureen.'

'Call me Mo. I love you. You're a bit mad, like, but I've took to you. And thanks for this, love. First time anybody's given me anything for a long while, I can tell you that. And, er...' She drops her voice. 'Our Sue. Twenty-four carat, she is. Something rotten's happened to her. I don't know what, but she's a lot better with you, Anna. She's nearly back to how she was before she had our Stephen. Look after her, and she'll look after you. I mean it.'

I nod.

'Do you know what happened to her?'

'She won't talk about anything,' I say carefully. 'Get this one taxed and insured, will you? Otherwise, you'll never be out of the woods.'

The Mini is finally abandoned after Mo 'blesses' it with a drop of holy water. Although she made the pronouncement last night that religion does no good, she clearly believes in the Last Rites. She goes into the house, brings Susan out, shows off her new car.

Susan admires it and goes to check on the children. I follow Susan into the house. The children are lined up on the sofa, and Susan is counting toes. For once, Stephen is not the buffer between my girls, and all three are watching and listening to Susan. Emily glares at Lottie a couple of times, and I know exactly how she feels. I remember. I

115

remember Kate and Beckie handed over to a stranger at Preston's of Bolton because I wanted them not to be a part of my family. Oh, yes. A place in me understands Emily only too well. Is this to be my punishment?

It happens very suddenly. One minute, it's This Little Piggy Went to Market, and the next is chaos. Emily has dug her nails into the back of Lottie's hand. I act too quickly and slap my bigger twin. She looks at me disdainfully and doesn't even bother to cry. Lottie makes enough noise for both of them. I pick her up and carry her out of the room. At the bottom of the stairs, we sit, Lottie and I. She sobs out her little heart while I weep into her hair.

A long time ago, I disliked intensely two little girls whose births caused my beloved mother to die. Did God disapprove of me for that? Has He watched me down the years, has He sent me a repeat prescription in the shape of Charlotte and Emily? Even now, with Catholicism fading to grey in my life, I still manage to believe in God. Also, I have read enough child psychology to begin to understand that my reaction to my sisters was not abnormal. But would Katherine and Rebecca have turned out differently had I loved them better, had our mother lived?

Susan joins us. 'She's fallen asleep. He's playing on the floor. Don't cry.'

I shake my head. 'Will Emily carry on like this?' I ask. I'm the teacher, for goodness sake – why should I need comfort from this young woman?

'I don't know,' she answers. 'But you shouldn't smack Emily. You should never hurt a baby.'

'She had to be stopped before she drew blood. Susan, it's getting worse by the day.'

'It will stop,' she says determinedly. 'I'll go and do us some fish fingers for our lunch.' And off she goes. And I'm still sitting here at the bottom of a blue-carpeted flight of stairs, Lottie in my arms, Emily on her own in the living room. So. I have to start leaving Lottie with Stephen so that I can spend quality time with Emily. I have to love her. I have to learn. Life's not easy, is it?

Susan is both brave and willing. She has taken out all three babies, Emily strapped to her chest, the other two in my twin pram. An hour without children is an island of bliss, but the strata in the rock include several layers of guilt. I sit doing absolutely nothing. I'm thinking, I suppose. About Den and his girlfriend, about Maureen, about this poor chap Alec Halliwell who is about to get a phone call from me. I hope Susan is OK, hope Emily behaves herself.

Here we go again. I am not allowed to be alone – the doorbell has just informed me of that. It's Geoff. Still young, still beautiful, still with come-to-bed eyes that crinkle in the corners. He got fed up waiting, he says. He has been driving past to make sure that Den wasn't here. He didn't like to keep phoning in case he woke the twins.

I hold the door wide. 'Come in. You're ruining Mothers' Hour, so you're committing a mortal sin.'

'Is it on?'

'No. It isn't even a programme. I offloaded the kids and got some time to myself.'

He's sorry and he says so. 'How are you, Anna?'

Edited highlights will have to do, so I skim over the surface of recent events. His face lights up when I tell him about the coming divorce. He thinks everything's so simple – move from one man to another, settle down, drink wine, have sex, go for walks. He isn't stupid – he's a very good deputy head – but he's a man, so he misses some of the detail.

'So you've had a bit of a rough time, then?'

'You could say that, Geoff.'

He asks me to go for dinner with him soon, and I tell him I'll think about it. There's no kissing, no cuddling, not today, not in a house that belongs to my daughters. It's like seeing the Hay Wain painted onto a tumultuous Turner seascape – Geoff is in the wrong setting. And I am becoming what Mrs Bee might term flummoxed. Geoff notices that. He does see some of the detail, then. Loving this man could be so easy. It could also be cradle-snatching – I'm twelve years his senior.

The side door crashes inward. 'I'm back,' yells Susan.

She walks into the house, looks at my visitor, says, 'Whoops,' and does a swift about-turn. Peace, perfect peace? Tell me about it.

He goes out through the front door. Susan, still wearing Emily, returns from the side. 'Was that him?'

Oh, not again. We've been through this before.

After a small silence, she says what she needs to say. 'Then the twins are definitely Den's.'

'Yes.'

'Because that other one–'

118

'Geoff?'

'Yes. He's black.'

'Is he?' I say. 'I never noticed.' Does she hear the sarcasm? No idea.

'Are you ... er...?'

'What?'

'Are you back with him, like?'

'No. I'm with me.' That's how it has to be for the foreseeable future. I have to love me before I can love anyone else. But Susan doesn't need to know that. She has enough to carry with that heavy twin of mine pinned to her bosom. I relieve Susan of her burden. 'Were they good?' I ask.

'Oh, yes. But Emily pulls some terrible faces. I had a job not to laugh. There's a funny little devil in there somewhere, Anna. Not just the naughty one. She's got a sense of humour.'

Ah, well. Where there's life, there's hope.

My cup runs over about an hour after supper. Susan is still washing dishes, while I have just walked downstairs after putting our children to bed. It's a lovely evening, with a spectacular sunset dipping away towards the Mersey plain, mackerel clouds, orange streaks resting on an improbable aquamarine. If an artist were to paint this faithfully, no one would believe that it had not emerged from the fevered imagination of a person who might have cut off an ear.

So. Now we have Den. He stands outside the front door, shoulders rounded, head bowed, hands clasped in front of his body. I half expect him to remove his shoes, because he seems to be begging admission to some holy place.

119

'What now?' I ask.

He looks at me. Paul McCartney eyes again. I've always preferred John Lennon, but that doesn't matter. 'It's all been a mistake,' he says.

My face is blank. At least, I hope it is. 'You'd better come in.' He follows me into the living room, but I haven't finished. 'I shall be talking to Mr Halliwell about his wife and her relationship with you.'

His lower lip hangs, puts me in mind of half an orange that has been sucked dry. Almost dry. 'Have I been followed?' he asks.

I use part of the truth. 'You've been seen by several people in the Highwayman with Mrs Halliwell.'

He seems to have lost a few inches in height. Height matters to him, because I am just about half an inch shorter than he is, so I've had to be careful with shoes. I've had to be careful with a lot of things, actually. 'Den, you came home with crab lice. You tried to kill me. You're fornicating with someone who's just about ready to start learning to read. This marriage is over, and I've a feeling hers will be, too. I hope you'll take responsibility for the poor soul when she's homeless.'

'I want to come back,' he almost whimpers.

'Well, you can't. This house is the twins' home. You can make a nice new life with Dolores.'

He gulps audibly. I can see that a future with a big bosom and no brain is not an attractive prospect in his book. Perhaps he'll run away and get a job on the continent, because some of his harem out there must be uninfected. Or disinfected, at least. Susan is going upstairs. She's quiet, but he hears her. 'That girl still here?' he asks.

'She helps,' I reply. 'And, if you hurt me again, I have a witness in residence. Don't mess with her, because she has a family who'll bend your membership card as soon as look at you. So. Is our business concluded?'

'I don't know you, Anna.'

'You never did. I, on the other hand, know you only too well.'

The thing that really hurts is that he doesn't ask to see the girls. Any normal man would grab with both hands the opportunity to creep upstairs and look at his children, but he isn't normal. My doctor, who should know better, has told me that my husband is mad, and I thought he meant mad for endangering his marriage, but I am not so sure now. Manic depression has been mentioned, as has a drug with an unpronounceable title. Den showed me the prescription before binning it a few weeks ago. I am pretty sure that he's seeing a psychiatrist.

'I've got a job in Lincolnshire,' he says now.

'I hope you and your other half will be happy there.'

His eyes dart from side to side for a few seconds. He's like a rat in a trap built by a world that is not being kind to him. He misses his mother. She was everything to him, and vice versa. 'I suppose it's best if we end the marriage,' he says. 'And I never, ever want to live with a clever woman again. You've made me ill. You've made me how I am.'

Perhaps I have contributed to his condition,

121

though I didn't create it. I don't like his way of life, his selfishness, his concern about image. I don't like the way he envies the rich and wishes them ill. He must be terribly insecure.

Suddenly, my mind is filled with images of us as we were, walking into the Med at midnight, our guts filled with cheap Spanish brandy. Looking for shells and finding someone's top denture in the sand, displaying said item in the living room when we came home. Stopping the Royal Mail in Kensington on rag day, placing items of ceramic bedroom furniture on the heads of Victoria and her beloved Albert, paddling in fountains, singing Land of Hope and Glory on the Mall, making dangerous cocktails with fruit juice and absolute alcohol. We did have a life. We have been young and yes, I have loved him.

'We've had some brilliant times, Den, but times change. I wasn't enough for you and wasn't right for you.'

'This is scary,' he admits.

'I know.' I want to hug him better, but I won't. I can't turn him into a brother, can't have him as a friend.

He leaves, and I sink into a chair and sob my heart out. It's like another death, another period of bereavement. He was so alive until he became a businessman. His humour was brilliant, he enjoyed the holidays, good food, nights out, the theatre. Now? He's an old man, and he hasn't yet reached forty-five.

'Anna?'

'I'm all right.'

'Then why are you crying?' she asks.

Why? Because part of my life just walked away, and I saw darkness all around him. He isn't steady, isn't right, isn't whole. Even now, I worry about him. But I don't tell Susan about all that, because she's probably too young to cope with the concept. I ask her to make a pot of tea while I watch the news. The cup that cheers, the English cure, the best medicine.

She comes back. I hear the kettle as it grumbles its way towards boiling point. 'Anna?'

'What?'

'Maureen's in the ozzy. Mam's in the kitchen crying. Maureen's feller beat her up and took the car off her.'

'What?' I am on my feet in a fraction of a second. 'Phone a taxi. Take Marie to the hospital and find out what you can. I'll get Juliet.'

It never rains but it pours. Have you noticed that?

I suppose it's not believable, but it's happening, so it's real enough. If anyone had told me – a year ago, say – that my beautiful big house was going to be filled with Scallies I would have laughed. But it's not funny. Juliet is now in charge of two divorces – mine and Marie's. Maureen doesn't need a divorce, as she never married her Jimmy in the first place, so that's OK.

The master bedroom I allocated to myself and my girls – they are in separate cots, of course. Emily is sleeping through, and I am not as tired as I used to be. The smallest room contains Marie and dozens of cardboard boxes. Her husband is drying out in some unit for alcoholics, and she is on the emergency list for a council flat in St Helens. She's had enough of her sons, her husband, and her wrecked house, so she's being fast-tracked up the list.

Bedroom two is for Susan and Stephen, while the third largest is occupied by Maureen. She has broken ribs and has recovered in hospital from severe concussion. The doctors and nurses were worried about bleeds and brain damage, but she woke after three days demanding a double brandy and a lipstick, so she's all right, thank goodness.

Our Maureen's Jimmy is on remand in jail. We got the car back eventually, and I had it restored to its former beauty, since it's the only thing of any value that poor Maureen owns. Marie is trying for a two-bedroomed flat so that Maureen can move in with her, because Maureen's kids are old enough to have moved on. 'Time they stopped depending on her, anyway,' Marie said yesterday. My house is busy, alive and happy. The post-natal depression is wearing thin, and I am on a lower dose of red things, while the yellow ones are now withdrawn. The doctor is pleased with me. I am pleased with Marie.

She is sorting out the Emily/Lottie business. It's slow, detailed and impressive. Had Marie married a different bloke, she would have made a hell of a good mum. And I never allow myself to forget that this woman produced Susan, who is a wonderful daughter. There is in Marie a deep well of knowledge, an intelligence that is rare in a woman from any background. Out of the depths of the old Dingle has risen a psychologist who

124

needs no letters behind her name, and I am in awe.

She never raises her voice, doesn't get cross, shows boundless patience. Marie is an 'oper' of whom even Mrs Bee might approve were she privy to the full details of my life with the twins. Working on a system that seems simple, Marie uses reward and deprivation with Emily. It isn't simple – it's quite complicated in reality, but my unexpected mentor follows a programme of which she is scarcely aware, yet she is an expert. I can only hope it works and that St Helens Council doesn't find that flat too quickly. I am learning, but I must learn with alacrity.

Sitting on our extra acre with three damaged women and three children, I am as happy as Mrs Bee's proverbial pig in muck. It's a bit like a commune, though we don't need a list of rules regarding tasks and responsibilities. It's as if each member of my household knows instinctively what needs doing and who needs help. The place is spotless inside. My heart overflows with gratitude.

Apropos of absolutely nothing, Maureen makes an announcement. She is going straight. Susan, after almost choking on iced tea, composes herself sufficiently to ask, 'Eh?'

Maureen's face is completely expressionless. 'Time I turned over a new leaf,' she says. 'I'm not as fast as I used to be, and a shoplifter needs to keep on the move. So I'm going into butties.'

'You'll need a big kitchen, Maureen, for the buttering and spreading,' I say.

Marie eyes her recovering relative. With a

125

family of such a size, a separate edition of Who's Who might be useful. 'Listen, our Mo. I've raised five lads and our Susan, and I've buttered more bread than you'll find in Warburton's Bakery. If you're going into sandwiches, you're on your own.'

Maureen places a hand on her broken ribs. 'After all what I've been through? You'll get paid. I'll give you a cut.'

'A cut?' Marie yells. 'Never mind cutting, get ready sliced. And I don't want nothing to do with egg mayonnaise. I can stand childbirth, drunks and thieves, but not egg mayonnaise. And you'll pay rent, lady.'

The gentle, good-humoured bickering lulls me to sleep, and I wake to find the chairs around me empty, the babies gone, and a blanket stretched over me. They'll be inside preparing food. Maureen, who is making the most of her temporary injuries, won't be doing much, but Susan and her mother are probably bathing kids and making a meal. It's a family, a proper family. Most people would run a mile from this clan, but I am strangely comforted by their various eccentricities.

Six

Anna was busy collecting newspaper articles. History was being made and, though it was unpleasant, she needed to save the evidence for the future.

'At it again?' asked Bert, ruffling her hair as he neared the table.

'We're winning,' she answered. 'It's nearly over. I'm sure it's nearly over.'

He shook his head. 'There'll be a fair amount of to-ing and fro-ing yet, love. It'll be one step forward and two back on many a day, but we can't lose. No way will Hitler rule the world, not while there's still a few of us standing. He's got to die. There's been rumours that even his own generals have been plotting to blow him up. He's mad, you know. Totally out of his mind.'

'Do the Germans know that, Uncle Bert? Do they know he's crackers?'

'Some do, some don't. Like Churchill, he's an inspirational speaker, gets people going. But he's bloody hysterical most of the time, just gets folk worked up and sends them to kill us. They'll catch on, pet. Wouldn't surprise me if the daft bugger got shot by one of his own.'

When was a murder not a murder, she wondered. Did war mean it wasn't murder any more? If Dad had killed a load of baddies, would he go to hell because of mortal sin, or would he enter heaven as a brave man? She carried on cutting and pasting. If she put it all together, she could read it when she got older, then she might get some answers. Until then, it remained a grey area that interfered with her religion.

'Uncle Bert?'

'What, love?'

'You know that final solution thing. Is it true? Can it really be happening? Can something so horrible be real?'

He removed his cap and stared through the window. So peaceful here, so quiet. 'I think it might be, sweetheart. Mr Hitler doesn't seem to like Jews or Romanies or people who're disabled. I am praying. I hope it's not true. If anything ever needed to be propaganda...' Then he found himself explaining propaganda. War was hard, especially when spent in the company of a seven-year-old. He spent more time on explanations than he did on eating his meals.

'So sometimes, what we read in the papers isn't true? Is that what you mean?'

He told her he wouldn't go that far, but that everybody saw things differently and sometimes news was exaggerated for a good reason. 'They try to keep our spirits up, you see. They don't want us all walking about with our faces in our boots, do they? They have to make us carry on smiling, love.'

'But they should write the truth.'

Bert smiled. 'And it shouldn't rain during the day, and the sun should shine from dawn till dusk. If you're looking for a perfect world, babe, you'll have to wait a long, long while.' He went to feed the chickens. At least chickens didn't ask questions.

Anna looked at the clock. Soon, it would be time for her to walk up to Berkeley Hall and bring back the twins. Auntie Elsie was working up there this evening, so the twins would be Anna's responsibility for a few hours. There was no point in moaning and groaning about that, she told herself. Everybody had to do their bit, and at least her bit didn't involve guns or bomb-making. Which was just as well, because she still felt like killing the pair of them at times.

They were two and a half now, and the half had been the worst. Tantrums. Screaming at each other in that weird language, breaking things, throwing food, banging their heads against walls. That was one of the most unusual of their behaviours, the synchronized head-banging thing. She failed to work out why they did it. Perhaps it was nice when they stopped? Perhaps they needed the pain to enjoy the pleasure when it was over? It was clear that Hitler wasn't the only mad beggar in the world.

She got out the big pram, because that provided the easiest way of getting Kate and Beckie from one place to another. She pushed the empty vehicle in the direction of the hall, but stopped halfway up the drive when she heard someone sobbing quietly. She parked the pram and pushed herself through a hole in a privet hedge. It was Linda Harris from the Land Army. She was curled into a ball and crying her eyes out.

Anna hadn't seen a great deal of Linda, because Linda was being courted by Roger, the son of Iris

Mellor, owner of Berkeley Hall. 'Linda?' she said hesitantly. 'Linda, it's me. What's the matter? Can I do something?'

'Go away, Anna. Please go.'

Anna wasn't going anywhere. 'No,' she said, her voice gaining strength. 'I'm not leaving you in this state. What's going on?'

Linda tried to dry her eyes. 'You sound more like Elsie every day,' she sobbed.

'What's the matter?' the child repeated.

'Nothing.'

So. Here lay a young woman who was crying for no reason whatsoever. The twins did that. Grown-ups did not do that. 'I don't believe you. Kate and Beckie cry for nothing, but you don't. Even I don't, and I'm only seven. You're crying because of something, not because of nothing.'

Linda scrambled to her feet. 'Roger. It's Roger. He's a few years younger than me, but he's turned eighteen and he's been called up. And,' she sniffed loudly, 'he's happy. He wants to go. He's happy about going away to fight, and I don't want him to go.'

Anna tried to reason with the distressed woman. 'A lot of them want to go, Linda. It's like a duty, like they need to defend their country – I've read about it. He's not the only one, you know.'

'He's my only one.'

Anna nodded. 'Yes, and my dad's my only one, but he's in some Western Desert, all sand and no water. It's everybody.'

'I know. I'm sorry. I'm selfish.'

'No, you're not. You're very worried in case somebody you love gets killed. You just have to

130

get used to it like the rest of us.'

Linda allowed a smile to live on her face for a split second. 'Yes, Elsie,' she replied.

Anna had to continue her journey, since she didn't want to be late – Mrs Mellor was a stickler when it came to timekeeping. She parked her pram at the bottom of the steps before walking into the hall. Nursery classes were held at the back of the house, and Anna had to walk through a deserted corridor to reach the rooms she needed. But she didn't get far, because there was a big row going on. And she heard most of it. 'I love her,' Roger shouted. 'I am sick and tired of repeating myself, Mother, but I love Linda. You can't change that. You can't change how I feel.'

'Nonsense – you're too young for that sort of thing.'

Anna stood very still.

'She's only three years older than I am. I'm probably going abroad, Mother. But I must tell you this here and now – if you don't stop being so damned horrible, I won't be coming back here even if I live. When it concerns Linda, you're a bitter, twisted woman. You are NOT my mother.'

The child fled. He was giving up his mother, while Anna would have sacrificed almost anything to have hers back. Roger loved Linda enough to walk away from his own mam. The concept was a total anathema – mothers were too precious for that sort of behaviour. So Master Mellor must have been very, very serious to threaten something like that.

When Anna returned to the corridor with her sisters, the office door was open, and Mrs Mellor

131

was alone at her desk. She was weeping. Apart from the possibility (according to Uncle Bert) of an eventual one-nil result for the Allies against Germany, this day was a vale of tears. She hesitated, opened her mouth, stepped back, stepped forward again. It was difficult to know what was right, what was the best thing to do. Oh, well. She was going in, and that was an end to it.

Without knocking, she entered the office. 'Hello,' she said when Mrs Mellor looked up and began drying her face on a lace-edged scrap of fabric. 'Linda's crying, too. She's in the big garden. She's very, very upset about ... about something or other.'

'I see.'

Anna addressed the twins. 'Touch anything, and you're dead,' she advised, her voice darkened by the severity of the promise. 'It's the war,' she told Mrs Mellor. 'Auntie Elsie says everybody's in a hurry to do everything and it's all because of bloody Hitler. Life's changed, she says. People haven't got the same ... er ... standards, I think she said. They're doing things differently.'

Iris Mellor nodded. 'A wise woman, Elsie Dixon.'

Anna approached the desk. 'If he gets killed – Master Roger, I mean – you'll wish you'd stayed friends with him. You'd never get over it. Auntie Elsie knows people who've lost sons, and she says they'll never get over it. She's a wise woman like you just said.'

'Yes. How old are you now, Anna?'

'Seven, soon be eight.'

'And you?' she asked the twins.

132

'Two and a half,' they chorused.

'And they'll live to be three if they behave themselves – that's what Auntie Elsie says.'

'Take them home, Anna,' said the weary Iris Mellor. 'Go along. Take them home. I shall be well, I promise you.'

The woman watched while the child pushed her younger sisters away from the house. 'Out of the mouths of babes,' she muttered before pouring herself a stiff whisky. 'Damn this bloody war.' Then she had another double before going out to find her son. As she walked through her little bit of England, she thought about Roger and what he might have to face once he got through basic training. And the girl wasn't too bad, she supposed. She was a bit older than Roger, but not enough to make any significant difference.

What the child had said was true. People grew up fast in times of war. And she, Iris Mellor, had to mature to the point where she could let her son go. Not just to the war, but into the arms of a young woman who seemed a little too grown up for him. 'Oh, well,' she mumbled. '*C'est la vie.*'

Linda burst into the house. She was still crying, but she was smiling at the same time, and her breathing was odd. Anna decided that had Linda been a weather feature, it would be rainy and sunny at the same time, with rainbows.

Linda fell to her knees. 'Thank you, Anna,' she said. 'Thank you for caring enough to march in and fight dragons for me.'

'Mrs Mellor's not a dragon.'

'I know. But you'd have gone in even if she had

been a dragon. Wouldn't you?'

Anna wasn't sure, and she said so.

Elsie had just returned from her shift, and she came in from the kitchen. 'What's happened now?' she asked with her customary bluntness.

'I'm getting married,' replied Linda. 'No time for banns, so we're being treated as a special case because of the war. We both hope you'll all be there once we've sorted it out properly. Oh, and there's the parachute. For my dress. Mrs Culshaw says she'll sew as fast as she can, but ... ah, Anna. How can I ever thank you?'

'What's she done now?' Elsie demanded.

'She made it happen. She had a word with my soon-to-be-Ma-in-law.'

'Aye, she would,' said Elsie in her matter-of-fact voice. 'Shall I put the kettle on?'

Another year passed, and the war continued. Anna made her First Holy Communion, and when the breakfast party at the church of Saints Peter and Paul was over, Tom Brogan drove her home. She was unusually quiet. Because of her tendency to think a little too deeply about things, he was slightly concerned. 'Well,' he said as they waited at traffic lights, 'that's you done and dusted and a full member of the clan.'

'Yes.' But she didn't feel any different. Something holy was meant to have happened, but it hadn't been holy at all. When she'd opened her mouth to receive the wafer, no light appeared, no warmth entered her chest. And, when she got back to her pew, the girl next to her had whispered and giggled all the while, and the boy to her left had spent most of the time playing with a matchbox containing two caterpillars. The Body and Blood of Jesus Christ had sat in the mouth of a boy who played with creatures in a Swan Vestas container.

'What's the matter, Anna?'

She sighed. 'It stuck to the roof of my mouth. I had to pull it down with my tongue, because otherwise, I think the Holy Host would have been there all day.'

'Sure, that's all right,' he said.

'It's the not being able to eat or drink,' she complained. 'And I went dizzy. Auntie Elsie calls it faint for lack of nourishment.'

'It's a law of the Church,' he explained. 'When you receive Jesus into your heart, you have to be empty.'

'It's my stomach that was empty,' she complained. 'My heart and my head were filled with Kate and Beckie terrorizing everyone. They're naughty. It's a special kind of naughty.'

'Ah, away with your bother. They're three years old with no sense of right or wrong. They're babies, Anna.'

Nobody would listen, it seemed. No one would try to work out what she was trying to say, because it sounded daft. Yes, they were babies. But there was something extra to them, something odd. They weren't identical. At least there was no problem with who was who and who was to blame. But they were so similar in character, so secretive and fastened together, so crafty...

'You'll never work it out,' he told her now. 'People are people, and no two are the same.'

135

'They're the same,' she said softly. 'And that's what makes them twice as bad.'

'You mustn't think like that, child. You'll see. Wait till they grow up a bit more and get to school – they'll be different altogether, so they will.'

When they reached the cottage, Anna went off for a walk. She told Father Brogan to go in for a cup of tea, and she would be back in a few minutes. 'I just want to think,' she said. 'About Communion and all that.'

The priest sat with the Dixons and watched the twins playing nicely at the table with their dollies. 'She's very mixed up,' said Tom Brogan.

Elsie nodded. 'You've got to remember what happened, Father. She sat with Frankie, cleaned her up, never went to the funeral because she was in hospital. The twins came along and her mother left. That's the sum total of it.'

The visitor lowered his tone. 'But she seems to think they're evil, Elsie.'

Bert spoke up for his best girl. 'Anna's got a lot of sense and she talks a lot of sense. They're little buggers, the pair of them – excuse me swearing, Father. But I can see some of what Anna means. Happen she does exaggerate a bit, but them two would try a saint. They've got their own language and their own rules. They listen to nobody, and don't give a fig for any of us. Me and Elsie are just servants – we clean them up, dress them, put food in front of them. There's no...' He paused. 'I don't mean thanks. I don't even mean appreciation. I think there's no love in them.'

'Love for each other?' the priest asked.

Bert shrugged. 'Who knows? They talk a language called rubbish, and I don't see them hugging each other. They certainly don't hug us or their sister.'

At that moment, the pair turned, looked at the guest and smiled.

A cold, but lightweight finger travelled the length of his back. Dear Lord, were these people making him fanciful? Had Anna's words in the car caused him to imagine things? It was their eyes – laughing, yet empty. It was nonsense, of course. They were only babies.

'It's true, Uncle Bert. Look.' Anna held up a newspaper. She read aloud. Some Jews in Warsaw had committed suicide rather than give in, and approximately 50,000 people had been killed. 'You know they have the same God as we have?' she asked. 'The Jews, I mean. Jesus was a Jew. Father Brogan told me we all come from Jews. This is just horrible.'

'Aye, and that was last year. Since then, there will have been a lot more, love. We have to hurry up, or there won't be a Jew left breathing.'

Anna looked at the piles of newsprint that surrounded her. She needed to hurry, too, because she wanted to get this war cut out and stuck down while it was still happening. She had nine very large scrapbooks filled already, and she was well into the tenth. But it wasn't easy, because she had to work while the twins were out, since they certainly kept a keen eye on her progress. 'I'm over a year behind,' she grumbled softly.

Bert watched his favourite girl as she read pieces

137

about the desert campaign, her lips moving when she laboured over names that were scarcely pronounceable. He loved her to bits. Elsie just plodded along, seeming to ignore or to miss the behaviour of the other two. But Bert knew what was what. If those little buggers could get their hands on Anna's scrapbooks, they would. Angelic faces sometimes hid naughty minds, just as the biblical whited sepulchre might conceal the gravest sin.

Elsie came in with the twins. Bert, standing in the kitchen doorway, gazed at the industrious eight-year-old with her scissors and glue. 'Anna?'

'What, Uncle Bert?'

'The books you've already filled – shall I take them up to the hall and ask Mrs Mellor to hide them?'

Anna smiled. Uncle Bert understood. He knew what they were capable of, and he was on her side. 'Yes, please.'

Elsie shook her head. 'I don't know what all the fuss is about. They've been as good as gold for weeks now.'

Bert stared at his wife. 'They wait their chance.' The words were pushed past narrowed lips. 'But I'm taking no chances with our Anna's bits and bobs.' He walked upstairs to get Anna's scrapbooks from their top shelf. 'It shouldn't be like this,' he muttered to himself.

Downstairs, Elsie was squaring up to Anna. 'I don't know what came first, chicken or egg,' she declared, 'but you and Bert see only bad in these two little girls. That could be why they're sometimes naughty, because they know you don't give

138

a damn for them. Three years old,' she said. 'You should be ashamed, both of you. They can't be held responsible for their actions at this age.'

Anna continued to tidy away her treasures. The twins were now causing rows between the Dixons, and that was exactly what they wanted. Auntie Elsie forgot things so easily. They had flattened the chicken run – fortunately, it had been empty at the time. They had thrown chicken droppings at washing on the line, broken two windows by throwing stones, dug up all Auntie Elsie's lettuces, picked the French marigolds. According to their foster mother, Kate and Beckie had high spirits and would grow out of this phase. After picking up all her belongings in order to carry them to her room, Anna made her reply. 'Did you find the bread knife?'

'No.'

'Well, I did. They'd been poking it between the planks of the coop. Perhaps they fancied chicken for tea.' She stalked out, head held high. Auntie Elsie wasn't as clever as Uncle Bert, so she hadn't yet seen past those pretty faces and beautiful curls.

Bert Dixon was sitting on Anna's bed and looking through the full scrap books. 'Four bloody years,' he said gloomily. 'Millions dead. All because of a madman. I ask you, Anna, where's the sense?'

'There is none,' she replied.

She was right, and they both knew it.

Anna's friendship with Linda Harris, now Linda Mellor, flourished anew once Roger had disappeared into the jaws of the war in Europe. Iris Mellor became unexpectedly fond of her daughter-in-law, and the change in her attitude was probably influenced by Linda's pregnancy. A beautiful boy was born, so the Mellor line was assured, and that mattered. Grandmother doted on Richard, while his mother found him to be so much fun that she nicknamed him 'Sausage'.

'Why Sausage?' Anna asked one day as they walked to the Post Office.

'Squidgy and fat,' came the reply from Linda.

Anna laughed. 'Steak puddings are fatter than sausages,' she said. 'Pudding's a better name.'

Linda shook her head. 'The war ruined your northern steak puddings, Anna. Where there was meat, there's now breadcrumb and gravy. At least we can still get a half-decent sausage if we play our cards right. He's a sausage. Aren't you, Sausage?'

The baby chortled and Anna shivered. How often had the twins laughed when being pushed in a pram? The only time they chuckled was when someone else was in trouble. They no longer needed Anna to read to them. They could both read for themselves, so their self-containment was almost complete. They slept together, ate together, bathed together, played together. No one was allowed to enter the world they had constructed so carefully just for themselves. It was a club with two members and no affiliates. Anna ordered herself to think about something else. 'Linda?'

'What?' She parked her pram outside the shop.

'Can you tell me what a shotgun wedding is? Only I heard people talking about it and wondered what it was.'

Linda coughed and bent down between pram and window.

'Linda? Why are you laughing? It's not funny. If there was a gun at your wedding, I never saw it. Don't pretend to fasten your sandal – I know it's not undone. Come on, give me an answer.'

Linda stood up and leaned on the Post Office window. 'You will be the death of me, girl.'

'What?'

Linda leaned forward and whispered. 'We had to get married because of Sausage.' She patted her belly. 'I already had Sausage in here.'

Anna decided to pretend not to have caught on. Living in the countryside had taught her a thing or two about bulls and cows, about how calves were made. 'There were no sausages,' she said in mock-seriousness. 'There was salmon, game pie, trout and salad. And some pork. No sausages and no guns at your wedding.'

'I was already expecting him.' The mother pointed to her child.

It was Anna's turn to laugh. 'I know. I knew, I knew, I knew all the time.'

They entered the shop together. Mrs Culshaw, local seamstress and postmistress, glared at Anna. 'There you are. I waited for someone to come so that I can go and get Elsie. I've shut them in the shed. Two pure-bred Persians I could have lost because of them.'

'Pardon?' said Linda.

'Them bloody twins. They shouldn't be out on their own, not at their age. Pinched two of my Tilly's kittens, they did, and they're nobbut two

141

weeks old. A few hours away from their mam, and they would have been dead. It's all right, I got the kitties back, but one of them little buggers of yours kicked me.' She stared hard at Anna.

'They are not mine.' These four words emerged slowly and clearly. 'They have the same mother and father as me, but they aren't mine. Everybody carries on as if I'm their mother – well, I'm not. I'm just a child.'

Edna Culshaw looked at Linda. 'Well, that's me told, isn't it? And this poor kiddy's right – she's not in charge of them. Well, she shouldn't be, but I know she often is. Can you stop here while I nip up and get Elsie? If there's owt you can't manage, tell the customers to take what they need as long as they have the ration points, and I'll sort money out later.'

Linda and Anna waited. 'They're getting no better then?'

'No,' Anna replied. 'They are terrible. Uncle Bert can see it, but Auntie Elsie won't.'

'Yet they're no trouble in nursery.' Linda looked through the window to check on Sausage. 'Good as gold, a mile ahead of everyone else, no problems. The teacher's thrilled to bits.'

Anna folded her arms in the manner of Auntie Elsie. 'The teacher should live at our house for a month or two, then. Let her do her washing twice because they've covered it in chicken muck. See, they're good if it suits them, Linda. If they think they're getting their own way, they're great. School must be something they enjoy. If they start doing something in class that Kate and Beckie don't like, it'll be a different story.'

Linda shook her head slowly. How could one woman give birth to a child like Anna, then to a pair of potential nightmares? But the woman had died, hadn't she? Perhaps the twins had always felt out of place, unwanted, sad.

'You can make up all the excuses and reasons,' said Anna. 'I've done all that myself. But they're not right. Naughty isn't enough, because they're more than that, worse than that.' Underneath all Anna had just said was another point, though she didn't care to make it just now. It wasn't her fault that Mam had died and that the twins existed. But it seemed as if half her life had been spent watching them, walking them, taking them to and from nursery. She was missing things. She wasn't sure what the things were, but she knew she was missing out.

Elsie Dixon bustled in, Mrs Culshaw hot on her heels. 'Weren't you supposed to be watching them?' Elsie asked Anna.

And it all burst out in that moment. It was as if the words had a life and strength of their own, because Anna could not control them. 'They aren't mine,' she told her beloved foster mother. 'And I can't play when I want to, because I often have them with me. It's not fair. If you can't manage them, give them to someone who can, because I've had enough.' On that note, she turned on her heel and left the scene. She was horribly angry, mostly with herself, but she was fed up with being in charge. Mrs Culshaw would understand, because she had cats, not kids. Linda would be sympathetic, since she had seen the twins in full flood during a visit to the Dixons' house. But

Auntie Elsie thought all children were the same and she wouldn't listen to any bad news about Kate and Beckie.

Elsie dragged the two miscreants into the shop and made them face Mrs Culshaw. 'Say sorry,' she ordered.

'Sorry.' They giggled after delivering the syllables in unison.

Mrs Culshaw stood in the shop doorway. No one was leaving until she'd had her say. 'Elsie, I know it's not been easy for you getting three kiddies when you were coming up fifty. I've no quarrel with Anna, because she does her best. But these two listen to nobody.'

Elsie shifted her weight from foot to foot. 'They said they're sorry.' Her voice was quiet.

'Aye, and I say the moon's green cheese, but do I mean it? Now, I DO mean this. Keep them two away from my shop. They've no right touching my cats. They've no right being out on their own at this age.'

Elsie sat in one of the customers' chairs. 'The gates don't stop them any more,' she said. 'I suppose we could fix padlocks or something, but it's treating them like animals in a zoo, isn't it?'

Linda stepped into the arena. 'Just don't blame Anna – any of you. She's worked hard, got them reading, counting, knowing their numbers. The nursery's never seen such clever children, and that's what Anna set out to produce, since her mother did it for her. But she's eight years old. We all forget that, because she's an old head on her shoulders.' She spoke to Elsie. 'Good luck, Mrs Dixon. You're going to need it.'

144

In June 1943, the U-boats lost heart. Depth charges, radar and warning systems developed by scientists made life impossible for the crews of these killer submarines. Allied aircraft were now capable of bombing U-boats out of existence, so another corner had been turned. Anna cut and pasted the news into her scrapbook. She didn't know where her dad was, though a letter had arrived weeks ago. Bert thought he'd be going for Palermo, capital of Sicily, but no one could be sure. 'As long as he's getting nearer to home, eh?' said Bert before going into the garden.

But Anna was worried about Elsie, so she heard scarcely a word. She couldn't forget how rude she had been in the Post Office, because, having thought through what she had said on that occasion, she had to admit that it wasn't Elsie's fault, either. Auntie had not contributed to Mam's death, and she was no blood relation to Beckie and Kate, so the care of those two mischief-makers had to be shared.

It was being shared now. Beckie, with her tongue poking from a corner of her mouth, was measuring the articles Anna wanted to keep. She then measured the page in the scrapbook, and made her calculations on a bit of paper. Anna stopped reading. At three-and-a-half, Beckie was coping with calculations that would certainly have flummoxed many of the students in Junior One.

Kate was reading. 'Pan-tell-eria,' she said carefully.

Anna looked at the piece. The island of Pantelleria was between Tunisia and Sicily. Did Kate realize that her father was in that area? How much did these two know? 'Yes, it was done by aeroplanes. The people surrendered before our army went in.'

'Bombs,' said Kate.

'Yes, bombs.' Anna carried on sticking.

Kate spoke to Beckie. 'Corra Anna borra kittle?'

Beckie shook her head.

'You're not having a kitten,' said Anna. 'And don't think for one minute that I don't understand enough of your daft-speak, because I listen. You're not fit to have a cat. You'd probably kill it.'

'No,' they shouted.

'Shouldn't that be no-plee? Or are you going to have a bit of sense and talk like the rest of us?'

There was no response. There was seldom a response, because they preferred their own world, their own company, their own plans. But they continued to help and no attempt was made to sabotage Anna's work. For some time, their older sister had known that they were clever; this was the day when she realized that they were more than that – they were unusually brilliant.

'Anna?'

'What, Kate?'

'Did he see us. The daddy – did he see us?'

'Yes, he came when I was ill.'

'And will we live with the daddy when he comes back from the war?'

Anna didn't want to think about that. The idea of having just one adult in the house was not attractive. Uncle Bert went to work, but Auntie Elsie was at home for most of the day. How would it be with just Dad? She shivered.

'Are you cold, Anna?'

She wasn't cold. Something had just walked over her grave, and she feared for the future. Their father would go to work, and who would mind the twins? Would it not be better if they stayed with the Dixons while Anna went to Dad? That had been Anna's intention – well – her dearest wish, but she was older now, and she realized that Dad would probably want all three of his children back when he came home.

She had to wait and see.

Seven

We decided to meet at the scene of the crime at one o'clock for a bite of lunch. The part-time amateur hookers come out to play only in the evenings, and his wife is one of them. She's the one who's currently servicing my husband, but there is no awkwardness when I meet her official other half.

He didn't do justice when describing himself to me. The only bit that fits is the Guardian crossword and a silver pen. The rest is – well – beautiful. And it's as if we have known each other all our lives, because we have similar humour and similar concerns. I order orange juice, he has a half pint of lager, and we settle in one of the private booths in which magic moments occur, but only after tea time. It's a tatty dump, probably looks a bit better when daylight fades.

'We're batting for the same side,' he tells me. 'I've two girls to bring up, and they'll be a damned sight better off without Dolores as an example. Unfit mother, you see. She says she's taking them with her, but I'll fight for them right to the end.'

'Good for you.' He is extraordinarily handsome. Like me, he has too much hair; like me, he has inherited good bone structure – what does she see in Den? He's staring at me. 'Sorry,' I mumble. Is he waiting for me to say something? 'Yes, I have two girls, but they're only three months old. So she's planning to go to Lincolnshire with Den? Don't you think we should warn the populace, get the town crier out?'

Alec grins. 'This is the first time she's actually come near to the point of leaving, so I'm keeping my fingers crossed and hoping for better luck this time. Holding a knife and fork's difficult, and it slows me down at work, but crossed they are and crossed they'll stay.' He makes a show of picking up his half of lager with crippled fingers. 'It's a bugger,' he sighs. I like this man. He's easy company, and wonderfully easy on the eye.

I tell him about the Dutch crab lice, and he asks how I know their nationality. 'Clogs,' I say. 'And their accent was strange.'

He shakes his head thoughtfully. 'That's why she was scratching, then. Thank God for small mercies, eh? Good job I can't bear to touch her.' He ponders for a moment. 'You know, they might not have been Dutch, because she's been with God knows how many men. Don't blame foreigners, Anna. The accent was possibly a speech defect, and the clogs – well – anyone's entitled to the odd fashion blunder. My wife's probably bred a strain all her own. I'm OK. I keep my distance.'

I like him. And the way he looks at me... I think he likes me, too. Alec Halliwell doesn't deserve any of this because he's a decent – and very attractive – man. And he loved her so much. When she had an evening job, he used to stand at a bedroom window and wait for her to come home. If she walked down one side of the avenue, he knew she'd come home on the bus; when she was on the opposite side, she'd had a lift – and the rest – from a man.

'I started having headaches,' he says. 'Blinders, they were. They stopped when I stopped standing at the bedroom window.'

'They stopped when you stopped loving her, Alec.'

'Undoubtedly. And now, I can't wait for her to go. But I must say, I feel a bit sorry for your husband. She's not the full quid – bottom stream of the Secondary Modern before they invented this comprehensive doo-dah. But she was beautiful, you see. And I fell for her hook, line and sinker when we were both fourteen. I've never quite managed to love anyone else. So far, anyway.'

As owner of a wild imagination, I have to keep my feet on the ground. But there's something about the way he's looking at me... I take a sip from my glass. Nothing is happening. He's talking to me, that's all. And yet ... those bright eyes are travelling from my face to my neck, then down to the rest of me. I should have worn better clothes.

After smiling broadly at me, he tells me about the obsessive cleaning that begins at six o'clock every morning. She attacks every room, windows included, is done by ten o'clock, then the rest of the day is hers. 'The gas fire has a grille in front that comes off, but she doesn't know that. She pokes her fingers through the slots and struggles with the duster–'

'You haven't told her it comes off?'

'Why should I? I can't be bothered,' he answers. 'When I'm there, I just watch her doing it and

150

smile to myself. But just before she leaves for good, I'll pull the grille off and say nothing. She may guess then what the smiling was about, though I have my doubts.'

I know exactly what he means. We rub along with friends, colleagues, neighbours and relatives even when they annoy, but the person closest to us is the one we punish once the love dies. The punishments may be small, yet they are calculated, continuous and deliberate. Den likes the toilet paper placed on its spool so that the loose end hangs against the wall. I always put it on the 'wrong' way round, and he inevitably turns it to suit himself. A small thing, but once combined with other annoyances, it is a weapon. We are cruel. Marriage can be extremely cruel. It can also be the loneliest place.

'I stopped loving him a long time ago,' I say. 'But when I stopped liking him, that was the end. We weren't supposed to be able to have children. Then, at the grand old age of forty, I had twins. He wanted a son, got two girls. Girls are a waste of space.'

'But OK for jumping into bed with?' he says dryly.

'And cooking. They have to be able to cook.'

He takes a photograph from his pocket and turns it over. 'See?' he says. 'That's Dolly.' She has written *Our holliday in Torkey* on the reverse side. Den will never cope with this. Although he swears he has had enough of clever women, he needs the odd game of Scrabble or bridge from time to time. I pass the item back to Alec, and our fingers touch for a brief, delightful second.

151

'Excellent,' I say. 'They'll do very well together.'

He agrees. I give him the details of a good solicitor based in Liverpool. 'Or you can share mine – I'll give you her card. Make sure it's what you want,' I tell him. 'Divorce is stressful.'

'So is living with her. I'd rather have dirty windows and less hassle.'

'And your daughters safe.' I notice the pain in his face whenever his children are mentioned. Unlike Den, he cares. He is terrified of losing them; he doesn't want them to turn out like their mother. This is a caring, gentle man who has always deserved better than Dolores. The longer our conversation continues, the more determined we become to push the two together. But I have one reservation, because Den will take no interest in Alec's girls. Would they not be better here, with their father? Even if Dolores had to stay, Alec could be around to influence his children. 'You may lose them.' I say. 'And to keep them, you may have to keep Dolores as well.'

But he convinces me that the older girl will refuse to leave. At fourteen, she will be listened to by the court, and there's a possibility that the same court will choose not to separate siblings. 'As for Dolly – Dolores – as far as I'm concerned, she's going for good.'

Time is flying by. We have a standard pub lunch of chicken and chips, and I don't want the meeting to end. It's silly. Haven't I enough on my plate with chicken and chips, Lottie, Emily, Susan, Stephen, Marie, Maureen and Geoff? Am I trying to establish a new nation? He's a friend, I tell my conscience. An accidental friend, and

152

they have a habit of turning out to be the best. Don't get too fond of him, I order myself firmly.

'No need to kill it,' Alec says. 'If you're lucky, that chicken was already dead before it hit the plate.'

I haven't realized that I am stabbing at the items in front of me.

'Angry?' he asks.

'Something like that. It comes over me in waves.'

'Not long since you gave birth, Anna. Bad time to get divorced.'

'There is no good time. If I wait, won't the girls notice their daddy? This way, they aren't going to miss him. He's away a lot, so they hardly know him. He's not interested.'

'And you're happier when he's abroad.' It isn't a question. He knows.

It's raining. We sit in his car and exchange vital information, promise to keep in touch by phone. He smells of soap. No aftershave. I have this strong dislike for perfumed men. Nice hands, soft voice, decent but casual clothes. Stop it, Anna!

'Whenever you need me, just shout,' he says. 'Anything round the house – have toolbox, will travel.'

We have four daughters between us. The atmosphere in this car is loaded, so I must get out immediately, if not sooner. I don't want to go. Then he takes my hand and we are both trembling. I don't know what to do, how to react. If I retrieve my hand, he'll think I'm offended, or that I don't want him near me, or that I'm an anal retentive who can't bear to be touched.

What shall I do? Will someone tell me?

'It's eased off,' he says.

What does he mean? 'Are you talking abut the rain?' I ask.

'Of course. What did you think I meant?'

'I don't know.'

He looks straight at me. 'Oh, but you do know. Something's gone a little haywire, hasn't it? It's been haywire since you walked in and sat with me.'

My mouth opens, but delivers no words. This is all too silly to deserve an airing – better to keep it inside under lock and key. And there's Geoff. And there's Alec's wife and my husband – too complicated. This can't happen, won't happen, as I can't and won't allow it. My willpower is legendary...

Such a sweet kiss. Not demanding, not threatening, just promising. My lips are still parted, but he takes no advantage. Nevertheless, it is the embrace of a lover, not a peck from a friend. 'Alec...'

'What?'

'Oh, Jesus.'

'Where?' he asks. 'When did he come in?' Another kiss, warmer, deeper, and a hand on my belly. Desire for him shoots through me like a bullet fired at close range. 'It's a long time since I did that,' he whispers. 'God, you're lovely, Anna. Did you know you wear your heart in your eyes? Can you bear to spend some time with me? Soon?'

My breathing isn't right. I have never suffered from asthma, and this is not a good time to start. Hands should do as they are told by the owner, but mine aren't listening. I am holding his face, can feel a light stubble trying to break through his skin. Good skin, quite dark for an Englishman. 'Alec, you're amazing,' I inform him. 'But this won't do.'

He agrees, and carries on agreeing until I kiss him back. 'We're even now,' I say.

'No. I did it twice. You owe me one, baby.'

I have read some daft books in my youth, and I recall 'long and lingering kisses' and 'kisses that melt the heart' and all that kind of trash. That kind of trash happens, because we cannot separate. His hands are inside my blouse, and I don't care, as now is the only moment that matters. In this state of lunacy, I am willing to lose anything and everything just in order to cling to him. For minutes, the kiss goes on. He's gentle. Needy, yet restrained.

It ends. Everything ends – I've noticed that.

He fiddles with a non-existent tie. 'That's another fine mess you've gotten me into, Stanley.'

Whatever happens, there is no chance that he will stop being amusing. Even when aroused and needful, he remains a clown.

Yet Den was like that. I must never forget how Den was and what he became, because it can happen all over again. But Alec can laugh at himself, so that's the difference. Perhaps we both need sex. In which case, we could get this business over and done with in an evening. However, I am forced to admit that for me, it would be more than sex. Love at first sight? It's just a legend, or an excuse for people who choose to behave like animals, wham, bam, thank you, sir. Or Ma'am. I am not like that. I have never been like that.

'When shall we three meet again?' he asks.

'Three?'

'It was you who brought Jesus into it. I'd say it was out of character for him to get involved in this kind of thing. Because it is a thing, Anna. Isn't it?'

I nod, don't trust my voice.

'When?' he asks again.

'I'll phone you.' It takes tremendous will power, but I am out of that car like an Olympic sprinter off the blocks. It's a frightening situation, because I am losing control and I have only just picked up the guide lines of my own life. Fingers don't work, and I drop the keys twice before opening the door. The left foot isn't much better, and the car leaps about a bit when I put it into gear and pull away.

He's still sitting in his car, and he's laughing at me. I don't mind. He's the sort of person whose kindness overrides everything. Just about. I put out my tongue, blow him a kiss, then turn towards the bypass. I'm a good driver. Passed my test first time, never had an accident, but there's always a first time, so I pull into a lay-by and repair my make-up. It's not easy. Hands are clumsy and I get mascara in an eye. Great. Now, I'll be driving half-blind.

Two buttons open on the blouse, thank goodness I notice, because Susan would have found plenty to say about that, I don't doubt. I'm in trouble, aren't I? Most people will understand that I didn't go out today to catch a man. I'd have dressed a damned sight more carefully for a start, higher heels and a better skirt. I just went to make sure that Dolores's husband was singing from my hymn sheet.

Elsie would be disgusted with me. Bert would wish me happiness. My twin sisters would crow, while Den would probably counter-sue. As for Mrs Bee – she'd have five fits and a litter of kittens. Yes, I know I've had an affair with the gorgeous Geoff, but this is different. It's odd. No one starts messing about with a man whose wife is messing about with... You see? Confusing.

Maureen's ice-cream van is not parked on the drive. From the moment I step into the house, I know it's completely empty. People, like furniture, absorb noise, and the place seems echo-y and sinister, like one of those films where men leave dehydrated, dead mothers in the cellar and run around outside with knives and evil intentions. Why am I thinking like this? We don't have a cellar.

Panic grips my throat. I can almost feel Den's hands throttling me. Upstairs, I find all rooms except mine are messy, as if folk have left in a great hurry. Something has happened. Have they been kidnapped by Maureen's Jimmy's friends, by Marie's sons, by the alcoholic husband? They're my babies, they're mine! And yes, I know what motherhood is at that level, when a cold hand reaches your heart and squeezes it dry of blood. I love them, I bloody do!

O my God, I am sorry, and beg pardon for all my sins. Act of Contrition? What's that going to achieve? Apart from the Dixons' double funeral, I haven't set foot inside a church since ... since the last time I set foot in a church. Three adults and three babies have disappeared from my house while I... Never mind about that. Don't think about it, nothing happened, nothing ever will happen. My kids are all that matter – everything else is salad dressing, and I prefer my lettuce free from slime.

'Are you there, Anna?'

Mrs Bee. 'Where are they all?' I scream.

'Doctor's,' she answers.

'What? All of them?'

She nods. 'They all just piled into that daft van and buggered off.'

'The babies?'

'Oh, yes. They took them all in case, you see.'

'In case of what?'

'Emily's rash.'

I sink into a chair. My legs don't belong with me any more. 'Rash?'

'Aye. They were worried in case it was thingummy. So they've got one baby each, because you weren't here. Where've you been?'

'She didn't have a rash, Mrs Bee.'

'Well, she's got one now. They don't run to timetables, babies. They're not like trains and buses, so– Where are you off to now?' she screams as my legs return to normal.

'The doctor's,' I yell. But the car turns into my driveway before I have stepped out of the side door. Maureen tumbles out. 'It's all right,' she gabbles. 'It's nothing.'

'What's nothing?'

She reaches into the car, grabs Emily and pushes her into my arms. 'That's nothing.'

I look at the more beautiful of my two babies. She's a bit spotty, and her left eye seems wetter than normal.

'She was worser than that,' Maureen informs me. 'A lot worser. It was like purple, wasn't it, Marie? And she felt dead hot. So we took them all in case it was menin... What's that word, Marie?'

'Meningitis.' Marie blows a strand of hair out of her line of vision. 'Can't be too careful, and we were in loco parentage while you were out. So we made a decision and went. Doctor says it's just a virus and there's a lot of it about. He grumbled on a bit about how breastfed is best fed and all that rubbish, but she just needs a bit of baby medicine and a lot of drinks. Oh, and keep her cool.'

Susan arrives with Stephen. 'Well, she's not going in the fridge, because I've had a go at that crème caramel in your cookery book, Anna. So that's tough titty to you, our Emily, because the bloody fridge is full.'

Our Emily – that is so touching.

I kiss my poor, sick little baby, and she smiles at me. Today, I shall spend every hour with her. For some reason best known to someone who certainly isn't me, this child was born with a chip on her shoulder. I have to mend her.

The fight for survival begins in the womb. I harboured two foreign bodies for the best part of forty weeks, and Emily was the stronger. The animal she used to be wanted all the nourishment, all the oxygen – it's natural. And, when foetus became

159

embryo, she continued in a uterus that was rather ancient for the task of maintaining a pair of semi-detached residences, and she fought for superiority. For that, she cannot be blamed, though I would prefer it not to have happened.

Today, I have learned that she needs me. Lottie is happy in almost anyone's company – I guess she is just grateful to be alive. But Emily needs her mum, so I shall have to do some very clever juggling.

I believe that personality begins to form before birth, that the unborn react to exterior noises, to the feelings and actions of their carrier, and to each other when the pregnancy is multiple. In that third trimester, they start to be people. This one was bigger, heavier, more demanding; Lottie was grateful to be away from the dark place in which, by some means, her sister clobbered her constantly. I must learn to live with this; I must keep Emily occupied while I draw out Charlotte, the shyer twin.

Living with Emily for the best part of a whole day, giving her medicine, keeping her hydrated, I see what Susan has seen. There is an imp in her even now, while she sweats and coughs, while she sneezes and holds my hand tightly. She's laughing at me. There's humour here, and not a little intellect. I have misunderstood. The kid is lovable.

'She'll be all right, Anna.' It's Marie and she's standing behind my chair. 'She's a little stunner, isn't she? There'll be a few hearts broke when she gets on her horse and hits town, eh? And the other one – she's very thoughtful, very deep.'

'Deep?'

'Oh, yeah. She thinks a lot. Quiet, like, but always thinking, never stops till she sleeps. They'll keep you on your toes, love. See, they're all different, and I thank God for my girl, because for the life of me, I'll never understand my lads. My girl's my treasure, and you're twice blessed. I've noticed with nieces and all that lot – no two girls in one family are the same. They all shine in different colours.'

For a so-called uneducated woman, Marie paints some lovely word-pictures. 'Thanks for everything, Marie.'

'Oh, go away with your bother. I've lived here in the lap of luxury for a couple of weeks, no rent, just a bit of housework – it's like I've died and gone to heaven. But the best bit – apart from being with my Susan and Stephen – was having Mo here. She's a cracker, our Mo. I mean, she can't be trusted in a shop, but she'd do anything for anybody what needs her.'

Susan comes in. She's anxious for me to taste her crème caramel before she has a go at baked Alaska. It's good, and I tell her so.

'Butties aren't enough,' she says. 'Our Maureen should be running a café, because she can cook nearly anything – can't she, Mam?'

'Start a business,' I say rashly. 'Call yourselves Third Party.'

Maureen arrives. 'What about fire and theft?'

We all tut at her. 'That's car insurance,' says Marie. 'Go on, Anna.'

What have I started now? I talk about women who are too busy to cook, people who work every day, but whose husbands expect them to produce a meal for friends or work colleagues in the blink of an eye. 'You meet with them, let them choose a menu, then you go to their houses and get all their serving dishes and so forth. Sometimes, you can cheat and cook a batch of something or other, stick it in the freezer, re-cook it and put it in their tableware. Juliet would pay a fortune for that sort of service.'

Maureen is catching on. 'Then we go round with the goodies and plant them in the house before husband and guests turn up.'

'Got it in one, Mo. Think big,' I tell her. 'Think shoplifting in reverse. What's your speciality?' I ask.

'Anything to do with pastry,' is her answer. 'I have a light touch.'

'Susan?'

'Puddings and cakes,' she replies.

'Marie?'

'No idea. Mostly Pimblett's pies and anything from the chippy. But I can wash up. Oh, I don't do egg mayonnaise.'

Susan digs her mother in the ribs. 'You do brilliant soups, Mam. Remember? When we had next to nothing and you got bones from the butcher? You just do the same and chuck a glass of wine in.' She studies me. 'Are you serious?'

'I don't know,' I tell her honestly. 'But we should think about it.' They need hope. They need to be good at something, to succeed, to become businesswomen. 'It's not impossible. When you get the flat in St Helens, some of the cooking could be done there. But most would be here, because I have the six burners and the double oven. It's a simple enough concept, and there'd be no bills for rent, heat and light in a business premises. We'll use a bit more fuel, but that can be accounted for with a proportion of the profits.'

'What about money?' Marie asks.

'Right.' I swallow hard. 'I'd have to invest, but I met a man today who's an accountant. He can look at the idea and give us an opinion.' He can also come here and see how full my house is. That will put a stop to any risk of him 'popping in while passing'. He'll come soon. I know he will.

Emily is asleep, and my left arm is dead. Marie takes her away and, when my arm returns to me, I pick up Lottie from the pram in the dining room. I am learning. Motherhood is like algebra, icing a cake and sex – you have to bloody concentrate.

My living room is sizeable – twenty-eight by seventeen, and it contains three sofas, some side tables, lamps, a massive coffee table and four women, but it's lost its carpet. I'm on my knees, as are Susan, Maureen and Marie. They've discovered my loose-leaf recipe holders and are sorting entrees from starters, soups from puddings, wheat from chaff. The chaff is being dumped in a cardboard box marked CRAP, and I am sad that some of my ideas and cut-outs from magazines have been relegated to the reserves bench. Some of the remarks passed are so cutting – I imagine that half of my extras won't even get to kick a ball.

163

'This here beef strong enough,' comments Maureen.

'Stroganoff. Keep it,' I order. 'I'm very good with nutmeg. I'm very good with main courses, actually.' Well, it's true – I do a lovely rack of lamb and am inventive even with offal.

Marie is laughing. 'What's this prawn hentail with a difference?' she asks.

I grant her a disdainful glance. 'I am ridding my life of the masculine, so the cock goes.'

'You mucky mare,' giggles Susan. 'Hey, Mam – she might be posh, but she's one of us.'

Posh? I washed my mother's body in a house with no hot water, no electricity, gas lights and few windows, since Hitler enjoyed another Kristallnacht in our back street, but I don't say anything. I tend to speak clearly and without much of an accent, have qualifications and know the order in which to use cutlery. Beyond that, I'm as confused as the next woman. Look at these three. Susan's a brilliant mother, Maureen's inventive and unafraid, Marie is stoic. Sometimes, they make me feel quite small and that's not easy – I'm five feet and nine inches tall, and rather larger round the equator since I had the twins.

'Talking of cocks of the walk...' Maureen throws a Magic Roundabout birthday cake in the CRAP box, '...Jimmy got eighteen months in Walton. Let's hope I'm done, dusted, settled and invisible when he gets out.'

'My feller's gone holy,' Marie says.

'Another hole in his head?' asks Maureen sweetly.

Marie shakes her head. 'Church. He's being

confirmed and taking the name Andrew. So he'll be Charles Andrew – must have gone royal as well. Whatever, he'll still be a right Charlie.'

We all sit back on our heels and think for a minute. I don't know why, but I nurture a slight suspicion that Charles Andrew could be on the right track. There's no hope for Jimmy. I think he may be on hard drugs, because the behaviour described by Maureen is a long way up the wall. 'Will you give Charlie a chance?' I ask.

Marie puffs out her cheeks. 'He's a mad bastard, but it could be the drink. I mean, when we got told our Sue was pregnant, he clouted her good and hard. I'm ashamed to say I was ashamed of her, but I'm not now. He was worse than me when we found out. The answer is, I have no answer, Anna. He could go either way.' She shrugs. 'I've prayed to God the Father and God the Son. Confirmation brings the Holy Ghost, so let's see what He can do.'

I take a sideways look at Susan. If the truth ever comes out, Marie will kill her son, and Maureen will be done for aiding and abetting before, during and after the act. Some dogs are best left to slumber. Oh, I forgot. 'Susan, I've got you a dog. Well, a bitch.'

She claps her hands like a five-year-old. 'What make is it?' she asks.

I am tempted to tell her Ferrari, but I don't. 'Golden retriever. She's a pedigree better than any of ours–'

'Couldn't fail,' Maureen interjects.

'And her name's Ellison Queen of Sheba. Ellison's the name of the breeder, and she has

165

four paws, a tail at the back and teeth like needles. That's the animal, not the breeder. But they'll drop out once she's eaten all my furniture. Her teeth, I mean.'

'Sounds like our Gary,' says Marie. 'His teeth are falling out, and it's all because he daren't go near a dentist. His breath stinks.'

Susan raises a hand to her face. She remembers smelly breath. It was our Gary. I distract the other pair by leaping on my game pie recipe. Iris Mellor started my collection with that one.

'Can you cook that?' Maureen asks.

'Of course. But we have to do a bit of deer-stalking, catch some rabbits, skin them and–'

'Shut up,' orders Maureen. 'Or I'll be sick all over your brandy chocolate mousse.'

I shut up, Susan seems to have calmed down. She leaves the room, goes to look at the sleeping babies. I won't follow her, because sympathy might make her weep, and she doesn't need that right now. If I thought I'd get away with it, I'd kill the creature myself. But I'm a coward. By a similar token, if I could do just one bank job and get away with it, I would. That's not out of common decency – it's because I don't fancy prison. Perhaps many of us stay on the right side of the law just to avoid incarceration. Perhaps one of us here in this room is more like her twin sisters than she cares to admit. Whatever, we're yellow-bellies.

Into the valley of death and recipes walks Alec Halliwell. 'I knocked,' he says, 'but nobody heard me.'

He's beautiful. I must remember to keep the side door locked. 'This is Dolores's other half,' I

166

tell the small congregation. 'Alec – Marie, Maureen and Susan, but Susan's upstairs.'

'Nice carpet,' he comments.

I inform him that we are starting a new trend, possibly a new business, and ask will he look at our proposals once I have them on paper.

'More paper?' His eyes are laughing.

'Don't get clever with me,' I advise him. 'Make yourself useful, find the kitchen, find the kettle and make tea.'

He leaves.

Marie is staring at me. 'You jammy little cow,' she whispers.

'I'm not little. Stick to your recipes.'

They are whispering about me, saying they feel love is in the air, laughing behind their hands.

'One word,' I warn. 'One word, and you are homeless. Both of you.'

He's back. 'Where's the tea?'

Maureen shakes her head gravely. 'Are they all daft, or what? It's in the small flour bin.'

'Of course,' he answers. As he walks down the hall, we hear him saying, 'Where else would it be?'

Maureen's eyes have bored all the way to the back of my skull. She makes a crude gesture with her hands. 'Are you and him...?'

'No.'

'She said that a bit fast, Marie.'

'She did. And she's gone red.'

'I've always voted Labour,' I say. 'Just shut up, or you'll be selling butties out of the back of that Hillman.'

Susan enters and asks about the gorgeous hunk

167

in the kitchen. If she doesn't stop, she'll be getting a mongrel and a black eye.

'We can grow our own vegetables,' I announce. 'And salad stuff.'

Nothing. Not a word out of any of them.

'We did old-time ballroom at school,' Marie informs us eventually. 'You had to change partners there, too.'

There's murder in my heart again, but I'm doing time for no one. I go to help with the making of tea. As I walk towards the kitchen, I convince myself that Alec wants to have sex with me just to get his own back with Den. 'What are you doing here? I ask him.

He doesn't know. 'I didn't think you'd have a meeting of mothers here. Or a wall-papered floor.' With no warning, he drags me towards him and traps me against his body. 'Anna.' He kisses me just once before releasing me.

It is very difficult for a person to maintain a clear head when desire floods the veins. But I manage. Just. 'Unless otherwise informed, Alec, always assume that I am busy. Don't make the mistake of taking me for granted. Den did that, and he's on his way down the road with both my size sevens planted on his rear. This house belongs to my children, and I live in it with them. Three of my friends are here, as well. Two are temporary, the other I'm not sure about. She has a baby, too. You can't just swan in here – ever heard of a phone? A letter? A pigeon?'

'Smoke signals,' he adds. 'I'll go.'

I scald the pot while he exits stage left, then I carry the tray through to the living room. 'He's gone,' I say airily. 'Forgot to bring some papers – divorce stuff. And I don't think he wanted to sit among piles of recipes. So.'

'So what?' Susan takes the tray. 'He fancies you, you fancy him – go and have a meal with him. Or something.'

'I had a meal with him yesterday lunchtime.' And something. But I don't mention the something. 'He'll be back. We have business to discuss.'

The three women line up in front of me. Susan taps the floor and counts the others in. Their rendition of Big Spender is interesting, but not perfect. 'Spe-e-e-nd a little ti-ime wi-ith me.'

'Sit!' I command.

They sit. 'Any more from any one of you, and there'll be no Third Party.'

Maureen can't resist it. 'No, but we can have fire and theft...'

I kid you not – this dog thing is clinically insane. Do they have mental hospitals for animals? She eats anything – and I mean anything. Shoes, chairs, skirting boards, carpets, loo roll, pram tyres, toys and doors. I am not prepared for this, not insured against wilful damage by a canine. I've never had a dog. Nothing against them, no phobia, no axe to grind. And she's so happy. Manic, almost. She runs everywhere, even when a wall is three inches away, she still runs. I swear she's going to end up looking like one of those boxer dogs – flat faced and drooling.

In spite of her tendency to crash, and despite all the tellings-off, Sheba is eternally optimistic. She sits in front of me smiling, tongue lolling, breath panting to and fro so that the tongue quivers. She's saying, 'Chase me,' because she suddenly dashes off, bangs into some other wall, turns and says, 'Why haven't you followed me?' I am holding one baby, sometimes two.

But – and this is the wonderful thing – when I place my children on the floor, a blanket spread beneath their bodies, she insinuates her fat little personage between them and she lies as still as stone. It's incredible. She does not bite babies, nor does she attack anything pertaining to them. Blankets, toes, clothes and fingers are all safe, because, in spite of being a mad creature, she knows where to draw the line.

She isn't Susan's dog at all, since she's chosen me. Susan accepts that with equanimity, though she does borrow the puppy from time to time because of the entertainment value.

Great. We now have four babies between two of us, and we pretend that it's perfectly natural for Stephen to share his pram with a two-month-old retriever. Why should we care? People talk, so let them talk. We have a life, they should get one.

The most wonderful news is that my home-made bolster is no longer needed. Propped up, Lottie and Emily seem to tolerate each other very well, especially when Stephen and Sheba keep pace at one side of us. I am coming to realize that dogs and children are a good combination and, though I have to tolerate some chewing and idiocy, the young bitch has added another dimension to the lives of our babies.

Maureen and Marie have moved out to a house

with two bedrooms. They were delighted to get a house instead of a flat, and they are settling in – arguing, of course – before attempting to launch the new ship named Third Party. Alec, who has gone all suit-and-tie professional – he's gorgeous in a suit – has looked at the idea, made a few suggestions and, apart from a couple of meetings with us, has kept his distance. He'd probably be even more handsome out of the suit. Juliet is finishing some paperwork, and we shall all be sweating over a hot stove when our first clients bite. I am a lascivious old cow. It's going to happen. I can't keep this up much longer.

Summer's thinking about moving on. The days are still lovely, but, when evening arrives, there's something in the air, a crispness that warns of cooler days to come. Sunsets are becoming spectacular.

I haven't phoned Alec, and he hasn't phoned me. The only contact we have had has been in the company of others, and I am beginning to feel saintly, because I resisted temptation. Or did I merely postpone the inevitable? I'm not sure, and I still nurse the suspicion that Alec may have tried to make a move on me just to get even with Den.

Oh yes, Den. He's left the area, and Mrs Dolores Halliwell is with him. She left her children in order to move in with an older child, one who is very high maintenance and unpredictable. Never mind. He may find it in his heart to tell her about removable parts when it comes to the cleaning of gas fires.

Susan comes in. 'All asleep,' she says.

'Good.'

'Can we have chips, Anna? It's ages since we had a chippy meal.'

We have one of the best fish-and-chip shops in the north-west. It's been taken over by a lovely Greek fellow who calls himself George, and he has the sense required to ensure that his cooking fat is as hot as hell before he drops in items to be fried. That way, you don't get as much grease clinging to the food. 'I'll go,' I tell her.

And it's as simple as that. I buy fish and chips twice, get into my car, drive home, and a certain Mr Halliwell pulls his vehicle onto the drive behind mine. So I just carry on into the house and close the side door behind me. Shall I lock it? No. That would be infantile.

George is generous, so there's enough for three. We eat in the kitchen, and Alec goes on about marketing, advertising, the need for discretion. 'We have to target the right people,' he says. 'And the best way is by word of mouth. So. We contact big, female bosses in the city and round here.'

'I know a few teachers,' I say. 'And a couple of lawyers as well as associates of Den's. How are your girls?' I add seamlessly.

'Joanna's fine, but Sarah's with my mother for a while. She got upset. But I'm doing my damnedest to keep her with her sister. I have a neighbour who'll look after her when I'm at work. It's not perfect, but—'

'Living with Den and Dolores wouldn't be perfect, either,' I say.

'What's that noise?' he asks.

'Just the dog falling downstairs,' Susan answers,

her tone casual. 'According to the book, she should have found her centre of gravity by now.' Sheba walks in. The tail is wagging the dog, as she loves visitors and fish, probably in reverse order.

Hope burns in brown, velvet eyes. But she's had enough for today. Like Labradors, English retrievers love their food, though for some reason that remains unexplained, they don't gain weight as fast as their Canadian cousins. 'Right,' I tell the others. 'Save one flake of cod each and let it cool. She's on a diet.'

When the dog has inhaled the flakes from her dish, Susan declares that she is tired, so she's off to bed. I try to glare at her, but she won't meet my eyes. I suppose I could develop paranoia and say it's a conspiracy, but I can't be bothered. Dividing my time between Lottie and Emily is taking its toll. I make coffee and carry it through to the living room.

He sits well away from me. Yet there's no awkwardness in him, no nerves. Alec arrived in this world, claimed his space and just got on with it. He's imaginative, but uncomplicated. 'Well?' he asks after a few sips of Nescafé.

'Well enough. The twins tire me, but I'm OK.'

The dog sits between us and reminds me of a spectator at Wimbledon, head turning to whichever one of us is speaking. 'Lovely puppy,' he remarks.

'Tell that to the restorer in Liverpool – this madam ate a leg on my Victorian lady's sewing table.'

'Oh, dear.'

I nod. 'Very dear. Major surgery. It's costing me

an arm and two legs, one in solid walnut, I think. But she can't help it. And she's wonderful with babies.' No suit and tie tonight. Just jeans and a flap-about grandad shirt with no collar. Startling blue eyes, laughter-pleats at the outer corners, tanned skin, brown leather strap on the watch, a small signet ring on the little finger of his left hand.

'Anna?'

'What?'

'Was it a moment of madness?'

I shake my head. 'About half an hour, give or take five minutes.'

'I've no agenda,' he assures me. 'You're a beautiful woman with brain and attitude. You've been brave enough to get rid of your husband while your kids are young enough not to be affected. And the way you took in those people–'

'They're my friends, Alec.'

He nods. 'And the business you're starting – amazing.'

Well, that's good. It's pleasing to be thought of as amazing from time to time. Perhaps I'll make him president of my fan club. 'Maureen and Marie are in St Helens now,' I tell him. 'They got a house rather than a flat. Unfortunately, Mo still isn't completely cured. She's "borrowed" a load of cookery books from various shops, and returning them anonymously is impossible. The cops have her fingerprints, and we can't take the risk. Too many pages to clean. Your wife's handbag was easy in comparison.'

He grins, and those laughter lines deepen. 'Leopards and spots? Yet I don't think she'll turn out to be work-shy, Anna. They've never had a chance, have they?'

'No.' I tell him about Susan wanting to be a vet nurse, but Alec thinks she'll be happy enough making puddings. 'Let her son grow a bit, then think again,' he advises. 'She must walk before trying to run.'

Silence descends on us as dusk deepens. I close curtains, switch on a couple of lamps, turn on the television for the nine o'clock news.

'Anna?'

'What?'

'It's worse than I thought. I'm afraid I love you.' His work is suffering and he isn't sleeping properly, can't read, can't concentrate, can't listen to the Carpenters. He thinks he's going out of his mind. I think he wants me to accompany him in that direction.

'I'm not ready, Alec. Not for you, not for anyone. Life needs to be uncomplicated, because I have twin babies, Susan – she's troubled – and a business to start. Apart from all that – think about the practicalities.'

'You're talking from your head,' he tells me.

'Yes. That's where my mouth is.'

'But not from the heart.'

It's very difficult to keep a straight face when a small dog is turning from one to another as if trying to take in what we are saying, but I must manage this. 'I just can't do it,' I say. 'Look, I'm already with someone – sort of. It's a colleague from work.'

'Sort of?'

I nod. Sheba gets fed up and goes to sleep.

Thank goodness for small mercies. 'I haven't been seeing him since Lottie and Emily were born. We've spoken, but no more than that. Please take me seriously when I say I'm not ready. Life's not easy for any of us, especially for those among us who're looking after injured young mothers, dedicated shoplifters, women with alcoholic husbands, a business, a house and two children. Very small children.'

He stands. 'So I'm in a queue?'

'Something like that. Sorry.'

He apologizes for bothering me, says good night and walks out of the house. I feel as if some superior being has tipped me up and poured me out – like the teapot in the nursery rhyme. I have done the right thing. And I'm sure I'll stop crying soon.

Eight

There were many, many full scrapbooks by the middle of 1944. Although Anna now distrusted the press because of what Uncle Bert termed propaganda, it was all she had. The wireless said the same things, and the wireless wasn't always working, because the battery needed to be charged by a man who lived over the hill. But she was learning to sort wheat from chaff, and the map of Europe she had acquired for her bedroom wall displayed more red pins these days. The red ones were for territory occupied by the Allies, while black-headed ones showed Hitler's conquests diminishing behind the double-edged sword of western democracy and Russian communism. It would end soon. It had to end soon.

Anna was nine, and there was a great deal of discussion about her future. Mrs Mellor wanted to send her to a boarding school in Liverpool, but Anna put her foot down. She didn't want to live at school. Attending on a daily basis was quite sufficient, thank you, so Bert and Elsie were pleased, since they wanted her to go to a convent grammar school in Bolton. Although she didn't embrace wholeheartedly the thought of a return to Cross and Passionists, the Bolton school was infinitely preferable to the Liverpool option, so she agreed to sit for a scholarship, but not until she was eleven.

'You'd pass now,' the teachers told her repeatedly.

That was all well and good, but Anna intended to stay with the easy life for another couple of years. There would be one year of overlap, as Rebecca and Katherine would start attending the infant department in twelve months, but that could not be helped. Five or seven years of secondary education would be quite sufficient, and she had no intention of serving extra time. Even when everyone told her she would catch up and be with older girls, she stuck to her guns. Who wanted to be with older pupils? Who wanted to be a clever clogs? She certainly didn't.

Things on the twins' front had taken a sinister turn, though Anna didn't have an ounce of tangible proof. The farm owned by the Harris family, grandparents to Linda, had lost a barn. It hadn't been bombed, hadn't been mislaid, of course, but it had burned to the ground. For days after the event, Kate and Beckie had huddled together, giggling and speaking their special brand of gobble-de-gook, while Anna had translated all she could manage. The Harris family had been good tenants, so good that the Mellors had allowed them to buy the farm some years earlier, and they were proud to be landed. Linda, who had come up from the south to work for them with the Land Army, was very distraught. 'Anna – who could do a thing like that?'

Anna shrugged and said nothing. They had new words now, and some of them were likely to be *matches, burn* and *fire.* They used language to disguise rather than to clarify a situation, and getting proof wasn't easy. So Anna's cutting and pasting had to be put on one side again, as she had decided to become a spy, and keeping up with them wasn't easy.

They were quick. They fitted into holes she could scarcely get a foot through, and she nursed a suspicion that they knew she was in pursuit of them. Furthermore, she felt that they knew that she knew that they knew – something like that – and they were taking the wee-wee out of her. This expression she had learned from Uncle Bert, who got into a great deal of trouble with Auntie Elsie when he showed off his own brand of swearing. Anna thought it was funny, although she would never, ever use those words in Elsie Dixon's presence. But thinking them was all right.

Lying on her belly with Uncle Bert's binoculars held to her eyes, she watched the twins. Ah. They were playing the old game again. She leapt up, sped across a fallow field and arrived at some acres of pasture where cows grazed. Beckie and Kate, who had deliberately opened the gate, backed off as soon as their older sister appeared. Anna latched the five-bar, made sure it was safe, then caught up with her sisters. 'It's time you were dealt with,' she told them. 'And Auntie Elsie won't do it, so it's up to me.'

She smacked the backs of their legs until her hand hurt, then she dragged them off home. Standing them in front of their foster mother, she told the tale. They didn't weep, hadn't made as much as a squeak when she had slapped them. They were tough. But so was Anna.

'You shouldn't hit them,' said Elsie.

'Really? Then who will? You tell me to keep an eye on them, and I'm supposed to control them and keep them out of trouble – how can I do that when they're setting fire to barns?'

A glance passed between the two younger girls, and Anna knew that she had struck gold.

'They didn't do that,' cried Elsie. 'It'll be some tenant who's jealous because the Harrises own their farm.'

'It was these two,' Anna insisted. 'And now, they're letting cattle loose on the roads.' She turned to them. 'Every cow is written down by the Ministry, every sheep, every pig. Your daddy is at war, and we have to do our bit by keeping England safe and alive with enough to eat. Do you know how much a cow is worth?'

No reply was forthcoming.

'Do you know how much a farmer pays to have a cow served by a prize bull, to get good calves?'

Elsie blushed.

'Pounds and pounds and pounds,' Anna said. 'And you are back to your nasty, selfish, stupid game of opening gates to let the stock out. You are naughty, disgraceful, horrible little girls. One of these days, you'll open the wrong gate, and a bull will get you. Even a young one could turn you into mashed carrot and swede in ten seconds flat. And I, for one, will not be attending your funeral.'

Elsie sank into a chair. 'Anna, love...'

'Too late, Auntie Elsie. I am telling you now that these two wicked creatures burned down the barn, and now they're back to one of their older tricks. They do whatever they like and get away

180

with it, and their behaviour's getting worse, because no one does anything about it. Uncle Bert knows they're not perfect, but he doesn't … doesn't deal with them. I shall.' She glared at them anew. 'Whatever you do, I'll know about it, I'll be there. And I'm bigger than you are.'

Only then did a response come. 'But there are two of us,' Rebecca said.

'Two of us,' Katherine echoed.

A thrill of fear passed through Anna's body. They were four and she was nine, but the time might well come when the pair of them could defeat her physically. Mentally, they were in a class of their own – quick, self-serving and completely unconcerned for anyone but themselves. They were warning her, but she refused to let them win at this point in time. 'Then I'll have to make sure I have friends,' she said coldly. 'Friends who will beat the living daylights out of you. My mother would be ashamed of you. I've had enough. I'm going up to the hall to find some sensible people for a change.' Her final remarks were awarded to Elsie. 'You're doing this all wrong,' she said quietly. 'They think they've been put in this world to take it over. Look at Hitler, and think of them.'

Elsie stayed where she was for a long time after Anna had gone. The twins had disappeared upstairs, and Elsie was left feeling hollow and sick. Anna had common sense enough for an army. From the age of three or four, she had seen the world clearly, had been fluent, far-seeing and exceptionally wise. But the twins had that extra edge, and at its core lay a quality harder than flint or steel. Bert wasn't over-fond of them, and he was a fair judge of character. Were they bad? Had they already committed arson?

She needed to think about something else, something practical. Jam tarts. It would have to be plum jam, because there was a war on.

'Sausage' Richard Mellor was a sweet child. He had a tendency to run everywhere and, with a sense of direction that was hardly a strong point, he had a habit of bumping into things, yet he was very lovable, since he seldom complained when enduring yet another of his collisions with furniture, trees or people.

When she arrived at the hall, Anna found herself in the corridor with a small boy wrapped around her lower half. 'Hello,' she said. 'Where's Mummy?'

'Noo-noo,' he replied. Oo had been his first vowel sound, so his grandmother was Noo-noo, and everyone thought that was charming. 'Mummy wiv Noo-noo and man,' he told her.

Linda, who looked very harassed, appeared in the office doorway. 'Keep him,' she said. 'The doctor's here.'

Anna noticed that Linda's hair was all over the place, and Linda had never tolerated untidy hair. 'I will,' she replied. 'Is everything all right?'

'Most definitely not,' answered Linda before disappearing into the office.

Anna took Richard out onto the lawn, where he pretended to be an aeroplane. He was capable of pretending to be an aeroplane for minutes on end, though his flying machine would move only

182

in circles, so the resulting dizziness caused a hiatus from time to time.

Linda came out and sat on one of the stone steps. After staring at her revolving son for a while, she joined Anna.

'What's the matter?' asked the nine-year-old.

'I don't know the name of it. But she's using all the wrong words, can't remember what happened yesterday or even half an hour ago, and she's getting angry and falling asleep.'

Anna swallowed hard.

'She went out a couple of days ago,' Linda continued. 'Came back with some holly to decorate the house...'

'But it's not Christmas.'

'I know that, Anna, and you know that. The worst thing was, she said she'd been to Africa for it.'

'Africa? Do they have holly in Africa?'

Linda wasn't sure. 'She didn't like me at first, you know. Thought I was too old for Roger and that he was too young for marriage. Then we got close, especially after Sausage was born. She's been good to me in her way. But over these past few months, she's been getting vague. Sometimes, she seems not to recognize me. Recent days have been the worst. It's a nightmare.'

'Well, I hardly know you today, because your hair's loose instead of in your usual victory roll.'

Linda smiled, but her eyes remained clouded. 'We're losing her,' she whispered. 'It's galloping right through her brain.'

'Not dying?' Anna's eyes were round.

'Just in her head, sweetheart. The body works,

183

walks about, sits, stands, lies down. She hasn't a lot of staff, because many have joined up, but those who are here are having one hell of a time. She needs dressing.' A tear crawled down one of Linda's cheeks. 'She ... sometimes, she soils or wets herself.'

'But she can't help it,' said Anna.

'No, she can't. But will you help me? I know you're just a child, but you're sensible, and school is closed for the next few weeks.'

'You know I will.' It would mean that she could not be as vigilant as necessary when it came to her twin sisters, but Anna had a strong sense of loyalty and the ability to prioritize. This was an emergency. If poor Mrs Mellor was going crackers, Anna would be there, because Linda had Sausage to mind, while the staff needed to keep clean the rooms that were used, had to cook and do washing, shopping, and a million other tasks.

'The doctor's going to try to get us a nurse. There aren't a lot to spare, but he'll do his best. Oh, you can talk to Elsie and Bert, because I know they'll want to do their bit. But no one else, Anna. Tell Elsie and Bert that nobody else should be informed. They'll all notice soon enough, anyway. This hall is the centre in our little area. The family's important and has its pride.' And she couldn't tell Roger. If he knew, he might worry, lose concentration and die.

So began Anna's summer of drudgery, though she chose not to view it in such terms. A terrible sadness settled on Berkeley Hall, and nursery classes were moved to a pair of hastily erected prefabs in the grounds. A nurse was found. She wasn't qualified, but had experience in the area of premature dementia, and seemed to be prepared to deal with Mrs Mellor and her problems.

Anna discovered a few tricks that seemed to work. Mrs Mellor liked Ludo, Snakes and Ladders, Snap, and dominoes, though she had to be allowed to win. If she lost, she threw a spectacular tantrum, broke things, wet herself and refused to be changed. The nurse attended to the practicalities, but Anna was the entertainment, and it was tiring.

Mrs Culshaw was in high dudgeon yet again. She marched up to the Dixons' door and rattled the knocker. 'I'll have you two hanged, drawn and quartered, I swear I will,' she growled at her companions. 'And if I don't get you, somebody will, because we're all fed up to the back teeth.'

Kate, on one side of the large woman, sighed resignedly.

Beckie, on the opposite flank, cleared her throat.

Elsie opened the door, and Mrs Culshaw pushed in the reprobates before entering herself without waiting for an invitation. 'Elsie,' she said, 'they're at it again. I've never known anything like them in all my born days, and that's the God's honest truth. They need a good belting.'

Two perfect angels stood in front of Elsie Dixon's fireplace. Scarcely blinking and not at all put out, they clearly failed to care about whatever was about to happen.

'I've a couple of wedding dresses on the go and a Post Office to run,' said Betty Culshaw. 'So I'm what you might call a busy woman. Any road,

185

this being Wednesday and half-day closing, I thought I'd do a bit of sewing. And I'm upstairs in the little back bedroom making the best I can out of muslin and a few inches of lace, when I hear a noise. So I look down, and there's Kate with bottles.'

Kate looked sideways at Beckie. Beckie leaned casually against the fireguard.

'There's pop bottles in yon yard what other people have brought back, and I've returned their deposit. Your two are pinching them and bringing them back again as if they're from your house. I'm paying twice.'

Elsie sat down and addressed Kate. 'In English, did you do it?'

Kate nodded.

'Why?'

'Bogga,' whispered Beckie.

'Never mind that malarkey,' yelled Betty Culshaw. 'You're thieves. And that language of yours, the secret stuff – it's just so none of us knows whatever you're planning next. They've been stealing, and that's all there is to it,' she advised her hostess.

'Why?' Elsie asked the twins.

'Saving up for Uncle Bert's birthday,' Kate replied.

'You can't save up with somebody else's money,' said Elsie. 'It's stealing.' She had finally had enough. 'Get upstairs now, both of you. And you can stay there. I'll bring jam and bread for your supper, and you've to stop in all week. I'm shamed to death of you.'

Hand in hand, the twins left the room.

'They've no conscience,' commented Betty. 'It's like the world's their oyster, and nobody else counts. Tell you what, though, I'm getting that back fence mended pronto. They've played one trick too many on me.'

'How much do I owe you?' asked Elsie, the words floating on a long sigh.

'I don't know. I got the bottles off them today, and I've no way of proving that they've done it before or how many times. But the bottles aren't the point, are they? Where's Anna? Can't she keep an eye on them?'

Elsie shrugged. 'She's working. Gets a pound a week off Linda Mellor for helping up at the hall.' Anna disliked her sisters, but Elsie wasn't going to give away any more family secrets. Betty Culshaw had heard enough that day in the shop, when Anna had said she was fed up with the twins.

Betty placed herself in an armchair. 'Is it true she's gone mental?'

'Who?'

'Iris Mellor, of course. She's not been seen at church for weeks, and nobody's heard a dicky bird from her. I've heard as how she doesn't know whether it's Tuesday or breakfast time.'

Elsie sighed yet again. 'Well, she's not herself,' she said carefully. 'Some kind of fever, I think. It's left her too tired to even dress herself, but we hope she'll get better soon. Anna talks to her and reads to her.'

'Hmmph.' Mrs Culshaw folded her arms and sat back. This movement made clear to Elsie that she knew better, and that she intended to stay until she got to the bottom of things.

'I've jobs to do,' said Elsie, rising to her feet. 'I like to be straight when my Bert gets home.'

Betty Culshaw, at a slightly lowered level of dudgeon, left the house.

Elsie collapsed onto the sofa as soon as she was alone. She had let down her neighbour and friend, Frankie MacRae. Without knowing how, she had failed to rear the twins properly. Anna, thank God, was nearly as good as gold, yet somewhere along the line, Elsie had gone wrong with Kate and Beckie. People weren't born bad, surely? But hadn't Anna been complaining about her sisters for long enough? So had they been like this from birth?

With no idea of what to do or where to turn, Elsie sobbed her heart out. They were listening. She knew they were listening. But they didn't care. They didn't give a damn, because they were ... different.

By the time Anna arrived at Berkeley Hall the next day, the police had been sent for. Linda, who trusted everyone in the household, could think of no one who might have done what the police called an inside job. Mrs Mellor's dead husband's gold cufflinks, tiepin and hunter watch were missing. Mrs Mellor's jewellery boxes had disappeared, as had a string of pearls given by Roger to Linda just before he went abroad.

Anna, who had been searching the grounds for her sisters, who had gone missing, ran to the nearest policeman. 'Our twins have gone again,' she said.

When she learned about the thefts in the big house, she tightened her lips and said nothing at first. It was like the barn – she just knew. But this time, she was one tiny step ahead. For a while, she had known about the hollow tree in Grantham Woods, and she had kept the knowledge to herself. But she needed a witness, someone who knew her and trusted her sufficiently to believe in her honesty. So she asked Linda and the policeman to come with her. 'It's the lightning tree,' she told them. 'That's where they've been hiding stuff.'

'Who?' asked the constable.

'That, officer, is the bit that's going to hurt. Let's go at Anna's speed,' Linda suggested.

The three of them walked across pasture and around the edges of arable land until they reached the rim of the woods. 'We have to be quiet now,' Anna said. 'Like me, they have very good hearing. In fact, you two stay here, and come when I shout. I'll start shouting if and when I find what I think I might find. Then you can put them in prison for me.'

'Put who in prison?' mouthed the constable at Linda.

Instead of replying, she shrugged. In her opinion, this was a matter of least said, soonest mended.

There wasn't a lot of brittle wood about, but Anna had to tread carefully and avoid branches that touched her body. There should be no movement, no warning, because this time, the police would get them. Birds fluttered here and there, but, apart from that, the wood seemed uninhabited. Until she neared the lightning tree. Struck years earlier by a bolt from the blue, the injured object had struggled to live. It had a hole in its base, and this was an ancient tree, so the bole was sizeable.

There was scarcely a sound, but she knew they were inside. The tell-tale signs were a pile of leaves to one side, and a heap of twigs on the other. These had been prepared in order to plug their hiding place after the thieves had made their deposit in this, their own savings bank.

Without bending, without looking to see what they were doing, Anna opened her mouth and screamed, 'They're here.' She did this repeatedly until Linda and the policeman appeared. Anna pointed to the hole. 'In there, you'll find my twin sisters, Katherine and Rebecca. They've been letting cows out of fields, stealing from the Post Office and I reckon they burned down a barn not too long ago.'

The policeman's jaw dropped, and he stood looking very silly for several seconds. 'How old?' he asked finally.

'Four and a half,' replied Anna tersely. 'With what Mrs Culshaw calls criminal minds, no time for anybody and, I'll bet you my Post Office book to your helmet, a load of jewellery.'

The young criminals crawled out of their hole. 'We were hiding it,' said Kate.

'From the Germans,' Beckie added. 'They'll pinch it if they come.'

Anna laughed, though there was no mirth in the noise she produced. 'No, they won't. Because you've already stolen it. How were you going to sell it?

The young constable shook his head. 'It's the magpie thing,' he said. 'Young kiddies like anything that shines.'

'Like fire?' Anna asked. 'Like returned bottles at the back of a shop? Did they shine for you?'

He knelt down, removed his helmet, and began to pull out the contents of the lightning tree. Mrs Mellor's jewellery boxes were followed by her husband's watch, tie-pin and cufflinks. Then came scarves, hankies, pretty nightdresses, Linda's pearls. But the worst for Anna were the last two items. She saw her First Holy Communion rosary, and a pearl-backed prayer book given to her by Auntie Elsie and Uncle Bert to mark the same occasion. She wasn't sure about being a Catholic, but these were gifts, and they had been stolen. Without thinking, she crossed the small clearing and hit her sisters' cheeks so hard that the twins stumbled.

'Hang on,' said the policeman.

Anna turned on him. 'No, you hang on. Hang onto them, take them away. They got born like this. Auntie Elsie and Uncle Bert have been good to them, good to all of us. Imagine what they'll be like in a few years.'

This was another statement that would haunt Anna for the rest of her days. It was as if she knew at the age of nine – as if she had always known – that there was something terribly wrong with her younger sisters. It would always hurt. Their very existence would be a constant source of worry. But on that day, in a wood with a rosary and a prayer book, she was just speaking words.

Anna was no prophet.

The stolen items were gathered up by the policeman, and the twins were taken away for questioning. Elsie was found, and she was chosen to act as responsible adult while the girls were questioned.

Meanwhile, Anna MacRae went to the hall and apologized to a woman who scarcely understood what was being said to her. But the apology was necessary. It was the first of many.

1945

It was over. It ended on 6th May in a small school in Rheims, but no one in England celebrated until the 13th, when the Mall in London was suddenly packed with revellers who cheered their beloved Winston as he drove to the Palace for lunch. Bells rang everywhere, people danced and screamed in the streets, there was weeping and laughter and, at cenotaphs and memorials the length and breadth of the land, men and women placed flowers for those who would not come home, and for all who had died in the second Great War.

A few people in Eagle Rise put out bunting and Union flags, but the celebrations were subdued, because for them, this was a spoilt day and they could not bring themselves to rejoice. A sad quiet descended on them, and they could scarcely bring themselves to express relief or joy when the news arrived.

Yes, the war was over. Yes, the men who had survived would be coming home to their families.

But a cloud hung over the place named by locals as the Big House, their manor, Berkeley Hall. A sad, black-clad Linda Mellor followed a hearse on Iris's last journey to church. Mrs Mellor, who had died of a heart attack, was being laid to rest on the very day on which peace had been officially declared.

This was bad enough, but there was even worse news. Roger, the young Mellor who should have taken over the reins, was dead. His grave would be in Italy, so Linda did not get to bury her husband. Instead, she followed his mother and treated the service as if it were for both the deceased. With untidy hair not quite concealed by a black veil, she stood before a full church and paid tribute to the dead. '...not only my husband and my mother-in-law, but all who have perished during these six long years of war.'

Anna wept quietly. Her sisters watched with interest, though they were not moved to weep. They never cried... 'On behalf of Iris, I thank you all for coming today to pay tribute to a fine woman and her brave son. I must now bear the burden of business until my son comes of age. I beg you all to pray for the family we have lost, and for all whose sons, brothers, husbands and friends are coming home injured. God bless.'

The church was deadly silent. All over the country, people were singing and dancing, but this place would scarcely notice peace. They would continue to plough and nourish, sow and reap, milk cows, collect eggs, breed pigs for market. In villages such as this one, the circle of life continued no matter what was happening in the political arena. A few people sniffed back emotion when the coffin was carried out, but no one said a word.

Anna dragged her sisters to the graveside. She hoped they were glad that they had apologized to Mrs Mellor for stealing her jewellery, yet there was no sign of emotion in either of them. They were making their mark in different ways these days, because the school had been required to bring in secondary level work for them, and they were sailing through algebra as if it were just another language, one they had always known. They were weird.

Mrs Mellor had not understood them, had not recognized them, yet Anna had forced them to make that apology. And here they stood, white blouses, grey skirts and socks, beautifully clean, not in the least way sad. Didn't they know about death? Didn't they understand loss?

At the hall, farmers, their wives and labourers were all given food and drink, but there was very little conversation. Anna spent her time keeping an eye on the twins, just in case they decided to pinch a couple of silver cake forks or a pretty plate. Her sisters were very clever, but Anna was the one who could read people. She could certainly read them. They were playing a long game, were acting as normally as they could manage, but Anna waited for the next explosion. And Dad would be home soon.

Linda and Anna spent a few moments together. 'I just want to go home,' Linda wept. 'But this is my responsibility now. Until Richard is a man, I have to run this place.'

194

Anna nodded. 'No, you don't. You get a steward, someone who'll manage the business.' She had overheard whispered conversation in Mrs Culshaw's shop. 'Then you can go home for a few weeks and come back again. When he's at school, you and Richard can travel to your mum's house in the school holidays.'

'What a clever girl you are, Anna.' Linda dried her eyes. 'Your sisters may be spectacular when it comes to learning, but you know how to apply what you know. And you're kind.' She touched the little girl's hair. 'Ten years old now,' she said absently.

Anna couldn't stay. She left Linda in the office and went to continue her vigil. Ah, there they were. As ever, they stood apart from the crowd, side by side, though not hand in hand. They ate nothing, drank nothing. Anna glanced at Bert and Elsie, who were talking quietly to some farmhands. She hoped that Dad wouldn't blame them for the way her sisters had turned out.

Her heart skipped a beat. Just the four of them – Kate, Beckie, Dad and Anna. One adult for three children, two of whom were ... strange. Dad didn't know them. All he had seen were two babies still red and angry after their recent ordeal. How would he cope? How would she manage with just one parent in the house? She found herself wishing they could all stay with Bert and Elsie. That was terrible, because Dad was coming back to a family, his own family.

This was the end of something horrible – a world war. Was it the beginning of yet another situation that would prove unpalatable?

Nine

Geoff phoned yesterday, and I finished it. He was genuinely upset, and I felt sad for him, but it's impossible. I can't afford an untidy life, and I was always aware that he was waiting somewhere just out of sight. He'll survive. There'll be no shortage of women for him. And Geoff's too good a guy to be messed about. So I'm feeling a bit sorry for myself today, like a kid who wants a certain toy, even if she's never going to play with it. Idiot.

Nothing to do with Alec Halliwell, I keep informing myself. I have to be a mother, the inventor of a new business, a dog-owner, a housekeeper and a sane woman. This is all possible if I continue to keep company with the Hughes family, who have saved my bacon several times, who make me laugh, and who keep my feet planted firmly on planet Earth. I actually love these people.

But. When I lie in my lonely bed, the pillow I clutch has a name. Sometimes, I talk to him; sometimes, he answers back, but I am asleep when that happens. That's when everything blurs and I start to run away from him or towards him. Lately, I have been inclined towards towards...

Susan Hawkeye Hughes notices everything. Then she tells the everything she notices to Marie and Mo, who are now sitting opposite me on one of the sofas. Marie says I should 'gerrit-overwith' and Mo tends to agree. 'Have a wild night,' suggests the latter. 'Posh room in a hotel, bottle of shampers, some nice massage oils, candles...'

Even the puppy woofs at me. She can keep her nose out, too.

'Shut up, Mo and dog,' I order. I am changing my mind about this family – they aren't helping at all. The Spanish Inquisition springs to mind, since I am being persecuted for no good reason. What next, then? The rack, the iron maiden?

'What about the caravan?' This suggestion is made by Susan.

I grant her a withering stare. 'What? With you lot standing at the back bedroom windows with binoculars, waiting for the earth to move?

'Oh, it won't move,' says Maureen. 'It's a dead posh van, that.'

'And he is gorgeous,' adds Marie. 'Lovely hands. Have you noticed his hands, Anna?'

'No.'

'And he's funny and interesting and–'

'He's an accountant,' I shout. 'All accountants are bores. They have to be bores to get into college when they do the course. It's a prerequisite.'

Maureen folds her arms. She usually folds her arms when I fire a few multisyllabic rounds of ammunition in her direction. 'Mrs Dictionary,' she mumbles under her breath. It is clear that Sheba agrees, because she starts to chew on one of Maureen's shoes.

I feel like a rare and exotic foreign film that has attracted a small, but dedicated audience. Glad I don't have subtitles, because if these three could read my thoughts... Things are coming to a pretty

197

pass when a woman can't sit in her own living room without being stared at. They won't go away. Well, if they won't go away, I'll let them act as babysitters while I go away. But why should I? Why should I allow myself to be chased from my own home? Calm down, Anna. This is Susan's home, too, and these people are her family.

Standing up suddenly, I inform my audience that the film will continue shortly when the projector is mended. Meanwhile, some incidental music will be played, and popcorn may be obtained from the foyer.

'What's she on about now?' asks Maureen of no one in particular.

'She's going out,' says Susan.

'Where?' Marie asks her daughter.

I am still here, yet they talk as if I have already left. So I leave. I know where to go when life gets a bit edgy. The camera crews are here when I arrive, dozens of people climbing out of cars just to capture that perfect moment. Tripods abound, and occupants of other cars watch the watchers while keeping an eye on the main event. This is where the Vikings landed. Here is where the sun bids fond farewell on an evening such as this, when the heavens are relatively clear.

Tonight, there is a dark smudge in the sky, a cloud whose efforts to obscure the sun's au revoir have failed. God has taken a pair of scissors and slashed the cloud in several places. Through these vents, blades of fierce orange light glare down in determined attempt to pierce the Mersey. It is truly awesome. Like Beethoven's Sixth, it moves me to tears. I often pray at the Crosby erosion.

This is more spectacular than any building, with or without the intervention of Michelangelo. The Sistine Chapel is amazing, but the art of whichever divine being created Crosby's sunsets is superior to the daubs of any human painter. Jesus preached out of doors for the most part, so, if He is the Son of God, He showed us the way. This is His church. Wherever two or more are gathered in His name – well – there are many of us here, plus cameras and tripods.

Plus Alec Halliwell.

Credo in unum Deum, Patrem omnipotentem. OK. Fair enough. So I sit here and pray, and He sends me my biggest temptation. Jesus was tempted in the wilderness, but He had a will of iron. I wish I had a will of stainless steel, because it's rustproof, and the tears are corroding my own supposed will that was fashioned from Earth's ores.

This is Susan's fault, not God's. She knows I come here when I need to think, pray, cry – whatever. The little madam has phoned Alec and sent him to join me. Yes, he's concentrating on the view, but yes, he has parked in the space next to mine. Rebecca and Katherine, where are you when I need you? You got rid of several of my suitors, even stole one or two for yourselves, but you aren't here now.

He's doing the stretching-of-the-legs bit, walking up and down near the rails. He'd better be careful, because some of these tripod bods are competitive to the point of ferocity, and only the best will get into the Crosby *Herald*. He turns, comes back and stands in front of my car, hands in pockets, half-smile on face.

Surrounded by redness, he looks like a saint who has a halo everywhere, not just above his head. I wish he'd go away. That is, I think I wish he'd go away. He moves to one side just as the moment arrives. A final act of defiance by a disappearing sun throws up the most amazing, incredible vision. This will not last and, in those brief seconds of supreme glory, cameras click wildly. The black cloud wears a scarlet frill, like a dancer from the Moulin Rouge. Apart from the clicking, there is no sound, no movement. Aquamarine darkens towards violet and navy. It is so quick, this ending. Ripples of pale, white cloud turn pink, then red. It's suddenly colder, because our star is moving now to create a fantasy somewhere else and, in a few hours, sunrise in a country far away.

People start to breathe again, move again. Tripods are folded, cameras packed away, engines start. One by one, the vehicles leave until there are just two remaining. He doesn't smile now. Those beautiful eyes bore into me, their heat in no way diminished by the metal and glass carton in which I sit. It's as if he has pinned me to the seat. But I am not afraid of him; I am afraid of me.

The fear makes me panic, and I have no yellow pills. Galvanized, I turn the key, grind my poor car's gearbox into reverse, and back away. It's a good thing that others have left, because I sure as hell might have hit something. I roar off past the Lifeboat Station, the golf course, the fancy houses at this superior end of town. But Lady Luck is not with me. Not that I believe in luck, but... The level crossing barriers drop and red lights show. So I am stuck at the edge of the Liverpool-Southport line, and I feel foolish.

Alec's car, behaving in a dignified fashion – as behoves the vehicle of a trained accountant – stops behind mine. In my rear-view mirror, I see his fingers tapping on the steering wheel. They aren't tapping in an angry fashion – I suppose he is just a bit fed up. The down train passes, but it's minutes before the up one goes by. Barriers are raised, and I drive on, taking a right without signalling and clogging my way down Merrilocks Road. There are speed limits, yet I carry on breaking them until I find my way into Waterloo. He won't come this way. He won't know this way.

He's cleverer than I thought. Outside the cinema on Liverpool Road, I see him again in my mirror. So I decide to concede, but not without giving the wretched man a run for his money. 'Get the bloody business done with,' I say aloud as I drive up the Formby bypass. He wants sex? I'll give him sex, then I'll bend his ear till it's L-shaped. This is a curvaceous road, probably made so by farmers who insisted on hanging onto a few extra yards of field. Walls near to the famous round house are scarred, because many people have crashed here. Legend has it that cars swerve to avoid figures who aren't there, that ghosts cause the accidents. Oh, well. Not to worry. The dead are the least of my problems just now.

Sand dunes are cold and hard, but I have several car rugs and a couple of bottles of Coke in case we get thirsty. He is right behind me all the way past Formby and Ainsdale. Now, we are on the Southport coastal road. I pull into a parking bay, get out of the car and drag rugs from the boot. He stops, stares at me, leaves his car and arrives at my side. 'What are you doing?' he asks.

'Preparation,' I reply. 'Sand dunes, invisibility, sex, get it over with.'

'Why?' he asks.

'Why not? It's what all the foolishness is about, isn't it? But I'm not doing it naked. It's too bloody cold, and I don't want a chill.'

He is laughing at me!

'What's the matter?' I ask, coating the words with a heavy layer of innocence.

He stops laughing. 'It was about sex, that first day in the pub. It's still about sex, but that's not the main thing any more. Look, I'd sell my soul for a night with you, but not like this, not in the sand dunes. We're not sixteen.'

'I noticed.'

He tears the rugs away from me and tosses them onto the bonnet of my car. 'Anna, it's not a game. Are you still sort of with the other man? The man you said you were sort of with?'

I shake my head. 'No. So that's another heart broken. Sort of. And I didn't get rid of him for you, I did it for me and mine. Too many complications – I'm still learning to be a mother.' My heart is all over the place. It seems to be trying to fly out of its cage.

He is standing about half an inch away from me. In the cooler air of evening, I feel warm breath on my face. If he moves any nearer, he'll be on my feet as well as his own. He's tall. When he draws me in, my head fits neatly under his chin, and I hear his heart. I don't want this. I do

202

need this. Loneliness is a terrible thing, and the desire for closeness with a person of the opposite gender is worse than terrible. Also, I have a feeling that this may be one of the right men for me. We all have several, but we seldom meet more than a couple. He has magic hands, firm, decided, yet respectful.

'Alec–'

'Shush. I love you.'

He does. I know it's silly after so short an acquaintance, but I also know he's right. It's something ... he's holding me so gently ... something that needs no apprenticeship. Had this been less than love, we'd be in the sand dunes now with my Cow and Gate-stained rugs and heavy breathing. The words he uses are beautiful, expressions that are aired only between lovers. For a long time, he just holds me and whispers, and I become impatient for closer contact. He knows what he's doing, all right.

Another kiss. Is this our fifth? He has to hold me tightly now, because my legs are suddenly frail. Silly novels, stupid words, drowning in him, tasting him, shaking when he teases me through my clothing. I am forty years old, and a shivering schoolchild at the same time.

He stops and I groan involuntarily. 'I have a new bed,' he says solemnly.

'Congratulations,' I manage.

'For us. The kids are going away with my mother for a few days. So I thought we'd have a fresh start. New sheets, too.'

I hesitate.

'I can show you how to take the grille off the

gas fire.'

That does it. I am completely won over, totally lost. And all because of a bloody gas fire.

After surviving a greeting by the puppy, I enter my domain. Bubble, Toil and Trouble are still sitting in the same places they occupied before I left for my unscheduled adventure. They look as if they've been planted, and I consider water and a drop of Baby Bio. A silence heavier than lead hangs in the air above them. Susan has the grace to blush, and so she should, because she is the perpetrator who has pushed me into the gas fire, and I think it's going to be hot in there. 'Where've you been?' she asks.

I sit down and ignore her question as she knows very well where I've just been – and who with. 'I shall need you all to stay here for a few nights soon,' I say casually. 'You'll have one baby each. I'll be here every day, but may sleep elsewhere.'

Three pairs of eyes are fixed on me. The silence is short, as they burst into loud applause until I warn them about waking the children. Sheba, a warm weight on my feet, lifts a lazy head, then drops it again. She isn't impressed. Neither am I. The next time I decide to do something daring, I'll get the town crier out.

There follows a verbal search of my wardrobe. This covers the full spectrum from what to arrive in to what to sleep in. Maureen has some unusual ideas about items I would never have dreamed of in a million years, but I manage to shut them up by informing them that everything will be new, but there'll be none of the interesting stuff mentioned by Maureen.

They don't shut up for long. 'Get a lovely negligent,' Marie suggests. 'With a bit of lace on.'

Susan, who thinks lace isn't elegant, believes I'll do better in plain oyster satin. 'And it's negligee,' she tells her mother.

'Marilyn Monroe wore perfume full stop in bed.' This is another contribution from Mo. 'Mind, it didn't do her much good, did it? Thirteen years, she's been dead.'

Well, this conversation's going from bad to worse, isn't it? 'Go and have a look at the kids, Susan,' I say. 'And, Mo, I'm not wearing nothing. I'm turned forty, I've carried twins and my belly looks like an empty shopping bag with irregular stripes on it.'

'You nervous?' Marie asks.

'Bloody terrified.' It's true. I should postpone the event, get fit, find my I Hate to Exercise book, eat just fruit and veg, go for a run every morning. The very thought of push-ups makes me sweat and—

A scream cuts through the air like a bolt from a crossbow. I meet Susan in the hall, and she is as white as a boiled sheet. 'Susan?'

'He's taken him. The side door isn't locked and—'

'Who's taken him?'

She swallows and tries to breathe at a more regular rate. 'Gary. Says my baby shouldn't be allowed to live.'

My girls are crying loudly. 'Marie?' I call. 'Go and calm them down, will you? Maureen, come here.'

Marie goes upstairs, and I know she isn't walking steadily. She heard some of it, but I don't know how much. I drag Maureen and Susan back into the living room. I have to be quick. There's no time for secrecy, not now. 'Maureen, go and find Gary. He's taken Stephen.'

'I'm going with her,' Susan sobs.

'Tell her, Susan,' I shout as they rush out. 'And I have to tell your mother.'

They leave, and I sink onto the bottom stair. That poor, sweet little boy who helped achieve armistice between my daughters, has been taken by his father, who is also his uncle. I hear Marie singing to my twins. Good people in a bad world. Gary, like his dad, is a heavy drinker. It won't take much. Just a blow to the little head or... The ducks are noisy. By this time of night, they have usually sorted out who's who and where the kids are and who should have which nest. Jesus!

I have a poker made in 1947 at the foundry in Bolton. It's of heavy iron with a brass handle that gets polished every other Thursday. I am armed, scared, and dangerous. Stephen. I rush across the grove and, in the dim light provided by a very few street lamps, I see the criminal. Big belly, T-shirt, nasty, ugly man. There is a murder in each of us, and this one's mine, so leave me to it. With a great deal of force, I whack the swine across the back of his pear-shaped head. Everything goes into slow motion. He staggers, rights himself, turns and looks at me. An inch at a time, he falls backwards with the child in his arms, and water splashes up. All this seems to have taken half an hour.

I jump in after him, grab the baby, scramble up the bank and run back home. Stephen's coughing, so he's breathing. Thank you, God, I shall never doubt You again. I lock the doors, tear off Stephen's wet clothes and wrap him in a few pram blankets. He's gurgling at me. I guess he enjoyed the ducks.

Marie comes into the living room. Her grandson, on the floor and in the company of a very friendly retriever, is poking a finger into a canine ear.

'Anna?'

Poor woman. What am I meant to say? Shouldn't we get an ambulance and phone the police? I may have killed her son. He's a waste of space, but he's still her son. 'Phone your house,' I suggest. 'Tell Susan her baby's safe.'

'We've no phone. Next door has one, but ours is—'

'Get them, Marie. Just get them.'

While she is dialling, the front door opens — Maureen has her key. They all have keys to my house — that's how well I trust them. 'Anna!' she screams. 'There's nobody in at our Marie's.'

'I have him,' I shout. 'Stephen's here with me and the dog. He's fine, I think.'

They make a circle round the child. I start to shiver. Noise escapes from my mouth, comes from nowhere, and I can't stop it. I am laughing and crying and my breathing isn't right. Susan dashes over and slaps me hard on my left cheek. 'Stop it, Anna. Tell me what happened.'

Crippled words emerge. There's a poker on the grass, and he is in the water. Stephen was in the

207

water, but he's all right now. Gary isn't all right, because I beat his brains out with my poker. It was made as a gift just after the war, but I can't remember who the recipient was, probably my mother-in-law, and should we get the police?

'What's she on about?' Marie asks.

'Our Gary,' replies Susan. She holds my hands in hers, and seconds pass before she speaks. This is one of the hardest moments of her life so far. Many beats of time are marked while she works her way towards the big finish. She swallows hard before speaking again. 'He forced me and put a pillowcase over my head. He's my baby's dad. I saw him in the village last week. He was pissed. He said Stephen should be put down like a dog. As if it was my fault. As if it was Stephen's fault.'

Marie is weeping now. Shortly, we'll have four hysterical women, an almost dry baby, and a dead man in the brook.

But I reckoned without Maureen. She stands up and walks out of the house. Just one order is issued before she closes the door. 'No police. Leave this with me.'

Susan kneels at her mother's feet. 'Now you know why I couldn't say who the father was, because Gary said he'd kill me.'

Marie nods.

'Stephen will be all right,' Susan tells her mother. 'Anna looked it up, and many babies born from incest are OK as long as it isn't the usual thing in a family. Why should an innocent kiddy suffer, Mam?'

Marie rocks back and forth like someone whose movements are restricted by a straitjacket. I can't look at her properly. Small hiccups of hysteria continue up my trachea and into the room. Maureen is outside with a dead body, and the dead body is my fault. No, it isn't. It was him or Stephen, and it was never going to be Stephen.

Marie speaks. 'Your own brother did this to you? And you never told me?'

'I couldn't. He would have said I asked for it, that I wanted what he did to me. And he would have killed me.' She doesn't mention the long months during which she expected her child to have two heads, no eyes and more than four limbs. Only I know what she went through, because we are close, Susan and I. Each has saved the life of the other.

Maureen hasn't come back. What are her plans for a corpse of such a size? I should have called for an ambulance and the police. What will happen to Emily and Charlotte if I go to jail? Then I remember. I'm post-natal. The doctor knows I've been a bit pots-for-rags... Crackers. I've been hormonally challenged. But a man may be dead. He had rights, inalienable human rights. So has Susan. He took away her right to bodily integrity, and that's high on the list – number two, I believe.

But I broke number one and, in a way, I mended the breakage by saving Stephen. Any adult would rescue the child and get rid of the man. We're programmed that way – it's something to do with the continuation of the species. Come back, Maureen!

As if in response to my unspoken request, Maureen enters with poker. 'He'll not be doing any more damage,' she said. 'I'll just wash this poker–'

'Is he dead?' I shout.

'Don't be soft,' is Maureen's answer. 'With a head as thick as his, he likely never felt a bloody thing – he was as pissed as a fart. He's gone home. And he's scared to bloody death of me, 'cos he knows I'm not nice with most men.' She sits on the arm of a sofa, still clutching the weapon. 'See, when you've been used as a parking place with fringe benefits, you look at them different. And soft shite knows I'd kill him as soon as spit on him. And I have friends. Some of them are armed and dangerous even on Sundays.' She reaches out and strokes Susan's hair. 'You've got us, kid. And better still you've got Anna.' She turns to me. 'You knew already. She trusts you, babe.'

Maureen has gone to wash the poker. She brings it back and tells me to hold it. 'Just in case. Your fingerprints would be on here anyway, you see.' Rubber gloves again. People with a criminal history are good to know, because they think of everything. 'Thanks, Mo,' I manage finally.

'Look at you,' she says. 'You're in a hell of a state. Here I am worrying about fingerprints, and you're as white as a sheet.'

So is Marie. She's gone very still and silent, though she's continuing to hold her beloved daughter. I open my mouth and force it to work. 'She may finish what I started,' I warn Maureen. 'Marie, I mean. No one gets away with messing up her girl.'

Maureen nods. 'Don't worry, queen. I'm in charge. It'll be OK.'

With that, I have to be satisfied. Maureen helps me upstairs and undresses me. 'Get in that bloody bed now, you,' she orders. 'Me and our Marie'll be stopping tonight. I'll get you a sleeping pill.'

'Are you on sleeping pills?' I ask.

'No. I buy them in a pub. They're good. You can't overdose. They've made them so you can't kill yourself.' She smiles at me. 'Working girls need them, so I get them for my mates. On the game, you've a lot to block out before you can sleep.'

I am in a room with my children and I am weeping into a pillow with a name. The best thought in my head is built on knowledge and instinct – if Alec were here now, he would simply hold me and comfort me. That's how I know it's love. That, and the gas fire. Smiling through saline, I fall asleep suddenly. The pills work.

Life, as they say, has to go on. Before the business with Gary, we had already chosen two of our guinea-pigs carefully, because both are on my side. One is Juliet Anderson, my lawyer; the other unfortunate creature is Alec, who is bringing with him his older daughter, Jo. Mrs Bee, the fiercest critic of my acquaintance, will also be among us. And poor Alec will be the only male. We couldn't think of a sixth, because most folk travel in pairs, so five will have to suffice. I have been nominated Minister without portfolio, and my brief is a roving one, in case anything goes wrong. I am to sit and eat until or unless otherwise ordered. In the background, Susan, Mo and Marie will be serving up just three courses. If my experience so far with this trio of women is anything to go by, the evening should be interesting.

We are summoned to the dining room, where Maureen is moved to make a short speech. By that, I mean that the other two have forced her into it. 'Third Party, without fire or theft, is the name Anna gave us. This is just a try-out, because normally, we wouldn't be here. Well, we might be here, like, in Anna's house, but we wouldn't be here in your house when you're eating. Any road, it's mulligawotsit, then chicken with olives and them dry tomatoes—'

'Sun-dried,' I say helpfully. I would never have chosen mulligatawny before chicken, but who am I to offer criticism? Just the only investor, that's all.

'Yeah – like she said. And I don't know what's for pud, because our Susan changed her mind about five times.'

At this point, I advise the guests that I have done none of the cooking, so any digestive difficulties should not be placed at my door. 'Wouldn't dream of it,' says Alec. He sounds like an accountant. 'I know where the loo is.' He doesn't sound like an accountant.

Juliet comes off worst, because while the rest of us drink water after taking a sip of the soup, she has bravely imbibed a whole spoonful. I never before saw her move so fast.

Marie's dulcet tones can be heard over the sound of my solicitor coughing and spluttering in the downstairs bathroom. 'Can you not read, you daft bugger? That's two teaspoons, not two friggin' tablespoons.' She puts her head round the door.

'Sorry,' she says sweetly. 'Just a small problem with the staff.' She disappears again. 'If any of that lot has false teeth, they'll be melted by now, you soft mare,' she screams.

I look at my majestic table with its elegant crystal, beautiful flower arrangements, pretty candles and good Irish linen. Mrs Bee is laughing until tears stream down her face, my soon-to-be lover is making sure his daughter has survived the experiment, and I am listening to poor Juliet who is still in the loo. 'Would anyone like some wine?' I ask innocently. That just about puts the tin hat on it, because everyone is suddenly helpless. Even Juliet, when she returns, is weak with mirth bordering on hysteria. 'Poisoners,' she manages to gasp before sinking into her chair.

Maureen comes in. 'Erm...' She exits quickly. Over gales of laughter, I hear her complaining, 'No use talking to that lot in there. They're all away with the bleeding mixer.'

We calm down eventually. And Mrs Bee fixes Alec with a steely stare. 'Is it you?' she demands to know.

He nods.

'Is it you what's wife's run off with Anna's husband?'

'Yes.'

'Is that your daughter?'

'Yes.'

'She'll be asking you to present your documents next,' I advise him. 'Plead the fifth.'

The chicken is a triumph, so things calm down in the kitchen. Juliet starts making eyes at Alec until I kick her under the table. 'If you have five minutes, I'd like to talk to you later,' she says. So I kick her again – what are friends for?'

The pièce de résistance is the third course. A mountain of profiteroles is carried in by a very proud Susan. She was determined to triumph over choux pastry, and she has certainly achieved that. Mrs Bee puts some on one side for her daughter and son-in-law. 'You, girl,' she says to Susan, 'are a natural pastry chef.'

'So's our Maureen,' comes the reply. 'Which is why she should have stayed away from Mulligatawny. It was our Maureen that showed me how to do profiteroles.' She lowers her tone. 'She's no good with soup. Me mam's the one for soups, but she's shy.'

Marie isn't shy at all. Marie is wondering when she's going to get her hands on Gary and who's going to help her kill him. So she hasn't been concentrating on Third Party, because she's upset.

Juliet and I repair to the garden so that we can talk and she can smoke without annoying anyone. Halfway between the house and the caravan, we have a rockery and an arbour with seats, so we sit there while she puffs on a Silk Cut. I have plenty to tell her, and she is on her second king size before I've dragged the baby out of the water. 'Where is he?' she asks.

'Upstairs asleep.'

'Not him. Don't get cute with me, Anna, just because that man in there is ringing your chimes.'

'We don't know where Gary is. But I'm worried that his mother might finish him off.' I take a

214

deep breath. 'You know what I tell you is in confidence, don't you?'

She nods. 'Of course.'

'He raped Susan, Juliet. She was a virgin, wanted to do exams and become a vet nurse, but he impregnated her and–'

'And that's why he tried to kill the little boy,' she finishes for me. 'He won't prosecute you – he's too much of a coward, I'd guess. But thanks for telling me, Anna. Jeez, what a time you've had. But that man in there – is that Dolores's husband?'

'Yes.'

'And you and he are...?'

'Not yet. We're still doing the mating dance – give me a drag of that ciggy.' I inhale, and it makes me dizzy. Glad I gave up. 'I am helplessly and hopelessly in love with him.'

She sighs. 'Don't give Den grounds for a counter-suit. Alec's daughter's old enough to tell her mother what's going on. Whilst there's supposed to be no guilty party, and while all divorces are based on simple breakdown, judges do judge. Don't endanger our position. Now,' she taps my hand, 'tell me about him.'

I find myself painting a beautiful word-picture of a man standing in front of a sunset, a man who is gentle, yet keen and powerful. 'He's good, Juliet. That's all I can say about him. He's a lovely, ordinary, extraordinary person with humour and good looks – have you seen his hands? So beautiful. I imagine them moving over the strings of a violin or the keys of a piano.'

'Or over you,' she says.

'Yes. Or over me with all my stretch marks and wobbly bits – yes. Falling in love with me has given him pain – he didn't plan this when we met for lunch. It's as if it was already there in that dreadful pub, part of the menu. I have to go along with it, have to see what happens next. It may burn out.'

She stamps on her cigarette stub. 'And it may not. Go to it, girl. But be very, very careful.'

It's Tuesday. I am a physical and emotional wreck; Gary, suffering from loss of memory and severe concussion, has been discovered in Providence Hospital covered in bandages and confusion. I did that. His brothers are planning to take him home and wait to see if a familiar environment will act as an aide mémoire.

Marie is shaken. Maureen is walking about with a face like a bad knee – all lines and wrinkles. Little Susan is scared. She's holding onto her son almost every minute of the day, and I wonder whether we should hire a bodyguard. I gather them together in the dining room. 'I want you all to stay here for a few nights. Not just because I may not be here, but because there's strength in numbers. Now. Do we have an our-somebody-or-other in the depths of Liverpool who's trustworthy? A man, I mean.'

Maureen shakes her worried head. 'We don't do men in our family. We do piss-heads, coke-heads, dick-heads and weedy bastards who couldn't swat a fly. Men? Not a one.'

Marie stands up. 'Gary's got at least one more night in hospital. They're not letting him out till tomorrow at the earliest.' Her face and voice are grim. Something's going to happen, but it won't be here, in my house. I stare at Marie and see that her eyes, while open, are closed to me for a few seconds. She's blank. We have all been shut out yet again, because there is stuff going on in her head.

'Marie?' says Maureen.

'What? Look, leave me alone. I have to deal with this, because he's my son and he's something else as well.' She straightens her shoulders. 'Let me put it this way – he won't be living in this village any more. I can guarantee that.'

The icy finger of fear traces a line down my backbone. I am hearing words she isn't saying, am sensing her determination.

She hasn't finished. 'Me and Maureen are going to take our Susan and Stephen to our house, and your two and the dog can come as well. There'll be nobody here, babe. We'll manage.' She sniffs, so some emotion is being allowed to return. 'After what you've done for me and mine, Anna, you've earned your time with yon feller. He loves the bones of you. You deserve him, sweetheart. You deserve that kind of love. So shut up and get on with it.'

Maureen is dabbing her eyes; Susan is smiling at me. 'Are you sure Gary doesn't know where you live?' I ask.

'One thousand percent,' is her reply. 'Anna, go and get a life. If you don't want to do it for yourself, do it for your kids. He'd make a smashing stepdad.'

I suppose he would. But there's a hurdle I

217

haven't yet seen – his younger daughter, Sarah, might not approve. And children are our biggest burden, as well as our greatest achievement. However, I am now convinced. If I don't go tonight, this lot will probably never forgive me.

They've gone. The house is far too big for me alone. I feel as if I'm rattling about like a pebble in a magnum-sized bottle. When I drop the wedding ring into a glass bowl, the sound echoes down the stairs. There's a mark on my finger. I don't tan deeply, but that unkissed circle is a testament to my adultery. In reality, I've only committed the sin with one person, while Den... 'Remember the crab lice and the marks on your throat,' I tell the woman in the mirror.

Why did I remove the ring? Why wait until now? Silly question. When I give myself to this man, it will be the real thing. I suspect that I've only just matured to the point where I can recognize true love – I've been too busy teaching and catering to a man whose mood was never predictable.

I am clad in dark blue velvet, strapless and with the bra built in. A single strand of good pearls is my only jewellery. The best thing of all is that I can, at last, wear high-heeled shoes. I've been practising in these shoes for over a week, and I can balance OK now. Arms are all right, no loose skin yet. The dress is short enough to display one of my better areas – the legs. This shoulder-length hair will have to go soon enough, because there's no worse sight than a woman of a certain age with long hair. Unless she puts it up, that is.

He'll be waiting. Will he be as nervous as I am? He won't be pacing about in new high-heeled shoes, that much is certain. And I can walk in them, I can. My stomach growls, because I have been too edgy to face food. There's a silly smile on my face, because I'm remembering him at the sand dunes when he told me that we aren't sixteen. And the way he talks, the words he uses, so strange dropping from the mouth of a well-spoken man. Perhaps his voice empowers the earthy language and makes it acceptable.

I close my house, making sure all bolts are in position, and I double-lock the front door before walking to the taxi. I can't allow my car to be seen in the vicinity of his place – Juliet would frown upon such carelessness. And I'm on my way to Eccleston, on my way into a future that is uncertain for all of us. I am doing the right thing. I think.

Ten

Sometimes, Anna had to admit that she was a little bit proud of her sisters. They won writing competitions, spelling tests, and always came top in arithmetic. Some of the work they did was for twelve-year-olds, and they seemed to grow cleverer with each passing month. Criminal events were fading into history, and the twins were adapting very well to school. Anna, lulled into a sense of security, concentrated on preparing for her scholarship and entrance exams for grammar school. Until it came to Jimmy Hardcastle and mental arithmetic.

Jimmy was a mouthy little chap with thick spectacles and a limp, as he had been born with poor vision and one leg shorter than the other. He was a happy child, and most of his peers accepted him, because he had been prepared at home by parents sensible and decent enough to help him minimize his difficulties and concentrate on his strengths. As far as Jimmy was concerned, he was as good as the next man, and he did well at school, since his brain, unlike his body, was in good order.

The twins bided their time until the days grew shorter. Dressed from head to toe in dark clothes, and with masks made out of old blackout material, they captured Jimmy, took him into Grantham Woods and tied him to a tree. Their final act before leaving was the smashing of his glasses, without which he was almost blind. They congratulated each other on their cleverness, hid their extra clothing and rushed home in time for tea. But there was no meal on the table. Familiar with the pattern of the Dixon household, Beckie and Kate made a light meal of bread, butter and jam, and drank Vimto instead of weak tea. Supper would come later, so that was all right. They did not pause to wonder where Elsie was, where Anna might be. They simply fuelled their own bodies and went upstairs in search of amusement.

In their bedroom, they communicated their glee at having put Jimmy-Game-Leg-and-Specky-Four-Eyes in his place. Because Jimmy had committed an unforgivable crime – he had beaten Rebecca in a mental arithmetic test some weeks earlier. He had to be punished. No one could be allowed to outdo the MacRae twins. Street-wise enough at five years of age, they had stopped stealing, but not because it was wrong. They hadn't got away with stealing; the kitten, the bottles and the jewellery had all served to put them in difficult situations, so they needed to get their fun elsewhere. Having held themselves in check for many months, they were now confident enough to pay back the crippled boy who had bested them.

The house was empty, so they spoke in English. 'What if he never gets found?' asked Kate. 'He's a long way into the woods, and not many people go there unless they're chasing rabbits or pheasants.'

Beckie shrugged. 'He'll die. Then his mental

arithmetic won't be any use to him, will it?'

Kate frowned. 'But what if they find out it was us?'

'How? We were just two people with hoods on.'

'But everyone always thinks of us, Beckie.'

'I know. Isn't it great?'

They giggled and carried on with the homework set for them by a teacher from the grammar school. They were singularly smart, and they would never get caught.

A matron was now in charge of the mother and baby section of Berkeley Hall, but Elsie still helped out, as did Maggie Chadwick, who had been nurse to the deceased lady of the manor. It was easier with the nursery classes off the premises, because it was quieter and a lot better organized. Many of the mothers and babies had returned home, so the war work allocated to the big house was being wound down. Maggie, who had met a decent farm labourer, was planning to marry soon, and she, too, would be leaving the hall.

Today, Elsie had brought Anna along to find Bert, who had begun to describe himself as a semi-steward. He and a man named Bernard Hanley were joint stewards, and they relieved Linda Mellor of most of the work involved in the running of several large farms. 'Why are we here?' Anna asked repeatedly.

'I need to talk to your Uncle Bert.' Elsie couldn't do this on her own.

'The twins'll be in the house by themselves, Auntie Elsie.'

'Never mind. Come on and do as you're told.'

So Anna was in the room she still considered to be Mrs Mellor's study when she heard about her father. Elsie had received a visit from a friend of Billy MacRae's who had explained it all to her. He wasn't dead, but he wasn't in his right mind any more. 'Like the twins?' she asked.

Elsie shook her head. 'No,' she said. 'He's had some shocks, and he thinks the war hasn't ended. He's going to need medicines and a lot of rest. Then they'll move him to a place up here, and we can go and visit him.'

'I want to go to Brighton. I want to see him, talk to him. If he sees me, he'll remember me and he might just—'

'Anna, leave it to the army and the doctors. They know what they're doing. Where your dad is, there'll be all kinds of clever people who know exactly how to help him. It may be too soon for visitors. Please, please wait.'

'I'm always waiting,' said Anna. 'I've waited years and years for my dad, years for the twins to start turning decent. I'm fed up.'

Things became confused after that, because a child had gone missing, and police came in to seek permission for the public to search the Mellor family's lands. It was already getting dark, so there was a degree of urgency in the man's tone. 'We need more than just the force,' he said. 'We're losing light. The child's vulnerable.'

Anna looked at him. 'Who is it?'

'Jimmy Hardcastle.'

The child nodded wisely and pondered for a few moments. 'He beat one of my sisters in some

223

test or other a few weeks back.' She turned and looked at Elsie. Anna, exhausted and worried about her father, didn't care any more. She held Elsie's hand before returning her attention to the policeman. 'They burned that barn, they stole – now they've taken a child who got one right answer too many. Ask them. Hit them – whatever you have to do. Jimmy has a bad leg and he can't see properly. Get my sisters. They'll know where he is. Because they will have put him there.'

The sergeant stared hard at Anna. She was talking about members of her family as if they were apprentice criminals. 'Are you sure?'

Bert stepped forward. 'She's sure.'

Elsie said nothing, because she continued to labour under the delusion that she had turned Kate and Beckie bad. Children were not born bad – they were made bad and, as she was in loco parentis, it was her negligence that had caused the twins to turn out so odd.

Anna pitied her foster mother. 'Auntie Elsie, it's not your fault – it's nobody's fault unless you blame my mam for dying. You remember how a sheep knows its own lamb? How they skin a dead baby and wrap the fleece round another one? The ewe believes that's her baby. I think Kate and Beckie knew you weren't their mam because you didn't smell like her. That was when it went wrong.' She had heard all this from a sheep farmer, and had applied it to her own familial situation. It made sense in some way.

Most of the police had already left when Anna caught up with their boss. She knew he was the boss because he had stripes. 'Try Grantham

Woods,' she advised. 'That was where they used to hide stolen jewellery and stuff. But first, try to shake the truth out of them. Oh – you'll need me there. I'm the only thing in the world they are afraid of.'

Bert, Elsie and Anna arrived home in a police car. 'Get down here now,' screamed Anna as soon as they entered the house. 'Now!' she repeated.

A pair of perfect children descended the stairs. Dressed in yellow gingham dresses and green cardigans, they looked like angels, round-eyed, innocent and beautiful. But their sister grabbed them and dragged them down the last two stairs, thereby depriving them of dignity and literally lifting them off terra firma. 'Where is he?' she demanded as she dumped the pair in front of the sergeant.

'Where's who?'

'Jimmy Hardcastle.'

They shrugged. They had no idea, because they never played with him.

'You don't play with anybody,' snapped their sister. 'Because there's nobody bad enough for you, not round here, anyway.'

'Steady, love,' urged Elsie.

Anna turned to her foster mother. 'He can't walk properly, can't see properly – he's the sort of person they'd choose. And if they've left him out there somewhere, he could be dead of cold by morning.' Once again, she focused on her sisters. 'Where is he?'

When no answer was forthcoming, Anna stood and looked into the policeman's eyes. 'Right. You can take them to that orphanage now, the one you told me about where they cure bad kids. We can't manage them any more. This time, it could be murder.'

Kate stared at Anna. Anna was a good actress. But she was also a part of their world's law, and she was not on the side of her younger sisters. Kate's eyes slid sideways in the direction of Beckie. 'Becks?'

'What?'

'Will they put us in an orphanage?'

Anna managed not to gasp. These two seldom displayed a chink in their armour, but she had slid a knife some way in on this occasion.

'No,' answered Beckie. 'We've got a dad somewhere.'

Anna exploded. 'Have we? Have we? The war's made him ill, too ill to come home. He's hundreds of miles away in a hospital. Nobody knows when he'll be well enough to come back and look after us, and he certainly couldn't be in charge of nasty people like you two. Uncle Bert's had enough, and Auntie Elsie's not able to cope with you. So tell us where that boy is, or this policeman will take you to a place where you can do least damage.'

The two younger girls turned as one person and walked out of the house. A strange procession followed, with the sergeant behind the twins, Anna hot on his heels, Elsie and Bert bringing up the rear.

When they entered the wood, the twins stopped and Beckie spoke. 'We saw the whole thing,' she said. 'Two people in black tied him to a tree and broke his glasses. It was terrible.'

226

'We'll get him,' snapped Anna. 'I'll deal with your lies later.'

Again, they had lost. Again, their older sister was the reason for their lack of success. She was storing up so many black points that she would have to become a target. No one did this to them; no one who committed such an act of betrayal could be allowed to get away with it scot free.

Elsie, not as quick a mover as the rest of them, was bringing up the rear. She was asking herself questions, and she didn't like the answers. Her love for Anna burgeoned as well as ever, but she didn't love the twins. She admired them, because they were intellectually superior to most other people, but she found it difficult even to like them. It had taken a while, but she was coming round to her husband's way of thinking.

Anna, crippled internally by the news about her father, was now worrying about a boy who was truly handicapped, a weakling with a strong mind, bad eyes and a good attitude. He didn't deserve this. It was as if the twins practised on easier victims before working their way up to more difficult people. Only too aware that she was setting herself up as a target, she began to call Jimmy's name. 'Shout, Jimmy,' she yelled. 'We know you've no glasses, so stay where you are and just shout.'

Other searchers responded to Anna's cries, and several joined the main party. Bert's partner, Bernard Hanley, led in ten or more labourers and they all stood by Anna. Not a word was spoken while they listened for a response. At last, a faint sound reached grateful ears. 'He's deep in the woods,' Anna told everyone. 'I know every tree in here, because I've had to keep my eye on certain people who regard this place as their own personal property.' She noticed that the twins didn't even flinch. They had no sense of shame, no idea of right and wrong. All they knew was winning, escaping, staying safe.

It was Anna who found him, held him and cuddled him. It was Anna who wept over him and wished she could have him for a brother. Because although his problems were visible, they were bearable. Years later, she would look back on the moment and realize that though she hadn't heard the word, this was the day on which she had known for certain that her sisters were clever psychopaths.

Later, when Jimmy had been taken to hospital to be warmed and watched, Elsie left the house and went to sit with Betty Culshaw. She was tired, and she had seen enough trouble today. Bert stood by and surveyed the scene with interest while Anna literally beat the truth out of the younger girls. They scarcely reacted, shed not one tear, but, when the whole thing became boring, they admitted their crime. Anna sent them to bed without supper, then sat in Bert's arms and cried till she slept.

Elsie returned. She hadn't been able to bear to stay and watch while Anna did what needed to be done. 'Betty asked a lot of questions, but I told her nowt,' she said. 'Jimmy's mam and dad'll spread it soon enough. Did Anna knock the truth out of that pair?'

'They want talking about, them bloody girls,' Bert whispered. 'What are we supposed to do?

They did it, all right.'

Elsie shrugged. 'I reckon they'll finish up put away.'

'No,' replied Bert, his voice low enough not to wake the sleeping Anna. 'They'll learn to hide it, go from strength to strength, then they'll likely kill somebody.' He glanced down. 'And I think I know who.'

Elsie shuddered. 'Get a lock for her bedroom door. She can have a key, and we'll keep one hidden. Anna's got to be safe.'

He stroked the child's hair. 'Her dad and this, all in one day.'

It was a big, old house set back from Chorley New Road, Bolton. It had a massive front garden with a fountain in the middle. This was in the shape of an angel holding an enormous sword, and the water came out of the sword. Anna looked at the item and judged it to be a symbol of war.

A huge lawn looked as if it had been manicured, and Anna felt obliged to talk to the gardeners. One was in a wheelchair, and he was weeding with the aid of a long-handled fork. A second man laboured with one remaining arm, while the third, whole in body but with a badly charred face, seemed to be in charge. 'It's lovely,' she told the scarred man. She looked him straight in the face, because instinct led her to know that he wanted and needed that.

'Thanks, love. The garden'll be resting for the winter soon.' He couldn't smile, because the lower half of his face was worst affected. 'Who

229

are you?'

'Anna MacRae, and this is Mrs Dixon. She looked after us when my mam died in 1940.'

The man squatted down. 'So you're Sergeant Macker's girl, eh?'

'Macker?'

'It's his nickname. Now, listen to me, young lady. Do you remember your dad?'

Anna considered the question. 'Very tall, kept lifting me up till my head was in the washing on our pulley line. Smelled of beer and cigarettes and had a noisy laugh.'

The man looked up at Elsie. 'He's not the same as he was, Mrs Dixon. I don't think he laughs, and this young lady should be prepared.'

'We've done what we can.' Elsie replied. 'But she's determined to come here and make him whole again. And, let me tell you, if anyone can, it's this little madam.'

The ex-soldier watched the two females as they walked the long walk to the doors of Hollybank House. He prayed inwardly that Macker would be calm, at least, that he would not go into one of his tantrums while his daughter was here. The one-armed man looked up. 'Good luck to them, eh? I think they might be needing it.'

The wheelchair turned until its occupant could see his colleagues. 'He broke two windows last night. They reckon he's smashed more glass than the Germans did with their doodlebugs. In a way, we're lucky. Better a broken body than a broken mind.'

Elsie and Anna were taken into an office where a doctor awaited them. He smiled, introduced himself as Adam Corcoran, then asked them to sit. He cleared his throat. 'Sergeant MacRae, isn't it?'

Elsie nodded.

'Ah. Here you are. Mrs Dixon.' He put a tick against her name. 'We had to give him sedatives last night. He forgot again, started throwing things. We can't let you visit him without supervision. He seems to be stuck in a place where one of his men died, and it may take some time for him to return to normal.'

Elsie stared hard at the officious dwarf. 'Last war, my husband served. He came back all right, but some of his shell-shocked mates were shot by their own for trying to desert, and others came home and either got locked up or dumped on their families. Empty shells, they were, because the shells sent over by the Germans took their minds away. Shells from shells, that's what we had to deal with. I was lucky. Bert had the strength to take it in his stride, but he never talks about it. Is it still the same? Do you do nowt for them once they come home? After they've saved their bloody country?'

Anna was shocked, because Elsie had seldom made so long a speech, and she wasn't often rude. And she hadn't finished.

'Fit for bloody heroes? Is it hell. This girl's father's a fine man, and we want him back in one piece, so get on with it.'

The doctor scarcely reacted. It was plain that he was used to dealing with attacks of this kind. 'We can only keep him safe, Mrs Dixon. From all accounts, he was an extraordinary soldier, so we

231

shall do our best. How can we do better than our best? The Americans are working on new drugs–'

'Drugs?' Elsie was almost screaming now. 'He wasn't on bloody drugs before he went abroad. Nearest he came to drugs was that much whisky – he fell from top to bottom of some stone steps, not a bone broke. Drugs. Hmmph.'

A twitch gave the doctor away. Anna knew he was trying not to laugh about the stone steps. 'He had a bottle in each pocket when he fell,' she told him. 'And they weren't broken, either.'

He smiled at her. 'Your name?'

'Anna MacRae.'

'Wear that name with pride, Anna MacRae. I've heard nothing but good about your father. Come along – let's see what he makes of you.'

They walked down a long corridor. At first, rooms along each side had doors opened to reveal men enjoying card games at tables or reading in armchairs. Some were playing darts and dominoes, and many had visible injuries. Then the corridor narrowed, and a huge iron gate had to be opened before the party could continue its walk.

At this end, the rooms were all locked. 'These are single rooms,' Dr Corcoran said. 'For soldiers who aren't yet ready to face the world and all its noise. Anna, my dear, hold my hand.' He looked at Elsie. 'I'll take her in,' he said. 'Let him deal with one at a time.'

Elsie sat on a chair outside the door to Billy's room. She wanted to be with Anna, but the doctor possibly knew best. 'God, I'm scared,' she told a Constable print on a wall.

Anna's hold on her companion's hand tightened. Her dad was a big man, but the person in the small room was thin. His hair seemed to have crawled away from his face to the back of his head, while his eyes were sunken into the skull.

'Billy?' said the doctor.

Billy turned and saw only Anna. 'Frankie?' he whispered.

Anna wrenched her hand free and ran to the poor creature. 'It's me, Daddy. It's Anna.'

'Anna.' A skeletal hand traced the contours of her face. 'You look just like her.'

'I'm lucky, then.'

'You are, love.' He stared at her for what seemed to be a very long time before speaking again. 'I took her to Blackpool once, you know. Before you were born. All the lads were looking at her, but she only had eyes for me. Where is she?'

'Tonge Cemetery.'

'Bolton?'

Anna nodded. 'She died after having the twins.'

'Yes,' he said. 'I remember.'

Dr Adam Corcoran was stunned. He hadn't experienced a conversation like this, not with Sergeant Billy MacRae.

'I live with the Dixons now,' Anna went on. 'They took all three of us – me, Katherine and Rebecca. They're six now. At school.'

At last, a smile. 'Are they as pretty as you?'

'Prettier. But very, very naughty.'

'Dixons,' Billy said thoughtfully. 'So you moved next door. Not far, I suppose.'

'We live in the country now, Dad.'

'That's nice.'

'Uncle Bert's a steward for some farms, and

233

Auntie Elsie looked after mothers and babies all through the war. We had to go to a Proddy school, because that was all they had up there, and we couldn't get far in the war. But I shall be able to get to St Mary's Grammar next month, because the trams and buses are running properly again. I passed the scholarship.'

'Of course you did. You've got your mother's brains as well.'

Anna touched the thin face. 'And yours, Dad. Will you come home soon?'

'When I find him.'

'Who?'

'Bobby Watson. He's very good with a camera, said he'll teach me as well. We can do weddings. Good idea, eh?'

The doctor stepped forward. 'Bobby died in Tunisia, Billy. Anna – tell him.'

Anna told her father that Bobby was dead.

'Are you sure?'

'Yes. Positive.'

'Tunisia?'

She nodded.

'I liked Tunisia,' he told her. 'And Egypt. But my first love's still India. I wanted to live there, wanted to take you all out with me. The Punjab. It's brilliant there. Is he really dead?'

'Yes. And India's going to have its own government, so we won't be in charge any more. This is home, Dad. Well – not here, not in this house. You could work with Uncle Bert. You have to get better. You can't stop here, you know.' She opened her little peggy-purse. 'There you are. That's a picture of me, and here's one of the twins. When

234

you forget where you are, and when you forget that your friend died, look at these photos and remember that Rebecca, Katherine and I are real.'

When Dr Adam Corcoran led Anna away into the corridor, he was drying his eyes.

'Are you all right?' Elsie asked.

'Yes.' He put away the handkerchief. 'She's his doctor now. He knew her. We owe a lot to Anna, because that's the most sense we've had out of him since he came back to Blighty.'

Elsie nodded. 'Sorry I was a bit nasty before, but–'

'Don't worry, dear lady. I'm used to it.'

Elsie put an arm around her foster daughter. 'We had a priest, a good man who was drowning himself in whisky. She put a stop to that, didn't you, love?'

'No,' came the reply. 'My mother did. We were at her grave, and that's where he poured the last of his drink. If there's a heaven, my mam's an angel. We both spoke to her. And Father Brogan never touched a drop again, though he still calls himself sorely tempted.'

The doctor smiled to himself. Out of the mouths of babes came some of the wisest thoughts. 'Do you have room for Billy when he gets better?' the doctor asked after sniffing back some drops of emotion. Sergeant MacRae was probably going to be a handful for the rest of his life, but he could not be contained for ever.

'I've sorted all that out,' Anna answered before Elsie got the chance.

'But we've only three bedrooms,' cried Elsie in pretended horror.

'And we've got Linda Mellor. Mr and Mrs Aston next door are going to live with their son just outside Chorley, and my dad can have their house. It's all arranged. They're even leaving most of the furniture, because they said a hero should have somewhere to sit, somewhere to eat and a bed to sleep in.'

Elsie smiled, but said nothing. She knew all about the arrangement, yet she allowed Anna to think she'd planned it herself. He would come home eventually. And, if he were to be protected from the twins and their ongoings, Billy would need a place of his own.

It was a big secret to keep, but Bert and Elsie would hold it tightly for the rest of their lives. There was a small legacy for them, and it had come into play only recently. They knew the deceased Mrs Mellor had arranged for the bequest to become available when Anna's senior education began. In an effort to conceal their own hidden wealth, which was in cash under a floorboard, they applied for the uniform grant and carried on as before.

Deeds for the two houses were lodged in a bank under Anna's name, while a sizeable sum was invested for her. The Dixons were to have access to all monies in case of emergencies of their own, or for Anna, but the bulk of the cash would go to the child once both foster parents had died. There had been no mention of the twins in Iris Mellor's will. Even then, when the older Mrs Mellor had been alive, the behaviour of Rebecca and Katherine had been spectacularly bad. Until

236

they needed to be good, that was, at which point they had invariably transformed into angels.

On the run-up to Anna taking her place among the elite of St Mary's, the twins were as quiet as mice. She scarcely noticed them, since she was occupied in the preparation of Dad's house after the Astons had vacated it. She scrubbed floors and polished furniture, washed curtains, placed family photographs on tables, raided her Post Office account to buy new pans and a kettle.

Tom Brogan was a man who did not give up easily. Giving up drink had been hard, and giving up on Anna MacRae was something he wasn't going to do. No. She was a good girl, a kind girl, so she ought to be a good Catholic. He knew what she was going through. Anyone with half a brain was bound to question something that had happened almost two thousand years earlier, and the Church was far from perfect.

Also far from perfect were her sisters. Having listened several times to a litany of their sins, he didn't hold out a great deal of hope, since they sounded crackers. Was there a difference between sinfulness and insanity? They knew what they were at, knew they were doing wrong, so they were liable and had clearly reached the age of reason. He'd heard it all from Anna, from Bert and even from Elsie, though she had been slower than the others to voice her concerns.

On the day of Billy MacRae's return to society, Tom blessed the house. He prayed in every room, and scattered Lourdes water all over the place. Anna watched, and hoped he wouldn't

237

spoil her polishing, but he was only doing what he knew, what he felt to be right.

When the blessing was over, they went outside and sat on their favourite wall. 'St Mary's, then?' he said.

'Mmm. Yes.' She was too busy watching for Dr Corcoran's car.

'Will you come back to your faith?'

She sighed. What faith? She wasn't yet old enough to read the books she needed to read and understand, so she had no basis from which she might start to work out her opinions. 'I'll do what the nuns demand of me,' she said. 'So that'll mean Confession, Communion, Mass – even Benediction. I'll sing in Latin and bring my prayer book – but I'm still me, Father. I listened to you, didn't I? I applied for St Mary's rather than the other schools. I'll work it out for myself.'

Anna would never 'do' blind faith, and he knew it. He'd read to her from the Epistles and Gospels, but nothing had worked. The death of her mother, the misfortunes of her father, and the ill behaviour of her little sisters made her question the very basis upon which Christ had founded His church.

He watched her now as she ran towards an approaching car, and he experienced little hope. Her father was here, and she would have a hard time believing in a benign God when Billy became difficult.

Sometimes, there was little to be done to rectify a situation. But he wouldn't give up. He would never desert her. He passed the Dixons' house and saw two small faces at the window. They made no move to come out and greet their father. It was all

238

going to be left to Anna.

Two men got out of the car, and Anna immediately grabbed the hand of the taller one, Billy MacRae. This was a big part of her future, and it wouldn't be easy for her. While he prayed for further guidance, Father Brogan approached the party of three. The doctor made no move towards the house, so the number was reduced to two. Tom would go with Billy and Anna into the house. It was part of his job. When doctors could do no more, the representatives of God had to take over. It had always been so.

Eleven

It's a between the wars semi-detached house on a long road, and it has many almost identical siblings. Attempts to make differences abound – stone-cladding, planks of wood between ground and first floor bays, wishing wells and cart wheels in gardens. This is a decent area of St Helens, far superior to the council maze on which Marie and Maureen have been parked. They seem happy enough, and the neighbours have been decent and helpful, but I know they would love it here – a broad avenue, trees on each side, good cars parked on most driveways.

Alec's house is plain, apart from white-painted pebble-dash on the upper level. His gate reminds me of my childhood – five-barred and with a horizontal piece holding it together. I notice a cluster of gnomes in a corner. These were probably the property of Mrs Halliwell, because they are now parked with their backs to the road, and I am sure that the master of the house has ill-treated them since the departure of their mistress. A large black-and-white cat decides to weave itself around my ankles, and this is not good news, since I am trying to be elegant as I stride up the drive in my high-heeled dyed-to-match-the-dress shoes.

The door opens. 'Winston,' Alec calls to the animal. 'Put that woman down, you've no idea

240

where she's been.' He looks into my face. 'Or where she's going to be in a few minutes.' His gaze travels the length of me, beginning with my hair, which I have almost managed to tame, pausing where my upper body disappears into the dress, then fixing on the legs.

Never before have I met a man such as this. He opens his mouth, speaks, smiles, and I go to pieces. I was a bit like this over Gregory Peck during my teenage years, but he never offered me a bed and a gas fire. And tantric what? He is wearing an apron over his clothes, and the item fails to make him look ridiculous. He's also clutching an enormous book with the title positioned so that it faces me.

'What's that about?' I ask.

'Can't you read?'

'I can read. But why are hanging for dear life onto that volume?'

'Biggest book in the library – makes a great doorstop.' He moves his lower hand to display the word sex. Tantric sex? For an accountant, he certainly counts more than beans. Has he been calculating chickens before they've hatched? There's a gleam in his eye, and I recognize it as mischief. Somewhere not too far below the surface, Alec is an adorable rogue and a torment. We are going to have fun.

'Have you read it?' I ask.

'Come in. And don't be daft – one paragraph was enough. I couldn't make head or tail of it. I'm still getting to grips with the Kama Sutra – they must all have been double-jointed, or deformed in some way.'

241

The place is testament to the taste – well – the disastrous choices of the recently departed Dolores. Garish carpets, ghastly curtains, little figurines of crinolined ladies on almost every surface. In the dining room hangs a print that had a run of popularity so huge that almost every idiot bought one. It's an Eastern woman who looks as if she has a bad case of food-cum-blood poisoning. Her skin is green. Three darts stick out of her forehead, so it is plain that Alec has found a use for the hideous object. He marches me into the living room and gives me a duster. 'This is a test,' he says sombrely. 'Go and clean that fire.'

I click off the grille and he pretends to write in his tantric tome. 'Can clean gas fire,' he mouths. He then bends down. 'What if I've read more than a paragraph? Do you mind being a guinea pig? It's all for the good of mankind, you know. We do have a responsibility to improve life for our fellow citizens.'

'Will I suffer unduly?'

He shakes his head. 'No. If there's any sign of that, we have chloroform. See, what is supposed to happen is that you linger on the edge of the abyss – you can even jump if you like. Several times. But I have to hang in there with my crampons on.' He shakes his head. 'This is not going to be easy. If I didn't worship the ground across which you totter in those delightful but very silly shoes–'

'Crampons? In bed?'

'They are figurative crampons, and you already knew that. But first, we have curry. I made it myself just for you, my darling. Not too hot, of course. We don't want you fighting for breath just yet, do we?'

Now, this is something else. There is one plate and one spoon, so he sits me on his knee and feeds both of us. I know now why he's wearing the apron, because he cannot control his state of preparedness. And it's not just eating, it's ... where are the words, Anna? It's sexual. There's no touching, no roaming hands – just me, him, the spoon, the plate and the food. It should be horrible. It should be off-putting and odd and savage and awful and ... other things, but it isn't. When a crumb of rice stays on my lips, he removes it with his tongue. I should feel sick. I don't feel sick, I feel aroused. The man is a torment, and I should go home. Immediately. But I can't go home, because nothing will stop me now. I want him, and I intend to have him.

And there's a noise, and it's coming from my throat, and I can't stop it. I never had this before, never felt a chemistry so strong that I scarcely need to be touched. In an effort to ensure that this embrace will be eternal, I hold his head and pull him hard against my face. It's our first all-the-way open-mouthed kiss, and it is not describable. My heart is demanding double pay, because it's working way beyond the call of duty. The man is in no hurry – there's almost a carelessness in him. Or perhaps it's acceptance, because he knows he's drowning.

'Jesus,' he blasphemes when we finally separate. 'Where have you been all my life?'

'I don't know. I can't remember.'

'Where, Anna?'

243

Come on, brain, get into gear. 'Bolton, Eagle Vale, Sale in Cheshire, Hesford and here.'

'And here,' he repeats. 'Are you still hungry?'

I shake my head. I am not hungry for food.

I'm a tall woman, and weightier than I used to be, yet he carries me easily to the stairs and places me about halfway up. Here, he undresses me very slowly. When he gets to the hold-up stockings with the black lace tops, he smiles at me and tuts. 'Naughty girl,' he says. 'Sweet, but naughty.'

The really strange thing is that I'm no longer bothered about saggy bits and stretch marks. He'll want me anyway, because he is trying to get into my head and my heart – the body is a mere channel to an end. How do I know this? I'm not completely sure, but I can see that this is not the face of a predator. His eyes give away his every thought. He is an honest man, and this – whatever this is – is not just about sex.

Soft as butterflies, firm as his hold on my heart, those hands begin making love to me. I was right – he's imaginative and decisive without demanding to take over. So different from any lover I have known, he begins his exploration. When he moves over my body, his eyes ask me from time to time whether it's OK, and it is. It's wonderful, and I am no longer on the stairs of an ill-dressed semi-detached in Eccleston, because I am no longer me. The kisses begin, and I start to moan. The noise I make urges him on, and I find myself enjoying sensations that are completely new to me. I am a forty-year-old teenager and I want him. Now.

I am dumped without ceremony on his recently acquired replacement bed. It has a scarlet coverlet, and the material smells brand new. This was bought for me, just me. He removes his trousers, folds them with excruciatingly slow care, then tosses them to the floor, where they lie in a crumpled heap. Helpless with laughter, I roll away to make room for him. Few naked men manage to be beautiful, but there's always an exception, and here it is. With all due courtesy, he begs to be excused, and I hear him stumbling down the stairs. What the heck is he doing now?

He returns and repairs to a chair near the window. Thank goodness the curtains are closed. It's that bloody book again. A lamp is switched on, and he studies a page, turning the huge tome as if trying to work out a diagram. 'Just a moment,' he says apologetically. 'I shan't be very long.' He looks down at his lower body. 'Long enough, I hope.' Every vulgar statement he makes fails completely to be vulgar.

I cannot cope with him. Never before has sex been a pantomime. Whatever he says, whatever he does, he makes me happy, makes me laugh. And he isn't afraid of me laughing at him. I remember the coastal road, the unusual terms and words he made acceptable, even welcome. Alec owns no inhibitions, and he removed most of mine on the staircase. But this performance is worthy of an Oscar. 'I think I need an eye test,' he announces after poring over the page.

When the book is on the floor next to the bed, he joins me and asks me am I sure. I shall kill him in a minute. He combs my hair with his fingers, kisses my face, my neck, begins his travels. And I'm waiting, wanting, urging him to complete what he has started. But he won't. He has read that bloody book from cover to cover, hasn't he? 'Where's the chloroform?' I ask when I find enough oxygen to produce words.

'Are you in pain?' His hair is tousled when he emerges, and he becomes a child who's been running about in the park all day.

'Yes.'

'How can I help?'

'You know how.'

'Oh. Right.' And he picks up that blasted book.

Why am I chuckling? Why, when every nerve in my body is screaming, do I lie here giggling in the manner of a two-year-old?

'It won't always be like this,' he informs me. 'I thought you needed a special treat.'

'A treat?' I shout. 'Making love with someone in a supposed state of transcendental meditation is not my idea of a treat. Especially when he needs to look at the instructions every five minutes. And what makes you so sure there'll be other times? You've been leaping about like a frog in a box. Put the book down and come here.'

'Yes, Miss.'

He lies down, turns again into a submissive schoolboy after a telling-off. And I know now what he has wanted all along, can guess the reason for the book and the jumping about. He needs me to be sure. To make himself sure that I am sure, he has teased me until I take charge. So it's my turn to play the game, my turn to make him beg, and it's easy. This is an evening I shall

246

remember for the rest of my life, because it's perfect. If I never make love again, I shall always know the possibilities, the seemingly endless joy, the after-tears from both of us.

He tells me he loves me, and I tell him the same. We must try not to lose each other. Even if we can't live together, we can meet, talk, laugh, find a place where we can be alone like this. He says he feels that we should have been together all along, and that our respective spouses (or spice, as he insists on terming the departed) have done us a favour. Then he asks me to give him more of my childhood, because my voice is wonderful. He's lovely.

'So what happened next?' he asks.

'I went to grammar school and got into all kinds of trouble about not going to church, et al. My father became my responsibility. The twins went to a non-Catholic school – Bert and Elsie weren't overjoyed, but I was. Because they would have been first formers while I was still in the sixth.'

'And where are they now?'

'One dashes around between London and Oxford, while the other is based in London and Paris. Very successful women. They've had at least one abortion each, and have managed to ruin several marriages. It's what they do. Ruination.'

I lie in his arms until we both drift into slumber. Occasionally, I wake to find him kissing my cheek or pulling me closer, but it's a wonderfully refreshing sleep. In the morning, he wakes me and presents me with what smells like bacon, plus an egg. The offering is on a tray with little legs. Am I an invalid? I sit up and rub my eyes. 'Breakfast isn't my thing,' I tell him.

'Try,' he urges. 'I did it all for you.'

I look at the plate. A runny egg lies between two pieces of something or other. 'What's that? And that?'

'Bacon,' he says.

'You cremated it,' I announce. 'I don't know whether to eat it or send flowers. A cup of tea will do, thanks.'

He goes away.

Not once during my marriage was I offered breakfast in bed. Not once did Den wash dishes, hoover a carpet, clean a window. I suppose I don't hate Den, but I never loved him, not like this, not like Alec. It's too hot to last in its current state, and I understand that very well. Because it's not just about sex, this should not worry me unduly. When I'm covered in baby-sick, when my hair's like a bird's nest, when I can't be bothered with make-up, this man will love me, the me that's inside. Whereas Den would be afraid of anyone seeing his wife in a state worse than Russia.

I listen as he clatters about in the kitchen, hear him talking to his cat. Above the dressing table, I see a wedding photograph. Underneath, he has posted a reminder to himself – THIS IS AS BAD AS IT GETS. He used to love her, but now, her gnomes are in the naughty corner, her green woman print is full of holes, and her wedding photo is a warning. She doesn't know what she's given away, does she? Perhaps she did not bring out this side of him, the playfulness, the teasing. I smile to myself. He needed an intelligent woman, and now, he has one.

Alec brings tea, serves me a heated croissant and gets into bed. The tea goes cold, as does the croissant, because we are occupied. On this occasion, he's in charge and he's wonderful, so caring, yet exciting. I am given words of love and words born of good, healthy lust. There's no laughter, and everything is urgent and fast. He knows more about women than any man has a right to know, and I believe this to come from instinct rather than experience. Or perhaps he reads a lot of books?

The thoughts disappear on a wave of excitement, because there is no reason in sensations as animalistic as these. Wonderful. I am in the arms of a man I love, who loves me, who, in a way, is me. Two halves of one whole, a meeting of minds and souls, the perfect couple. Yes, as I come to my senses, I am pinching words from novels I discarded twenty years ago. Perhaps they weren't so silly after all.

He drives me home, and there's no one here. I imagine Susan, Mo and Marie struggling in a two-bedroomed house with three babies and a young puppy. But I don't feel guilty, because I need this man – even I deserve a break from time to time. He leaves me making coffee while he weeds the rockery. With his sleeves rolled, he reminds me of men who worked in the fields where I grew up. He's a chameleon, and I love him in any or all of his colours. And it's true – love hurts. Happiness hurts. These feelings are painful, because everything is finite. From such

249

certainty comes the work of every romantic poet who struggles and starves while trying to express the fleeting moment we spend on the planet. I look at Alec and my heart is full; it is also afraid of becoming empty again.

When we sit at my kitchen table drinking Kenya blend, it's as if he belongs here. We talk. He asks more about my childhood, about the troubles caused by Katherine, Rebecca and my father. I tell him that Linda Mellor finally revealed the truth, that there was no pools win, that the lady of the manor loved me enough to go some way towards providing for my future, and for my foster parents. He speaks about the disastrous Dolores, his mother, his children, his gut-grindingly boring job.

'How will Sarah take this?' I ask him.

He stares into his cup. 'She misses her mum too much, Anna. I have to let her go. Sometimes, love means letting go. Jo's OK. But she'll steal your babies, because she's a born mother. Aside from that, she thinks you're cool, man. I could put her right, tell her you're a red hot momma, but I'm her father, and fathers don't do sex.'

'I'm sorry, Alec. About Sarah, I mean.'

He shrugs. 'I'll have access, but it's hardly the same. She'll be reared by a mother who can't spell Torquay and a man who sees women as an aid to masturbation. And you think he has a psychiatrist as well?'

'Yes.'

'Any proof?'

'No. There was a weird prescription for some drug or other, but he threw it away. And he'll put up a good fight, because the rational side of him is super-clever. But I do know this – he isn't as ill or as devious as my twin sisters.'

'And you feared your own twins when they were born?'

'God, yes. Especially when Emily carried on with the behaviour she'd practised in the womb. I think what she did was connected to the survival instinct. It stopped. She's no longer a bully, so I'm no longer afraid of a repeat performance. In fact, she shows a sense of humour already. I think she's going to be my little clown, and Lottie will be my philosopher.'

'You thought they'd be like your sisters?'

'It wasn't thought, Alec. It was a feeling, a terror.'

'A phobia,' he says. His eyes are embracing my soul – God – stupid novella-speak again. 'Don't ever lose me, Anna. There's more to us than a roll in the sand dunes.'

'Or cleaning a gas fire,' I say. 'Or a green woman with three double-tops scored in her forehead, or tantric sex with a side dish of burnt bacon. I do love you. Making things work with two babies, your daughters, a pending divorce and a new business won't be easy. Could you live here?'

He shakes his head. 'No room at the inn just yet, sweetheart. And you can't throw Susan out, because that brother of hers will be waiting. I am a patient man. Accountants have to develop a doggedness, as the work can get bloody tedious. Actually, it's not the work, it's the explaining to clients that numbs the mind. Budgets, tax years, claims, interest, how to be creative with money before the government steals it.'

'Then do something else.'

The eyes twinkle. 'Will you pay me to lie down with you every night?'

'Is it tax deductible?' I ask. 'Will it be worth your while?'

'Do you need an answer?' he whispers. 'Don't you know already how much I'd give up to be with you?'

'Yes, I do know. We have to find a way around this, though. And the "this" we have to find a way around is complicated. If Den were to find out...'

'Hang onto the last fifteen hours,' he orders. 'I never experienced anything like that in my life – it was good, it was perfect and I want it all again.' He looks at me for several seconds. 'When it's all over, will you marry me?'

'Yes.'

'What?'

'Yes.'

'Say it again.'

'Yes.'

He stands. 'I'll finish the weeding, then.'

After depositing a kiss on the top of my head, he goes outside again. This time, he removes his shirt and I remember that vertebra just below his neck, can feel it now under hands that don't want to let go. I have touched the skin that stretches over biceps and triceps, have threaded my fingers through that shock of hair, have kissed his throat.

Discovering one's sexuality at the age of forty is better than failing to find it at all. But how I resent the wasted years, all that time with Den and his expectations, his perfunctory love-making, his total selfishness, his adoring mother. Geoff led me

252

out of the wilderness, but Alec was the one who stood in the light provided by Earth's star; it was he who was with me when the sun went down, and when it came back this morning. Yes. Love hurts. But it's worth it.

Bedlam arrives in an estate car that does look very like an ice-cream van. Sheba is the first to make her presence known, and she dashes off to 'help' Alec with the weeding. I daren't look.

Maureen stuffs two babies into my arms and asks if she can have the caravan. She's had enough, she's going back on the game and the van would be ideal for the entertaining of clients. 'I can't work for Third Party with her while she's in that mood.' The her in question walks through without a word to anyone. Marie has a face like thunder, uncombed hair and odd slippers.

'See?' Maureen cries. 'She's gone like a bloody zombie, and we've three parties booked. Tell her, Anna.'

I wait until Marie has wandered off. 'Mo, she's got so much on her mind—'

'I know, I know. But the only way to snap her out of it is to kick her up the bum. I understand her – she's part of my family.'

'Her son raped her daughter,' I say quietly. 'She doesn't know whether she's coming or going...'

'She's going,' Maureen answers. 'She's going out all the while looking for him. He signed himself out of hospital a day early, and she's like a cat on hot bricks.'

'Then go with her when she leaves the house,' I advise.

'I couldn't leave our Susan last night with three babies and a lunatic animal what was eating the sweeping brush. I mean, I know you have to make hay while his kids are on holiday, Anna so...' She stops and stares hard. 'Well. I can see you've had a great time.' She takes a step nearer to me. 'Was he any good?'

I hand Lottie over – these two are getting heavy. 'He's brilliant. Sorry to have put you out, though, but I didn't know that Marie had gone hunting. I shan't stay with him again – I'll be here.'

'Don't you want to be with him?'

I have allowed Emily to slide down to my hip, and I realize that I am copying a stance used by women since time began. Emily feels like a part of me. She's warm and giggly and I love her. I'm glad she's turning out a bit silly. We all need a silly daughter. 'Mo, I want to be with him for the rest of my life, so the next few days aren't going to matter.'

We both turn and look through the window where a half-naked man wrestles in the grass with a small retriever. 'He's so nearly perfect, it scares me, Mo. I wonder when I'll find his faults and how much difference they will make. More to the point, what about when he discovers my deficiencies?'

The hard-faced kleptomaniac prostitute sniffs back a tear. 'Just hang onto him, love,' she says. 'I wish I'd...'

'You wish what?'

'That I'd ever felt as happy as you look now, queen. That I'd met a decent man who'd take me as I am and love me no matter what.'

254

'Maureen, I–'

'She's going to kill Gary. Our Marie. She says she brought him into the world and did a bad job, so she has to remove him. Then she shut up. And shut down.' Mo is crying openly now. 'I can't do nothing with her, Anna. Even our Susan can't. It's like living with a photograph, because Marie's not really there, and I'm scared. If I go out with her, do you think I could stand there while it all goes off? He's more likely to kill her than the other way round.'

I place Emily in the pram and look for Marie. As she's nowhere to be found on the ground floor, I make my way upstairs. She's in that smallest bedroom, is curled on the bed, cardigan and odd slippers still in place. All her little bags and parcels have disappeared into the St Helens house. She looks so small, and she may be asleep or may be pretending to be asleep. Whatever, she isn't open for business.

Downstairs, Maureen has placed the sleeping Lottie on a mattress in the playpen. She's looking down at my daughter, a sad smile playing on her lips.

'Mo? Are you OK?'

She nods.

'Where's Susan?'

'Outside with your feller. Isn't Lottie beautiful? My kids are grown and cheeky and all over the place, old enough to look after themselves. I never really looked at them, you know. I was too busy keeping one step ahead of Jimmy, pinching from shops, getting enough for them to eat. Anna?'

'What?'

'I love them, but I think I might have forgotten to tell them.'

I put my arms around her. 'It's never too late, Mo. Go and find them and tell them. If Marie budges, I'll follow her. And if she's not fit to cook, you, Susan and I will cope. We will, you know. It's amazing how we survive, isn't it?'

Her head hangs low. 'Glad I met you,' she mumbles. 'You're clever, you are.' And she dashes off to tell her children... Oh, God, this is a sad world.

Chaos continues while we do our pale imitation of Martha Stewart. Using the client's dishes, we set up a rack of lamb with the leg-frills placed to one side, since the hostess will need to heat the rack all the way through without burning its paper decorations. Maureen is doing vegetables, Susan is repeating her mountain of profiteroles, while Alec – God love him – is doing a great job with avocado and tissue-thin slices of smoked salmon.

This is a large kitchen, but it's suddenly the size of a bathroom cabinet, as we all seem to be falling over each other. 'I can't breathe in,' Susan complains. 'Mo? Any chance of me having room to drizzle my chocolate?'

Maureen is placing her vegetables into hostess trays designed to keep the contents hot and fresh for up to four hours. They'll have to go into the estate car, of course, but we'll plug them in again as soon as we get to our destination. She's smiling. She's smiling because she drove all the way to

Liverpool to tell her offspring that she loves them and would die for them.

'Hang on, Susan,' I advise. 'You'll have room enough in a few minutes.'

'The chocolate's ready now,' she moans.

'Just wait.' I say. 'Or I'll set Alec to beat you with his big book.'

He turns away and faces the wall, but his back is shaking with laughter.

'What big book?' Mo's eyes are wide.

'Don't ask,' is my answer. 'It's a state secret.'

'Behave yourself, Anna,' he warns. 'Because I'm going home soon to feed my cat, and God knows what I'll bring back with me.'

Work ceases. Two pairs of female eyes are fixed on me. 'What?' I ask the women. 'What?' Not a word is born. Maureen and Susan are as still as two of the uprights at Stonehenge. 'Yes, he's staying here. You and Marie will go home, Maureen. The twins can go into Marie's room, and–'

'Mam,' mutters Susan. 'Is she all right?'

'I'll go and look.' Upstairs, I open the door and look inside. She isn't here. Four neglected cups of tea are lined up on the window sill. We have a problem. Marie is out there somewhere in an odd mood and in odd slippers. And we need to deliver food for a function that begins in two hours. Which means we must also set the client's table and leave serving instructions hidden discreetly in a pre-arranged place where she alone will look.

I re-enter my kitchen. The profiteroles are drizzled and everything seems to be in order. 'Alec – will you stick this lot in the back of the estate? Maureen, you'll have to do this one on your own

257

– well – with Alec...' I look at him and he nods. 'Susan, you stay here and mind babies. I'm going to try to find your mother.'

Susan starts to weep, and Alec holds her in his arms. I don't know where I'm going to start, but I have to appear confident and decided. I turn to Maureen. 'Look, Mo – it doesn't matter any more who knows what. Agreed?'

She nods.

'Fetch Mrs Bee. Susan can't be alone, not if Gary's on the prowl. Mrs Bee might be old, but she'd frighten the skin off a rice pudding at forty paces.' I speak to Susan. 'All Mrs Bee needs to know is that your mother's upset, missing, and not quite herself. This may sound hard, but the business can't be allowed to fail at the first hurdle. Third Party is for your future, and for Stephen, too. Alec – fill the car. Maureen, you drive, because you're used to the vehicle. Alec, sit in the back and make sure the food stays where it's put.' I sound like some bloody-minded Sergeant Major in a particularly filthy mood. So he'll know now that I am bossy, but that can't be allowed to matter. 'Oh, and feed your cat on the way back.'

Ten minutes later, I am on Church Road and I can see Marie. She's in the telephone kiosk outside the Eagle and Child, and she's talking. Fear plunges its cold knife into my chest, and I can scarcely breathe. I don't need to hear what she's saying, since I already know. This is the moment. She's making it happen now. I pull into the pub car park and wait. I'm old enough to remember the days of a judge's black cloth, the square he placed on his bewigged head before issuing the death penalty. Marie has no black cloth. Just odd slippers and an empty stomach, since she hasn't eaten all day. And I'm praying, just as I prayed when Ruth Ellis was hanged for killing a man who had treated her appallingly for years. She did it in what was seen as cold blood, since she emptied the gun of all its bullets in order to ensure that he would die.

She replaces the receiver, and I get out of my car. When I reach her, she smiles at me. 'Hello, Anna.'

'Hello, Marie. Susan's waiting for you.'

'Yes.' She pulls the cardigan tight. 'Gone a bit chilly, hasn't it? And you know what? I'm dead hungry.'

I take her arm, lead her to the car, and put her in the passenger seat. When I start the engine, she speaks again. 'Anna?'

'What?'

'I need a grand. Cash. Used notes, fivers and tenners.'

'All right.'

'Do you know what I've just done?'

'Yes. You've saved two lives – possibly three if we include your own. I can't condone what you've made happen, but I sure as hell understand it. Will he be ... found?'

She nods. 'He's in a gang. Some of the others have already been beaten halfway to kingdom come. It was part of the plan, Anna. But he'll... Well, let's wait and see. I fancy scrambled eggs on toast and a nice cuppa.'

Maureen has taken Marie home. I think they all

know what's happened, though no one is speaking about it. Marie ate her eggs and toast as if food were going out of fashion and she needed to stock up. Susan and Stephen are at the other end of the house, while my girls are next door, in the room that was Marie's.

I am in bed with my lover, and he is trying to massage the knots that have formed in my shoulders. Magic hands. He bestrides me and attempts to rub away the tension. He guesses that something unusually bad has gone down, but he asks no questions. After spending an evening cleaning my kitchen, he now works on my back, and he is not gentle. He attacks muscle and bone, bringing blood and oxygen into each section and giving me the chance to relax and sleep. He could take this up professionally, and I tell him so. Talking isn't easy, because I appear to have gone completely limp.

'Surely you wouldn't want me to do this for other people? Half of them women?'

He's right, of course. Again.

'You have a map of South America just above your left buttock. Is this a sign? Do we emigrate?'

'No.' It's just a birthmark, and I am British, couldn't imagine myself living elsewhere, couldn't even move south in my own country. But I'm far too sleepy to put any of that into words. Is Gary dead yet?

'You've tensed again, Anna. Clear your mind and think only of a Crosby sunset.'

'Love you,' I manage just before sleep claims me.

He wakes me with tea and one slice of toast.

I've had another night of good, refreshing sleep, and I accept now that he is the reason.

'I'm going to feed Winston,' he says. 'He attacks chairs if I don't give him a good breakfast. Speaking of which, I've fed and changed your daughters, and they're downstairs with Susan.'

I owe him an explanation. It's not my business, yet it is affecting me, and I trust him totally. He knew already that Susan was terrified of her brother, but I tell him why. A man who will help run a business, who will clean my house and give me breakfast, who will attend to my twins, deserves truth. 'Marie did what had to be done.'

He chews thoughtfully on half my toast. 'There are times when justice and the law don't marry. A case would have exposed Susan's little lad as the result of a dreadful action, and he doesn't deserve that – neither does his mother. And, of course, the lovely Gary might have repeated his performance on some other girl, or on Susan yet again. No wonder Marie was odd yesterday. Is he dead?'

'I don't know.'

'Look, I'll be back. Are we doing a Third Party job tonight?'

'No.'

'Then we'll feed the Hughes family. Get them here, and I'll cook.'

'Curry?'

'Perhaps.'

'Can we have our own cutlery and plates, please?'

'I shall take your request under consideration.' He kisses me on the mouth, but almost chastely,

261

then leaves me. I feel cold without him. With no Alec in my life, it would always be the dark time after the sun has fallen away behind the Mersey. So I'm keeping him.

Babies are time-consuming. Susan and I spend yet another daft morning playing peek-a-boo with teddies and blankets, crawling around the floor to show our amused audience how it's done, singing nursery rhymes – Susan's tone deaf, by the way – and generally making complete prats of ourselves. When the kids are exhausted, we put them down for a nap and make lunch. Alec hasn't returned yet, so there are just the two of us.

I eat my sandwich in the living room so that I can watch News North-West. The scene is there, the blood is there, the hospital is there. Stephen's father/uncle died in the ambulance and was confirmed dead on arrival at the Royal. Several members of his gang were beaten up the night before, and a senior policeman is telling us about gang problems in Liverpool. The body has yet to be identified, but I know who it is. Dear God, I am paying for that murder! I realize I've almost stopped breathing, and I inhale a few crumbs. This causes me to cough, and Susan rushes in with a glass of water.

By the time the bout of coughing and spluttering is over, the news has moved on, and a weather girl is telling us to take umbrellas, because meteorology remains an inexact science, so I suppose she's just trying to hang onto her job. I am not going to say anything to Susan, as it's not my place, and I wouldn't know where to start, but I am assuming that Marie must have heard by now. Therefore, I need to get to the bank before it closes.

Leaving Susan in charge yet again, I carry out the necessary transaction, and the bank manager has to become involved. I am not fond of small, moustachioed, pigeon-chested little farts. So I tell him to mind his own bloody business, or I'll take mine to the Midland. Sometimes, I can be so ill-tempered. I suppose the temper is something Alec will discover at some stage, but he's not a small, moustachioed, pigeon-chested little fart, so he won't be on the receiving end of it – he'll be a mere witness.

When I get back, Alec is here, but Susan has disappeared with the babies. She's trying to give us some time alone, and he is clearly grateful. He closes the living room door and, just like before, presses me against it. He is the young buck again, is claiming his territory on a patch of wall in some darkened alley. I really could kiss this man for ever. I suppose we'd have to come up for air, food and water, but apart from all that...

'Tonight,' he whispers, 'I shall turn you over after your massage and...' And. The terms we seldom use, those that are usually employed as swear words, drift on warm breath into my ear. He is extraordinarily graphic and wonderfully exciting. I should not like to live in a world that did not contain this clever, sensitive, desirable soul. But oh, how I wish my legs could be steadier in his presence...

'Where is she?' Alec and I place the twins on Maureen's hearthrug. There will be no curry tonight, because we've scarcely had time to think.

'Identifying him,' replies Mo. 'The cops sent an unmarked car for her. She wouldn't let me go with her, but she's told me. About you giving her the money. There was no other way, was there? No other way of making sure that Susan and Stephen will be OK.'

'And Marie. She might have become a target. Or, if he was developing a taste for rape, some other poor females might have suffered. I know what's happened is wrong, Mo, and I know I am making a contribution, but I could see no alternative without the whole sorry mess coming out. Susan's stronger now, and—'

'Does she know? Does our Susan know Gary's dead?'

I shake my head. 'I'm not sure – she may find out while we're here, so we can't stay long. I won't have her weakened again. I don't want to see her in the state she was when I met her at the clinic. His death means the story doesn't need to come out. Perhaps I'm not family like you are, but...'

'You don't know, do you?' Maureen asks, her voice suddenly shrill. 'Susan thinks I'm Marie's sister, but I'm not. No, Susan isn't my niece, *she*'s my sister. Marie's my mother. She was fourteen when she had me. See? Scum of the earth, so why are you bothering with us, eh? We're the sort of people who get gang-raped when we're thirteen, then we hand the baby to our parents and pretend she's our sister. And she grows up knowing she's different and goes off with the first man who looks at her. And he puts her on the game

264

because he needs the drugs, so she gets too fat for the game and becomes a shoplifter. Why are you mixing with frigging criminals? Eh? And you a teacher, pillar of the sodding community.'

Alec holds her while she sobs her heart out into his shoulder. This is not a bad woman. This is a woman who did what she had to do, who never fitted in anywhere, whose identity became a confused, dark secret. And I understand Marie now; I know her better, can see where her anger came from, and why she had to do this terrible thing. Marie remembers rape, and the product of her suffering is now howling in my lover's arms.

The police come in with Marie. The remaining sliver of reason in my head tells me I'm glad that Maureen is crying, because these officers will think it's grief attached to the murder of her ... nephew. That's right, he's supposed to be her nephew.

'We'll look after them now,' I tell the detectives.

'We're very sorry,' says one. 'It's the gangs. We do our best, but...'

'I know. Thanks for bringing her home.'

They leave. Maureen pulls away from Alec and drops into a chair. 'They know all of it now, Marie,' she says. 'They know you're my mam, but Susan doesn't need to be told, does she?'

'That's up to you, love. I'll put the kettle on.' Marie is strangely calm, but not robotic this time, thank goodness.

I lie down with my babies and tickle their faces, but my eyes are on Alec. What the hell have I dragged the poor fellow into? He's an accessory after the fact, as am I. No, I'm worse – I'm a part

265

of the fact. He shouldn't be here among weeping women in a house with virtually no furniture, peeling wallpaper and a board where one of the windows used to be.

But he's smiling down at me. 'I had a thought,' he says. 'Unusual, I know – especially in view of the fact that I had a thought yesterday as well.'

Maureen's giggle wears a hysterical edge.

'When everything's over – the divorces and so forth – Anna and I will live together, probably in her house with the twins and one of my daughters. Susan can stay or go – whatever she wants to do. But I think the three of you – four, counting Stephen – should use my house.'

Marie is in the doorway with a teapot in her hand and a half-smile on her face. 'In Eccleston?'

'Yes.'

'Is it posh?'

'It thinks it is.'

She sits at a table, her hand still clutching the teapot. 'Is Eccleston ready for us?'

No one answers, because she's still talking, almost to herself. 'He looked as if he was asleep, you know. Not a mark on his face, but white and stiff, like a statue lying down. And I stood there and told them yeah, it is my son, and my belly hurt, like I could feel him being born. Then I thought about our Susan and her little lad, and I knew I'd done the right thing.' She nods. 'The wrong thing was the right thing. Crazy bloody world. Does anyone fancy a suggestive?'

Maureen explains. 'She means a digestive biscuit. She's the same with them self-assembly shelves and suchlike, never reads what she calls the destructions.'

So, that's the first hurdle cleared. I stand and follow Marie into a grim cupboard of a kitchen, and I give her the envelope. I tell her that the bank manager tried to get clever over the size of the sum, and why I needed it in used notes, and that I wiped his eye for him.

'That's a Liverpool expression,' she informs me.

'I know, Marie. I've made myself an honorary member.'

Dolores has accepted a lump sum settlement, while Den, having fought the good fight with all his might for weeks, has been forced to concur with the proposal by Juliet that Emily, Lottie and their mother should be allowed to remain in the house until the twins have completed their education. Fortunately, Jo has kept her mouth shut about Alec and me, and Lincolnshire is far enough away to hold our respective spice (oh, Alec) out of our hair until the decrees nisi come through.

Mrs Bee marches in with a beef pie, a chicken pie and an apple crumble. 'Hello, love,' she says to Alec, who is becoming part of the brood she insists on looking after. She sees him as the other victim, and views the pair of us as conspirators in search of revenge, a concept of which she approves. 'These pies is for Marie and Maureen. You don't feel like cooking when someone as young as their Gary gets murdered through fighting. Was he one of them there football hooligans?'

'Probably.' I relieve her of her burdens and go to put the kettle on. But she follows me. Like a gas, she seems to permeate everything everywhere. 'Anna?' she whispers.

'What?'

She closes the door silently. 'He's a grand looking man, that Alec.'

'Yes. I suppose he is.'

At my side now, she whispers, 'I reckon he's sweet on you, girl. I've seen him. Looking at you. Hey, wouldn't it be funny if you and him finished up wed, and his wife and your Den ended up separated and lonely? It's like that there poetical justice when summat like that happens.'

I switch on the kettle and plant a kiss below her left eye. 'I love him, Mrs Bee.'

Those wise eyes fill with tears and she fishes in a pocket for her handkerchief. 'And I can't tell nobody about that news, can I?'

'No. Not till we're properly divorced.'

Jo bursts in. She has a baby in each arm and is wearing the blue dress I bought when I went to seduce her father. She advises me that it will fit her if her boobs grow a bit, and I tell her to go and show her dad how she looks in it. Mrs Bee, who never misses a trick, asks me whether it's a special frock, and I tell her it is.

'Is she part of the package?' the old woman asks.

I won't laugh. I'm remembering when he told me I was well-packaged that evening when we first got together. He made me feel like a rather special and unexpected parcel left by the Royal Mail. 'Yes, she is. Sarah's with her mother now, but Jo says my clothes fit her better, so Dolores lost the fight.'

'No!'

I laugh. 'Mrs Bee, it's a joke. She's a daddy's girl and I don't blame her. He's a special man.'

She dries her eyes and mutters something about scones in the oven and Jenny being prone to neglect when it comes to cooking. Mrs Bee is happy for me, for us. Alec comes in for the tea tray. 'Jo wants us to sleep here tonight, Anna. She's working on taking over your babies.'

'And?'

He smiles. He has a glorious smile. 'She's accepted me and you, sweetheart. But. If you lend her that dress, I'll probably kill you. She could meet some dirty old man – like you did – who'll peel it away and–'

'And read a book on tantric sex?' I ask sweetly.

He draws himself to his full height, which is six feet and two and a half inches. He won't allow anyone to forget that half inch. 'Listen, Sugarplum. There is no other man like me. I am unique, imaginative, handsome, sweet-natured and very, very humble.'

I shall love this silly, wonderful man until the day one of us dies. Because sex has moved down the podium to silver medal status. For both of us, it's the being together that matters. Actually, sex is probably reduced to bronze, because our children are high on the list of priorities. To be together, we will pay any price. Apart from allowing Jo to wear the blue dress, that is.

Twelve

School was heaven and hell rolled into the one package whose colours of brown and gold were on the backs of over three hundred of Bolton's cleverest Catholic girls. For Anna, the heavenly parts were French, Latin, maths and English. Hell came in the guises of religious instruction, which was on the menu daily, and science. Science turned out to be hopeless because it consisted of a couple of pipettes and the odd Bunsen burner. The nuns were here to create young ladies, so they concentrated on the arts, because the arts were feminine.

These young ladies would leave school, marry, and produce many good, Catholic children. Among that number would be more girls, who would come along and fail to learn any physics or chemistry, because the subjects were a bit messy. Domestic science was untidy, but the lessons had to be endured, since no good Catholic girl would catch a good Catholic husband unless she had the ability to cook, wash and iron for him.

Anna learned to shut up, which wasn't easy for her. Having argued openly with Sister Beatrice on the subjects of transubstantiation, Limbo for the unbaptized and hell for Protestants, she was sent to the office of a fierce little nun named Mother Gertrude, headmistress.

Here, she was given a lecture on the evils of

Henry VIII, who seemed to have started the whole slide into perdition by cutting off heads and getting divorced. Protestants could not enter the Kingdom and that was an end to it. Transubstantiation had to be accepted via an Act of Faith. Anna was used to those because of Father Brogan. The Communion host was not a piece of bread, it was the living body of Jesus, and she felt nauseous. Was this cannibalism? Limbo was yet another Act of Faith, so Anna should be ashamed of herself and, should the bold child have any further questions, would she kindly make an appointment to see Mother Gertrude instead of inciting dissent in the classroom. Such appointments, should they be required, were to be obtained via the school secretary, and Anna was dismissed.

At home, life was far from easy. Billy MacRae, having sat in his house for several months, decided it was time to venture forth. He ventured off for four days and three nights, and Anna found herself in a state of desperation, since no one in authority would listen to her.

She used the telephone kiosk to speak to Mother Gertrude. 'I'm sorry, Mother, only my daddy's gone missing.'

'But you can't stay away from school, Anna.'

'I know, Mother, I know. But he came back from the war in a bad state. They had to look after him for a long time in hospitals and rest homes. The police say he's a grown man and there's nothing they can do. Ask the sisters to pray, would you?'

'Of course, child. We'll all pray. Come back to us soon, and I shall make it my very own business to take from your teachers all you have missed, and you can work from notes and text books. God bless, Anna.'

Anna opened the kiosk door to find Bert standing on the pavement. His face was like thunder, and he grabbed her arm as soon as she emerged. 'They've done it again,' he said, his words forced through tightened lips. 'We've a tent missing, one that Master Roger used to play in when he was a lad.'

'Who ... what do you mean, Uncle Bert?'

'Them bloody sisters of yours. They've been visiting him before you're back from school. And there's been a bit of giggling. I reckon they've talked him into going to find the enemy during the night, and he's buggered off with yon tent and God knows what. Elsie's got stuff missing from the larder, and we've put two and two together.'

'I'll kill them,' she said.

'You'd have to stand at the back of a very long queue, and that queue will get longer with every year that passes. They've refused to make their First Holy Communion, because they want to go to Bolton School. St Mary's is good enough for you, but not for them.'

Bolton School was a private school, and very few scholarships were available. 'They're clever enough,' Anna said.

'Aye. So imagine what sort of grown women they're going to turn into. It'll be either the House of Commons or a prison cell, no half-measures.'

'He has to be in a clearing in the woods,' said

Anna, almost to herself.

'Nay.' Bert shook his head. 'They've been caught out too many times in yon. They'll not make that mistake again.'

'But he might, Uncle Bert. My dad wouldn't go where they told him to go, because he forgets what people say to him. And that wood's deeper than I've ever been – there have to be clearings.'

He shook his head in despair. 'We've got to start somewhere, I suppose. I thought he'd never leave the house – he didn't want to come to work with me, did he? But he's vulnerable, Anna. He knows his mate's dead, because we've drummed it into him, but he's not ... well, you know what I mean.'

'Not predictable,' Anna finished for him. 'Dr Corcoran says he's still all there, but he chooses what he hears. Something about a defence mechanism.'

They went home to change into walking boots, Bert chuntering all the time under his breath, because he didn't know what the world was coming to, and he'd half a mind to get over to the school and drag them two little hellions out of their class for questioning.

Anna hadn't a great deal to say for herself. She felt weary, worried, disappointed and sorry to have to take time off school if this was yet another of the twins' tricks. Then she remembered Jimmy Hardcastle with his bottle-bottom glasses and his weak leg – had she not rattled the truth out of them, Kate and Beckie would have left him there to die. Would they do that to their own father? No. They weren't strong enough to fasten him to a tree. But they were sufficiently wicked to put the idea of camping into his head.

Her main concern was for her father, who had shown marked signs of improvement of late. She'd managed some good and meaningful conversations with him, and he had even become animated when talking about his dead wife. Although he seldom asked about the twins, he knew who and where they were, and seemed happier with Anna. Sometimes, she spent the night in his house, and he appeared glad to have her with him. And now, he had gone missing.

Bert joined her. 'You ready?' he asked.

Anna was thinking. 'Will you wait for me, Uncle Bert?'

'Why? Where are you off to?'

The days when she could slap them and detain them until they gave up the truth were long past. It was 1947, so they were great big seven-year olds, sturdy, well-fed and as stubborn as she was. She had to be clever. The fight would go on, but it needed to be psychological. 'I'm going to the big house. If Linda's in, I'll ask her to take me to the school.'

'Well, I thought of that, but they'll be in lessons.'

'Yes.'

'The teachers won't like it.'

'Neither will my sisters. That, Uncle Bert, is the idea. They're terrified of Linda Mellor ever since she said she was going to put their names all over the place. Remember? When they took my bike to bits?'

'I remember. Took me the best part of a week-

274

end to put the bugger back together. Don't tell Elsie I swore.'

'As if I would.'

'Any road, I'll come with you. I don't see why Mrs Mellor should have to deal with our troubles without us being with her.'

They came out of the house and saw Billy strolling down the street, a bundle on his back and a broad smile on his face. He had been out. For the first time since ... since he didn't know when, he had got out of the house and breathed fresh air.

Anna grabbed Bert's hand. 'Leave it to me,' she said quietly. 'I'll get to the bottom of it.' She followed her father into his house and closed the door. 'You've been gone four days,' she said.

'What?'

'You've been missing for three nights and four days, Dad.'

He dropped his backpack and sat down. 'Did they not tell you?'

'No, they didn't. They never tell anybody anything. Where's the tent come from?'

'They gave it to me. Kate and Beckie.'

'Dad?'

'What?'

'Look at me.' She waited until he was concentrating. 'They stole it. The twins took that tent from a storage shed on the estate.'

'Oh.' He wiped a hand across his brow and thought back to the last time he'd seen the twins. 'I was here with them and they were telling me about – what's it called? Agoraphobia. They said it's Latin, something to do with fields and fear.

275

They'd looked it up and decided that if I stayed in here any longer, I'd never be able to set foot outside. So I told them I'd lived under canvas for years, and they said they'd get me a tent. And they did. So I went.'

'Where?'

'In the woods. It was great. It was like it used to be when…'

'When your friend was still alive. But that wasn't a good time, Dad, because it was a war, and the war killed him. That war's over and done with now. And you should have told us where you were going, because they don't do messages.'

'I'm back, anyway. And I've got a chance of work. That gamekeeper's putting in a word for me. I'm good at creeping about and catching people.'

Anna shivered. As long as he didn't forget and shoot somebody… Would he have a gun? Did gamekeepers carry guns? It probably didn't matter, because Linda Mellor would have more sense than to employ Dad in a position that involved weapons.

'I'd better take the tent back, then,' he said.

'It's all right, Dad. The people who stole it should take it back.' The twins needed her to know that they were the culprits. Every time she hit them or scolded them, they had won. But Linda Mellor had the power, the real power. As the last remaining member – albeit by marriage – of a notable family, she sat on several boards and committees. 'Are you all right for an hour, Dad? There's eggs and milk in the kitchen in case you're hungry.'

'I'll be fine, love. I did enjoy that few days outside.'

She left him.

Richard 'Sausage' Mellor, born during the war, was going to attend one of the feeder establishments for Bolton School. Linda was on the board of the private infant/junior school where her son would be put through his paces. He wouldn't need a scholarship, because Linda Mellor could afford the fees; all that was necessary in Richard's case was a pass for the entrance exam to one of the best private schools in the north of England. But Kate and Beckie required a full grant from the ratepayers. It was time to get clever.

So Anna made two decisions on that day. She would fix the twins like a couple of beetles pinned in a glass case. And she would move permanently into her father's house.

Having prepared Linda during a private meeting, Anna arrived at the manor with two seven-year-olds, a tent in a bag, and her father. Things were going to change. There was a lead weight of guilt in the older girl's chest, because she would be leaving Elsie and Bert to deal with developing criminals, but she had to look after her dad, and had to stay sane. And she would be next door, wouldn't she? And Dad liked Elsie's cooking, so there would be plenty of visits.

Linda, seated at her mother-in-law's desk, removed the spectacles she had come to need of late for reading and writing. In her dark suit and crisp, white blouse, she appeared officious and rather daunting, which impression pleased Anna while seeming to have no effect whatsoever on her companions.

'What now?' Linda asked.

'Brought your tent back, Mrs Mellor,' said Anna sweetly. 'They lent it to my dad after stealing it from you. They can't deny it, because he's better now, and he remembers them giving it to him. I think they probably hoped he'd get lost and never come back, but he did come back.' She dumped the tent on the floor.

'Thank you, Anna. Is your father here?'

'Outside in the corridor, Mrs Mellor.' This was definitely a 'Mrs Mellor' occasion. It was too serious a subject to be ruined by familiarity.

'Leave us, please,' Linda asked. 'And I shall need to talk to Mr MacRae later.'

Anna left and sat next to her dad, who held her hand rather tightly.

'Is there something wrong with them?' he asked quietly.

Over the years, she had worked that out as well. 'More Beckie than Kate, I think, Dad. Beckie's the one who sets things in motion, and Kate goes along with it. But when she chooses to do that, she's as bad as Beckie, so who knows? From the start, they resented being brought up by Uncle Bert and Auntie Elsie. If Mam had lived – again, who knows? They've been talking in their own language, like a code, since before they could walk, and they listen to nobody unless they need information. So they listen at school. They're already doing grammar school subjects.'

'Are they confused, like I was?' he asked.

'No, Dad, they're geniuses. According to the

psychology doctor who sees them from time to time, there's no way to measure how clever they really are, but brains like theirs get hiccups. The hiccups mean we all suffer.'

'She would have lived if I'd been there. I'd have shifted the snow.'

The twins appeared, faces as white as a new fall of the substance under discussion. They stared hard at Anna, then at their father before walking out of the house. Linda opened the office door and motioned Billy and Anna to come inside the room. Still hand in hand, they placed themselves on a pair of chairs that continued to remember bodily warmth from the recently departed twins.

From the other side of the desk, Linda Mellor spoke to Billy. 'Don't worry about those two,' she advised. 'They would survive a Hiroshima, and to hell with the rest of us. Mr MacRae?'

'Yes?'

'Keep the tent. It's yours. And feel free to put it in the woods, though there is a wooden cabin for you in case you need shelter.'

Anna's heart missed a few beats. Surely he wasn't going to be a gamekeeper? With a gun? After all he'd been through?

'The woods are the property of my son, Mr MacRae. There are footpaths, and I encourage people to use them, because there's a great deal to be learnt about nature in there – the schools come, you know.'

'Yes,' Billy replied. 'There were kiddies in there while I was camping.'

'Quite.' Linda leaned forward. 'Visitors to the area have to be safe. We have trees that are half-dead, trees that need lopping so that younger ones might thrive. I should like to offer you a post as woodsman.' She picked up a book. 'This holds all you need to know about arboriculture. You keep my son's property beautiful and healthy.'

Billy gulped. He was being offered a proper job, not just the come-to-work-with-me that Bert had suggested. 'And I get paid?'

'In cash, Mr MacRae.'

'I'm Billy. Or Macker. I don't know how to thank you, Mrs Mellor.'

'You're welcome, Billy.' Linda knew a good man when she saw one. He'd been through Purgatory, and the woods were to be his reward.

'You lost your husband, Mrs Mellor?' he asked.

'Yes. He was one of the last to be killed.'

'I'm sorry.' Billy stood up and shook her hand, picking up the book before turning to go. 'I'll leave you two to talk woman-talk,' he said, his head already in the volume that would teach him his new trade.

When only Anna remained, Linda allowed a huge sigh to escape. 'Your sisters are cool customers.'

'Yes, I know all about it. And thank you for giving my dad some work. He needs a job. He needs dignity and confidence.'

'You're welcome.' Linda paused and tapped a pen on the table. 'Having said that they're cool in crisis, I think I may just have fixed your little ogres. Though Beckie did accuse me of blackmail. How do they know all this stuff? They should be out scrumping apples and playing ball.'

Anna shrugged. 'They get the bus to town and go in Bolton Central Library – and it's not the children's section. They make notes. In code. In fact, it could be in Greek for all I know, because I've seen some of the symbols before, but...' Anna grinned. 'It's all Greek to me.'

Linda remained serious. 'I can get their notebooks looked at by someone who read classics. No one comes to mind, but I know people who know people.'

'My headmistress teaches Greek to a handful of sixth formers. But she's a nun, and God alone knows what those two are writing about. Plus, they've hidden their notes somewhere out of Uncle Bert and Auntie Elsie's house.'

Linda explained that the twins now feared for their places at Bolton School. She had implied that she could have them black-balled, and they weren't happy. 'Moving into Billy's house is a good idea,' she said. 'He loves and needs you. He must have really loved your mother.'

Anna nodded. 'So did I, Linda. So did I. But I feel terrible about leaving the twins with Uncle and Auntie. It's as if I'm betraying my foster parents. But I've homework to do and books to read I want to have some peace. They'll still cause trouble, but I– Oh, Linda. I think Auntie Elsie's frightened of them, and Uncle Bert's scared he might just flatten them one of these days.'

'Few would blame him,' Linda said.

'The courts wouldn't forgive him,' Anna replied. 'Nor would the hangman.'

With that, Linda was forced to agree. But Anna needed her space. She would continue to care for the Dixons, of that, Linda was certain. But the twins would find their own way to the devil, no matter what.

Katherine and Rebecca MacRae passed their scholarship examinations at the age of nine and, by 1950, they had spent several months ripping through the Bolton School curriculum like whirl-winds. They learned chess in days, took up the violin and had the bulk of homework completed by six o'clock each weekday evening.

Since the afternoon of reckoning with Linda Mellor, there had been no more incidents. But the Dixon household was not a happy one, and Anna still suffered guilt because of that. She looked after her father, cleaned and cooked for him except when the pair of them ate next door, did washing, ironing and shopping. Elsie helped, but she developed rheumatism and, as time went by, she did less and less. She visited, because the oppressive silence next door drove her out of the house, but some household tasks became too much, and Bert was forced to pull his weight.

The twins did nothing apart from school work and extra-curricular reading. They now lived and ate upstairs, using as excuse violin practice, homework and chosen areas of study. When they did play their borrowed instruments, people would stand stock still in the street, because they were good. Everything these 'bad' children did was good. They entered chess competitions, defeating people older, wiser and more practised at the game; they played in the school orchestra which, apart from solos or duets delivered by the twins, sounded like a hundred cats in terminal agony. Algebra they had already overcome, while physics and chemistry were a breeze.

Then the school secretary sent a letter to Billy. He was invited to come along and discuss with head and form teachers a matter of some delicacy, and his appointment was set outside school hours. Reading between the lines, Anna gathered that the staff wanted Kate and Beckie to be off the premises when the meeting took place.

Billy shook his head. 'There's something not right,' he said for the umpteenth time. 'They're not like other girls their age.'

'They're not like anybody any age,' Anna replied. 'It's just becoming more noticeable to us as they get bigger. I wonder what they've done now?' Surely they wouldn't upset any apple carts in the exclusive halls of learning at Bolton School for Girls? It was a place that fed their intellectual hunger, and they would respect it accordingly. Wouldn't they?

Billy, who was now what he described as almost sane and nearly 'fully-furnished' in the upstairs department, went on the bus to meet the educators of his children. He didn't know the twins. Anna, so like her mother, was easy to read, but the other two were special in several ways. Folk clever enough to teach at a private school would know all kinds of stuff like child psychology, so he entered the hallowed portals of the impressive sandstone building with a heavy heart.

When he returned to Anna two hours later, his feet were as leaden as his innards. 'Oh, Anna,' he said, laying his trilby on the table. 'Oh, God.'

283

'What? What have they done now?' she asked.

'Nothing. They've done absolutely nothing to damage the school or their classmates. They suck up everything they're taught like a couple of vacuum cleaners, never put a finger out of place, model students, no complaints about most of their work, but...'

'But what, Dad?'

'Well, for a kick-off, their compositions – essays, I think they're called – are strange. The teacher showed me some. Just facts and reports of events. No feeling. Nearly no opinion. "The house burned down and everyone inside was consumed by the flames. Not even bones remained, just piles of ash where the kitchen used to be." Stuff like that. It's like reading Edgar Allan Poe, only worse, because they're children.'

'Perhaps they've no imagination?' Anna had an imagination, and could not have coped with life had she not found a means of escape within her own head. 'They're mirrors for one another,' she said quietly. 'Beckie is the main source of ... of light. Kate's more a reflection. Yet they will have to separate at some stage.'

Billy stared at the floor. 'They've no friends. Nobody likes them. I get the impression that while their teachers are a bit in awe because the girls are cleverer than they are, they don't think much of Kate and Beckie.'

Anna stood up and did what she termed an Auntie Elsie. 'I'll put the kettle on.'

'Anna?'

'What?' She looked at her father and saw the depth of his misery.

'That's not all, love,' he said. 'They've started to compete. With one another. And whoever gets the better marks is beaten up by her twin. So they're going to be split up. They've forty-odd in the top stream, which means there are two classes. Beckie is more competitive than Kate. She's the one that's being shifted, and she's not happy. They've had to be pulled off one another during what they call rec – recreation break. They fight in secret places, but they have been found. And now, they're being watched.' He paused and wiped his eyes with a handkerchief. 'They even fight in a way that doesn't show. All the bruises are on their bodies, but they've been seen by the physical education teacher when they were changing. The poor woman was sent to spy.'

Anna forgot the tea and sat down. What would become of her little sisters? Because, no matter what, they were the daughters of Billy and Frankie, just as she was. 'I hope I never have twins,' she said. Years later, she would look back on that day when she and her father sat huddled over an empty grate. Had she ever made the tea? She couldn't remember.

But what she would never forget was that this was the day when Dad found the Shepherd's Crook, a small hostelry over the hill. Weakened by war, made sane by the regularity of days in the country, he could not take on board the knowledge that his younger daughters were, in truth, not right. He renewed his relationship with beer and whisky, joined in small talk, played dominoes and came home in a state that would have shocked his daughter had she been awake.

For months, he held himself in check and limited his intake. Sometimes, he slept in the woods, either in his tent, or in the cabin provided by the estate, always with a bottle of whisky as his companion. But Billy's descent into alcohol dependence had begun, and it would never be completely reversed.

It was all down to Linda Mellor yet again. Anna had accepted long ago the concept of having two mothers – three, if she counted Dirty Gerty, as the pupils of St Mary's termed Mother Gertrude. Elsie was the cuddle-mam, Linda was the mother who made things happen, while Gertrude was a support when it came to learning.

Linda was the power. She could train her sights on the twins and fire at will, but even she was slightly flummoxed on this occasion. 'Anna, while they're killing one another, the rest of the world is safe.'

'They're my sisters.' Sometime, Anna didn't quite understand herself, because she found it difficult to hate her mother's children completely. As for her dad – he was behaving strangely again, and the twins had been the cause of that, so everything in Anna's head was as cluttered and disordered as an attic filled with centuries of junk. She didn't know how she felt.

But Dad? It was as if they weren't really his, since he hadn't been there from the start. But they were his. The bonds of flesh and blood were elemental and strong, which factor was probably the reason for him beginning to fall apart again. 'I'm worried,' she told her friend. 'They're getting dangerous. Elsie's had to give Kate my old bedroom, because they're not getting on with each other.'

'Don't they practise their violin music together?'

Anna nodded. 'Oh, yes. Together, but not together. When one starts, the other starts, but they deliberately play different tunes. It's been sudden and very nasty. Auntie Elsie and Uncle Bert are living in hell.'

Linda walked to the window and stared out at the gardens. 'Perhaps they should be split up. You could go back to Elsie's and let one of them stay with your dad.'

That could not possibly work, and Anna said so. She did all the chores, while neither of the twins did anything in the house. And the cacophony of two violins competing at a slightly greater distance might prove disastrous for the whole neighbourhood. Dad neither knew nor liked them, their teachers couldn't stand them, and Anna had taken enough. 'It makes me tired,' she said.

Anna stood up and joined Linda at the window. 'It's as if that snow brought a curse with it. It fell from heaven, but it originated in another place that's meant to be too hot for that kind of weather. I can't concentrate. My own school work has to be done, but it's hard trying to make sense of Latin declension when all this is going on.'

Linda put an arm across Anna's shoulders and drew her in. 'I shall write to them. Two separate letters, but the twins will come here together. I hate threatening people, yet nothing else will work – no point in appealing to their better nature, as they seem to have been born without a good side. Go now, my dear. I have some telephone calls to make.'

Linda stayed where she was for some time after Anna had left. She had no calls to make, but she intended to go out very shortly and deal with Billy. Over the months, she had become rather too fond of the man. Since the death of Roger, no one had appealed to her in the least way. Until now. He was an employee, as she repeatedly advised herself. And pity was akin to love.

She pulled on a pair of boots and a coat, marched briskly down the drive until she reached the edge of Grantham Woods, stopping to listen after a few more strides. Nothing. There was more to woodsmanship than the chopping down of trees, but Linda's worry went deeper than mere concern about forestry. She made for the cabin, opened the door to her property without knocking, and there he was, a half-bottle of whisky gripped in his right hand.

He jumped to his feet. 'Just putting a drop in my thermos,' he said. 'Keep the cold out.'

Linda slammed the door home. 'You let that girl down, Billy MacRae, and as God is my witness, I'll kill you.'

He forgot himself for a moment. 'Eh? You what?'

'You heard me well enough. I love Anna, and I'll do almost anything for her. If that has to include separating you from your whisky-tainted breath, so be it. One of my staff will take over the house, do shopping, cooking and chores. Anna's a skivvy, no more than that – just an unpaid serf who waits on you hand and foot. She wants to be a teacher – how's she going to manage that with a weight like you to carry?'

He closed his mouth with an audible snap.

'You're in the Shepherd's Crook almost every night, you're drinking on duty, and no alcoholic should be let loose with a saw and an axe.'

Billy swallowed hard. 'I'm not an alcoholic,' he said.

'Denial,' was her reply. 'That's where you are right now – in denial. You can't go a day without a drink, and well you know that. It's time to stop before you find yourself drinking a full bottle of spirits every day. What will happen to her when you die of alcohol poisoning or cirrhosis of the liver? Elsie and Bert are getting no younger – and look at you. Burying your head in a bottle while your little girl tries to set right all that's amiss in your life? I thought you were a man. I liked you, enjoyed talking to you. But I'm not wasting my time on an old soak.'

She slammed her way out of the hut and found that her legs weren't working. For about five minutes, she sat on a tree stump and tried to compose herself. He wasn't even handsome any more. His skin had grown rougher, while the male-pattern baldness was threatening to leave him looking like a pink snooker ball, but…

Cupid was notoriously unpredictable and, whenever he intended to fire an arrow, he should perhaps prepare himself via an eye test. Billy MacRae was poisoned meat, and she should begin to dine elsewhere. Not that he knew, of course. Not that he felt anything in return. His attachment was to Johnny Walker, and he was too selfish to sever the connection. Linda had seen it all before in her family from the south. Billy MacRae had begun to kill himself.

They were not quite eleven years old and dressed in school uniforms. Both managed to look like Anna, while failing completely to resemble each other. They didn't blink very often, and Linda found herself thinking of that old friend named Adolf Hitler, who had owned staring, probing eyes.

The bull whose horns Linda grasped took the form of a large tome on the subject of mental health. They knew all the words, so they had better look at this one. These were children, yet they weren't, so the risk had to be taken. It was for Anna's sake, she repeated inwardly several times. It was a cruel act, but Anna mattered. Didn't they matter? How beautiful they were, how cold those eyes.

Linda had to keep Billy out of the equation; she didn't want the dreadful duo to know that their father had been to the school. She passed the open book to Beckie and asked her to read aloud the marked section.

Beckie cleared her throat. 'Psychopathy,' she read without any effort. 'This is an antisocial personality disorder manifesting itself via aggression, perverted, criminal or amoral behaviour, no empathy, no sympathy, no remorse. Psychopaths are manipulative and capable of remaining outwardly normal. Those of high intellect may achieve success in a career, but seldom in domestic life.'

Beckie looked up. 'Then there's a list of drugs, some stuff about research and a bit about treatment.'

Linda retrieved the book. 'I have spoken to the school board,' she said. 'And they say your teachers are concerned about the two of you fighting, and about the total lack of imagination in your English essays. Your essays are dull, because you cannot imagine the feelings of anyone except yourselves. You don't care enough to wonder how others feel.'

A half-smile played on Beckie's lips. 'We haven't got that,' she announced smugly, pointing to the book. 'The doctor says we haven't got it. We're not psychopaths.'

Linda kept a tight rein on her temper. 'The doctor is one man, and a very old one. Others might see you differently. And you don't fit in at school, do you? While at home, you create chaos and cause misery. I wonder how your headmistress would react if she knew your history? The burning of a barn, the kidnap and attempted manslaughter of a child, the stealing, the—'

'All right. What do you require of us?'

Linda shook her head in near-disbelief. Beckie talked like a forty-year-old, while Kate seemed to be keeping her counsel for the time being.

The lady of the house passed a list across her desk. 'The rules,' she snapped. 'Keep to them, or I'll have you out of that school faster than water down a plug hole. I mean it. I'm not going to sit here while two evil creatures destroy Anna, Bert, Elsie and Billy. I shan't allow you to undermine that wonderful school. You think you're clever, don't you? But you're just a collection of knowledge, with no sense of how to apply such learning. Ten and ten makes twenty, but twenty what? Loaves, fishes, people? All the same to you, all consumable, all there to be stamped on by the nastiest pair of children it has been my misfortune to meet. Get out. You make me sick.'

Beckie made for the door, but her twin remained for a while. She wanted to ask how to learn to behave, but she couldn't, not with Beckie near enough to hear. So she followed her sister out of the house, and went home to learn the rules.

Linda Mellor wept. She cried mainly for Anna, but also for Billy. A decent man, he was on his way to hell in a handcart, courtesy of a Scottish distillery and two difficult little girls. And there was no more she could do.

Thirteen

Charlie Hughes is sitting in a corner in the Throstle's Nest, and he is nursing a pint of orange juice with a few ice cubes rattling against the sides. He has the shakes, and I don't know whether it's still from withdrawal, or whether seeing his son going into a hole in the ground has caused the tremors. Whatever, he looks lost, lonely and upset. Something needs to be done. All my life, I've been a sucker for sob stories, but my interest in folk has always repaid me tenfold, so I've few regrets.

So I go and park myself next to him, because I don't quite trust this lot – they look as if they've been let out for twenty-four hours because there's no full moon. Are they armed? Will we all be standing at the wrong end of a machine gun in an hour or so? I don't want any of them slipping him a mickey, since he's doing well. Which is more than can be said for the cabaret.

An Irishman of indeterminable age is propped up by the bar and is murdering *Silver Threads Among the Gold*. The fact that he knows very few of the words isn't helping a great deal. When he finishes, a collective sigh of relief emerges from a dozen or more of us, but he's starting on *Danny Boy*. Some almost sober bloke gives the would-be warbler a double whisky, so that's all right for the moment.

Across the room, Marie is watching over Susan,

while I am getting to know Charlie. Charlie Hughes has found religion, and I envy him. The child I used to be never managed to handle the so-called one true Faith, but Charlie is like a newly converted Catholic, so he is in danger of becoming evangelical and tiresome. And yet...

And yet, he's funny. He has some hilarious anecdotes about life in an alcohol-free zone, and he even makes the DTs amusing. I remember Father Brogan doing the same after his escape from Ireland. 'I could have worked with pink elephants,' Charlie tells me. 'Or anything any colour any time – purple rabbits, green lions – bring 'em on. But it was the real people that scared the shit out of me – excuse my French. Bloody terrifying, they were. Nuns everywhere, priests drying out – and climbing out at night to get some booze. One priest broke into the chapel one afternoon and stole the altar wine. It was Ribena, so his luck bombed. Another fellow broke his leg when a drainpipe gave way, but he wasn't a priest, he was just a plonker. Sorry I swore.'

'It's all right.' Didn't Tom Brogan tell me that the worst part of recovery had been nuns?

'All that praying. I got used to it, like, and I'm down for confirmation, because it started being all I had. Faith, I mean. It was the nuns that got me straight in the end, but they were frightening. I've never seen the point to nuns – who needs 'em? But when you're trying to come off the piss, they'll scare you into going teetotal.'

We've had curly ham sandwiches, peanuts and crisps. There was a disagreement earlier on over a few sausage rolls, but they've all disappeared.

Needless to say, Third Party didn't cater for this event. Gary's brothers aren't here, because the neighbours complained, and the lads are on remand for malicious damage. They were in church and at the graveside, but each had become very attached to a policeman, so that was that. The house has been boarded up, and they will be sent down, or sent to live in hostels.

'I hear you've done a lot for our Susan,' Charlie says. 'Thanks.'

'She did a lot for me.'

'Aye, she would. She's a good girl. They're living in St Helens?'

'Marie and Maureen are, yes.'

'I've no home now,' he says mournfully. 'The lads've been chucked out.'

'Marie had had enough, Charlie. She was worn to a shadow.'

'I know, love. I know. Mind you, none of us gave Marie an easy time. Except for our Susan, and she got up the duff, didn't she? I was pissed when I hit her.'

'She's forgiven you.'

A fight breaks out near the door, and one fellow chucks another into the street. 'Are they with us?' I ask Charlie.

He shrugs. 'Well, one of them isn't any more, that's for sure. Who knows, eh? They all look the bloody same to me – they'll be cousins or some such articles. It's not a proper funeral without a fight. Weddings are very much the same. After a while, they get blurred round the edges because of the booze, and it all turns into a bit of a free-for-all. It's a normal fight, only with chairs, stools, bottles and glasses. Speaking of recognizing folk, where's our Maureen?'

'Babysitting my twins and Susan's Stephen.'

Charlie tells me that Maureen could never stand their Gary, and I can't explain why her hatred has grown to the point where she couldn't attend the funeral. The truth about what happened to his daughter might push Charlie back inside the beer barrel, and I don't want to be responsible for that. 'Go and talk to Marie, Charlie. She knows how hard you've tried to get yourself back on track.'

'Oh, I don't know, I–'

'Just do it. She knows you're trying your best in that place, that you're making a real effort to change. Go on. Take your orange juice. If she thumps you, I'll sort her out.'

While he walks across the bar floor, I see how thin he is. The dark navy trousers flap, and the matching jacket is wider than his shoulders. Dad was like that at the end, because he stopped eating. It occurs to me that Dad may have sent Charlie to me, just as Mam sent Marie and Susan. These people may be my chance to do something right.

I gaze around the pub and look at all the men and women who have gathered to say goodbye to a thug. And I listen to their conversations and their jokes and yes – they're exactly like the rest of us. I was wrong – they're not loonies having a day off. In fact, they're quite smart when it comes to quips and put-downs. When is somebody going to do something with them? If the energy in this tiny pub could be channelled, we might get a shock, because your day-to-day, common-or-garden

296

Scouser is as sharp as a pin. But in the year of Our Lord 1975, no one wants to know.

My Alec walks in. I didn't know he was intending to come, don't know how he found out where we are, but perhaps he just followed the debris. He stands in the doorway, hands in the pockets of his today-I-am-an-accountant suit. He looks delicious. 'Oi,' he calls to the barman, who takes no notice.

Oh, God, here we go. Alec puts fingers in his mouth and delivers a whistle fit to crack every glass in the joint. Silence reigns. The Irish singer shakes his head as if trying to rid himself of the noise, falls off his stool, and nobody else moves. He just lies there and either goes to sleep or passes out. Not a soul cares, because at least he won't be singing.

The barman gives his full attention to the suit in the doorway. 'What's up?' he asks.

Alec's mouth twitches, because he and I have a secret joke about 'what's up?' and it's not for general consumption. He can't look at me, or that twitch will become a laugh. 'Sorry to bother you,' he says in his best English. 'But I noticed blood and guts outside here. About ten people in all. I counted legs and divided by two.' Well, he is an accountant. 'They're all tangled up together, and I think we may need an ambulance or three.'

The barman pushes his way to the door and peers out. 'Oh, they're all right,' he announces. Then he looks Alec up and down. 'It is a wake, you know, lad. This is what we call normal round here. Did you want a pint?'

Alec carries his pint to my table. 'Do you want

anything, darling?' he asks.

'No, thanks.'

'Was it grim?'

I nod. Susan was hysterical, Marie wore a face like stone, but at least her shoes were a pair, while I stood there feeling guilty because I'd funded the mess.

He leans close. 'Both nisi will be through our letterboxes in a few weeks. Of course, we have to appear in court because of the twins. After that, I think the final takes another couple of months, then we're free. Oh and my mother says to tell you thanks for coming to tea, you're a lovely woman, and she wants to see a lot more of you. You made her laugh, babe.'

He's trying to cheer me up, but I feel so low. I keep telling myself it was all for Susan, then I remember the poker and how hard I hit him. My sisters are psychos? What about me? I saved the baby. I have to keep telling myself that I saved the baby, saved Susan and, possibly, Marie as well.

'Come on,' he says. 'I'm taking you home.'

'We've a taxi ordered,' I tell him.

'Let Marie and Susan have the taxi – you're coming with me.'

So I make my good-byes, hope that someone will keep an eye on Charlie, who is sitting with his family, at last. We leave by a side door, because Alec doesn't want to take me through the bodies on the pavement. I love the way he holds me when we walk, arm round my back, hand firmly on my waist.

He follows a route I know well, along Stanley Road and through Bootle, on to Seaforth and

Litherland. In Waterloo, he stops for petrol and buys me a small packet of Maltesers. He knows they're my favourites. And I'm suddenly crying and trembling like a leaf in a spring breeze. Sometimes, a small kindness from a loved one breaks the dam.

He drives without speaking till we reach the erosion, and we watch a sunset that is less dramatic than the one we saw months ago. No, it's weeks. I have known this man for weeks, and he has become my rock, my comfort, my love.

'Are you all cried out yet?' he asks.

'I don't know. There were moments when I thought Susan was going to explode and tell everyone, but Marie did a good job.'

'Marie is a good person. Anna, you did what anyone in his or her right mind would have done. You saved the child twice. Come here.'

We sit until the light dies. In his arms, I am safe from everyone and everything. The Maltesers are shared, and he makes a big deal of biting the last one in two so that we have exactly half each. Yes, it's the little things. Like when he brushes my hair till it shines and acts more like hair, and when I get his scrambled eggs exactly right. He's the better ironer, so he does my blouses (blice, of course) while I'm the expert at putting plugs on electrical things. We please and help each other. And usually, we laugh a lot, but not tonight.

'Thank you for choosing me, Alec.'

He's smiling when he replies. 'I didn't choose you. My body chose. That first day, in that terrible pub, my body chose. Fortunately, there was a table between us. And my mind and soul followed my body, which was why I refused to demean us in the sand dunes. By that time, my illness was beyond cure.'

It occurs to me that love like ours, which breaks all speed limits, should be arrested, but there's never a policeman when you need one. And nothing can stop us now, because the man is not merely in the circle of my life; he has become its fulcrum.

The drive home is quiet, because there's little to say. That's another thing – it's good to be with someone who can share a silence with no awkwardness.

Maureen is at the front door before we've parked. 'Are you all right?' she asks.

I nod, too weary for words.

'Only he's been.'

'Who's been?'

'Your feller. Him what has departed, as you put it. Wanted to know who I was and what Jo was doing here. So we had to make it up. Jo said there's work going on at home because of a flood and the electrics. She's fast off the mark, that daughter of yours, Al. I said I'm the babysitter, which was true. But I think he's suspicious.'

'Too late,' Alec pronounces. 'Nisi stage. We've sworn before Commissioners of Oaths, and that's that.'

'Are you sure?' I ask.

'I think so.' He turns to Maureen. 'Where is he now?'

'Staying at a friend's. Says he'll be back to see you tomorrow.'

Alec walks into the house. 'Come on, Jo. Pack

your stuff. When Den arrives tomorrow, we shan't be here.' He returns to me. 'Just to make absolutely sure, I have to go back to the house. Sorry, sweetheart. Phone me at work when you can. Be brave. If he touches you, I'll kill him.'

I'm alone now in this great big bed I bought for us. I feel lost. So I get up and look at my babies, so beautiful, so perfect. I've discovered of late that I can hang around here for hours just looking and listening to their breathing. No one in this world has babies as beautiful as mine. It's two in the morning, and I'm still sitting here on a cushion that's gone a bit flat for comfort. So I go back and try to sleep on Alec's half. If I bury my head in the pillow, I can breathe him in.

The door opens. 'You still awake, love? Only I heard you walking about.' It's Marie.

'Come in. Has Maureen gone home?'

'No. Snoring like a pig. Good job the bed's a three-quarter, or I'd have been out the window – she's like a bloody octopus, that daughter of mine.' At last, she has managed to say it. Maureen's her daughter, and to hell with the world. She perches on the end of the bed. 'You know what Alec said about us renting his house?'

'Yes.'

'Did he mean it?'

'Of course he did. He doesn't say things he doesn't mean.'

'Right.' She's agitated. I can feel her legs swinging against the bed. 'What is it, Marie?'

She inhales as if preparing to read out a bill in Parliament. 'Would he mind if Charlie came? Because it was all the booze, you know. If he's on the wagon, he'll be OK.'

Now that I've met Charlie, I realize he's either going to make a success of it, or die trying. He sat in a pub full of people, and he stuck to orange juice. 'We'll ask him, eh?' And if I know Alec, he'll say yes. And I do know Alec very well.

'Thanks, Anna.'

'For what?'

'Everything.'

'Bugger off, Marie. If you start crying, I might just join you.'

I've always considered the dawn chorus to be a wonderful thing, but today, it's unpleasant, because it's delivered from the throat of Den Fairbanks, who is a fully-qualified twerp. It's half past seven, Susan and I have catered for the babies, while Maureen and Marie are still in bed, lucky devils. And he's standing here like some lovelorn loon with face-ache, and he's saying he wants me and the twins to move to Lincolnshire, because he's made a mistake. Great. My cup truly runneth over, and it's spilling arsenic.

I'm never at my best in the mornings. Physically, I am not a pretty sight. I have the sort of hair that goes into a spin during the night – if a cuckoo were to pass, she'd stop and lay an egg in it. My face doesn't settle back onto its skull before midday, and the veins in my hands show through like little blue ropes. The infamous MacRae temper is at its shortest until after the second cup of coffee, and I still haven't had the first. Jesus. A funeral yesterday, now this. I don't know which is worse.

'You'd better come in.' I widen the door to

allow him to pass. 'Where's Dolores?' I ask as casually as I can.

'Gone back to her husband,' is the answer.

I must say nothing. I don't need to say anything, because Alec loves me and he won't have her back. 'The answer is no, Den. I am not moving to Lincolnshire. I've nothing against Lincolnshire, since it's done me no harm, but you're there, so I'm not,' I tell my soon-to-be ex-husband. 'The decrees nisi are completed and all we need now is to sort out the children on our day in court. We've accepted the terms, and I declare this marriage over. It's finished, Den. It's kaput.'

His jaw drops and I see the wet inner side of that inflated lower lip. 'The nisi gives us all the chance to change our minds,' he advises me.

The dog runs in, and Den backs off. He couldn't possibly co-exist with something that deposits hair on his clothes. It's all too much for me, and I go into the kitchen, pour out one cup of coffee and carry it to the living room, slamming it onto a side table. I make a mental note to mop up later. Then I pick up my girls from the playpen in the dining room, and take them to visit their father.

'They're bigger,' he comments. 'And there's no sugar in my coffee.'

There's a time and a place for bad language, and the company of two babies means I can't shout, but I sure as hell can use the words. In a quiet voice, I tell him that it's my bloody coffee, and he can ... well ... I give him advice on sex and travel. He looks surprised and hurt, because people don't talk to him in such a fashion. I place the twins on the floor and they cuddle their puppy. It's probably unhygienic, but it's OK with me, because they love that little dog and she adores them. And let's face it – the kids would probably pick up more germs in that baby clinic. Also, I've made sure she doesn't have worms, because worms can–

'Anna I–'

'Bog off,' I say. 'My life's sorted. I've registered a new business, I have excellent partners, a good accountant and a brilliant lawyer. If you don't get out, I shall apply for an injunction, since this is harassment.'

The phone rings, and I dash into the hall to pick it up before someone else does.

'Anna?'

'Yes.'

'Is he there?'

'Yes.'

Alec is speaking normally rather than quietly, so I gather that Dolores has left. 'She was here when we got back last night, and Jo told the same lie – we've had water and electricity trouble. Anyway, I've thrown Dolly bloody Daydream out. She slept on the sofa. Sarah's with her gran. Can you talk?'

It's a big house, but I daren't risk it. 'Not really,' I say.

'Phone me as soon as you can,' he pleads.

Marie and Maureen are hanging over the banisters like a pair of marionettes with limp strings. 'Who the hell was that phoning at this time of day?' asks the latter.

I put a finger to my lips, then point towards the

living room. 'Den's in there,' I mouth.

They disappear as fast as two seasoned sprinters. Wish I could do the same.

When I return, he isn't even looking at his daughters. He doesn't care about anyone, and I am fairly sure why. When a woman gives birth, she gets as much responsibility as the managing director of ICI. She's in charge of a unit, what- ever the size. His mother taught him that he was a god, that he could do no wrong, and he expects every other woman to step aside while he does exactly as he pleases. There comes a time when a mother puts her foot down, and that occasion teaches her son that he's not quite the big deal. Men are our fault – I gathered that years ago.

'Why is the house full of people?' he asks.

I scarcely hear him, because I'm remembering stuff I'd rather forget. At least I have a new bed now. But I can still recall the laboured breathing, the hung-open mouth, the absence of expression in those dead eyes. I was just something he used, like a handkerchief, because I was a mere receiver of bodily fluid and something he played with. A toy, a handkerchief and a hot dinner – they were the items he needed. 'Go,' I say now.

'Who are they?' he asks again.

'Business partners. And friends. Yes, I have friends now. I'm not stuck with Round Table and Ladies' Circle and you. I don't even hate you, Den. You don't merit the energy required for strong emotion. I am divorcing you. As far as I know, Alec Halliwell is divorcing his wife. So, unless one of your other concubines is willing to step in at short notice, you're stuck with her and

305

that poor child.'

'I want my life back,' he says, eyebrows knitting in the middle.

'So do I, mate. And you are not, not, not destroying me again. You are your mother's creature. Get the pills from the psycho before you go off the rails.' Yes, his mother created this shambles of a man. My sisters, on the other hand, were born odd. Is there a chance that Den might have been all right with a different mother?

The situation deteriorates further when a taxi screams round the corner. Dolores alights. She looks a perfect fright in one of those terrible coats with fur attached to every edge, and loops of cord stitched round buttons and button holes. When she blinks, I swear I can feel the draught from all those false lashes. I stand outside my front door. 'Come in,' I say sweetly as she pushes me out of the way. I like this woman's style – apart from her choice of clothing and interior decoration, that is. She takes him by the hand and drags him outside – thank you, Dolores. Den pays the taxi driver before Dolly hurls my dear nearly-departed towards his car. Meek as a lamb, he opens the passenger door and she gets in. There is a God. And thank you, God.

Susan emerges from the dining room and tells me she's been hiding under the table behind the long cloth I bought in Ireland. Fair enough. That's pretty normal for these parts. Stephen is with his grandmother, so Susan minds my pair while I phone Alec.

'Did he hurt you?' is his first question.

'No. But I think I ruffled his feathers. Your wife

has dragged him off.'

'You're my wife,' he tells me. Little shivers dance all over my body. When someone you love says that sort of thing, you feel marvellous, don't you? 'Jo's livid,' he continues. 'Worried about her little sister – she's gone round to my mother's, so I'm guessing school won't see her today.'

'Alec?'

'What?'

'I love you so much, my toes curl.'

A round of applause from above puts an end to the nonsense. The puppeteer has tightened his marionettes' strings and they are celebrating something or other. 'You tell him, love,' Marie yells. Maureen does a whistle not dissimilar to the one employed yesterday by my lover. Susan starts to sing, 'She's getting married in the morning.' Her voice shows no sign of improvement.

'Is that our audience?' he asks now. 'Throw them out, my darling. Not Susan, of course. Tonight, I want you all to myself. I'll bring champagne and we'll have an orgy.'

I replace the receiver and shake my head. Isn't an orgy some kind of group therapy? And aren't bunches of grapes required? Another mental note – buy grapes. And find those old linen sheets – they'll do as togas.

It's been such a whirl this morning, swinging from despair to hopefulness, but we still have to do our thing. So it's Susan, me, Maureen and Marie acting the rubber pig (as Mrs Bee terms it) in an effort to educate our children. Halfway through *If You're Happy and You Know it Clap Your Hands*, I stop and look at the other madwomen.

They're doing all the actions – as was I a moment ago, and they look as if they should be having treatment. And I'm not sure what we're achieving here, because three babies and one retriever are fast asleep on the floor. Life's a mystery. I'm going for the grapes.

Jo has stayed with her sister and her grandmother. According to Alec's mum, Den and Dolores will pick up Sarah at the weekend. So only Susan and Stephen remain, and they're at the other end of the house. It seems that Den has accepted his fate and, while Dolly may be thick, she's certainly up to dealing with him a damned sight better than I ever managed.

The threatened orgy doesn't happen, because we're both exhausted, and we lie top-to-tail like sardines on the biggest of my sofas. We've eaten the grapes, at least, so that's OK. We war babies don't like to see anything wasted. I'm happy and frightened in roughly equal proportions. He's here now, we're together and safe, and the curtains are closed. But the world is still out there, isn't it? I can't lose him, daren't lose him. Because his face is at the opposite end of the sofa, I get down on the floor and crawl nearer to him. When I am settled, his arm comes to life and squeezes me. It's all right, Anna, I tell myself. It's real. He's real. I'm more than a toy, a handkerchief and a three course meal. I'm an electrician as well, and he's a bloody good ironer.

He wakes. 'Anna?'

'Hello.'

'I forgot,' he says sleepily.

'Forgot what?'

'Don't know. Can't remember.'

I kiss his hand and he opens it. There's a small box. A ring box.

'I remember now,' he announces in triumph. 'I was going to put it in the champagne, but I bet you would have swallowed it.' He gets up, kneels next to me and proposes for the third or fourth time. The little white band where my wedding ring sat for years is almost covered when he and I become engaged. The ring's white gold with seven diamonds in the shape of a flower. 'The wedding ring matches,' he says. 'Fits round the stones. It's in a safe at work, and there it will stay until we have our day. And I didn't forget at all.'

Of course he didn't. He drags the sofa against the door in case Susan wanders. More magic. And I've learned things, like I can travel, too. I am allowed to become an explorer, and there's no wet-lipped face hanging over me while I fulfil a role dictated by a man with the imagination of a tranquillized snail. There is, however, a hand over my mouth. Was that noise really coming from me? He's laughing at me. Even now, we laugh.

But there is a serious side to this. I am almost forty-one, and I am trying to give this man a son. We spoke about it briefly and only once, and if it's a fifth girl, she'll be loved. I just want the chance to be the one who hands over a healthy little boy to a man who deserves his wish to be granted.

Alec shudders, groans, his eyes still on me. He never does the shut-eyed thing at the end, when

309

some men appear to blot out a partner's face, perhaps imagining a different one. I stay where I am and look down at him. I'm no psychic, no foreteller of the future. But I know something. I have just become pregnant.

The first test comes back negative, but with a question mark attached. This is odd, I suppose, because a person is either pregnant or unpregnant, and question marks should not happen. Two weeks later, I have a positive. I didn't need it. I already knew that question mark was a dastardly impostor.

When I started with the twins, I was odd from the moment of conception. Not exactly ill, just different. And this is the same – it's the same difference, I mean. There are no cravings for coal with thick cut marmalade, but I do have a passenger, and I can't stand tea or cigarette smoke. I won't tell Alec yet, because there's many a slip during the first trimester, and I couldn't bear to disappoint him. So I hug my secret and hope my belly stays flat-ish for a while.

On my day in court, which is several weeks later than expected, the judge congratulates me on our civilized arrangements. Huh? She hasn't seen me with my bird's nest hair, wasn't there when I told Den to eff off back to Lincolnshire. She doesn't know I'm Alec's very willing and pregnant lover. But I had to come to court, because of my babies. They're six months old now, very amusing and almost as good as gold, and I am taking full custody with open access for their father. Not that he'll be interested, but I sometimes make an effort to be fair. Juliet is elsewhere and has sent one of her clerks. My divorce is so simple and well constructed that she isn't needed. Den hasn't turned up yet. He's good at missing unimportant occasions like this one.

Alec is also here, because he will be seeking full guardianship of Jo, and will be asking for access to Sarah. Even our court dates have dovetailed, and I take that as a good sign, although I'm not sure about who sends signs and whether the sender has my best interests at heart.

We are divorced. Final decrees will follow in a few weeks, and we are free at last. Outside in the street, Alec lifts me up and swings me round as if I am a child. Then he drags me into the nearest hostelry, because we don't want to bump into Den and Dolores – we've had enough of the pair of them.

The place is buzzing with lawyers. Briefs are handed – possibly for the first time – to silks by solicitors. Over a whisky, a barrister will discover who he is supposed to defend and against which charge. I'm fairly sure this shouldn't be happening outside chambers, but it is, so who am I to try to change the system?

'Champagne?' Alec asks.

'No, thanks,' I reply.

'Have you gone teetotal, or what?' he demands to know. 'I can't remember the last time you had a glass of wine.'

That's the other thing that happens when I carry a child. I can't drink alcohol or tea. No idea why, but there it is. 'I'm not teetotal,' I say. 'I'm or what. And, when I'm or what, I can't drink,

311

though I did enjoy the occasional glass of Guinness when I got to about seven months with the girls. They must have needed the iron.'

He opens his mouth and breathes in an enormous amount of air. Alec's face is so easy to read that I can just sit here and watch emotions colliding in the eyes. I see joy, fear, more joy. And I see tears welling from a heart as big as Africa. He's still in shock. 'Anna,' he says several times.

'Yes? That's my name.'

'But...' He swallows. 'We've been...' He leans closer. 'We've been having sex.'

I laugh. 'That's how babies are made, sweetheart. You see, the man and the woman get together–'

'I love you.'

'You'd better. Because in about six and a half months, our baby will be making its debut. Now, don't go all excited on me.'

'But I shouldn't have – we shouldn't have–'

'And don't talk daft. Any child of yours and mine can withstand a battering. It's very well cosseted, lying in a bed of fluid inside a bag tough enough to carry a ton of shopping. We won't lose a baby by making love. Now, get me a St Clements and we'll say no more about it.'

He seems to have been poleaxed to his chair. One of his tears goes on its travels, and he dashes it away, since we are in a public place. At home – our home – he would have allowed it to find its own way south. 'Oh, God,' he whispers.

'No, the name's still Anna. You know, darling, it's so easy to work with all our nearest and dearests' names – they're unforgettable. Alec and Anna,

Den and Dolores, Susan and Stephen, Maureen and Marie – so wonderfully alphabetical.'

'How long have you known?'

'I learned my alphabet at my mother's knee.'

'Don't be obtuse. How long?'

'A few weeks.'

'Then why…?'

'In case it came to nothing, I kept it to myself. I love you so much, I couldn't have borne your pain.'

'But you will bear my child.'

'Of course.'

I have heard people say that it's terrible to see a grown man cry. It is no such thing. There's no point in trying to hide so profuse a flow, so he just allows it to happen and waits for it to stop. You see, that's my Alec. Stuff happens, and he waits for it to stop. I know he's embarrassed, yet in another sense, he is way past embarrassment. We both are. A man in shirt sleeves and a waistcoat passes a whisky to me. 'See if he'll drink that,' he says in a clipped, legal voice. 'Divorce can be a dreadful business.' The man puts on his jacket and picks up a briefcase. 'Don't worry, old chap,' he advises Alec. 'It'll all be for the best, you'll see.'

'I don't know what I did to deserve you.' The words stumble past tears.

'You're good in bed. In fact, you're excellent.'

There's a rainbow now, sun shining through raindrop tears. He has a wonderful smile – I'm always saying that. 'Am I really good?' he asks.

'You know you are.'

He's stopped weeping. 'Well, that's brilliant.

313

But only with you. Only ever with you.'

I tell him that his book on tantric sex must have worked wonders for him. 'It did,' he answers. 'Because my silliness put you in charge that first time. I was terrified and inadequate. You're one quality woman, and I wasn't good enough.' He reaches for my hand. 'If I have never told you what you did for my self-confidence, I am sorry. You've allowed me to become me. It was ... difficult. I loved her, but it was the love of one young animal for another. I changed, she remained the same. She hurt me and I curled like an autumn leaf. You were the bringer of springtime.'

Oh, bugger. Now it's my turn to cry.

He passes me a handkerchief. 'Stop showing me up,' he says. How well he knows me. The truth is, we don't give a fig what anyone thinks, which is just as well, because Den and Dolores are here – brilliantly tardy, of course.

'Are you all right?' My ex offers a brief imitation of concern.

I dab at my eyes. 'Fine,' I tell him. 'I'm pregnant.'

Den shrugs. 'Too late. I hear we're divorced now.'

Alec stands and shakes Den's hand. 'Thank you for removing the thorn from my side, old fellow. Oh, the baby's mine. We're getting married very soon.'

The soggy lip hangs again. 'What? All this time you've been– Hell's bells.'

Dolores turns and pushes her way out of the crowded bar. Alec and Den are squaring up to each other, but I know nothing will happen. If something did happen, Den wouldn't cope. He

314

hasn't coped since his mother died. He stares at me, and I see only hatred in eyes I once thought beautiful, so dark that the pupils don't show. He leaves.

'That's that,' Alec pronounces.

'You enjoyed telling him.'

'I'm proud, Anna. He knows what he's lost, and he's learning what he's gained. Dolly may be daft, but she's controlling. He'll be lucky to get supper tonight, because she'll be mithering him for a wedding ring. Sex is something she trades in – for clothes, shoes and so forth. But marriage scares him.'

I agree. 'He should have married his mother. She liked him.'

Now, we're both laughing. So that's better, isn't it?

Nothing lasts.

We've told everyone who needs to know, and most females are knitting. Even Jo's having a go at a matinee jacket. All our bedrooms are filled, so Maureen and Marie stay in St Helens. Sometimes, they sleep in our living room, but, for the most part, they go home after doing their Third Party jobs. The two smaller bedrooms here contain my twins and Susan's Stephen. Jo shares with my twins, and we need a bigger house. Alec and I have the master, and Susan sleeps in the second. There's no more room at the inn.

When the next baby comes, Susan will need to move out. If she doesn't want to go to Eccleston, she can have the caravan. Because if Charlie and Marie have Alec's main bedroom, Maureen and

Susan will need to share a room, while Stephen can have the smallest. I am sick of all this mental juggling. I'm looking at the architect's plans for three further bedrooms and another bathroom. They've been passed by the authorities, and work is due to start any day now. The bedrooms will have to be propped up by something underneath, so we're having yet another reception room and a large study. At the present time, I have Charlie in the caravan and–

And the doorbell's ringing.

I open the door, and my hand flies of its own accord to my throat. 'Katherine.' I can't move. No. Nothing lasts. I feel as if somebody has nailed both my feet to the floor. She's beautifully dressed and gorgeous, and I don't want her in my house, near my babies, near my life. They must both go away and stay away for ever, because I cannot be near what they are.

'May I come in?' She kisses me on both cheeks and I remember Judas at the Last Supper. Alec's at work. My girls are asleep, while Susan has gone out with Stephen for some bits of shopping. I am alone with one of my enemies for the first time in years. She is disconcertingly beautiful. Now thirty-six, she looks like a fresh-faced teen-ager. 'How are you?' I ask. I don't know why I enquired, because I have managed for so long not to care.

She stands in the doorway to the living room. A small movement in her forehead displays minor agitation. 'Tell me they're not like we were.'

I am confused. 'What?'

'Your twins. They're not like Rebecca and me?'

316

'No. Not at all.' I remember my fears. I don't want this woman to bring them back to me.

She sits and stretches those amazing legs to one side. 'You never noticed, did you? You never saw that it was all Rebecca and that I was terrified of her. Yet I remain so scared of being as sick as she is, I aborted my second baby last month, because I'm afraid.'

This isn't easy. The thing to remember about sociopaths is that they are often super-intelligent, yet unaware of their own condition. They are believable, even likeable. They function well and hold down great jobs – this one lectures in Latin and Greek at Oxford. Greek. I remember the Greek. 'Dad found the tin with your codes in,' I tell her. 'They were in the woods. And I took them to Mother Gertrude. It all shocked her, but the repeated "KILL ANNA" meant that she had to translate that bit for me so that I could watch my back.'

'Quite.' Not a flicker on the face, just beauty without lines, an empty shell. She's a painting. 'I had to dance to my sister's tune, or my name would have joined yours in the tin. I was not allowed to show fear, happiness or anything between those two extremes. Even now, I often act as if she's watching me in case I show weakness.'

She is opening her blouse. Between her breasts, a capital K is entwined with an R. 'She did this with a needle, a small knife and Indian ink. She has the same on her chest. Rebecca wrote my essays, because she said mine were foolish. Perhaps I betrayed the fact that underneath it all, I had feelings. The fights – I was defending myself. In the end, I stopped competing – it was easier. You have to start believing me, Anna, because she is mad.'

I don't know what to think, what to feel. She folds back the flap of her designer bag and hands me a brown envelope. 'That's from Harley Street – read it if you like. He says you can phone him and talk to him. I haven't got the illness. Rebecca has. She's extremely unwell unless she takes three million tablets a day. There's a list of what's wrong with me in there.' She waves a hand at the envelope. 'There is a lot wrong, and it's all because of Beckie. But I daren't have a child in case it turns out like her. What if I carry the gene?'

'What if I do?' I ask.

She asks me what my blood group is, and I tell her it's A positive. Then she drops the bombshell. 'Anna, don't get upset. Dad was O rhesus negative, the universal donor. He had a card from when he was in the army. If he hadn't been such a soak, he could have kept people alive through surgery until the hospital got their own group sent up from the blood bank. I believe that you have Mother's blood group, because they were definitely together when you were conceived – the war hadn't started, and he hadn't gone for re-training.'

I am shaking. 'What do you mean? Tell me, Kate. Tell me now!'

Her face is not as still, not as perfect as it was when she arrived just minutes ago. And she's talking, talking, talking. About private detectives and people who lived in Broom Street and the night our mother was raped because Dad was

318

away on combat exercise. And a rare blood group, and having to be careful, having to give her own blood in case she ever needs it. On and on and on... Then I'm gone. I descend gratefully onto the sofa on which Alec and I made this baby, and I hear no more.

I am calm. I am calm. I am in Ormskirk Hospital, and my baby is fine, and Alec is here. Kate is not here. They've done a load of tests and I've been shifted about like a wooden thing – sit, stand, give me your arm, you're going to feel a little scratch, have you seen any blood when you've been to the bathroom – blah, blah, blah.

And all I can think is that Susan and Marie were sent to me by my mother, that it was all meant to happen the way it did, because Susan and Marie, like my mother, were raped. The one woman who knew about Mam is still alive in an old folks' home in Bolton. Perhaps I'll visit, perhaps I won't. For the first time, I am truly glad that my poor father is dead. I can see him now watching Kate and Beckie from his front window, a look of puzzlement in his eyes. They aren't yours, Dad.

I wonder whether my mother wanted to die. It would have been hard for her to raise the twins, harder still for her to keep the truth from me and my father. Yet she couldn't have told him right away, because he was going to war, and she wanted him to live. He would probably have gone AWOL anyway, so that he might find the villain and kill him. He, too, carried the slow-burning but don't-be-there-when-it-happens MacRae temper.

As for the rest of the story – the snow came, and the doctor came too late, and she died. Fate. Is that the answer to all of it?

My darling Alec keeps talking to me, but I'm not hearing much. I think they gave me some sort of tranquilliser, maybe phenobarbitone. They can use that on pregnant women. I think it's really for epilepsy, but it quietens the screaming nerves. The architect's coming. I think Susan will be in. There's bread in the chest freezer in the garage. Building starts soon. I hope someone makes sure Charlie's all right, because he'll never recover. Alcoholism is for life. There's no cure, only abstinence.

Emily's teething again. Susan knows where the stuff is.

'Anna!' He is squeezing my hand.

'Yes? Get me out of here.'

'But you've had a shock, and–'

'Now, Alec. I mean it. She'll destroy us. She broke my bike.'

A doctor arrives. The points on his shirt collar have curled upwards. He has no Alec at home to iron for him. He's smiling at me. I can't see anything to smile about, but to each his own. 'You may go home,' he says.

'I was going anyway,' I advise him. There are things to be done, and only I can do them. Sitting up isn't easy, because I'm a bit dizzy, but never mind. I may even ask Mrs Bee for her gun once my head clears. Kate must go. If I have to pepper her plump, pretty little backside with shot, I bloody well shall.

Must have slept all the way here. He's carrying

me over the threshold and placing me on our baby-making sofa. The architect's here. Nice man. He takes one look at me and volunteers to leave, but I tell Alec to deal with it. Plans to be submitted, house to be extended. Sleep.

Jo's holding my hand when I wake. She's trying to smile through unshed tears. I am lucky. So many people love me. When I open my eyes for a second time, Susan has taken over the vigil. Such a strange day. Pheno-wotsit has made me limp and dizzy and I can't keep up. Then it's Alec, eyes boring into my head, shirt open at the throat, not an accountant today. So very tired.

I am in bed, and I don't know how I got here. Yes, I do. He is behind me, his body hard against mine. We are like spoons in a drawer, and he isn't asleep. I can tell from his breathing that he is awake. And he knows I'm no longer in the land of Nod, because this man and I have been familiar with each other since long before we met – we remembered us from the future. It's a circle, you see. We climb aboard and try to find our place, but some of us are lucky, and the one we happen to cling to is the right person. The rest have to settle for what's there – I did that with Den. Those who meet the wrong folk are the people who lose their balance and fall off the circle, God help them. We're back to God. Again.

'What did they give me?' I ask.

'Nothing, darling. I think you're allergic to your sister. You went into shock. But they didn't give you any drugs.'

'And our baby's all right?'

'Fine. But, my love, I really think you should

321

hear Kate out when you feel up to it.'

'Hmmph.'

'What?'

'Has she tried to get you into bed yet? Even at the age of thirteen, they pinched my boyfriends. Then I found Rebecca having sex with Peter – I liked him a lot.'

'But you didn't find Kate.'

I think about that. 'I never found her, but that doesn't prove she wasn't at it. They were nightmares. They plied Dad with drink – leave it, Alec.'

'All right, stay calm. Mrs Bee came in to see you, and she was crying like a child. She's on to her second cot blanket, and you'll have to buck up.' He pauses. 'So they're your half-sisters?'

I turn and face him. 'Probably. The nutcase who ... who attacked my mother is likely to have been their dad. Susan is part of my bit of the circle. She landed in the same area as I did.'

'What?'

'Never mind. It's a theory.'

'Please tell me, Anna.'

He has to live in my head, doesn't he? 'You've heard people say what goes around comes around?'

'Yes.'

'Are you keeping me talking just to make sure I'm OK, Alec?'

'No. Carry on.'

I take a deep, shuddering breath. 'Mam was raped. I could do nothing for her when she bled to death. I just washed her hands and face, combed her hair and waited for someone to come and help me with the body.'

'Right.'

'So she sent me Susan and Marie. They landed in my part of the circle.'

He's smiling. I can hear him smiling. 'I love the way you think, the way you talk. So you have to do the paying back? You are responsible for all the sins in the world, and your dead mother makes sure you pay your dues?'

'Listen, Long Shanks. If you don't want the answer, don't ask the question. I know what I mean.'

'So do I, darling. So do I.'

A few hours ago, I was on a hospital trolley wearing one of those open-all-the-way-down-the-back designer overalls, so elegant and stylish. My belly was prodded, my child was listened to, and my mind had taken a holiday without picking up passport and ticket. They weighed me, measured me, stole a gallon and a half of blood, and I was fed up to the back teeth. Those medics did sod all for me, so I'm turning now to my proper doctor. When I began to love this man, I started to love myself. And, through loving Anna, I learned to love my children with such ferocity that it hurts.

It's a circle. Tender loving, careful, slow and sensual – that's my medicine, Dr Turned-up-Collar. I can live without the bloody hospitals. But not without the man who whispers softly while he brings me back to the only life I want. His life. My life. Ours.

Fourteen

Billy MacRae's fight against alcoholism was a lonely one. He would jump on the wagon and stay there for a few weeks, but reality hurt, and he needed his medicine. Another possible reason for his continuing descent was that although he loved Anna with all his heart, he could not take to his younger daughters, and that worried him. They were odd. Each had a look of her older sister, yet neither one resembled the other. Dead eyes. And several times, they brought whisky for him. He had no idea of its provenance and was not inclined to enquire, since the answer might have pushed him further into the dark and isolating world of dipsomania.

Anna stopped yelling at him, even Bert and Elsie gave up the fight, while Polly, the housekeeper sent by Linda Mellor from the big house, said not a word on the subject. A kind enough woman, she told herself that she was here to cook, clean, wash, iron and shop so that Anna would have a chance of an education. Polly Fox wasn't hanging round to separate him from the booze at the end of a hard day's work. So, with that pragmatism known to most people in service, she got on with it all and kept her mouth shut.

By 1953, Anna MacRae, having reached the age of eighteen, was studying for her advanced

School Certificates. She had gained nine subjects at the lower level, and was now working on English Literature, French and History. With no need and no desire to attend university, she had been accepted at Didsbury Training College in Manchester, where she would be prepared for a future in educating infants and juniors. A people person, she wanted to teach children, not subjects, and it was her intention to study Religious Education, Physical Education and English at college.

Deciding on RE as her main area of study had not been difficult, since there were a few things that had been omitted during her seven years at St Mary's. The Old Testament had been ignored for the most part, as had other Christianities, Buddhism, Islam and Judaism. There was more than one way to heaven or hell, and she needed to know.

Dad was driving her crackers. She needed college, needed not to be here, since she could do nothing constructive to alleviate the problem. Like Polly Fox, Anna was forced to accept the knowledge that it wasn't worth it, wasn't her job. She loved him, and she was watching him die. Had he been dying from cancer or some other horrible disease, she might have coped. But this was slow suicide, and she couldn't manage to accept it. Mam had died by accident, and this was different, because Dad wouldn't seek help.

Living with a drunk drove her out of the house. She often did her homework in Bolton Central Library, which had become a haven of peace where she was left alone to do her own thing with no interference from staff. She was at the library when she met Den Fairbanks, who relieved her of her virginity within weeks and who became her shadow thereafter. He loved her. He said repeatedly that he loved her, and that was what she had sought. Love. She wanted someone of her own, so she kept him away from Dad and away from Kate and Beckie.

The twins, at thirteen, were sexually active. Anna knew that, since she had found Beckie with Peter Simpson, who had been Anna's third or fourth boyfriend. She wouldn't give him sex, so Beckie had stepped in and spread herself beneath him in a place in which she was almost certain to be found by her older sister. Sometimes, when Anna closed her eyes, she saw the look of triumph burning in Beckie's face. With the boy labouring over her, she had fixed all her attention on Anna, because this was another game of chess, and she had won again.

Fine. If the twins wanted to get themselves pregnant, that was OK with Anna. She hadn't seen Kate on that fateful day, yet something told Anna that Kate had been watching her sister and Peter at play. Anna believed that once Peter had recovered, Kate would take her twin's place and commit the same deed. Anna remained their target, but she was going to Manchester so, as far as she was concerned, they could do as they liked.

She went just once to see Dr Corcoran, who had looked after Dad before he had been released into the community. 'He's drinking himself to death,' she said. 'He's drunk at work, at home, and in the pub.'

Dr Corcoran nodded. 'He's not the only one, Miss MacRae. And I know you have always demanded the truth from me, so I must tell you now that alcohol has become his drug of choice.'

She fiddled in her handbag with the rosary she was given at school. Although she didn't regard herself as a dyed-in-the-wool Catholic, Anna remembered that a good woman had spent almost half her life with these beads at her waist. Sometimes, she spoke to God and asked for help, yet she knew in her bones that no creature, living or dead, would improve the behaviour of Billy MacRae.

'How much is he drinking?' the doctor asked.

'No idea. There are boxes of bottles all over the woods, and I find them in his bedroom, under the kitchen sink, in the shed – all over the place. I can't manage him.'

'Nor should you attempt to do that. He has to go alone for help, or alone to his death. He is not your responsibility.'

'He's my father.'

'Yes, and you have a life to begin, your own adult life. University?'

'Training college. I want to teach younger children.'

'Good for you. Now, listen. Do nothing for your father. Let him look after himself and, once you have gone to college, leave him all alone. There will be nowhere for him to turn except to doctors. This may sound cruel, and he might well stop eating and concentrate solely on the booze. Whatever, he won't listen to you.'

'We have help in the house. Meals are made for us.'

'Then get rid of that help when you move to Manchester.'

It seemed cold and cruel, yet Anna understood what the doctor meant. Screaming, pleading, reasoning, asking – none of these had worked. So Dad had to do it for himself. There were places where he could be helped – Dr Corcoran had said so, but Dad had to go by himself. No one could make the decision for him, and no one could steer him towards the right thing. She hadn't been able to save Mam thirteen years ago, and she couldn't save Dad now. But it still hurt. It would always hurt.

It was a lonely feeling. Anna, at eighteen, was teetering on the brink of womanhood, and all she saw around her were the props that had held her upright during some difficult years. She was the only one left. The rest of the upper sixth had escaped, and were having a party in the house of one of the rich girls. Anna could not attend, because she had her unpredictable and sick father to deal with, and her boyfriend to meet in a couple of hours. She had been summoned by his mother, and his mother was not a woman to be denied.

She walked past the statue of St Francis of Assisi, the soft footfalls of her indoor shoes leaving no echo of the past. Washrooms and sixth form lavatories to the right, gymnasium-cum-assembly hall straight ahead. Silver-edged stairs led up to art, gold-edged to the science that never happened. Upstairs was the music room, desks and chairs tiered steeply like the arrangements in some of the better football grounds. She would never come here again, because she hadn't remained completely Catholic, since it didn't make full sense. It was over. She should now know everything about being an adult. She knew next to nothing.

The Bishop of Salford had granted permission for her to attend a non-denominational college, and Anna resented that. Why should she need permission? Many girls her age were working or married, some were mothers. At eighteen, she was old enough to join the forces and be killed, but she needed to plead with a bishop for a place at Didsbury. Silly.

It was inevitable that Gerty would find her. A part of Anna needed to say thank you and goodbye, but her cowardly side wanted to run, just as the others had run. Mother Gertrude had been very patient and kind to this almost non-believer, so she would face the nun, because facing up to whatever came along was part of being grown up.

'So it's there you are,' said a little Irish voice.

Anna turned. 'Yes, it's here I am, Mother.'

'Did you say farewell to Pauline and Rita?'

'I did.'

'And here's you off to a non-Catholic college with every intention of studying comparative religion.'

'Yes, Mother.'

'Why?'

'Because it exists, and I have to know.'

Mother tutted. 'But when you're at the end of your rope, it's a priest you'll be sending for. A pity your friend Father Brogan died. Perhaps he might have knocked some sense into you.'

Anna chuckled. 'He tried for years, but my skull was too thick to allow it all inside. I think I'm too ... analytical by nature to just accept what I am ordered to accept. But, having studied moral philosophy in the sixth, I can now lay claim to the third right of man, which is, as I'm sure you know, the right to have a family and to educate them in accordance with my own chosen beliefs.'

'Will you come with me to chapel before you leave?'

'No, thank you, Mother. I stayed just to tell you I'm grateful. And to look at the place that has housed me for so long. It's all very ... brown, isn't it?'

'Huh. Still the bold girl, is it? Well, you have been a credit to us and I'm proud of you. All the same, I wish...' The voice died, and the little, black-veiled head shook slightly. 'God bless you, Miss Anna MacRae.'

'And you, Mother.'

The nun left the building and walked across to the convent. Now, only Anna remained, though a distant clatter of buckets announced the advent of those nuns who cleaned, because they had received no education. Tears pricked and threatened, but she held them at bay. So alone. Dad was on his way to death via alcohol, Bert and Elsie were tired, while her sisters were ... were her sisters.

There was only Den and his dreaded mother, his lovely father. They would have to be her family now. She needed him, because he was there.

330

He was a way out, and she would grow to love him. His mother was rather frightening, but perhaps that was the way mothers acted when their children grew and went off to London for an education. Or when they brought home somebody who'd attended a Catholic school. She had no blueprint, no mother of her own with whom she might compare the protective Mrs Fairbanks.

She walked for the last time down to Deane Road and waited for the bus to town. Adulthood loomed, and she didn't feel ready. She was going to college, and she didn't feel equipped for that, either. No bells would ring to summon her from lesson to lesson. There would be choices to be made, decisions to be taken. Suddenly aware that there was almost no one on whom she might lean, she was filled with fear. Thank goodness for Den, she thought as she walked onto the bus. This was her final journey as a child. Tomorrow, Anna MacRae would be a woman. And that was official.

I'm thinking about having my hair cut shorter, but Alec wouldn't like it. He loves to brush it, play with it, and use it as an anchor when we make love, since he likes to look into my eyes during the act. I'm thinking about all kinds of things, actually, because I won't allow my mind to settle on Kate.

Glad the house extension has begun. No one needs seven bedrooms, I suppose, though we do have rather a lot of children between us. Even little Sarah, who visits infrequently, deserves a small space of her own. Juliet is drawing up something

331

or other, so that when we leave the house, more of its value will come to me, as I have spent some of my legacy on the project.

Alec and I are to be married in a few days. It will be low-key, though I fear there may be a plot afoot, and the Hughes family will have instigated it. God help us. It could turn into another fight with chairs and drinking vessels. Perhaps we should elope?

Charlie is doing OK in the caravan. He's not intrusive, though he enjoys a meal with us a couple of times a week. He's moving in with his wife tomorrow. And always, always, there will be a room in my house, or in a caravan, for Susan. She's become more of a little sister to me than...

When my hair is wet, it behaves in a manner commensurate with its position in life. I can scrape it back in the style of a flamenco dancer, because I have my mother's bones, and the slight puffiness of morning has long disappeared from my face. I look good. It is suddenly vital that I look good. A pair of large, gold hoops depending from my ears completes the picture. Had I been less blonde, I might have looked Spanish.

Dressed in a kaftan that hides my little bump, I descend the stairs. I hear them talking. In the shower when they arrived, I felt the intrusion, though I could not hear it. She got here when I was rinsing my hair. How did I know? No idea. It's an automatic thing that developed during childhood. It is a sixth sense job.

Judas kisses me again. He is dressed this time in a deceptively plain suit that must have cost several arms and legs, and he is disguised once more as a

332

woman. The woman tells me I look beautiful, and her companion informs her that Anna always looks beautiful.

We sit. For the first time ever, there are tears in Kate MacRae's eyes. Has she been in the company of onions? But there's stuff happening in my head, little pinpricks of memory returning, and I am uncomfortable. It's as if I have spent the past few years under some kind of canopy, a sunshade, perhaps, and the light is fighting its way through tiny holes. I once told someone – can't remember who – that Rebecca was the light, and Kate was the reflective surface from which Rebecca bounced and gained strength. But I was a kid then, and what do kids know?

'Where is she now?' I ask suddenly.

Kate shrugs. 'Well, you'll probably get a visit from the police any day now. Interpol is looking for her, but I doubt they'll have any success. She's disappeared with a man and about five million pounds' worth of French francs. It'll be South America. We won't hear of her or from her again, because she's clever.'

'I see.' Bert once said that they'd end up either in Parliament, or in jail. 'So they'll be somewhere that won't extradite them.'

Kate stands, crosses the room and hands me a sheet of paper. 'Her final letter to me. Read it. You're at the core of it, anyway. You always were at the core. Posted in Paris three days after Rebecca and the man left. That's what the police told me, anyway.'

So I read. I read aloud about their secret society, so exclusive that it had only two members. I learn

333

that Kate was never any use, in spite of the training given to her by the superior twin. *You always loved her more than you loved me. Pretty Anna? She can't hold a candle to either of us in the looks department. A pity you didn't listen, because you could be sharing the high life with me. I watched you watching her. Always, you wanted her good opinion. Well she's all yours now, and I am out of here.*

I look up. 'You loved me when we were children?'

She nods. 'God knows I tried to please her. But, as my psychiatrist says, when my ego and super ego kicked in, I became a balanced person. Until she unseated me repeatedly.'

'While Rebecca's id remained in charge,' I say. 'Strange. I was talking to myself just the other day about Freud's theories, but I was applying them to him.' I jerk a thumb in the direction of my lover.

He clears his throat, which didn't need clearing. 'So I'm *him* now? Wonderful. She is marrying this him in a few days, Kate.'

Kate smiles. 'Shut up, Alec. Be a witness, by all means, but don't make me laugh, because laughter will turn to tears.'

And in that moment, I know. There's no point in asking myself why and how I suddenly know, because I've always been quick to act and react. My instincts are seldom wrong, as I have been studying people, albeit subconsciously, since Mam died. Some folk collect ships in bottles; I bypass the ships and collect people. Some are given to me, others are chosen. This one is a bit of both, I suppose. Given to me the day my mother died, Kate is now picked by me. 'I'm sorry,' I tell her. 'I was just a child, and I didn't dare look too closely. Come here.'

And I sit with my sister on the baby-making sofa. She touches my face for the first time in thirty-odd years. 'Anna borra,' she whispers. 'Inside and out, Anna borra.'

'Welcome home,' I tell her.

The article I have agreed to marry is melting at the other side of this large room. Although I am busy with my sister, I make time to thank goodness yet again that I have a man who can cry without loss of perceived dignity. He's human, delightfully so.

'Alec?' Kate leans forward. 'Are you all right?' She can ask people how they are, is capable of caring. How can I have missed so much? It's because I moved in with Dad. During their teenage years, I was scarcely there, and that's how I got it all so wrong.

He blows his nose on something that looks like it was born in a cow pat – ah yes, he was changing plugs in his car before the meal we failed to finish. I smile at both of them. 'He isn't just all right, Kate. He's a star. But never lend him a handkerchief.' And she bursts out laughing, and it's real laughter and yes, the tears come. It pours from her in fractured sentences, the odd sexual behaviour, Rebecca's determination to turn Kate into a clone of herself. 'Until I was fourteen, I thought I was a lesbian. She did things, made me do things...' Kate glances at Alec.

'It's OK,' I tell her. 'He's unshockable – he lives with me.' But I am not unshockable. However, I

335

will not let that show.

Alec announces his intention to make coffee, and leaves the room.

'He's lovely,' says Kate. 'I never cared much for Den. And you did the right thing. Every time she was in London, he arranged a business meeting and slept with Rebecca. I wouldn't have said anything, but now that you're divorced, I–'

Alec is back. He is in the company of a large piece of wood, a retriever and a bemused expression. 'She's eaten a leg off the kitchen table.'

'Teething,' I tell him.

The dog isn't bothered. Knowing herself to be beautiful and irresistible, she launches herself at new company, pawing at a very good suit and slobbering all over our visitor's hands. My sister's hands. But Kate is not daft, and she deals quite competently with the… Oh. Well, she was doing OK till the pup leapt onto the sofa, parked herself next to the newcomer, leaned her full weight against her and started to pant. As dog owners, we are failures.

I look at the piece of wood. 'She's teething,' I repeat.

'So are our twins, but they don't chew legs off things.' He shakes what's left of the newish table's fourth limb. 'Naughty girl,' he says. 'Everything slides west now. I wouldn't care if you were starved, but why can't you be good?'

'Are you taking to me, dearest heart?' I ask.

He waves the lump of wood once more. 'I'll deal with you later,' he threatens. 'I am going to make coffee. Definitely this time.'

Kate is smiling – she's one stunning woman.

'He's the right one, Anna.'

'Yes. He's delightful.' He's going to deal with me later. Sometimes, this man of mine can be a bit much for a pregnant mother of twins. Even so, I shiver inside at the thought of being dealt with later.

'Anna?'

'Yes?' I like having a sister, but I shall take it slowly.

She won't. 'I'm due a long break, and my assistant lecturer is capable,' she tells me. 'May I come to your wedding?'

'Of course. Mind, there'll be some rum folk there – Scousers with attitude. If you're staying for a while, come tomorrow and meet your nieces. And there's another one.' I pat my belly. 'This one's Alec's.'

She tells me how lucky I am, explains her abortions once more. It's in her genes, so she daren't breed. I can understand that. No one knows Rebecca as well as Kate does.

It's late when she leaves with Alec. I tell myself several times that I mustn't worry, that she'll be fine, that I am lucky because I have a whole new relationship to explore. Then I clean my teeth, remove make-up and wait for him to come home. Because he promised to deal with me.

Dad hadn't bothered to wake up. Again. He was becoming less and less reliable, and he should not be let out with axes. Anna called him from the bottom of the stairs and, after three unproductive shouts, she went up to fetch him.

Trying not to breathe, she stood in his bedroom. It wasn't just the smell of whisky and beer; Dad was filthy. He lived for days in the same clothes, slept in them, ate in them. Well, he pretended to eat, but most of his food went for pigswill, and he probably thought no one knew.

He was eating less, drinking more. The whites of his eyes were yellow. Even the palms of his hands were advertisements for his condition, since they, too, were jaundiced, and they bore other marks – bright red ones that spoke volumes on the subject of liver failure. Capillaries had exploded all over his face, and he looked like a tramp. But he was her dad, and she had to keep him going during these last few weeks before college.

She shook him. 'Dad? Dad?'

There was still no response. 'Don't panic, Anna,' she said aloud.

For half an hour, she sat with him, holding one of his unclean hands in her softer ones. The not going to work didn't matter any more, because this man needed to leave the village today. His daughter wanted him to die peacefully, in comfort and in a clean bed.

Polly stood in the doorway. 'Has he gone?' she asked in a whisper.

'Not yet. Would you run up and ask Mrs Mellor to phone Dr Corcoran? He's in charge of a few rest homes for ex-servicemen. He'll know what we should do. The doctor needs to be told about the blood, the not eating and...' She swallowed. 'I think he's had a stroke – his mouth's crooked.'

Polly ran. Anna noted blood on the floor, was fairly sure that there would be more in the bed, and she'd seen what happened when he used the lavatory, because he often forgot to clean away the bright red décor in the bowl.

Time went out of order. One minute, she was holding her father's hand; the next found her alone in that filthy room. Elsie brought the village doctor, who gave Anna an injection.

When she woke, she was in her own room. It was almost dark, and Elsie was sitting next to her. And the memories returned as if borne on a powerful gust of wind. The ambulance men wrinkling their noses because of the smell, her sisters standing and staring when the stretcher was pushed into the vehicle. Their dad was dying, but they might as well have been watching an old Laurel and Hardy, since their expressions were almost always the same. Kate's face was the more mobile of the two, but both were quite wooden.

'Anna?'

'Yes?'

'He died, love. He took a second massive stroke and went.'

Anna gulped. It was over, and she felt nothing at all.

'I'll stay with you tonight, pet. The doc says that injection can make you woozy for a while. Now, I'll make us both a cuppa. Oh and don't worry over the funeral – Bert's been to the Co-op.'

Anna didn't feel much until the day before the funeral. Then the whole bloody shooting match moved in on her, because both her parents had died covered in the stuff. In the arms of Polly Fox, Anna allowed her grief to pour. Then Linda arrived and took Anna to say goodbye to her father in the chapel of rest at the Co-op funeral parlour. Neither of them mentioned taking the twins, because they were not fit company, even for the dead.

Linda wept. 'I tried to look after him.'

'We both did. There was no more to be done,' Anna said. 'And see how normal he looks now – almost beautiful.'

'He was beautiful.'

Anna knew then that Linda Mellor had lost her heart to a hopeless drunk, and that fact hurt almost as much as Dad's death. 'He's all right now, Linda. No more pain.'

'Yes. Come on. Let's go home.'

Billy MacRae was laid to rest on a beautiful day. Birds sang, the sun shone, and everyone wept. Apart from the twins, of course. They employed themselves by reading names and dates on surrounding headstones. Anna barely glanced at them. She knew, but was unable to prove that they had given Dad alcohol. They were demons from hell, and they had no right to attend a Christian service.

Billy was placed above his beloved and long-dead wife. On that very spot, Thomas Brogan had poured the last of his supply of whisky; now, Frankie was in the company of a man she had loved, a man who had been incapable of facing withdrawal from booze. But they were together at last, and Anna drew a small amount of comfort from that.

It was over. She had done this all alone, because Den was sitting exams in London and had been

340

unable to attend. She could do some things alone, it seemed. Perhaps growing up would not be too bad after all.

Fifteen

The thing about weddings is that they creep up on you like muggers, vagabonds, and that landmark birthday you've always dreaded. You're confident that everything's under control, and you're going to be fine, because nothing's happening for six weeks, a month, a fortnight. Then suddenly, when you were least expecting trouble, it's going to be next Saturday and oh, my God, are we ready? The answer is almost invariably that we are definitely unready.

Lists. You start off with lists and end up with lists of lists, and the dog's eaten them all anyway, so there was never any point. You thank goodness Maureen's making your dress, the marquee is ordered, your twin babies have at least three changes of clothing in case they vomit in the registry, and you are very grateful that every neighbour in the area has opened up heart and freezer in order to accommodate the food.

Oh, hell. You promised to phone his mother, who owns two new suits and which one shall she wear? She's so pleased for us that she will weep again on the phone, and I am dangerously near to spilling saline of my own. But the call has to be made. I prefer the lovely, cuddly woman in the blue one, so I ring and tell her so. You see, if I had a list, I could cross that one off. Dry your eyes, Anna, you'll look like a panda.

342

Booze. Has your intended ordered it? He was last seen crawling with twin girls in the living room, but he's disappeared and how much is champagne these days? Flowers. Not having bridesmaids helps. Your sister will walk you into the place, but she's having trouble finding something to wear that won't clash with your stuff. Because you've gone bonkers and chosen something so unusual that people will need sun glasses when you walk in. The dress wants a volume control, and you should have gone for a nice dove grey or a creamy beige. He would have hated it, but it would have been nearer to normal than the thing Maureen's making.

Then you wake up one morning, and the wedding's tomorrow. At this point, a false feeling of calm descends, because there isn't a thing you can do to mend any of it – it's too late. It's a bit like going into hospital – you panic till the last moment, then you just go with the flow, because there's no choice.

And here I am, on the eve of my wedding, trying to fight my way out of the house. He doesn't want me to go. Marie is coming to look after the twins, but he still doesn't want me to go. I don't want to bloody go. I'd rather lie down with him than sleep alone in his tantric sex bed at the other side of the bypass.

'I'm younger than I look,' he moans. 'I can't be trusted by myself overnight, because I need a motherly bosom to which I might turn when–'

'Behave yourself, Alec. Embedded somewhere in ancient folklore is a rule that bids me leave this house before midnight, and–'

'Why? Will you turn into a glass slipper?'

'No. Probably a pumpkin and six white mice. Now, let me pass.' He is blocking the doorway. 'Your best man and favourite client will be here, Mike Wotsisname. He'll look after you.'

'He has no bosoms. And there's my bump. How can I manage without Bump?'

Alec has started to educate Bump already. He/she is currently learning the three-times table. The two-times has been done, as have the colours of the rainbow, The Dong with the Luminous Nose, elementary statistics, and the Tudor dynasty, which, according to the father of said Bump, was all the fault of Yorkshire. Because I am still attached to Bump, I am force-fed the same educational soup, and I love the server of this sustenance more with every mad thing he does. 'Let me go,' I beg. 'It's only for a few hours. Oh, and what's all the whispering about?'

He leans his head to one side and tells me that he can't hear anything and should I see a doctor? But I know he understands what I mean. There's a plot on. Everyone but me knows what's afoot – even my newly-retrieved sister is in on it. 'I'll slap your face again,' I promise.

He looks at his watch. 'No time for what follows that sort of behaviour. Unless you stay. Stay with me, hit me very hard, and we'll make up for a few hours.' More of his delightfully vulgar whispering in my ear is followed by, 'Please, Anna. I bathed the twins and I–'

I launch myself at him and inflict the torture he often uses on me. Yes, he's bigger and heavier than I am, but I can still pin him against the door and pretend to be whatever is the female equivalent of a young buck. A buckess? Oh, dear. I shouldn't have done this ... I want to stay. I want to drag him off upstairs and– Shut up, Anna.

We separate. And my serious Alec arrives. 'Before you leave me – I am so proud to be marrying you, Anna. You are the most wonderful, delightfully silly woman I have ever met. We seem to have been designed for each other, yet I can't believe my luck. I thought you were too good, too classy for me. I expect I believed Dolly was all I deserved.'

I touch that beloved face. 'No, I'm the fortunate one. I never truly connected with anyone since my mother's death. Den seemed a safe place, and I tried so hard to love him, but,' I shrug. 'But he wasn't right for me, and I was no good for him, because I refused to worship the man. You are my light and my life, but Marie and I need to change places now, just until morning. Stop the game now, Mr Halliwell. The next time you see me, I shall be Mrs Halliwell.'

One more kiss, and he lets me go.

I sit on the wall and wait for Maureen. She arrives and deposits her mother on the path before going back to the car in order to retrieve Marie's clothes for tomorrow. Stress crackles in the air – this lot takes weddings very seriously. No smiles, just dark looks. 'If my suit's creased, I'll leather you, lady,' Marie promises. Sounds great, doesn't it? Oh, yes, I am really looking forward to tomorrow.

Maureen drags me away. Everything I need is in Alec's ex-home, where I shall be sleeping tonight. Charlie, who is now an official resident alongside his wife in the Eccleston house, has made room for all invading females by retreating once again to the caravan. I don't blame him. Susan is in Eccleston with her son, and Kate arrives just after Maureen and a tired, pregnant bride. 'Bed,' my sister orders as soon as she sees me. 'You look shattered.'

'Bed?' I cry. 'I have to try on the dress, because Bump's expanding in all directions. Mrs Bee says it's a boy, since I'm carrying high or low or something. Her daughter says it's a girl, and I say it's a pest if I can't get into the dress. Anyway, this is my last night of freedom.'

I get into my dress. Another thing I have learned about Maureen is that she is an excellent, instinctive and self-taught seamstress. She has done some clever drapery over my bump, and I don't look too bad, though I know my hair will be hard work – it's always bloody hard work. Why I had to be endowed with enough for two people I shall never know.

We're having what is usually known as a hen party. Everyone except me can get drunk, and I know from past experience that a sozzled Maureen is not a thing of beauty, nor a joy to treasure. Susan stays reasonably sober for the sake of Stephen, so I'm not suffering completely alone. Winston is with us. Visited regularly by his 'dad', he seems to be settling well with his new servants. My dog would never have survived Winston, since the cat is arrogant, spoilt and very feisty.

So, I can't enjoy a drink. But what I can do is

346

watch an interesting phenomenon. My sister, who was supposed to be a mental case and a genius, is developing a relationship with Mo, ex-prostitute, shoplifter, brilliant cook and dress-maker. Now. This *is* a thing of beauty. Maureen, on her third double vodka diluted with something or other, is in full flood. 'See, we told her she hated him, but she still wanted him back. So we had to go looking for him. Again. We found him with a stripper at the back of the Grafton – he'd been chucked out of grab-a-granny night. Welded to her, he was. I'm not kidding, you couldn't have got a postage stamp between 'em. And they were – you know – doing it.' She drops her voice for the last two words, and I wonder why. Perhaps it's because Kate seems posh.

'In the street?' Kate asks. 'What time of year was it?'

'Bloody freezing time of year, but he was managing. 'Er tassels looked a bit stiff, like, but there he was, doing his best, and Mary Hall, what's never been any use since her hysterical rectum, shouted, "Oi! John Hooton – your wife wants you back." We flew out of there – couldn't get away quick enough. One of me mates got wedged between a wall and a badly parked Reliant Robin. No.' She shakes her head and gulps another gallon of vodka and whatever. 'Never get involved with divorce, Kate. It's not worth it – bloody murder. One way or another, you end up being the meat in the butty.'

'What's a hysterical rectum?' my sister asks.

'Hysterectomy,' I reply.

'And what happened to her?'

'Who?' Maureen is well on her way to tired and emotional.

'The one whose husband was frozen to a stripper.'

'Oh, her. Well, she went all Avon cosmetics and introduction agencies, finished up with a plumber from Warrington with five kids and a wart on his nose.'

At this point, Kate ceases to cope. She literally falls from her chair and rolls about in agony. I understand all about this syndrome, as I have suffered from it for most of my life, and there's no help for it. I know she has placed the five kids alongside his wart, and I am sharing her mental picture of a man with several children depending from his proboscis.

Maureen delivers a scathing look to the figure on the floor. 'Have you seen the bloody state of this here? Oxford don in Greek? She's like you, Anna. Weak as water and hysterical. The future of our country depends on people what are being taught by the likes of that.'

She's like me? If she's like me, she's nowhere near Rebecca, then.

Kate struggles back into her chair. 'Listen, you,' she says to Mo. 'That's nothing. You have clearly never had the pleasure of Professor Harrington-Fielding-Smythe, OBE. It was in one of those lecture theatres where the seats rise in layers until they reach the back of the room. Students look down on their educators in more ways than one.'

'Too bloody right,' Maureen slurs. 'Power to the people.'

'It was King's College, London, I think. So

there was a huge screen on which some film of an archeological dig was to be shown. But something went wrong, and the screen collapsed to reveal the prof buggering a friend.'

Maureen is not impressed. 'And?'

Kate smiles. 'There were only about half a dozen students there. One of them, a bespectacled swot, came down and pointed to a sign. "No smoking," she said to the pair below. So the prof put out one fag and continued to engage with the other. He was loopy, of course. He disappeared the following week, as did the friend. Rumour has placed them in some retreat in Polynesia. Smoking is so bad for you.'

Maureen grins. 'You are like her. You're exactly the bloody same, all posh words and mucky minds, the pair of you.' She pauses. 'Is that what buggery means, then?'

'Yes.'

Maureen grins at everyone. 'See? Stick with her, and we'll learn something new every day.'

Susan takes my hand and asks me whether I am nervous.

'No. I'm excited, because I love him so much, and I think we need to be married. But he's up to something. You're all up to something, aren't you?'

Susan smiles. 'I daren't say.'

I nudge her gently. 'Go on. I won't tell anyone.' Then I realize that the other two are staring at us.

'I never said a word,' Susan announces.

'She never said a word,' I repeat.

Maureen shakes a fist. 'Better not. It's taken a lot of careful planning.'

'Kate?' I say sweetly.

'No chance. Sorry, sis. I like your style, but you're not getting anything out of me – or Maureen.'

'And our Susan doesn't want a broken arm, do you, love?'

'No.'

Right. I've had enough, and I'm going to bed. It's a bed I've used before. The tantric sex study chair is still here, as is that brand-new-at-the-time scarlet bed cover. But he isn't here, and I'm lonely. Stupid. After tomorrow, he'll be there every night. The baby might get up to five-times table before birth. Was Henry VIII Yorkshire's fault? No idea. Mother Gertrude said that he was not a good man... Thoughts merge and lose focus. I'm going, going, gone.

And it's morning. And everyone's running round me with scrambled eggs, coffee, make-up, brushes, combs, heated rollers. There's a warm-ish debate about a French pleat or a loose chignon, and I make my exit in the middle of all the discussions. I know how he likes me. No patterns, positive colours, hair pulled away to show my face. I shower, wash my crowning-rather-less-than-glory, scrape it back into his favourite flamenco style, then place on my eyes the slices of cucumber I took from the fridge. The girls find me eventually lying on the bed. I get the feeling that I am incidental, that they didn't really miss me until they found nowhere to put the dress.

'You'll ruin your hair lying down like that,' Maureen says.

'It's the only way to lie down. I don't know any

other way. Just get lost and let me iron out these suitcases under my eyes.'

They get lost. Deprived of the sense of sight, my body moves into listening gear. They're whispering. They're excited. Something monumental is happening today, and it won't be at the register office. I pick up the phone next to his bed and dial my number. To do this, I have to remove one cucumber slice, but risks have to be taken sometimes. Is it all right to talk to him instead of seeing him? Am I cheating? Tough, because I have to tell him. He must be the first to know.

'Anna soon-to-be-Halliwell's phone,' he says.

I'm grinning like the Cheshire cat. 'Alec?'

'Darling?'

'Bump kicked. He's moving.' I won't cry, because that will mean I've wasted the cucumber. 'Bump's a person now.'

'Oh, God, I should have been there. Love you.' He's almost weeping. 'See you later,' he says. I hear another catch in his voice. When I put the receiver down, I have a word with my belly. 'Be a boy. I'll love you whatever. But do try to be a boy.'

For my second wedding, I chose drama. There was no point in wearing pastels or cream, because he wouldn't like them. So here I stand, a scarlet woman with gypsy earrings in gold, everything else in red. The dress sweeps the floor at the back, sits just above my knees at the expertly draped front. My red shoes are not new, but my dress is. The blue is where no one can see it. A minute Immaculate Conception medal given to me by Gertrude many years ago, is pinned to my bra.

And I have borrowed a small clutch bag from Maureen. 'Don't carry money in it,' she tells me cheerfully. 'There's an 'ole in the bottom.' Par for the course, what?

'I look like a pillar box,' I tell everyone.

'You look bloody gorgeous,' Maureen insists as she pins a red rose in my hair. 'And I've covered your bump and sewn all them crystals on by hand, so one word about changing, and you'll be collected by the council when they come for the bins on Monday. Don't start.'

Kate is dabbing at her eyes. 'When we were little, I always thought how brave you were. When things ... happened, I was sure Anna would put them right. And throughout all the fear, I knew I'd be rid of Rebecca in the end, and that I'd find you. You look absolutely stunning. It's the colour of bravery. Now. Go and get your hombre, senorita.'

As I pass through the hall, I catch sight of a tall, blonde Spanish woman in the mirror, and it's me. Yes. They're right. I look wonderful, and he'll love this outfit. We get into the car, and everything is fine. In thirty minutes, I'll be Mrs Alec Halliwell.

I need to savour every moment of today, because I scarcely noticed my first wedding. That was all white lace, yellow roses and disappointment; this is the real thing. But the person I fix on right away is not my darling Alec – it's his best man, Michael Wotsisname. He has turned and is watching Kate, his mouth hanging open and almost drooling. She's in black satin with red roses at her waist. Although a slight woodenness lingers in her facial demeanour, she is a perfect picture. I cross my fingers. Perhaps she'll be happier with a northerner, because she's never managed to settle with anything from below the non-existent waistline of our plump little country.

Alec looks like a delicious James Bond. His best man is dressed in similar style, all the way from a real bow tie to shiny shoes, but he can't hold a candle to my 007. I look into Alec's eyes and can see that he loves the red. It's the same shade as the bedspread he bought for me when we first began to be us.

And I miss the whole bloody thing again. All I'll remember afterwards is saying the words, signing Anna Fairbanks for the final time and making everyone laugh. Two things distract me – three if I count Lottie's whimpering. Firstly, I truly cannot believe my luck and, for the first few minutes, am unable to take my eyes off the man I'm marrying. Secondly, something's happening. It's a bit like being in his car for the first time, except we're not in a car, and it isn't us. There's stuff hanging in the air between Kate and Michael Wotsisname. He really does answer to Wotsisname, since no one can pronounce his real one. It's Greek! Oh, my God! I glance over my shoulder. She lectures in Greek – perfect.

'Anna?'

'What?'

'Are you going to let me put this ring on your finger, or have you turned chicken?'

The place erupts. I'm not sure that eruptions are usual in a place licensed to kill – I mean to marry. James Bond is another slight distraction. I give him my hand and he twinkles at me. Oh, how I adore a man who twinkles. 'Wrong hand,' he says, mock-patience hammered into the words. This statement of his brings forth another wave of laughter from the audience. Perhaps I should have been a comedienne, because I would have been paid for such a performance.

I do the necessary swap, and we're married after a bit of paperwork.

Confetti, confusion, photographs. Then I am whisked away at lightning speed in an ugly black Cadillac with my husband, my sister and Wotsis-name. We are travelling in the wrong direction. Everyone else is on the way back to Hesford, while I have been kidnapped and am on my way to God alone knows where. Kate and Michael are OK, because I think any direction would suit them. I don't believe this. What happened to us is happening to them. 'Why are we going west instead of east?' I ask.

'Shut up, Mrs Halliwell,' orders my husband. Such a polite bridegroom he turned out to be.

There's no point in blindfolding me, because I know now where we are going. There's something about the sound around Anfield on a match day. It's like a choir that isn't rehearsed, because noise rises and falls in unequal measures and in many different tones. It hangs in the air like a cluster of balloons, then drifts away on the breeze. Thousands of voices have been heard in this hallowed place, and I am sitting now next to gates built a couple of years ago as tribute to Bill Shankly, one of my greatest heroes. 'What's happening?' I ask.

Alec leaves the car and shakes hands with an official. And I'm in the trophy room, in a corridor, on some stairs, on the pitch. And a voice that defeats all others announces the arrival of one of our back room boys, Mr Alec Halliwell, club accountancy committee, with his bride. There must be thirty-odd thousand witnesses when I am carried to the penalty spot, Kop end. Oh, yes. Red was the right colour for this glorious day. I can scarcely breathe. I am with the man I love in a place I love, and it's all too perfect. Only now do I understand all the tension and the whispering. It's all been worked out in minute detail, because we had to arrive at exactly the right time.

And they cheer. God, please let this mascara do what it says on the box. He stands me near the spot, removes my high-heeled shoes in deference to the pitch, picks up a ball, sets it down, and scores into an empty goal. They cheer and whistle again, stamp and clap until we are almost deafened. Then he closes in on my left ear, tells me he knew he'd score, as he's sacked the goalkeeper, and that he loves me more than he loves this place. That means something, because my own love affair with Liverpool FC has a long history. So I give him a big, sloppy kiss, and that sets the crowd off again.

He could not have presented me with a better wedding gift. He already gave me a silly paddling pool as he could not afford a swimming pool, a diamond pendant that matches the engagement ring, plus some studs for my ears. He has style, because he knew not to buy earrings in the shape of flowers, since that would have made for a cluttered effect.

It isn't over, because we're back in the tunnel and I am given my shoes. Kick-off is in two minutes, and I'm glad I have the shoes, since I am kissed by every red and every blue in the lines, and these are tall men. Gorgeous legs, too. It's Derby day, and Everton is our little brother from next door. Reds and blues – perfect purple when mixed, perfect rivals and friends in a city that bears no grudge.

Kate hugs me. 'He knew you'd love it, Anna.'

'I did. That will be in my heart for the rest of my life. Everton, too – I still don't believe it. I felt the grass under my feet – wonderful. And I saw how big a pitch really is, Kate. We watch, but we've no idea of the size of the job they do. Terrifying.' I turn my attention to my better half. 'Why didn't you tell me you work for them?'

'I like to maintain an air of mystery,' he replies.

I laugh and Kate laughs. But Michael Wotsisname is too busy lusting after my kid sister, so he delivers just a pale smile. He'd better watch out. I'm married to a bloke who knows a lot of big men – I just kissed most of them.

College was a walk in the park after Advanced levels in the sixth. There was reading to be done, and it was tedious, since experts in education stated the blatantly obvious, couching it in fancy language as if icing a plain cake just to make it look good. But the work had to be done, since the blatantly obvious was easy to forget, though Anna MacRae found her own way through teaching practices, as she realized from the start that the place to begin was with humour, not with books. For exams, she studied the experts; when teaching, she drove from the heart.

Faced with forty hungry little faces whose names she would have difficulty remembering within the allocated fortnight, she breezed in and made life fun. She used brighter kids to prop up the slow learners and, occasionally, she had the good fortune to be there when a child began to read for the first time. As she would admit for the rest of her life, she wasn't sure that she actually taught any of them to read; she simply presented them with the necessary materials and waited for the magic to begin.

Miss Millichamp was Anna's supervising lecturer. She visited without warning, and she made note of this girl's methods. Never a fan of Montessori, Anna applied discipline with kindness and innovation, a fact that went down in writing. When sent to a school in Stockport, Anna was shown by the headmistress a letter from Miss Millichamp. 'I'm not supposed to let you see this, but...'

Thus Anna learned that she was calm, industrious and inventive. '*She is mature for her age, and children enjoy her teaching. If she continues to obtain good results from the application of her home-grown theories, I shall carry on believing that this is a gifted student who will gain a distinction in Principles and Practice of Education at the end of her time at Didsbury.*'

Like any young person, Anna was encouraged by the news that someone valued her. She was managing her chosen subjects – Scripture with

Comparative Religion as main, English and Physical Education as her secondaries, so college was more fun than hard work.

Den Fairbanks, whose time in London was over, visited her several evenings each week, drove her home every Friday, and back to college on Sundays. She leaned on him, since he was going to be her means of acquiring a family away from the dreaded twins. They were still there, of course, when she went home, but she lived next door in the house that had been Dad's, taking some meals with Elsie and Bert while the twins continued to eat upstairs.

Den learned to hide his car, and they had very careful sex in her bed whenever they could. Or, to be more precise, whenever he needed it. Anna accepted his performances and, at first, wondered whether this must be a woman's lot, as she gained little pleasure from the activity. It seemed that something was always promised at the start, though it was never delivered, and she couldn't understand why he enjoyed himself to the point of puffing, panting and shuddering, while she had to be satisfied with so much less. She decided that she was nervous because of Bert and Elsie next door, and that she would improve when more privacy was available. It was her fault, of course. He knew about everything, so he had to be right.

His mother was a powerful person who cooked him a three-course breakfast every morning, cleaned his shoes daily, and spoiled him to the point where he knew he could do no wrong. Anna pretended not to notice, since she was so grateful to be a semi-detached part of a family that she might have tolerated almost anything. He would change when they were married – if his mother ever allowed him to be married, that was.

Strictly in the interests of research, Anna MacRae, in the year 1954, decided to put herself about a bit. It was a mixed college, and the wings were joined via the common room, so assignations were commonplace. It was just the sex, she told herself repeatedly. If someone else could do it well, perhaps she would be more likely to enjoy it with Den. And she wasn't engaged, wasn't hurting anyone as long as she didn't get pregnant. It didn't work, so she concluded that she was frigid, and she had better forget about ever having the earth move for her.

She got distinctions in all subjects, left college in 1955, and was wed within a week. Although she felt guilty once again about abandoning her foster parents, the urge to escape and survive was stronger than the self-blame.

The married life of Den and Anna Fairbanks began in a small house in Cheshire, and they moved on to Hesford within a few years. Den turned out to be an excellent businessman and a womanizer, but Anna managed to hang in, since she wasn't sure what else might have been done.

When his mother began to demand grandchildren, Den followed orders and did his duty rather too frequently for his wife's liking. Anna was scared. A child would fasten her to him, yet she could see no way out. When she went to the doctor to ask for tests, he ordered her to send her husband in first. Thus they discovered that Den had insufficient live sperm, though she complied with his wish to pretend that it was her 'fault'. There was still a chance that pregnancy could be achieved, but they were advised by medics not to bank on it, to enjoy life and accept whatever happened.

Stuck in a loveless marriage, Anna submerged herself in work. For almost twenty years, she toiled at the coal face, since she preferred to remain a classroom teacher with no particular responsibility beyond her debt to those she taught. She cooked, cleaned, went out to work and lay obediently underneath her husband whenever he insisted. His day-to-day behaviour worsened after the death of his mother. He endured two nervous breakdowns, and his wife began to realize that he was suffering from a little more than simple depression. Den was either as high as a kite or as low as a snail, no half-measures.

Then she met Geoff. His father was Afro-Caribbean, while his mother was a Liverpool girl. Despite a huge difference in their ages, he pursued her relentlessly, finally wearing her down after a pub quiz at which the staff had been a team. They won. Anna celebrated by giving herself to a lovely man whose teaching skills extended way beyond his classroom. The decision to allow sex had been made before she left home that evening, and she was protected by a Dutch cap, while he completed the belt-and-braces law by making his own arrangements.

At the age of thirty-nine, Anna found the truth. It was simple, yet she had clearly been too stupid to work it out. Before love, there was chemistry. A person had to desire another person – that was the law. But there needed to be affection as well, and she did love Geoff in a way. The sex was glorious, but she would never commit to him, as there was still something missing. That missing factor was probably total, unconditional and very romantic love.

When she became pregnant, she was almost certain that the child had to be Den's, since she and Geoff had been so careful, yet the part of her that still asked questions accepted that her marriage would be over if the baby came out dark. She left it to fate. During the early months, she continued to enjoy a relationship with Geoff, ending it only when her blood pressure became slightly unstable. He hung around for a while, even coming to see her after the babies had been born, but she eased him out of her life and coped as best she could with what had been termed post-natal depression.

In one sense, Anna was sorry that the twins were Den's. He had wanted a boy, and he took little notice of his daughters. Throughout those first weeks, fear took up residence in the new mother's heart, because Lottie and Emily didn't seem to get on. They hadn't liked each other in the womb, though the idea had been tut-tutted whenever she had spoken of it to medics.

This was when complete terror moved in. It was also when Anna decided that Den should move out.

Marriage altered us. It isn't that we're closer — we're just easier. This is what was wanted, what we lacked. When a relationship is solid and real, the need to commit can be overwhelming, so we did it. I now own a larger bump, a bigger car and a house that promises to be enormous. He's just the same as he ever was – he's *there*, and you see what you get and get what you see.

Mrs Bee is here today. Well, she's here most days, but she's very much here today. 'What the bloody hell's that?'

I carry on as if everyone has a paddling pool in the middle of the living room. 'Alec bought it.' I daren't tell her why, because most of our reasons are daft.

'What for? They can't even crawl proper yet.'

'I know. I think they'll walk before they crawl – I believe I did, as did my sisters. As for this daft article on my floor – Alec was a bit ... premature.'

I stare at it. He inflated it last night to see if it had any punctures. Fortunately, I managed to prevent him from filling it, because this is a good carpet. He deliberately chose the most garish, ugly item he could find. It's covered in pictures of buckets, spades, sandcastles and beach balls. 'It'll keep,' I say calmly. 'Perhaps he got it for a good price.'

She hmmphs. Only Mrs Bee can produce a hmmph of such quality. 'Have you not got enough on with yon builders and Jo's music?'

'I don't mind.' At least he's stopped going on about newfangled birthing pools.

'That's a blessing, then. Have Susan and Stephen gone?'

'Sort of. They come and stay sometimes.'

She's working her way up to it. I can tell when she's working her way up to something, because her nose gets coloured. I have no idea why, but there it is. At last, here it comes. 'So what's this about your sister, then?'

'What?'

'Her and Michael Wotsisname. I could tell there was summat on at your wedding – he looked as if he could eat her on a butty.'

'Oh – that.'

'Yes, oh, that. How long have they known each other? And what's she doing marrying somebody called Wotsisname because nobody can get a grip of his handle?'

I won't laugh. I don't want Mrs Bee to know about my errant mind, though I have to admit that the thought of trying to get a grip on a man's handle is the sort of thing that–

'Anna?'

'What?'

'Why did she marry somebody she didn't know, somebody with a name nobody can say?'

'Neophytou. It isn't that hard. She's a scholar in Greek.'

The arms fold themselves. 'In bloody Oxford? And him a fish and chip shop typhoon up here?'

Don't laugh, Anna, I tell myself. 'She's coming to live in Crosby. He can do his chips while she teaches in one of the public schools.'

'He'll never keep up with her on an intellect – intellectualitive level.'

'Intellectual, Mrs Bee.' The teacher in me will never die. 'He's a very bright man – he just happens to come from a family of fish and chippers. It was love at first sight, and I know how that is. Anyway, he's studying law as well as cod and

363

mushy peas.' I sigh. 'People say these things won't last, but I've served three months of my sentence, and she's done a couple of weeks.'

The old woman's eyes narrow. 'Are you taking the wee-wee out of me, Anna Fairbanks?'

'Halliwell.'

'Are you?'

'Yes. Now, it's my twin time. You may stay and join in, but it's not compulsory.' I lift them from the playpen, and Emily walks. She just stands up, lets go of my hand and walks. Lottie, not to be outdone, does the same, though she clings to my hand like a little limpet. Camera. 'Mrs Bee, hold onto these two, will you?' Like Kate and Beckie, they walk on the same day, yet they are not like Kate and Beckie. Thank goodness.

For the rest of my life, I shall treasure that photograph. It shows a very happy old lady whose walking is not as easy as it was, and she's in the company of a couple who need L-plates. Wonderful. So glad I had film, or this momentous day might have gone unrecorded.

They don't sleep all afternoon. They fall over the dog, a rug, and their own feet. I get the feeling that they fear forgetting their new game if they sleep. Alec goes to bits when he arrives home early, tears tripping one another down his cheeks. He didn't make these little girls, but they are his. They walk and fall, walk and fall until he drags them off for their bath. I don't know how I ever managed without him.

Now, I'm waiting for my sister. Because there is one last thing we have to do. It's important for Kate, and she needs me to be there when she meets the woman to whom Mam ran after the rape. I don't know whether this is wise, but I have to go along with her. I watch the newly-weds get out of their car, and I need no x-ray vision to see the love between them. Mike is to stay here with Alec. They both volunteered to accompany us, but it didn't seem right. This is old family business, and we need just each other this evening.

'You're seven months pregnant,' says Alec accusingly.

'Now, he tells me. I wondered why I got so fat. And I didn't get this way on my own, Halliwell. I'm fine. And it's now or never. Kate took a while to work her way up to this, and we're going.'

He shrugs and mutters something about not being wanted, and finding someone else to play in the paddling pool. Alec's a great one for mentioning private business when in the company of others. But I can't say anything, because it would make it worse, and anyway, I use the same trick from time to time. I kiss him before going out to sit in Kate and Mike's car. Yes, I'm nervous, but I need to be strong for her, for Kate. She's my sister.

We're on our way home. Home? 'Kate, why didn't you come to the Dixons' funeral?'

'She was with me.'

'Ah. So you're still scared of her?'

Kate nods. 'You don't know the half of it. No one knows how awful it really was. But when I need to talk, you'll be there for me.' She knows I'll be there. In spite of the fact that I was never quite bright enough as a child to work out what was truly happening, the woman loves me. I have apologized to her so many times that it's begun to sound hollow.

On that first climb to the rim of the bowl in which Bolton sits, we catch a glimpse of the hills across town. This landscape is what I miss, because Merseyside is as flat as a pancake. But no one can have everything. I have the river, the ships and my football team. Oh, and my children and Alec.

'You're smiling,' she says.

'I'm happy, Kate. Not about what we have to do in a few minutes, but just ... happy.'

She is, too, and she tells me so. 'He wants a baby,' she informs me. 'I've told him everything, but he believes in nurture over nature. Such a huge family, the Neophytous. I'm turning Greek Orthodox – it's only a nod away from Catholicism.' She pulls into the kerb for a break. 'Anna?'

'Yes?'

She pauses for a few seconds, is clearly deep in thought. 'When we were kids, she threatened to kill me if I made my first Confession and Holy Communion. Because she knew I'd talk to a priest about us, about her and the things she forced me to do.'

'But a priest is bound by laws, Kate.'

'I know. She trusted no one except herself. She was always the same. It was hell, Anna. You were in Purgatory, but my address was hell.'

'I know. I wish I–'

'No.' She looks into my eyes. 'I knew it was a long game. And I knew I'd win in the end.' The engine's still running, yet she shows no sign of continuing the journey. 'The police never came

366

to see you, did they, Anna?'

'No.'

'Didn't you think that was strange?'

I shrug. 'To be honest, I try not to think at all when it comes to the subject of Rebecca.'

It pours from her, spills like water rushing at Niagara. She has lied to me from the beginning, but she can't do it any longer. Saying that Rebecca had fled Paris with a man and several millions was a fantasy, a not-quite fairy tale that seemed to be for the best at the time. 'But you have to believe me, Anna, when I say I wasn't there when she died.'

The child lurches in my womb. I think he/she's experiencing a rush of adrenalin, because the landlady has accidentally flooded the premises with it. My heart feels odd. I'm cold, yet I'm sweating. What am I supposed to believe? 'Who wrote the letter?' I ask. 'That final letter from her to you that was sent from Paris days after her exit?'

'I wrote it,' she replies.

Who is this person? Is she so cleverly psychotic that she has fooled me into believing her to be merely depressive, into thinking of Rebecca as evil? 'At this particular stage in pregnancy, Kate, I could have done better without such news.' Why did she wait until we were alone, until I was at my most vulnerable and with no Alec to defend me? Is it my turn now? Will she kill me and my baby? Has she studied more than Greek? Has she watched people and learned how to imitate normality? 'Who are you?' I ask.

'I'm Katherine, of course. We weren't identical.

Yet the moment her heart ceased to beat, I knew it.'

I must stay calm. 'Then tell me everything now.'

'We're expected. Mrs Latimer will be waiting for us, and she's very old.'

'If she's old, she can wait a while longer,' I reply.

'But you're pregnant, and–'

'Yes, I'm heavily pregnant, and you have made me feel extremely ill. I may as well hang around for your next trick. Do your worst, whoever you are.'

So she opens her door and runs away. I sit here wondering what to do, knowing that I am in shock and far too ill to drive. I watch while she dashes through a side street, and I'm sure that I'd never find her, because at the back of Derby Street there are mazes fit to compete with Hampton Court. So I kill the engine and try to get my bearings.

There's a phone box. When I try to take change from my bag, fingers go on strike and everything falls to the floor. Bending in a restricted area is not easy with a bump. Think, think. Mam, stand by me while I deal with this. Keys. Get out. Lock the car. Phone. Reverse charges. 'Alec!' I scream. 'You have to come now, both of you.'

'What's the matter, sweetheart?'

'Everything. Bring Michael. Get Mrs Bee and Jenny for the twins. Come now!'

'Darling, calm down. Come where?'

'Derby Street, Bolton. You know it. It's where we come for our Indian spices and chapatti flour. I'm parked outside the sari shop. There's a Co-op nearby.'

'Where's Kate? Is anyone hurt?'

'No. Alec, shut up and come. Now!'

For forty minutes, I sit in a locked car and await the arrival of my hero. For the first time in ages, I crave a cigarette. But that's all right, because I was the same once or twice towards the end with the twins, and I managed not to indulge. There is one thing I can do, though. After picking up enough of my money, I repair to a little off-licence and buy myself a small, ice-cold bottle of Guinness. The child probably needs this as badly as I do.

Beautiful, black manna from heaven, sour yet sweet, creamy while sharp. It's so long since I had a drink that the effect is almost immediate. I shall always thank the manufacturers of my chosen nectar, because I'm sure they stopped me delivering my child on the spot. Doctors? They've no bloody idea when it comes to a crisis. Sometimes, the wrong answer is the right answer, and there's never a blinking doctor around anyway when you're in real life trouble. Like policemen, they're thin on the ground till we don't need them, at which point they're suddenly everywhere.

I decide to play dumb where my sister's husband is concerned. When the men arrive, I tell them that Kate panicked and ran off, because she feared hearing what Mrs Latimer had to say about our mother's rape. Mike relieves me of his car. I climb in next to Alec and tell him what's happened. Kate's husband has gone in search of her; I beg Alec to get me out of this town as quickly as he can. The future is something over which none of us can ever take full control, but I sure as hell can deal with the present.

'So,' he concludes as we drift on to the East Lancashire Road. 'You don't know who's the baddy and who's the goody?'

I nod. The cowboy movies were so easy, because bad wore a black hat, while good wore a white one. 'Kate seemed so ... so real.'

'She is real,' he tells me. 'She's probably protecting the true murderer.'

'What?'

'Look, Anna. I know I'm only a man and haven't the instincts of womankind, but she seems right to me.'

I am sick to death of telling people how hard it is to sort wheat from chaff when IQs in the Alps are factors. Psychopaths – sometimes termed sociopaths these days – are good at pretending to be normal. The man who mends your car, the other who drills your teeth, the girl who cuts your hair – any one of those could be insane while appearing to be normal. 'Alec, you are naïve. You've met good people and bad people, but not bad people who appear to be good.'

'What about Maureen?'

I feel like screaming. I won't, since I'm a passenger carrying a passenger, and I don't want the driver to crash, because I love all of us. 'Maureen did wrong. But she never pretended to be anything other than what she was. Kate, Rebecca – God, I've no idea.'

'Then I'd better send for the police.'

One of the many aspects of character that attracted me to Alec in the first place is his calm, his down-to-earth-ness. Sometimes, just sometimes, his view is too clear and uncluttered. 'Life

370

isn't black and white, love,' I tell him. 'There are shades of grey.'

'Meaning?'

'Meaning she's still my sister. Meaning she might have had a huge panic attack when I accused her of upsetting a pregnant woman. Meaning she presented herself with a fight or flight situation, and she took the latter course. She's ill, but that doesn't make her a murderer.'

He pulls into our driveway. 'We go to bed and sleep,' he commands. 'We'll give her a chance to come back and explain herself. But if you have any idea that she might have killed Rebecca, you must tell me, and I'll get the cops. OK?'

'OK.'

While Alec faces Mrs Bee and Jenny, I answer the phone. 'I didn't, I didn't, I didn't.' Kate is beyond hysteria. 'Jean-Paul. I can't do it. Prison. After what she did...'

'Quiet!' I shout. Mrs Bee and Jenny look at me inquisitively as they walk out of the house.

When the side door is closed, he snatches the phone from me. 'Listen, lady,' he says quietly. 'I don't care who's done what or who's said what, but if you upset my wife or endanger my child again, you'll be wearing your kneecaps as earrings. What?' A pause follows. 'Until you get your head screwed on properly, stay away. When you've stopped being cross-threaded, we'll deal with this. I don't know who the fu- who the hell Jean-Paul is, but this is no time to be bringing foreigners into it.' He slams down the receiver and holds out his arms. 'Come here, Anna.'

On our baby-making sofa, he lies me down,

371

makes sure my back, knees and ankles are supported, then sits and strokes my face until I sleep. Each time I wake, he's there, where my waist used to be, and he's whispering to his baby. 'It will be all right, Mummy just had a little shock. We'll take you to the zoo, and I promise that if they already have some like you, and no one wants to save you as a protected species, we'll bring you home afterwards. Now. After Harold fell off his horse with an arrow in his eye, this here William bloke took over. He was a Frog who invaded us – a bit like Hitler, but with a slightly better accent and without the funny walk.'

He's so daft, so adorable, so unfazed by life.

He won't leave me for a moment. Working from home means a dining table covered in ledgers, bits of receipts, paper clips and piles of tax forms. Susan is living here on a paid basis until my baby has been born. The freezer is full, as is the order book, so Third Party takes over the kitchen at least twice a week, though we are becoming inventive when it comes to puddings, which is where the freezer is a boon.

I am left out of everything. Susan is run off her feet by three toddlers, while I am confined to barracks except for twice a day, when Alec takes me and my children for a walk to the village, or to visit horses on the farm. When Alec's Jo comes home from school, she steps in and relieves poor Susan once the homework has been completed.

Not a word has been heard in weeks from or about Kate and Mike. Members of the Neophytou family are concerned, though they have been lucky, since they received one message of reassurance from Mike on the night of their disappearance. He and Kate will be back, Mike said, when some urgent business has been dealt with. So we wait while trying not to talk about the fact that we are waiting. Alec, between dealing with paperwork and phone calls, treats me like some Victorian female disaster that's gone into decline.

Then comes the call Alec can't take for me, since the caller refuses to talk to anyone but Anna MacRae. He places me on the stairs, sits behind me and massages my shoulders for the duration. It's Mrs Latimer, the old woman we were supposed to be visiting when Kate ran away.

When it's over, he takes me back into the living room, sits me down and places himself on the floor beside my chair. 'Well, I got some of that,' he says. 'But what did I miss?'

'What?' I'm miles and years away. I'm washing the dead face of a woman who should have remained the centre of my existence. I'm looking at two angry, newborn little girls who will never have a mother. I'm rescuing a small boy from a wood, watching my dying father, looking into Elsie's eyes, where all hope has perished.

'Anna?'

'What?'

'Tell me. No matter how bad this is, you have to talk to me.'

I know that. He didn't need to tell me that. It's just that once I say the words, it will be too real, and I don't want it to be real.

'Please, darling?'

I am dragged back to the here and now by two

373

occurrences. My back hurts, and the chair is wet through. 'My mother knew her rapist. It was Mrs Latimer's husband. He'd already left her, because he was planning to dodge the draft.' Fingers of pain are beginning to make their way round to the front of my body. And my labour is in overdrive. 'He hanged for murder in 1948 after raping and killing a young woman in Northampton. Mrs Latimer had no children, so Kate and Rebecca don't have half-siblings from that household.' There might be dozens of them, but we don't know where, so there's little point in worrying. 'Mrs Latimer said he was mentally ill – she'd been ill-treated for years. And I'm in labour.'

'What?'

'The baby's on its way.'

He jumps up. 'I'll get your case.'

'Don't bother, Alec. Go for Mrs Bee and get a doctor. I appear to have skipped stage one. And forget the bloody birthing pool.'

A robust child is born just minutes later on the floor of our living room after a swift and vicious labour. The on-call doctor, when he arrives, is unknown to me. Mrs Bee is wiping her face on her apron, because tears begin to mingle with per-spiration, and her face is very damp. It was hard work for her, too, but we both coped quite well, I think. The afterbirth is delivered whole, and I am told that I can stay at home, because mother and baby are well. 'You may prefer to go to hospital to be checked, but your blood pressure, et cetera – all OK.'

Alec, my knight in gleaming armour, has gone to pieces. This, our fifth child, is our first son. He is Alexander David Halliwell, and we intend to use his middle name. He is tiny, although the doctor has estimated the weight to be above the seven pound mark. My beautiful boy is in the arms of my beautiful man, and both are crying.

I smile at the doctor. 'Excuse my husband. He's had a rather difficult pregnancy.'

The doc laughs and says he's seen the syndrome before.

Jo and Susan come in and comfort Mrs Bee. Jo is radiant – she has another baby to fuss over. He will be totally ruined, of course. She rushes off to phone her grandmother and half of St Helens. By the time she's finished, we'll probably get a film crew from the BBC.

We are complete. Alec and I have each other, plus five healthy kids. Kate and Mike are filed away in a dark, dusty cabinet somewhere behind our shared consciousness. I am the child who lost everything, the woman who accidentally took first prize. Beyond Alec, I have scaffolding of the strongest kind – the Hughes family, Alec's mother, and the wonderful Mrs Battersby from next door. I suppose those two women are my mothers now.

Sheba is a big girl, though she remains a puppy. Retrievers need to be eighteen months old before the light of common sense begins to dawn. She does her best, bless her. While tormented by the twins, she appoints herself guardian of the newborn, and only those she knows are allowed near him. Although not completely sure of what she might do if someone did try to take him, I notice how she bares her teeth and growls at people she fails to recognize. I think she's all talk. Well, I hope she's all talk.

An impromptu party happens when David is six weeks old. It isn't organized – everyone arrives at about the same time, and the celebration simply follows. Juliet comes first – I believe she's getting broody. Maureen, Marie and Charlie roll up next, then Mrs Bee, who seems to have a *very* roving brief these days, puts in an appearance. She brings wine. Dear God, save me from Mrs Bee's wines. Amen. I can't drink, as I am breastfeeding this time, since I have just the one child to nourish, but I fear for the company. Alec keeps an eye on his daughter, who is eminently capable of imbibing when left to her own devices – he has already had words with her on the subject. Jo's a good kid – she just tests the boundaries from time to time. Susan has the sense to stick to orange juice, because she, like me, has learned the hard way.

The babies are all asleep by the time the party gets going. David is in the dining room, as he will need one more feed before I take him upstairs, so I leave him where I can hear him. Because of that, the party is held in our living room and in the almost-completed extension.

Maureen is 'on one', as Marie describes her daughter's impromptu performances. Revealing yet another of her vast store of abilities, Mo produces a ukulele and makes her way through most of the repertoire of George Formby, who was a family entertainer. Maureen is not a family entertainer, so what she sees *When I'm Cleaning*

Windows differs greatly from the original version. She is a hoot. Mrs Bee, though blushing behind her hands, is laughing like a drain. Charlie, who hasn't had a drink in months, sticks to orange juice and to Alec, as my husband is the only other man in this posse of females.

Maureen stops playing. 'Dog's barking,' she announces. Yet another gift – the woman has superb hearing.

Alec goes to look at his son and to calm the hound. When he returns, I see his grim face, and my heart lurches. 'Alec?'

'It's all right, darling,' he says before asking everyone else to keep quiet. 'We won't be long,' he tells them. Then he takes my hand and leads me to the kitchen, warning me before we get there. 'They're back,' he whispers.

He doesn't need to say the names. 'Oh, God,' I breathe.

'With the Frenchman.'

'OK.' Is it OK? Is my sister going to be arrested tonight? Will I be the final means of the undoing of Katherine?

They are seated. Katherine is pale, but calm, hands folded in her lap. Mike seems to have aged, while Mr Hedouin, an absolutely beautiful man, is in a bad way, eyes darting all over the place, forehead dampened by sweat, fear written all over the handsome face. Our dog sits as still as stone and watches over the newcomers. She is sufficiently intelligent to trust no one without proof of character.

'He ran,' Mike explains, waving a hand in the direction of the stranger. 'We had to travel the length and breadth of France to find him, and we employed detectives. It's a big country.' He sighs heavily, and I notice grey hairs above his ears. The MacRae twins have had this effect on so many people.

'I speak not well the English. Katherine will speaking for me,' announces the captive. He's not here voluntarily – that's very plain.

In that dull, flat tone used by both during childhood, Kate tells me what happened to her twin. 'They were living together in Rebecca's flat. Jean-Paul and his daughter moved in.' She looks into my eyes, and I see a void in her face. There's nothing there. She reminds me of an empty house that awaits new residents. A cold finger traces a sharp line down my backbone. Alec supports me, a strong arm around my waist. I am safe. While he is here, I am always protected.

Katherine inhales deeply. 'Rebecca hated the attention he gave to his daughter. Marguerite – that's her name – was discovered at the foot of a long flight of marble stairs. She lay in a coma for almost three weeks. But she suffered no loss of memory, no permanent damage to her brain. When she woke, she told Jean-Paul that Rebecca had pushed her. We think Rebecca had stopped taking her medicines.'

'*Ma fille ne marche pas,*' says the Frenchman. 'Marguerite – broke back. Sit in chaise now. She has only ten years and she not walk no more.'

'*Et vous avez touer ma soeur?*' I ask.

He nods just once. 'These ... two people are black – *qu'est-ce-que je voudrais dire?*'

'Blackmail?' I suggest.

He almost smiles. *'Oui, Madame – c'est vrai.* Blackmail. Until I am come in Angleterre, they say get police, tell them I am kill Rebecca. So I am coming to here.'

I leave Alec and take the man's hands. *'Je suis tres triste pour vous et pour votre fille.'* My French is no longer as thorough as it used to be. *'C'est le fin ce soir. Allez. Marguerite a besoin de Papa.'*

And he cries. I have not said enough, because there are no words for this in any man-made language. His daughter lives in a wheelchair, and Rebecca did that. I have told him I am sad, that he must go to his daughter, since she needs him. But what the hell will that do for the poor man? He killed my sister; I cannot blame him. Had she harmed Lottie, Emily or David, I would have done the same.

Kate doesn't move. She simply stares at the table.

Mike takes my hand. 'Anna, she's tranquilized. I bought street drugs in Marseilles – I didn't know what the hell to do. If I'd taken her to a French doctor, God alone knows what she might have said. She was so raw – she could have blurted it out. And you know her French is perfect. I have watched over her for twenty-four hours each day.'

In his eyes, I see echoes of the hell he has lived through.

'Where's the body?' I ask. I am amazed by my serenity.

'Underneath another in a Paris cemetery,' Mike replies. 'Jean-Paul's brother's an undertaker. So he's another accessory after the fact. We are all accessories now. If Jean-Paul goes to jail, there's a chance he'll be joined by his brother. As for us – oh, God.'

Being an accessory is something to which I was forced to become inured when Gary was killed. I am a criminal. Sometimes, criminals are the good people. I saved Susan. I saved Stephen. I saved Marie. Now, I am saving a heartbroken Parisian. And I will, by God, I will.

'Her things?' I ask.

'Destroyed. She is supposedly back in England, got a job here. She wasn't employed at the time, so that helped make the story good.' Mike sighs. 'Lie, after lie, after lie.'

The old station clock on my kitchen wall needs winding. There are dirty dishes everywhere. And my sister is dead, killed by the man whose daughter she tried to murder. My other sister is drugged, yet a lone tear tracks down her left cheek. That tear is all I need, because it contains the truth – she is basically normal, yet unsteady because of Rebecca.

As soon as I touch her, she howls. It's a horrible sound, though it changes when the dog decides to provide musical accompaniment. This is hysteria now. While Alec leads Sheba away, I hug what is left of Katherine. My mind is racing. We need to keep her here, where life is normal by her standards. She and Mike are going to need a massive support system. Yes, we are all guilty, all accessories after the fact.

When I look into Jean-Paul's eyes, I see the misery that was contained for so long in the face of Elsie, our foster mother. But my job is to look after Kate. 'Kate? Kate – look at me.'

She sobs, but manages to comply.

'I have a son. You have a little nephew. We'll look after you – Mike, Alec and I. While one of us remains alive, you will never, ever be alone.'

'Anna borra.'

'Yes, darling. Kate borra, too.' I know in this moment that she will never have a child, and that she will always depend on me. I can also see in her husband's face the urge to distance himself from recent nightmares. Will he stay with her, or will he move on to someone without so much baggage? How shall we cope if or when the authorities finally discover that Rebecca is missing? Questions, questions, and no answers.

Whatever, Kate will always be with me.

A long time ago, a mother gave birth, and responsibility was passed to me within minutes. I am a lucky woman, because I am with the right man, and I know I am one of the few. Alec will never desert me, no matter what happens. But I stand in a messy kitchen with Kate's head pressed into my body. She will be there for ever. In my heart, in my mind and in my soul, Kate is my precious and beloved burden. It's a circle, you see...

X

The publishers hope that this book has given you enjoyable reading. Large Print Books are especially designed to be as easy to see and hold as possible. If you wish a complete list of our books please ask at your local library or write directly to:

Magna Large Print Books
Magna House, Long Preston,
Skipton, North Yorkshire.
BD23 4ND

This Large Print Book for the partially sighted, who cannot read normal print, is published under the auspices of

THE ULVERSCROFT FOUNDATION